UNTRODDEN
Book One of
THE TRAILS OF TRUTH

UNTRODDEN

Book One of

THE TRAILS OF TRUTH

HADLEIGH GARRARD

Proprio
Vigore
Press

A publication of Proprio Vigore Press
www.ProprioVigorePress.com

Author Hadleigh Garrard
www.HadleighGarrard.com

First electronic edition: 11 January 2012
ISBN: 978-0-9848975-0-6

First paperback edition: 21 February 2012
ISBN: 978-0-9848975-5-1

Cover illustration © 2011 by Joan Doyle
www.theHouseArtist.com

Cover design by Hadleigh Garrard, Michelle Santee, Joan Doyle

Edited by Michelle Santee
admin@ProprioVigorePress.com

Proprio Vigore Press logo © 2011 by Proprio Vigore Press

Drawing A Line of Emperor Penguins by Rsperberg4

Coming in 2012: *Unveiled: Book Two of The Trails of Truth*
A publication of Proprio Vigore Press

The first one is for Bill Hansen: He would have enjoyed the journey.

Contents

➤➤ Prologue ➤➤

It was sufficiently late on Halloween night that the moonlit streets near the beach had emptied of revelers; the make-believe ghosts and goblins were tucked away safe in bed as the mist rolled in, gradually obscuring the full moon. A brief burst of brilliant white light split the fog-shrouded scene. A young man with long brown hair pulled back in a ponytail stumbled as he passed behind a weather-beaten stone bench that sat on the bluff above the beach. He hesitated and scanned his surroundings before sprinting south on the path that snaked along the bluff. A dark form emerged from the shadows of a clump of scrubby trees and followed stealthily as the young man raced through the twisting streets.

After a few blocks, the young man yanked open the door of a ramshackle brick apartment building. He darted up the rickety wooden stairs and pulled to a stop at the first door on the landing. Throwing a quick glance over his shoulder, he placed his right hand flat against the door and frowned in concentration. Long moments later, midnight blue light flashed at the margins of the door; it edged open, and the young man slipped inside, fighting for breath. A woman hastily closed and locked the door as an older man drawing on a robe entered the room.

"You must leave," the young man wheezed, "Tiergan ..."

Suddenly the apartment door burst open with a blinding blaze of light. All three pivoted. The woman gripped her necklace. The older man jerked a gemstone out of his pocket as a massive, black-clad, knife-wielding figure surged across the threshold and sprang at the woman.

The young man wrenched at the thrusting arm but was effortlessly tossed aside. The older man brandished his stone, and a beam of deep crimson light shot at the intruder, only to be absorbed by the black cloak. Soundlessly, the stranger drove a dagger into the woman's chest. Clutching futilely at the knife, she crumpled to the floor.

The gold-handled dagger glinted in the dim light as it was pulled smoothly from the wound; blood spurted in its wake. The young man leapt to his feet and hurled himself onto the assailant's back; he was lobbed across the room. The intruder lunged through another shaft of crimson and slammed the dagger directly into the older man's heart. Pausing for a fleeting instant to withdraw the dagger and gather the edges of the cloak, the killer began to spin, faster and faster, then vanished.

Winded and stunned, the young man scrambled to the woman's side and tried to stem the flow of blood from her wound with his hands.

"No ..." she croaked feebly, "too late."

"I'll get help."

"No time ... must ... hide the baby. ... They can't know ... she lives." She gasped and continued with great effort. "A veridictrix ... must ... survive!" The woman labored to breathe. "Take her ... to Greer. Tell ... tell her ... don't go back ..."

"You can't die," he pleaded.

The woman looked into the young man's eyes and, with her last bit of strength, said clearly, "Promise to keep her safe."

Tears streamed down his cheeks as the young man picked up the woman's limp right hand and held it palm-to-palm. "With all my heart, I so promise." He drew a calming breath and gently unclasped the woman's necklace. Placing a kiss on her forehead, he pocketed the pendant.

He got shakily to his feet and plucked a pale stone from the floor near the older man's still body. In the bedroom, he reached with unsteady hands into a crib in a corner of the room, scooped up a sleeping baby, and wrapped her in a blanket. Snatching a small box from the dresser and stealing one last grief-stricken glance at the lifeless pair, he dashed from the apartment.

The young man again sprinted through the narrow, murky streets, stopping this time at a tiny wooden house on the verge of the beach. Once more, he placed his hand flat against the door. Too quickly for the occupant to have been asleep, the front door was flung open by a grey-haired woman in a long, flowing garment.

"What's wrong?"

The young man brushed by her and staggered into the house, breathing heavily.

"You're covered with blood!"

"They're dead ..." the young man choked out.

"No! How? What happened?"

"An assassin ... must have followed me. ... She said to hide the baby."

"Hide her? But how …"

"There's no time! Take the baby. I'll go back for her cistella."

"Wait, come here." She pulled a colorless stone from her pocket. "Let me get rid of that blood."

"Quickly!"

"I should hide her?" The woman waved the gemstone over his garments.

"She said it's not safe to go back."

"Then you must destroy the baby's things." She tucked the stone away and added, "I know where I'll take her."

"I've got to go." The young man thrust the baby at her and bolted out the door.

He sped back, slowing as he approached the apartment building. With no one in sight, he bounded up the stairs. The apartment door stood wide, its latch shattered. He swung the door shut behind him and hastened to the bedroom, struggling not to look at the bodies. He crossed directly to the dresser and pushed aside the clothing in its lowest drawer. The wail of an approaching siren could be heard. The young man's mouth tightened, but he continued with his task. He seized a small green box bearing a raised crest. Pulling a ruby from his pocket, he rushed to throw open the screenless window and held the gemstone and the box aloft. After a few seconds, the box dissolved in a shimmer of intense indigo light.

Returning to the open dresser drawer, he gathered baby clothing and other paraphernalia and pitched it into the crib. Shoving it under the window, he grasped the sides of the crib firmly and stared hard at the ruby tucked into his left hand, a look of fierce concentration on his face. Eventually the edges of the crib softened and glowed indigo, then started to waver and blur. The young man continued to stare intently at the ruby, exerting great effort. The crib finally disappeared altogether as the door of the apartment crashed open and someone yelled, "Police! Don't move!"

∽ Chapter 1 ∽
Omnia mutantur, nos et mutamur in illis
(All things change, and we change with them;
proverb)

The fourth day of August was hot and muggy in Burning Springs, Pennsylvania. Sigrun Nyman was mechanically picking string beans along a row that stretched seemingly endlessly across the field while the sweat trickled slowly down her face. Her brown hair, which usually hung in thick unruly waves around her shoulders, was tucked into an untidy bun in a losing battle to stay cool. Philip Schlichter, Sigrun's best friend, had folded himself into the meager shade cast by the battered pickup truck parked at the edge of the field and was fanning his flushed face with the bandana he had been wearing to protect his neck from the blazing sun.

"Come and sit down before you faint," called Philip.

"No, it's too soon to take a break," she said with a laugh. "We'll never get the field finished if you stop every fifteen minutes."

"We won't get the field finished if you have to drive me to the emergency room with heat prostration either."

"All right, you rest – I'll pick your share as well."

He heaved himself to his feet with an exaggerated sigh. "No, I can't let you show me up."

"But, Philip, these are the last of the vegetables your mother wanted for the market tomorrow; if we finish early, we can get in a ride before dinner."

"I'll be too worn out to think about anything besides bed by the time we finish," Philip muttered as he resumed picking the row next to Sigrun's.

The sun beat down relentlessly as they worked in companionable silence. Untethered by the mindlessness of the repetitive task, Sigrun's thoughts turned, as they frequently did of late, to her father, William. Two months earlier she had suddenly heard a thud and had run upstairs to find him collapsed on the floor. Although he had been 74, he had seemed so healthy and had stayed so active that his death had come as a complete shock. She had not yet fully convinced herself that he was gone.

"Feeling down again?" Philip asked after a while.

"Yeah," Sigrun said. "I keep trying to think about being at law school, and all I can focus on is how excited Dad would have been. I guess ... well, I can't really see myself there without having him to share it with."

"I know, but remember how proud he was when you got accepted by UCLA."

She stopped picking. "That's what makes it so hard. It was **his** dream. From the time I was tiny, he told me he wanted me to go to law school so I could go out and save the world. ... I'm not so sure I want to do it on my own."

"Come and sit down." Philip headed back to the shade of the truck. "So you're still thinking about not going?" He untied his bandana and wiped his dripping face.

Sigrun took a long drink of tepid water and brushed escaped strands of hair off her face. "I just don't know. If I'm out in California – what about the Farmstead?"

"Like I've told you before, we'll take care of things – that's not what's really bothering you."

"Maybe not ... but it's so sad to have to sell the goats."

"I wish I could keep them – but I don't have time to feed and milk a dozen goats."

"I couldn't let you do that. I feel bad enough having you watch the house and everything. I mean, you've got too much going on this year with the entrance exams."

"Don't worry – I'll get my brothers to do most of the work. I'm a master at passing off my chores to them."

"But if I went to law school at Dickinson instead, then I could keep the goats and take care of the place."

"Hey, as much as I'd love to have you stay home, I can't let you walk away from your scholarship without being sure that's what you really want."

"I'm not sure about anything."

"Right. So stick with our deal: You promise to try your best at UCLA for a year, and I'll do my best to get into vet school."

"I suppose," she said doubtfully, "I should at least see what it's like."

"Exactly." Philip got to his feet. "Let's get this torture over with."

The day wore on. The sun gradually became obscured by

high clouds, and the pair picked at a rapid pace. Nonetheless, the afternoon slipped by more quickly than did the rows of beans.

"Finally," Philip said, picking the last beans in the last row and straightening his back. "I don't think we have time for a ride after all. I didn't tell you, but Mom baked you a cake, so we shouldn't be late for dinner."

"Oh, that was sweet. But … I just don't feel much like celebrating."

Philip gave her a quick hug. "I know, but we can't let your birthday pass unnoticed. Besides, Mom wants to spoil you a bit before you leave."

Philip hefted the last buckets of beans into the back of the truck. "Come on, if we hurry, I'll have time for a shower, and everyone will be much happier if I do."

⟩⟶⟵⟨

The temperature had continued to drop from the heavy heat of early afternoon, and a cooling breeze had sprung up. Sigrun decided that, even though she was tired from the long hours in the fields, the weather was perfect to walk the mile or so that separated the Schlichters' place from the century-old house and 10-acre patch of land that was all that remained of the Nyman Farmstead.

Strolling up the long gravel drive at the farm, she heard a voice call out, "Yo, Sigrun." She peered through the deepening shadows cast over the chicken coop by a row of tall maple trees bordering the drive and spotted a gawky 15-year old with hair a shade lighter than Philip's sandy blond. "Hi, Donald, I didn't see you there."

"Hey," he said as he loped over to join her, "thanks again for your father's chickens. It's funny – since I brought them over, my egg count has really improved. I think my girls are jealous and are trying hard to outproduce the newcomers."

She laughed. "I'm glad you were willing to take them."

"Willing – no way. I was thrilled. I mean, I have to do all the work to take care of mine anyway; so with almost twice as many birds, I should make nearly twice as much money with only a little more effort. Seems like a no-brainer to me."

"Well, I'm thankful they have a good home." They stepped into the kitchen. "I see you found time for that promised shower," she said as she spied the freshly-washed-and-changed Philip.

"When have you ever known Philip not to have time for a shower and clean clothes?" asked Donald. "I swear he changes clothes twice as often as Mom does."

"Watch it – I'm bigger than you," Philip said in a mock-threatening tone as he tucked Donald's head under his arm. At 21, Philip was still somewhat gangly, not quite grown into his hands and feet, and not as athletic as either of his younger brothers. As he and Donald wrestled, they bumped into the sturdy table in the center of the room, causing the dishes stacked upon it to rattle alarmingly.

"Stop that!" Sigrun laughed as she ducked out of their way. She caught Philip's arm and pulled him away from Donald. "Come on guys, behave and help me set the table." She grabbed a pile of plates and headed to the dining room.

"Happy Birthday, Sigrun," said an affable middle-aged man who was an older, heavier, and grayer version of Philip. "Come and chat; let the boys do some work for a change." Otto Schlichter settled himself in the living room. "I'd rather not bother you on your birthday, but I wanted to make sure that everything is okay."

"I'm fine." Sigrun reflexively brushed her now-unbound hair back from her face. "Well, I am worried about leaving the Farmstead empty – but Philip assures me that he and the boys will take care of it."

"We'll make sure nothing happens to the place while you're gone. By the way, I ran into Ray at the feed store and asked him how things were going. He said he's got the probate just about done. I asked him to keep me informed. I hope you don't mind."

"Not at all. I'm really grateful for your interest."

"Ray told me there'll be enough money to keep the Farmstead running while you're in school. So you don't have to rent it out yet. And Sigrun," Mr. Schlichter leaned forward and said earnestly, "always remember that we're here for you if you need anything. You know Mother and I think of you as a daughter – why, you've spent almost as much time over here as Philip since that summer you moved next door."

"Thank you," she replied warmly. "You know I think of you as family."

"I hope so – otherwise I'd have to marry you to keep you around," Philip said genially from the doorway.

His father laughed. "Why Philip, that's a grand idea."

"Sorry to interrupt, but I was sent to call you in to dinner."

"We're done," said Mr. Schlichter, getting to his feet.

"Happy Birthday, Sigrun!" chorused Norman, Donald, and Ernestine Schlichter as they entered the dining room. Dinner was a

spirited occasion; the conversation never strayed from cheerful sub-
jects, and Philip and his next-younger brother Norman strove to
surpass each other's comical stories. Sigrun allowed herself to be
swept up in the celebration. A harmonious rendition of "Happy
Birthday," led by Philip's impeccable tenor, was followed by the cutting of the cake.

ᗊ ᗤ

"Why don't you stay a while," Philip suggested after the rest
of the family had headed to bed.

"No, I'd better get home," she said. "I want to tackle some
packing tomorrow. I've been putting it off all summer, and now
there's only two weeks left."

"Don't remind me." Holding the front door for her as they
stepped outside, he gave a searching glance around the driveway.
"You walked?"

"Yes, it's a lovely evening."

"I suppose. But I've had quite enough fresh air today. I'll
drive you."

"Don't bother – I don't mind walking."

"Of course not. What would Mom say if she found out I
let you walk home alone at night?"

"So, all you care about is what your mother would say?"

"No," Philip responded smoothly, "but I figured if I said **I**
was concerned for your welfare, you'd think I was coddling you."

She laughed. "Okay, you can drive."

Sigrun settled herself into the passenger seat of a 1968
Mustang, a gift from his father upon Philip's graduation from high
school. The car had been Mr. Schlichter's pride and joy since his
own high school years. Philip had embraced the role of caretaker
for the car with an enthusiasm that continued to confound Sigrun.

"You know," Philip said as they drove down the driveway,
"Dad meant that – they do think of you as their daughter."

"I know … it means a lot to me."

"And it's not only my folks; my brothers adore you and
would do anything for you. … As would I," he added gravely. "I'll
even help you pack."

"But – don't you have things you want to do?"

"There is nothing in the world I would rather do than spend
time with you," he intoned solemnly.

She laughed as they approached the Farmstead. "Really –
I'll start taking you seriously if you don't stop."

"But I am serious," he protested, "I want to help pack."

"Then I'd love your help. And Philip, thanks for making my birthday special."

⚶⚶

Although she had turned her alarm off, Sigrun awoke as usual at dawn. As she was free of picking chores that day, she considered going back to sleep, but then she remembered her vow to start packing. The thought immediately cast her into gloom and banished all possibility of sleep. Best get an early start, she thought with resignation.

After a quick breakfast, she girded herself and entered her father's bedroom. It wasn't that she hadn't been in the room all summer – it was that packing his things would substantiate his death to an extent that she wasn't sure she could handle. Her sorrowful gaze lingered on his collection of "lawyer stories," as he had called them. William had loved novels about lawyers, especially ones with courtroom drama. She sighed. Now she'd never be able to describe for him what it felt like to give a closing argument in front of a jury. She didn't want to disturb the books. Maybe the clothing. Sigrun opened the closet and eyed the rather sparse and tattered contents; it had always been a struggle to get her father to replace anything that wasn't falling apart. She sighed again. She was planning to donate the clothing to charity, but not today.

With the whole day stretched in front of her, she thought, maybe it made sense to start on something more substantial. She wandered aimlessly down to the sitting room. She then headed to the kitchen and poured herself another mug of coffee, staring blankly out the window while she drank it. What about the attic? Clearly she would need somewhere to store the things she wanted to keep when she did rent the place.

Sigrun briskly ascended the two flights of stairs to the attic and struggled to open the tight-fitting door. The space was rather more crowded and chaotic than she recalled. She randomly started on one of the untidy stacks of boxes. After a while, it occurred to her that some of her mother's things must be around. Her mother had died before Sigrun and her father had moved to Burning Springs, and the Farmstead bore few traces of her. But knowing her father, he would have packed her belongings and brought them along.

She eventually worked her way to the back of the attic and found a large unfamiliar old-fashioned black steamer trunk. After clearing away the stuff stashed around it, she was able to pry the lid's rusty latches open and prop it up on age-weakened hinges. Inside, as she had suspected, were what seemed to be her mother's things. Rubbing the worst of the dirt from her hands onto her jeans before pushing the hair off her face, Sigrun contemplated the remnants of the life of someone of whom she retained only the faintest memories. Did it make any sense to look at this now? Standing there adrift, she became aware that she was hot and hungry. Maybe she should reconsider her plan of action over lunch.

As she ate in the shade of a tall beech tree, Sigrun watched the goats milling about in their nearby pasture. Her father's soft goat-milk cheese had been much in demand at the local farmers' markets, and she had found a rival cheese-maker who wanted to buy the herd. Once they were gone, she realized with a pang, she would be alone at the Farmstead.

She blinked back her tears; she didn't want to succumb to depression. Maybe it wasn't the most logical use of her time, but if she could empty that trunk, she would have a good place to put her father's things. And besides, since she didn't need to rent the house before next summer, she had plenty of time to pack. Fortified by lunch and focused on her goal, she returned to the attic determined to dispatch her mother's trunk. She lifted the top tray and settled to the floor; it held bundled letters.

She was pulled out of her absorption in her mother's long-ago correspondence to Sigrun's grandmother by the far-off ringing of the doorbell. That must be Philip, and, she thought in exasperation, she had forgotten to unlock the front door. Maybe he'd check the back. She waited, straining to hear something to indicate that he had let himself into the kitchen. Nothing. She descended the stairs and unlocked the door.

"Well, hello," she said to Philip's back.

Philip lazily unfurled his lanky frame from his position leaning against the porch post, his guitar slung carelessly across his back, and gave her a sheepish grin. "Hi, guess I missed the morning."

Struck by the image Philip presented backlit by the brilliant sunshine, she ran her eyes over him, from his scuffed shoes and worn and faded, but snug-fitting, blue jeans to his still-crisp, freshly laundered white T-shirt with its sleeves rolled up to expose more of his deeply tanned arms. The long summer in the fields had produced not only the rich color of his skin, but also the sun-bleached highlights in his tousled blond hair. The blue of the sky was re-

flected in his cheerfully sparkling eyes. "My, you do casually dishev-
eled well."

His grin widened. "I didn't think you'd notice."

"I always try to appreciate beauty when I see it," she said
dryly. "Are you coming in, or are you just dropping by on your way
to a gig?"

Philip ambled into the house. "I'm here to keep you company as long as you'll have me."

"What about your promise to help pack?"

"Oh, that too." He took off his guitar and set it on the sofa
in the sitting room. "But I thought we'd like some entertainment
later ... while we're resting."

"Haven't you rested all morning?" she quipped as she started
up the stairs.

"That's unfair. Well, I did sleep in a bit 'cause I stayed up late
last night working on a new song, but Mom left me a list of chores
for my 'day off', and then I ran into Dad in the barn while I was
tending the horses, and he wanted to discuss whether Estelle was
off her feed. So, no, I haven't been resting."

"Is she off her feed?"

"Yeah, but I think it's the heat. What have you been up to?"

Sigrun shoved open the door at the top of the narrow attic
stairs. "I tried Dad's room first, but I couldn't face that. I haven't
been up here in years and look," she said, gesturing at the dusty disarray, "it's a mess."

"Mmm – that it is. What's your plan?"

"Actually, I got side-tracked by a trunk of my mother's
things."

"Your mother! Anything interesting?"

"Sort of – I was looking at her letters. I can't decide what I
should hang onto."

"You don't really remember her, do you?"

Sigrun pushed a box aside to make room and handed Philip a
letter she had been reading. "I have a few memories, but I'm not
sure – they might come from photos. I was only four when she
died, and the cancer was pretty horrific."

While he read, Sigrun glanced through the package of letters
and opened one near the bottom of the pile. "Oh," she exclaimed,
"this one must have been written soon after I arrived. She wrote to
her mother, 'Sigrun is growing so fast! We can't believe how fortu-
nate we are that she was so young when she came to us'."

"How old were you when they adopted you?"

"Just a few months I think." She gave a rueful laugh. "Dad never wanted to talk about anything that even hinted that I wasn't his child, so I don't know much. ... Now I guess I never will."

"But you know, there might be loads of information buried in that trunk – be careful what you throw out."

"I suppose," she agreed absently, still reading. Then she set the letter down and looked at Philip somewhat helplessly. "What should I do?"

He got to his feet. "I say we take some of the stuff from the trunk downstairs so you can sort through it in comfort. Let me look around, but I bet if it's organized, there'll be plenty of room to bring up what you want to store."

As Philip assessed the attic, Sigrun combed through the trunk. Apart from the letters and a couple of old photo albums, the only thing she thought might have any connection to her infancy was a small blanket that was made of some extremely soft, unfamiliar material. In the end, she took only the letters and albums.

Time passed quickly as they rearranged. After carting down those items identified as trash, Philip trudged back up the stairs and sat down in the doorway to watch as Sigrun stacked the last of the boxes. His appraisal had been correct; once organized, the attic was no longer crowded. "Not a bad day's work, I'd say."

She laughed. "I think we're done, what do you think?"

"Definitely done."

🐾

After their delivery-pizza dinner, Philip sat on the couch in the sitting room strumming a quiet melody on his guitar and nursing a beer. Sigrun, curled into the softest chair in the room, had lapsed into silence.

"You know," she reflected, "I've never been away from home."

"You never took vacations, did you?"

"No – Dad didn't like to travel, and we always had chores, so we only ever took day trips. ... I can't really imagine living in Los Angeles."

"I can't imagine you not being here," he said glumly. "Who else can I confide in?"

"Oh, Philip." Sigrun sat up in her chair. "You can call me."

"I plan to – every day I expect. But ... you'll be out in the big city, meeting new people, having new experiences. I'll just be

here and … we'll grow apart."

"No we won't. You know I don't like meeting people, and I don't expect I'll like living in a big city, and anyway, I don't know how I'll get by without you."

Philip shook his head skeptically. "As Emerson said: 'We change, whether we like it or not'. … Anyway, there's something I want to play for you – my adaptation of 'Dead Man's Hill'. It really resonates with me." He struck up the opening measures of a rather mournful melody.

Silence reverberated as the last chord faded.

"Me too," Sigrun said eventually, wiping away tears.

Philip took a swig of beer. "Enough melancholy – this is for you, too."

She laughed as she recognized "California Girls."

It wasn't until two days before Sigrun was to leave that she finally confronted her father's clothing. She and Philip had discussed plans for her semester break during a long ride the previous evening. She was propelled into action by the vision of coming home to a room preserving the charade that her father was still alive. It was time, she told herself purposefully, to accept that he was, in fact, gone.

Sigrun folded the last shirt into the last box. As she contemplated the tidy room, her eyes fell on a framed photograph on the dresser of herself on a horse when she was about six. Her father had always said it was his favorite photo; she took it into her bedroom and set it on her dresser next to her baby box. She glanced at her watch. Damn, it was a quarter past four, and she had agreed to meet Philip at four.

Sigrun waved at Donald as she passed the chicken coop before parking her father's ancient pickup by the barn. She entered the dim coolness of the spacious building and followed the sound of voices until she found Philip and his father in a stall.

"I'm not too worried." Mr. Schlichter stepped out of the stall. "Hello, Sigrun."

"Is Estelle still not eating?"

"Well, she just isn't thriving the way she should be," Mr. Schlichter said. "I'll see you kids later – I have to get to bank before it closes."

Sigrun entered the stall and stroked the white star on the forehead of a large chestnut mare. "How's she doing?"

"She still hasn't gained weight, so I guess the vet had better check her out," Philip replied. "I'm done – why don't you get saddled."

Sigrun slipped out of the stall and set off down the wide aisle, but then she turned. "Hey, I finally did it."

"What? The clothing?"

"Yeah, it's packed and ready to be picked up."

Philip joined her, and they headed toward the tack room. "So how do you feel?"

She considered for a moment. "Good." She grabbed a brush and took her saddle and bridle down from their peg. "I think you were right: I was still vacillating about UCLA, and I was giving myself a safe haven by leaving the room intact."

"So, you've resolved to go?" He followed her into the adjoining pasture, put two fingers in his mouth, and gave a piercing whistle. The small herd of horses clustered under a clump of trees at the far end of the field flung up their heads and galloped over.

Sigrun laughed as several large heads thrust against her in search of treats. "Don't be greedy, girls," she said, handing out carrot pieces. She pushed through the milling horses and grabbed the halter of a dainty young chestnut mare with vibrant red highlights in her mane and tail. She gave Ellie a carrot and led her over to the fence.

After weighing Philip's question, Sigrun replied, "I think I have." Then she laughed. "How's that for an equivocal answer?"

"But it was just an illusion," he said unexpectedly. He swung his saddle onto Arabella, a frisky dark bay mare he had tethered next to Ellie.

"What was?"

"The room. You've been clinging to the fiction of continuity. But the reality is – your life **has** changed, whether you stay here or go to California."

"Thanks for pointing that out." Sigrun finished tightening the cinch on her saddle. "Let's go for our ride, and let me stave off reality for one more night."

🙠🙡

⌒ Chapter 2 ⌒
Actus primus
(First act)

"And did I mention the palm trees?"

"Yes Sigrun, several times," said Philip with a long-suffering sigh.

"Well, I think it's cool that I can see real live palm trees out my bedroom window."

"As opposed to dead ones?" he asked sarcastically.

"**No.** As opposed to the movies – I've only ever seen palm trees in movies."

"I guess you didn't come that time we went to Disney World?"

"No Philip, that was your family's vacation."

"Sorry, I forgot. You know, there aren't many things in my life I've done that didn't involve you; until now, of course."

"I've only been gone two days," Sigrun said in exasperation.

"So, I'm anticipating."

"Maybe you could try anticipating that my classes go well."

"Hey, has the presumptive roommate appeared?"

"No, I guess she's waiting until classes start."

"Isn't that in less than 12 hours?"

"Yeah."

"Plenty of time …"

"Wait – I think that's her now. Anyway, someone's talking next door."

"Then you should go and be sociable," he prodded.

"I suppose so," she said grudgingly.

"Yes, Sigrun, at the very least, you've got to be friendly to your roommate. I'll call you tomorrow to see how classes went."

As she tucked her cell phone into her jeans, she thought reluctantly that Philip was right, she should make an attempt at being sociable. She knocked lightly and opened the door into the adjacent common room, which contained a tiny kitchen and two moth-eaten but passably comfortable lounge chairs. A rather plump but pretty young woman with long, curly brown hair was talking animatedly into a cell phone. Catching sight of Sigrun, she waved, concluded her call, and stuffed her phone into a large green messenger-style bag slung over her shoulder. Her gum cracked audibly.

"Hello, I'm Sigrun Nyman."

"Glad to meet you. I'm Maria Guadalupe Contreras – my mother's rather old-fashioned – I go by Lupe. When did you arrive? I skipped the intro stuff."

"I came a couple of days ago for orientation," Sigrun replied, fascinated by Lupe's ability to talk so rapidly while chewing gum.

"Oh, well, you know," Lupe waved a hand dismissively, "I took a class at the law school last year, so I know my way around. And my boyfriend, Diego, well, he's over at Cal State LA, and his classes started already, so, like, we had to move him in, and we only have one car. Hey, you know, I've got the car this week, so if you want to go anywhere, I can take you."

"Thanks," said Sigrun, struggling to keep pace with Lupe's swift conversational shifts. "Were you an undergrad at UCLA?"

"Oh yeah, guess you wouldn't know." Lupe laughed cheerfully at herself. "I was a political science major here. But, you know, Diego couldn't get in – he's in his fifth year as an undergrad. Where're you from? Hey, did you have dinner?" She glanced at her watch. "I thought I'd go grab something before the cafeterias close – wanna come?"

Sigrun, not interested in going anywhere, recalled Philip's admonishment. "Sure," she said, trying to inject enthusiasm into her voice, "that sounds like fun."

"Great! We'd better hustle. And I'll show you around campus on the way back. Have you had time to see anything yet? You know, Westwood's only a couple of blocks away, and it's a pretty happening place."

As they left the suite, accompanied by a non-stop flow of friendly advice from Lupe, Sigrun found herself weighing one of Philip's favorite quotations: "You don't get harmony when everybody sings the same note."

❧～❧

"Sigrun Nyman?"

"Here," she replied as the Contracts professor fixed her with piercing blue eyes for an instant before moving on.

"Quentin Quinn?"

"Here," responded the earnest-looking student seated to

Sigrun's left.

Sigrun's attention wandered while the row call continued. She was still slightly flustered from the morning's rush to class. The previous evening, she and Lupe had discovered that they had been assigned to the same one of the four sections of first-year law students. Because first-year classes were scheduled by section, that meant they would have the same classes all year. Thereafter, Lupe could not be politely deterred from her insistence that they walk to their first class together. Unfortunately, their first class happened to be Contracts, which started at 8:30 on Wednesdays, and Lupe, it turned out, was not an early riser. Sigrun, although ready early as usual, waited too long to knock on Lupe's door. By the time Lupe had dressed and they had scurried across campus, they had barely had time to locate their assigned seats from the seating chart posted on the door of the lecture hall. She had slipped into her seat just as the stern-faced elderly professor strode purposefully to the lectern.

"Milton Teague?"

"Here," a reedy voice called from a seat near the door.

"Mr. Teague, why are you not in your assigned seat?" asked Professor Ida Acorda irritably, jotting a note on her chart.

"Uhm ... I didn't know we had assigned seats," he said, sounding bewildered.

"The chart is plainly posted. From now on, you will arrive on time and be in your proper place." Without giving the student time to respond, Professor Acorda moved on to the name of what appeared to be the last student, "Regan Wren?"

"Present," responded a woman's lilting voice from the back.

Professor Acorda shuffled her papers. "Welcome class. Before we get started, I'd like to go over some of my rules. First, attendance is mandatory, and I will deduct points if you consistently miss class. Second, I will randomly call on students and expect all students to be prepared with the day's assigned cases. Third, do not interrupt me; I will take questions at times that are convenient.

"So, Mr. Teague, could you tell me the essential elements of a contract?"

"Uh ... well, I ..." The sound of a book hitting the floor echoed through the hall. Several students giggled. "Sorry," Milton stammered sheepishly. "Let's see ... uhm, mutual consent, an exchange, uh ..."

"What is he missing, Mr. Quinn?" the professor asked briskly.

"A lawful objective," stated Quentin decisively.

"Yes," Professor Acorda said. "And, of course, an enforceable contract must be executed by competent parties. Ms. Contreras, what did Mr. Teague mean by the term 'exchange'?"

"I really couldn't say," Lupe said. "Some sort of swap, I suppose?"

"No," the professor said disparagingly. "In contract law, it has a precise meaning. And what is that meaning, Mr. Higginbotham?"

"But excuse me, Professor," Lupe said, holding up a book she had opened, "it says right here in Black's Law Dictionary that 'exchange' is 'to barter; to swap'."

A murmur of muffled laughter rumbled through the room. "Please do not interrupt," Professor Acorda snapped. "I do not dispute the general definition of the word. Mr. Higginbotham?"

"A contract requires consideration," Livingstone Higginbotham said smoothly, "that is, some bargained-for benefit must be conferred."

"Exactly," the professor said. "Turning to Dougherty v. Salt; Mr. Higginbotham, why is his aunt's promise to pay Dougherty $3000 at her death not a contract?"

So far, Sigrun thought with a sigh while rapidly taking notes, law school was shaping up to be loads of fun.

⤳ ⤳

The section had an hour-and-a-half break after Contracts. Sigrun checked her mailbox in the student lounge, more for something to do than because she expected to find anything. Her box, however, contained a folded piece of paper. The lounge was beginning to fill with students, so she went out to the adjacent patio and found a shaded seat at an empty table. It was still early, but the day was working itself toward hot.

She read the note of welcome from Emma Ehrlich, one of the few students her father had kept in touch with from his days teaching high school in Lancaster before they had moved to Burning Springs. She was his favorite success story – having gone on to graduate from Harvard Law School after Sigrun's father had encouraged her to become a lawyer. Now a professor, it was on her advice that Sigrun had selected UCLA. She made a notation on her calendar to stop by the professor's office that Friday afternoon after her last class.

⤳ ⤳

By Friday, Sigrun was beginning to get into a rhythm of going to classes and the library. Friday was a good day because she only had one class, Contracts, and it started at 10:30 rather than 8:30 as it did the other three days a week it met. Already, she and Lupe had reached an unspoken agreement that it was best not to walk to class together since their internal comfort levels for timeliness differed so significantly. She arrived at the Law School by 10:15, checked her mailbox, and was in her assigned seat with ample time to review the day's assignment.

The class quieted quickly when the professor reached the podium, with the exception of one intense conversation toward the front.

"Mr. Higginbotham," Professor Acorda said sharply, "Mr. Hawke. If you two would like to carry on a private conversation, please leave the room."

"No, professor, sorry," Tony Higginbotham said nonchalantly, settling back in his seat and appearing not the slightest embarrassed at the dressing down.

"Well then, Mr. Higginbotham, why did the court in the Plowman case find a lack of consideration?"

"Because the employees' past performance, exemplary or not, was completed prior to bargaining and therefore couldn't constitute consideration for a new contract."

"True," the professor said, "but why doesn't the company's moral obligation to provide for their employees suffice?"

"Moral obligation isn't something bargained for – the employees didn't give anything in exchange. But I don't see why the company can't be held to their promise, not as a contract, but because they induced the employees to quit."

"Good question," Professor Acorda said, sounding almost complimentary. "Ms. Contreras," the professor shot out, "can you tell us why the employees' agreement to quit is not sufficient for consideration?"

"No, Professor, I have no idea," Lupe said casually from her front-row seat.

"Perhaps if you had done the assigned reading, you might have a chance," said the professor testily. "Ms. Nyman, can you answer my question?"

"Because the employees didn't give up anything – they were going to be laid off anyway?" Sigrun ventured nervously.

"Exactly. So there was no exchange."

The hour-and-a-half class passed, Sigrun thought, quite quickly. As the class filed out of the lecture hall – voices exuberant at the onset of the weekend – Lupe called, "Hey, Sigrun, wait up. A bunch of us from the section are going for pizza in Westwood. You've gotta come, you know, I want you to meet Diego. How about it?"

"Well ..." Sigrun said uncertainly, hesitant to put herself in a situation in which she knew she would be uncomfortable; she always felt gauche and tongue-tied in groups of people she either didn't know or didn't know well.

"Hey, no excuses!" Lupe snapped her gum loudly. "It's Friday night, and you're new in town – you've got to get out and have some fun. Be ready at 7:30."

Slightly nonplussed, Sigrun watched Lupe dash down the hall. Well, she certainly didn't have any plans for the evening. She rechecked her still-empty mailbox before heading over to the closest cafeteria to pick up a sandwich for lunch.

It was 1:30 by the time Sigrun found her way to Professor Ehrlich's office. She paused nervously at the closed door, trying one more time to compose an introductory comment before knocking. Just as she raised her arm, the door was flung open. She leapt back quickly to avoid being hit by the intense young woman, dressed all in black, who backed rapidly out of the office, swinging her backpack onto her shoulder.

"Okay, thanks, Professor, I'll catch you next week," the woman was saying. She turned quickly and nearly ran into Sigrun, who was still attempting to get out of her way. "Sorry, I didn't see you." The woman hurried down the hall.

"Can I help you?" a courteous voice called from the office.

She stepped into the doorway. "Uh, hi – I'm Sigrun Nyman, I ..."

"Sigrun!" The thirtyish woman seated behind the heavily laden desk jumped to her feet and hurried over to shake Sigrun's hand warmly. "I'm so happy to meet you. Take a seat. I can't believe you're actually here – and grown up. The last time I saw you, I think you were four years old." Professor Ehrlich sighed. "I can't believe that Mr. Nyman is gone either. Of course, I hadn't seen him for years – but I have an image of him in my mind as fit and energetic."

"He was," Sigrun offered quietly, letting her hair fall forward to hide her face. "He seemed healthy up until the day he died. ... I guess it was better that he didn't suffer, but it was so unexpected ..."

"He had a heart attack?"

"Yes, without warning. Or at least nothing he ever mentioned."

"Very sad." The professor shook her head and sighed again. "But, on a more pleasant topic – how do you like law school?"

"It's okay I guess … it's rather early yet."

Professor Ehrlich laughed. "I suppose it is. I have to confess that I'm one of the few people I know who loved law school. Over the years, however, I've come to appreciate that few students feel the same."

"I'll have to wait and see. I was taken aback by the rather combative nature of some of my classes."

"You know, Sigrun, I remember my first semester at law school – it wasn't **all** that long ago – and how difficult it was. But it was fun once I'd gotten used to all the reading."

"I hope so," she said doubtfully.

There was a knock on the door, and a young man stuck his head in. "I'm sorry to interrupt, Professor, but we have an appointment."

"Yes, so we do. I'm sorry, Sigrun, I have to meet with another student." They both stood. "Please do stop by any time. I'm so happy to have finally met you."

"Me too … and thanks."

Sigrun **was** happy to have finally met Professor Ehrlich – but, on the other hand, the conversation had depressed her. In the bustle of new classes and a new routine, she had mostly succeeded in pushing her loneliness to the back of her mind. Now she felt an aching emptiness at not being able to call her father; he had been so excited at the prospect of her meeting the professor. She blinked back tears and quickly stepped outside. She had planned to go to the library, but it was another warm and brilliantly sunny day, and the thought of being stuck indoors was too much at the moment. Perhaps she could study in the Sculpture Garden, which she had happened upon earlier. She threaded her way through the crowds until she found a shaded spot at the base of one of several large sculptures scattered in the grassy open space. She had to admit that, so far, she was not at all sure she shared the professor's view of law school.

She pulled out her cell phone – maybe she could catch Philip before dinner. But the call switched to his voicemail. "Hey, you'll be happy to hear I'm going out to dinner tonight with Lupe and her friends. Call me if you get this before ten or so your time."

>⟶〰⟶<

At 7:20 that evening, Sigrun went into the common room. It had been quiet in the suite ever since she had returned, and Lupe was sure to be late. But she was ready early and decided she might as well wait in the common room. Tired of studying, she had brought out a novel, James Ellroy's *Black Dahlia*, that a college friend had recommended upon hearing that Sigrun would be going to school in Los Angeles. She had impulsively purchased the book at the campus store while buying supplies. She hadn't yet found much time to read, but she soon became engrossed.

Sigrun checked her watch when she heard a key in the outside door and was amused to note that it was nearly 8:00.

"Sorry we're late," Lupe said cheerily as she hurried into the room trailed by a rather short, sharply dressed, clean-shaven young man carrying an overnight bag on his shoulder. "This is Diego Flores – he's grumpy tonight because he wanted to have me to himself." Lupe laughed. "But I told him, like, we have plenty of time for that, and I want him to meet my new friends. So, you two chat."

Lupe vanished into her room, leaving an awkward Sigrun to greet Diego. "Hi, I guess you've gathered that I'm Lupe's suitemate?"

"Hi," he responded agreeably and looked around with a slightly vague expression. "No – what do you mean?"

Sigrun was disconcerted by his apparent lack of comprehension. "I share the suite with Lupe. My room's through there." She gestured to the closed door.

"I didn't know Lupe was sharing again." He sounded acutely disappointed. "I kinda thought she'd have her own place, I mean, she's not an undergrad anymore."

"Well," she said patiently, "we only share this room – we have our own bedrooms."

"Oh good." He set the overnight bag down.

She cast about for a conversational gambit. "Lupe said you're at another university?"

"Yeah ... Cal State LA. ... You in law school too?"

"Yes, I'm in Lupe's section."

"Oh," he said with no apparent interest and ambled over to examine the contents of the small refrigerator.

"So ..." she tried again, "do you like living in Los Angeles?"

He shrugged. "It's okay."

They lapsed into silence. Lupe's return rescued Sigrun from her struggle to scare up a subject to which Diego might respond.

"Ready? We should be off." Lupe swept through the common room. Sigrun paused to make sure the exterior door was locked and had to hurry to catch up. "I'd better call Hawke to let them know we'll be late. You drive." She tossed a set of keys at Diego as they approached a bright teal Sunfire coupe illegally parked in the loading zone in front of the dorm.

During the animated discussion of an acceptable division of the dinner bill at the pizzeria, Sigrun's cell phone vibrated in her pocket. She pulled it out and peered at the screen in the dim light. It was a text message from Philip. Holding the phone just below the top of the table, she unobtrusively read: "Just in. Call. Ok if late." She checked the time, almost 11:00, and smiled. What had Philip been up to so late?

As they filed out of the still-crowded restaurant, Lupe leaned past Diego to attract Hawke's attention. "Let's go check out that new bar, over on Manning, did you hear about it? It's supposed to be the hottest."

"Sure," Hawke said amicably. "You game, Tony?"

"Yeah, why not."

"I think I'll head on back," Sigrun said hastily.

"But, Sigrun, it's early," protested Lupe, "come on."

"No, I'd really rather not. I can walk, it's not far."

"Okay then," Lupe yielded. "You know how to get back? Just stay on Westwood Boulevard, and you'll end up on campus."

Sigrun watched as the rest trooped down a side street. She had tried, but she never seemed to have anything to say, and, to be honest, she would rather have read her novel. After a few blocks, she found herself in a vaguely familiar part of campus and located the law school after a bit of searching.

She pulled out her cell phone; Philip had said she could call late.

"How was it?" Philip asked in greeting.

"Dinner was fine," she said tersely. "I'm walking home; they went to a bar."

"I see – not your cup of tea?"

"Not really. But, on a more interesting topic, why were you out so late?"

"Oh," he said innocently, "just out to dinner."

Sigrun snorted. "Yeah, right, until two in the morning? You're holding out."

"Well …"

"Philip! Come on – who are you seeing?"

He laughed. "I wouldn't go that far. I mean, it was a first date, and it was a spur-of-the-moment thing, but ..."

"Tell me the details."

Sigrun closed her Torts case book with a sigh and looked at her watch. She was startled to discover that it was after eleven. She hadn't planned to stay at the library so late; she had been absorbed in trying in vain to understand the distinction between actual and proximate cause, but she was just not getting it. She hadn't been paying attention to the time because she thought she'd leave whenever Philip sent his nightly text message – usually around nine or so on a weeknight. Concerned, she packed up her belongings, hurried outside, and called Philip as she headed toward her dorm.

"Hi," he answered after several rings.

"Hey, you never called?"

"Yeah, well," he said listlessly, "I figured you'd call when you were done and, anyway, I've been struggling to capture a song that was sparked tonight."

"But, wait, didn't you have a date?"

"Yeah. Yeah, I did." He sounded dejected.

"What happened?"

"We were hanging out at Furnace Hill. And ... well, the state troopers came by and ... well, we had open bottles of beer. It caused quite a scene at home."

"Oh, Philip," Sigrun said softly. "Was he very angry?"

"Of course. You know Dad – the worst part about his anger is how quiet he gets. He makes you feel so small."

"What did he say?"

"Oh, pretty much what you'd think – how disappointed he was, and how he expected me to set a better example, you know, being the eldest, and so on."

"Did he ... was anything said about who you were with?"

"No, I don't think he was thinking about that. He was focusing on my having lied to him, the public humiliation, getting a criminal record, not getting into vet school ..."

"Were you charged with something?" Sigrun asked in alarm.

"Only violating the open container law. So, I have to report to a magisterial judge in a couple weeks. I guess I'll get a fine or something; it's not a big deal."

"What horrible luck."

Philip gave a humorless laugh. "Yeah, well, it could have been a lot worse, you know."

"I know. How could you be so stupid!"

"Well, thanks for the sympathy."

"Hold on a minute, I have to let myself in." Sigrun took the phone away from her ear long enough to unlock the outside door and then the door to her suite.

"I'm back," she said into the phone. "Philip, please, could you try to …"

"Use some common sense?" he suggested wryly.

"Yes, exactly."

"Yeah, well believe me, tonight shut down that incipient relationship. So, I guess I'll adopt your approach of all school work, all the time. … I'm grounded anyway," he added gloomily.

"Really! Did you argue?"

"No. I mean, I am living in his house, I did lie to him, and, like you so bluntly said, I was being an idiot. So, yeah, I deserve it."

"Well, that's true." Sigrun had to agree. "Did you talk to your brothers?"

"No. Fortunately, it was late enough when I got home that they were both in bed. After he'd calmed down a bit, Dad agreed we didn't have to create a drama out of it as long as I promised to tell them that I would have to 'pay the consequences'."

"I'm so sorry, Philip. I wish I could be there …"

"Me too." He sighed heavily. "But let's not dwell on my stupidity. Tell me about your day."

⌒⌒

Despite being on the phone with Philip until late the previous night, Sigrun still managed to arrive at Contracts fifteen minutes early. She was brooding about his plight and, she had to admit, feeling acutely lonely. She typically reviewed the day's assignment before class but, today, she simply sat staring into space. Her musings were interrupted by hurried footsteps.

"Dude!" Hawke called. "I've been looking all over for you."

"What's up?" Tony said from the front where he was chatting with Chun Chang.

"Surf's up, that's what. I'm not sitting in this shrew's class when 12-foot waves await. Let's go."

"Awesome! Bye Chun." Tony strolled up the aisle and caught Sigrun's eye. "Wouldn't care to join us, I'm sure?" he asked caustically.

"No." Sigrun hoped she sounded disdainful. "I'd rather be in class."

"So jejune," Tony said.

"What?" asked Hawke.

Tony laughed. "Never mind – we're outta here."

Sigrun remained depressed and distracted as class started. Fortunately, Professor Acorda launched into her lecture mode and only called on a few students; Sigrun was not among them. Even in Con Law – usually her favorite class – she found herself unable to concentrate, pondering instead whether she would be happier now had she switched to Dickinson.

After Con Law, Sigrun took her lunch up to her favorite spot in the Sculpture Garden, figuring she'd see no one she knew there. She made another attempt to sort out the question of causation, but it continued to elude her. And, the way she felt, she was bound to get called on in Torts.

Driscoll Campbell, the Torts professor, was a stooped and restive man who rarely stood still. Sure enough, as soon as a student stumbled in her response, the professor darted back to the podium and, after a quick glance at the seating chart, called on Sigrun to explain how a "superseding cause" impacted proximate causation.

"Well," Sigrun said fairly confidently, "if the chain of causation is broken, there's no proximate cause."

"But does the superseding event have to be distinct in time?"

"No," she replied more tentatively, "if the injury isn't the foreseeable result of the first act, the superseding event ..."

"No, no," he cut her off, "you're going in the wrong direction."

"But," she tried again, "if an unforeseeable intervening event occurs, then there can't be proximate cause."

"You're focusing on foreseeability," the professor said with a shake of his head, "I'm asking about directness. Really, class, it's not that tricky."

The only redeeming aspect of the day was that Tony, apparently still out surfing, was unavailable to advance his usual astute and articulate analysis as to why Sigrun's answer was wrong. The class concluded before anyone had come up with an acceptable explanation. Afterwards, Sigrun headed to the library, determined to craft a better response in case the professor called on her next class.

⤞⤝

Sigrun was in her seat checking her notes for Contracts Friday morning when Lupe uncharacteristically raced into the lecture hall with a couple of minutes to spare.

"Hey, Sigrun," she said breathlessly, "I missed the last two days, and I just know she'll call on me straight away. So, like, can I borrow your notes?"

"Well, I like to …"

"But you don't need them, you always know what's going on," Lupe cajoled. "Come on, I'm sure she'll call on me."

"Wouldn't it be better to come to class," Sigrun suggested a bit testily.

"I suppose," Lupe giggled, "but you take such great notes, I do better with them. Please? You know I'll give them back right after class."

"All right." She reluctantly handed her notebook to Lupe.

"Thanks, Sigrun, you're the greatest." Lupe rushed to her seat just as the professor entered the classroom.

Sigrun got out a blank notebook. Now, she thought peevishly, she'd have to copy her notes into the proper notebook after class. She wished she'd refused, but she didn't want to be rude to Lupe, who, she believed, was genuinely trying to be friends.

➤➤ Chapter 3 ➤➤
Inculpatus
(Blameless)

After Lawyering Skills the following Thursday, Sigrun debated skipping the library for a change. She only had Contracts the next day, and she didn't feel like being indoors. Maybe she could go for a walk before dinner – it seemed like all she did these days was sit in class, sit in the library, and sit at dinner. As she paused at the corridor that led to the library, she noticed Professor Ehrlich talking to a student. Just then, the professor looked up and caught her eye. Sigrun nodded before heading toward the exit.

"Sigrun, hold on," the professor called. As she caught up, she said, "I haven't seen you for weeks. How are things?"

"I'm fine," Sigrun said, feeling a bit guilty for not having stopped by. "I've been busy with classes."

"Have you had a chance to see anything of Los Angeles yet? I've got some free time on Saturday – why don't I show you around, and we can get dinner?"

"No, really, I don't want to impose."

"I insist," said the professor. "I'd like to get to know you and hear more about your father's retirement years. Why don't you come by my office Saturday around one o'clock? I need to take care of a few things, but then we can have the rest of the day."

Feeling she couldn't refuse, Sigrun said, "Well, if you're sure – it sounds lovely."

➤➤➤

Saturday's whirlwind tour of Hollywood and Beverly Hills ended at Venice Beach, where they watched the sun setting over the ocean from a beach-front restaurant.

"This is so thoughtful of you, Professor," Sigrun said. "I haven't had such a nice day since I got here."

"I take it you're not having a great time, then?"

"Oh," Sigrun said quickly, "it's not so much school as the fact that I don't know anyone, and I … well, I don't seem to have much in common with most students."

"Not liking law students too much, is that it?"

"Well, since I am one, I guess I can't say that – but no, not most."

"What drew you to study law?"

"My father really," Sigrun said. "But also, I like to figure out how things work. I was a physics major undergrad for that reason. It seems to me that law plays such a fundamental role in how a society functions, yet most people take it for granted."

The professor laughed. "No wonder you're not making many friends. In my experience, most law students aren't interested in such … intellectual questions."

"So I've noticed. Everyone seems to be focused on passing the bar and finding a high-paying job."

"Not all! I teach a clinical course on habeas corpus, and I think, all modesty aside, that my course attracts the best and brightest students. At least, I get the ones whose interests are broader than test scores. As it happens, I've arranged a lecture next Thursday by someone from Advocacy for Innocence – have you heard of it?"

"I don't think so."

"Well, it's a nationwide project that's helped free dozens of wrongfully convicted prisoners. For someone concerned about the ramifications of the legal system, I'm sure this will be a thought-provoking lecture. Why don't you come?"

"Thanks, I'd love to."

"Good. I think you'll find it intriguing, and, if you want to consider taking my course as your required clinical next year, I'll get you started on a case now. The cases take so long to wend their way through the system that, to have any hope of seeing results – which I admit doesn't happen often – it's best to begin in your first year."

"Have you ever won the release of a prisoner?"

"We've had our minor victories, but we mostly handle capital cases, and, so far, we haven't had any success there. The work, however, is extremely rewarding."

"I'm sure my father would have found it fascinating."

"You know, Sigrun, I wouldn't be here if it hadn't been for your father."

"Really?"

"Absolutely. He encouraged me to look beyond my small, insular world. If he hadn't pushed me, I know I would have settled for a local college and never even considered law school. But enough about me, I want to hear about you. I remember the first time I saw you; maybe a month after they got you, your father brought you to a holiday party at the high school. He was glowing – I'd never seen him so happy."

"Do you happen to remember how they came to adopt me?"

"Uhm ... no, I don't think I ever knew that," the professor said thoughtfully. "Or perhaps I've just forgotten. Sorry."

"That's okay. It's just that my father and I never talked about it, and I'm curious."

"Well, next time I visit, I'll ask my mother. Maybe she'll re-member."

✂✂

The evening of the lecture, Sigrun took a seat not long before Professor Ehrlich called the room to attention. "I have the extreme pleasure tonight to introduce Professor Marshall Barrie from Golden State School of Law. When he taught in Illinois a few years back, he was instrumental in initiating a groundswell of support for a moratorium against capital punishment there. Now he's turned his attention to California – where we have over 600 inmates on death row, by far the largest number of any state in the nation. With that, I'll turn over the podium."

"Welcome," Professor Barrie began. "I'm heartened to see so many in attendance tonight. My goal here is two-fold: to draw attention to the prevalence of wrongful convictions and to build momentum for legislative change. I hope that I can motivate you, as law students, to use your privileged position to work for justice. Oh, I don't mean you all have to go out and become public defenders," he paused while the ripple of laughter passed, "but you can work now as students and later as well-educated and influential members of society to raise the public's awareness of the reality of wrongful convictions. Moreover, some of you will be in positions some day to make the laws that you are now studying. My aim is to get you to stop and think about the possibility that the person who is on trial may actually be innocent. Our legal system is predicated on the principle that every accused is innocent until the state meets the heavy burden of establishing beyond a reasonable doubt that he or she is guilty of the charged crime. But, unfortunately, injustice is not infrequent.

"It is an irrefutable fact that innocent people have been sent to death row all over this country. In California alone three men have been released from death row based on evidence of their innocence. Since 1973, approximately 100 people have been exonerated from death rows across the country. In the 1990s, the pro bono Advocacy for Innocence was created to assist inmates who may be able to prove their innocence with new DNA testing. They have had great success, and, in their wake, a broad network of programs has sprung up around the country. Some of them – such as the one run here by Professor Ehrlich – assist inmates in trying to establish their innocence whether or not evidence exists that can be subjected to scientific testing.

"Again, here in California, the Courts have decreed that more than 200 people have been wrongfully convicted since 1989 – not all were on death row, not all were convicted of murder – but these numbers reveal that our criminal justice system has a significant capacity for error.

"And don't believe for a moment that the sole problem lies with faulty scientific testing or the lack of testing. Any number of factors play into wrongful convictions. For example, according to their case records, false confessions were instrumental in more than 20% of the exonerations won by Advocacy for Innocence. Accused men – and they are mostly men – confess for a number of reasons, many having little to do with the truth. Juries have trouble accepting that an innocent person would ever confess if he weren't guilty of something. Further, and perhaps more sobering, nearly 80% of exonerations involved mistaken identifications. In fact, controlled studies have shown that an eyewitness is as likely to be wrong as he or she is to correctly identify the perpetrator of a crime just witnessed. As what happened fleetingly in front of the eyes is repeatedly replayed inside the head, it becomes embroidered, reinforced, and finally entrenched.

"Then there are the problems with prosecutors. First, let me assure you that I do **not** believe that the vast majority of prosecutors **ever** intentionally set out to convict someone they are not absolutely convinced is guilty. To the contrary, most problems arise when prosecutors believe so strongly they are prosecuting the right person that they exclude potentially exculpatory evidence, fabricate useful evidence, and use inflammatory rhetoric that prevents the jury from fairly considering the evidence presented.

"The people who have been wrongfully convicted are just that – people. They had lives and families before they got swept up in the swirl of a criminal prosecution. Of course, I'm not going to try to convince you that every person wrongfully convicted is an upstanding citizen; some of them are guilty of other crimes. But in this country we have a constitution that protects the civil rights of the accused. If our constitution is to remain strong, we must ensure that every individual – no matter their criminal history, no matter how unlikable they may be – is secure from wrongful convictions.

"And sometimes, the net of an over-zealous prosecution pulls in an individual with no involvement in any past crime and no connection to the charged crime. One example of the many, many, moving stories of those who've been convicted of crimes they did not commit is that of a California prisoner who recently won his release after serving more than 20 years of a life sentence for murder. He's a former soldier who had received an honorable discharge and was attending a local community college. Down on his luck and drinking heavily, he had the misfortune of living near where a man was shot to death late one night. Based on the dubious testimony of an elderly woman who thought she saw him shooting a gun into the air outside his residence a couple of nights after the murder, the mistaken identification of a neighbor eyewitness who probably recognized the guy from having seen him on his nightly beer excursions, and – the coup de grace – the testimony of a career jail-house informant, the jury convicted a man with no tie to the deceased and no criminal record. Despite the absence of a gun or any physical evidence linking him to the murder. It took many years of work by the prisoner and the eventual assistance of a private investigator to track down the eyewitness, who then recanted, to win his freedom."

As the lecture concluded, Sigrun sat back, stunned by his passion and sincerity, enthusiastic applause ringing in her ears. Wondering what her father would have thought, she waited until the crowd had thinned to join the group of students clustered around the speaker. Her father had always been a proponent of the death penalty; would these statistics have made him reconsider?

"Sigrun," said Professor Ehrlich, "I'm so glad you came. What did you think?"

"I'm sold," Sigrun said. "I'd like to get involved."

"Why don't you drop by my office around 2 tomorrow. I'm meeting a student about her case, and I think you'd enjoy working with her."

🐾🐾

The following afternoon, Sigrun knocked on the partially open office door.

"Come on in," Professor Ehrlich called. "Sigrun, I want you to meet Blythe Jordan. Blythe, this is Sigrun Nyman, the student I was just mentioning."

"Hi, Sigrun," said the thin, black-clad woman sitting in front of the desk, the tight curls of her black hair forming a loose cloud around her head. "The professor was telling me that you want to work on a habeas case – that's terrific."

"I think the two of you will work well together," said the professor. "And since both of you are volunteers, you won't have to worry about any deadlines. Blythe's a third-year student; she completed the clinical course last year."

"I've only just started," Blythe said. "It's been really hectic so far this year since I'm writing grant proposals for a public interest job."

"Yes," the professor said, "Blythe is looking for a position with an Advocacy for Innocence group. Unfortunately, they have no funding, so she has to try to win a grant."

"I'm hopeful," said Blythe, "but I'm not optimistic. It'll be great to have help on this case, though. It looks like the guy might have some decent claims."

"I think so," the professor said. "This case is a federal petition for writ of habeas corpus by a person in state custody – that's the state of California, obviously. The petitioner – that's the person who's been convicted – has filed a habeas petition seeking release from what he contends is unconstitutional imprisonment. Keep in mind that we're not representing the prisoner; he filed the petition pro se – or on his own behalf. Our interest is to see whether he has viable claims that he was wrongfully convicted.

"Sigrun," the professor continued, "I realize you don't know anything about this area of the law, and, unfortunately, I've finished my introductory lectures already this term. But it's actually much easier to learn with a concrete example. So, I suggest that you go through the case file with Blythe. Come in when you have questions and I'll give you a quick tutorial on the quirks of federal habeas corpus jurisprudence."

"All right," Sigrun said hesitantly, thinking it all sounded rather complex.

"Don't worry," Blythe said, "I think I've got it, and the system really does make more sense with some context. Want to get started?"

"I'm done with classes for the day," Sigrun agreed.

⤚ Chapter 4 ⤚
Occasio furem facit
(Opportunity makes the thief; proverb)

"Our petitioner," Blythe began after they had settled at a table on the patio, "is on death row for a double murder and robbery that took place 20 years ago up the coast in Cambria ..."

"Twenty years!" Sigrun interrupted. "He's been on death row for 20 years and is still claiming he's innocent?"

Blythe nodded. "That's not uncommon. In this case, he's on his second round of petitions because he's raising claims based on newly discovered evidence. First, he appealed his conviction in **state** court. Next, he filed a series of habeas petitions there. After being rejected at all levels in the state courts, the petitioner moved to the **federal** system and filed a habeas petition in the district court, the lowest level. Then, he appealed that rejection first to the Ninth Circuit Court of Appeals and, finally, to the United States Supreme Court. With me so far?"

"I think so."

"Good. So, ordinarily, that would have been the end of it. In this case, however, the petitioner somehow tracked down a witness who had been interviewed by the police right after the murders, but the record of the interview was 'lost'. He eventually found the witness and obtained a declaration that he used as the basis for a couple of new claims. But he had to start over in state court."

"Why couldn't he stay in federal court? I mean, isn't the whole point that he's claiming his conviction violated the federal constitution?"

"True. But, you've got to keep in mind that federal habeas jurisdiction is quite limited – the sole question for a federal court on habeas review is whether the federal constitutional rights of a prisoner have been violated during state court proceedings. Federal courts can't hear a claim raised by a state prisoner unless the state courts have had an opportunity to consider it first. So, our petitioner had to return to state court to raise his new claims before he could raise them in federal court."

"I can see that."

"So," Blythe continued, "the prisoner filed his second round of petitions – all rejected – in state court. Then he filed a second federal habeas case. And that's where we are now: at the federal district court with a petition raising new claims pertaining to the witness he found. As the professor said, the petitioner filed this petition on his own behalf, but it's pretty clear that someone on the outside wrote it. I haven't read many, but this one is so well done, I can't believe it was written by a prisoner."

"Is that unusual?"

"No idea. But I have a bunch of questions, and I've been considering contacting the petitioner to find out who his helper is to see if I can get some answers. So, do you want to start reading the transcript, or would you rather I gave you a brief overview?"

"Oh, the more information you give me the better, I think."

"All right. Just after midnight on November 1, 1982, police officers responding to a 911 call arrived at an apartment to find the front door ajar and the occupants stabbed to death. In the bedroom the police found a young man who appeared to be trying to flee out the open window. The drawers of the dresser had been ransacked, and police recovered a necklace and two gemstones from the petitioner.

"The trial," Blythe continued, "was pretty quick. The prosecution offered forensic evidence and the testimony of the police officers. No murder weapon was ever found, but the prosecutor argued that the petitioner had had time to throw the knife out the open and screenless bedroom window, and a passerby must have picked it up before the police managed to search the area. The only evidence presented by the defense was an expert witness who testified that the type of wound that killed each victim would have required considerable force, but he couldn't rule out the possibility that the petitioner was capable of delivering such a blow. So, he's clearly guilty, right?"

"I'd say," Sigrun agreed.

"Ah, but now it gets interesting," Blythe said. "The prosecutor argued that the petitioner was part of some cult and had murdered the victims because he wanted their jewelry to perform some unspecified ritual."

"You've got to be kidding; where'd that come from?"

Blythe laughed. "Well, the prosecutor talked it up to the press and argued it in court, but the only real evidence he offered was some unexplained burn marks on the front door and the testimony of a neighbor from one of the lower apartments in the building. She identified the necklace found on the petitioner as belonging to the wife, who, the neighbor testified, always wore it. The prosecutor speculated that the petitioner must have seen the woman wearing the unusual necklace and decided to kill her for it. In addition, the murders took place just about midnight on Halloween. Apparently that was enough to spook the prosecutor – no pun intended. The defense dismissed the prosecutor's theory as pure fantasy and argued that no evidence connected the petitioner to the murders."

"Apart from his presence at the scene of the crime."

"Well yes," Blythe conceded. "But you'll see his point after you've read the transcript. The bodies were in the living room and there was blood everywhere – except on the petitioner. Add to that the missing murder weapon and the fact that the petitioner's fingerprints were found on the bedroom dresser, but nowhere else. So, my personal theory is that the guy happened by after the murders, noticed the open door, and grabbed an opportunity to engage in a little burglary."

"Interesting. I gather the petitioner didn't testify?"

"No," said Blythe. "Of course, you can't draw any inference about his guilt from that, but it makes me wonder if he had a juvenile record."

"Really? How old was he?"

"He was just 18 when he was arrested, so if he had had a criminal record, it would have been confidential. Had he testified, though, the prosecutor could have tried to get his prior crimes admitted to attack his credibility. But it's only a guess."

"Okay," said Sigrun. "So … you think I should start with the transcript?"

"Yeah. Why don't you read through it – it's not that long – and then move on to his claims. I want to review his earlier petitions to better understand the scope of what he's raising here." Blythe pushed a pile of bound transcripts across the table.

Sigrun opened the first volume. It began with a series of short hearings concerning pre-trial issues that she skimmed quickly. Then a potential jury panel was assembled, and the charges were read prior to jury selection. Eventually, the jury was sworn in, and the attorneys presented their opening statements. Sigrun quickly became absorbed. This was the first time she had read a trial transcript; she was surprised that the personalities of the prosecutor and defense counsel came so clearly through the unadorned record of words spoken in court. From the manner in which they posed questions to the witnesses, the objections they raised, and the exchanges they had with the judge outside the presence of the jury, she developed an image of the prosecutor as clever and exceptionally well-prepared, but earnest to the point of fervor. In contrast, the defense counsel, who came across as comfortable and confident before the judge, seemed lackadaisical and aloof in front of the jury. No wonder, she thought in dismay, that the jury bought the prosecutor's bizarre theory.

"Hi, Blythe," said a male voice behind Sigrun.

"Zvi," Blythe said. "Gee, is it time for dinner already?"

Sigrun turned: The man who had joined them was tall and heavy-set, with dark curly hair and a neatly trimmed beard that just hinted at grey. In his early forties, dressed in tailored slacks and a wrinkled, button-down shirt, he did not look like a law student, despite the case books tucked under one arm.

"I can come back later, if you're busy," he said amicably.

"No, no," said Blythe, "I want to keep to my schedule. Hey, have you two met?"

"I haven't had the pleasure," he said cordially to Sigrun. "I'm Zvi Ziegler."

"This is Sigrun Nyman," Blythe said. "She's a first-year, and she's joining me on my new habeas case."

"Ah, another bleeding-heart liberal."

"Zvi," Blythe chastised. "Don't mind him, Sigrun. He was my partner on our loser of a habeas case. He likes to hide it, but he's quite sympathetic to the downtrodden."

"Now, Blythe, just because I believe that justice should be meted out without bias does not make me a radical reformer like you."

"It's an ongoing debate," she explained to Sigrun. "Zvi's a business executive who decided he wanted to understand what the lawyers he hired **did** for all the money he paid them, so he came to law school. We've been friends since our first term, and I convinced him he should broaden his perspective by taking the habeas clinic with me."

"Did it work?" Sigrun asked.

They both laughed.

"Not really," Blythe admitted ruefully.

"No," said Zvi. "I remain a firm believer in the morality of capital punishment and the guilt of the majority of those sentenced to die."

"Of course," Blythe added, "it didn't help that the case we had was a disaster – the claims were totally fabricated and the facts were ghastly. Anyway, Zvi's here to join me for dinner. If you don't have any plans, why don't you come along?"

"Oh, no, I couldn't intrude," said Sigrun hastily.

"Don't be silly," Zvi said mildly. "My family is out of town for a few weeks, and Blythe is taking pity on a lonely old man. Indulge me in the singular pleasure of having two pretty young women entertain me."

Blythe laughed. "Here, Sigrun, take the transcripts, and I'll keep the rest."

Sigrun stuffed her notes and the volumes of the transcript into her backpack and hoisted the bag onto her shoulder. "Wow," she exclaimed as she followed Blythe out of the courtyard, "that adds a bit of weight."

"Yep," she agreed, "I'm glad to be rid of some. But we're not going far – the North Campus Center is the best spot for dinner."

"Only," Zvi said disdainfully, "if the metric used is the food served by campus cafeterias – all of which I find deplorable."

"Zvi," Blythe explained, "has only consented to eat on campus because I insist on going to the gym on Fridays nights."

"Yes," he added with a sigh, "and she has to eat early so she has time to do whatever it is that she does at the gym."

"What do you do?" Sigrun asked.

"I work out with weights a couple times a week, and I try to catch a kickboxing class twice a week. I have to struggle to stay in shape."

"Oh," Sigrun said in surprise, "you look quite fit."

"Exactly," said Zvi. "I keep telling her she's too thin."

"And I keep telling him that his ideal Rubenesque woman is unhealthy."

"Not true," he protested. "You see, Sigrun, young women today – they want to be so skinny, but they never think about what happens if they get sick or can't eat. They should maintain a healthy reserve. You too – you could use some padding."

"I'm afraid," Sigrun said, "that I'll have to side with Blythe on this as well. I most certainly do not need any 'padding'. To the contrary, I need to lose some of the weight I've gained since coming here and becoming largely sedentary."

"Let's eat," Zvi said, "all this talk of exercise has made me hungry."

⤙⤚ ⤙⤚

As they left the cafeteria, having already taken leave of Zvi, Blythe asked, "How about joining me at the gym?"

"Well," Sigrun said thoughtfully, "that's an idea. I used to be pretty active at home, but now I mostly sit. I don't know, though, I've never been to a gym."

"I'm happy to show you around. What are you doing for exercise?"

Sigrun snorted. "I don't do much of anything besides go to class and study."

"Sigrun!" Blythe sounded dismayed. "You need balance in your life – it can't be all school all the time. You should think about coming to the gym."

"Maybe I will." Sigrun turned toward her dorm. She pulled out her cell phone; Philip hadn't called, and she'd wanted to wish his brother Norman a happy eighteenth birthday.

"Hey, am I too late to catch Norm?" Sigrun asked Philip when he answered.

"Yeah, he's gone to bed – but we were just talking about you."

"Why?"

"Oh, you know, just a bit of bartering – chores at the Farmstead in exchange for use of the Mustang."

"Ah, I see. How did you fare?"

"Favorably. The Mustang commands good consideration, as you would say."

"But I thought you were grounded?"

"True. But I control the keys."

"Stellar, Philip! It's your brother's 18th birthday, and you're not going anywhere, but do you magnanimously offer him the use of your car? Nooo, you haggle with him."

"Hey, I have to keep him in line. So, what have you been doing?"

"Well, let's see – since we spoke yesterday morning, I've attended a soul-stirring lecture, agreed to assist an amazing third-year student, taken on the tribulations of a young man condemned to die for murder in furtherance of a satanic cult, debated the desirability of capital punishment over dinner, and possibly signed on to start weight training. You decide which you want to hear first while I go inside."

"And your choice is?" Sigrun asked after she had settled herself on her bed.

"That depends on the gender of the 'amazing' third-year."

"Ah. No, unfortunately, Blythe's a woman."

"Okay. In that case, I'll pick the young man's story."

"Really," she asked curiously, "does your mind always turn first to sex?"

"I'm wounded!" Philip said in mock dismay. "I'm only looking out for you."

"Right. Okay then, the young man it is. Although – come to think of it, he's no longer a young man. Let's see, he must be about 38 now. But he was 18 when, according to the prosecutor, he spied and subsequently coveted a pentagonal necklace worn by a young woman living in Cambria, a small, sleepy, beach community north of here. Late one night he used an unidentified explosive to blow open the door of the woman's apartment and stabbed her and her husband to death – killing each with a thrust to the heart. Interestingly, the husband was a pretty solid guy, and the defendant was tall, but thin. There were only minimal signs of a struggle. So, somehow our young man ..."

"Hey, what's his name?" Philip interrupted.

"Fremont, uhm ..." Sigrun paused while she pulled her backpack over to the bed and extracted a volume of the transcript to read the caption: "Zareh Fremont."

"Sorry, go on, I just wanted a name to go with my visualization."

"Hold on." She rooted around in her backpack until she located the first volume of the transcript and flipped through it to the prosecutor's opening argument. "So – to maintain neutrality – the victims were a husband and wife, Eireen and Edoardo Durante."

"Do you know how old they were?"

"I think he was about 30, and she was a bit younger, if I recall correctly. So, back to the story. The young man took the woman's necklace and two loose gemstones. He was still searching the bedroom when the police arrived and arrested him."

"What do you mean by loose gemstones?"

"Well, I've only read the opening arguments and some of the forensic testimony – so I'll have to get back to you on that. But one thing that caught my attention – and on which the defense focused – was the nature of the wounds. Each victim was killed with a single, clean, stab wound."

"Wow! What did he use?"

"No weapon was found. But the doctor who conducted the autopsies testified that the wounds appeared to have been inflicted by a short – maybe six-inch – blade that was razor-sharp and appeared to have been used with considerable force by someone who was taller than either victim."

"Which Fremont was? But how could someone so slight have been capable of using enough force to kill an older, stocky man with a single thrust of a short blade?"

"Good question. Apparently that was the crux of the defense. That and the fact that the petitioner – or Fremont if you prefer – bore not a trace of blood."

"What! That's impossible."

"Seems like it, doesn't it? I just started the testimony of one of the first police officers on the scene, so I'll have more details in the next installment. And I'm curious about who alerted the police. The autopsies placed the time of the deaths less than an hour before they arrived."

"Hey, this is pretty cool. So you're working with a third-year student?"

"Yeah, she's great. Oh, that reminds me, she wants me to join her at the gym."

"Good idea."

"You think so?"

"Absolutely – it'll make you a better rider."

"Maybe," she said dubiously, "but I'm not sure …"

"Sigrun, you're a tiny thing – you need to develop the assets that you have."

"But I **am** strong."

"Yeah, you're a lot stronger than you look, but only because of all the riding. If you just sit around studying – you'll lose it."

"I suppose, but …"

"No arguments," Philip said. "If you have someone to show you around, go for it."

"Okay," Sigrun said somewhat reluctantly, "I'll give it a try."

"What are your plans for tomorrow night?"

"Plans? When do I ever have plans on a Saturday night?"

"You do now. I want to play you the song I've been working on."

⌒⌒

Sigrun reached her seat just as Professor Acorda reached the podium. She sighed in relief as she assembled her book and notepad; she hated to be late for class, especially Contracts. During that morning's meeting on the case, she and Blythe had become so deeply engaged in their discussion that they had lost track of the time.

Lupe rushed by and slipped quickly into her front-row seat.

"Ms. Contreras," Professor Acorda said coldly, "your attendance is a pleasant surprise. Is it too much to hope that you've read the assignment?"

"Actually, Professor," Lupe said, "I believe that's highly unlikely."

A ripple of muffled laughter swept through the classroom. Sigrun caught her breath at Lupe's audacity.

Professor Acorda scowled as she scrawled on her chart. "I fail to understand why you people come to class unprepared. Mr. Teague, perhaps you might be able to tell us the holding in Sherwood v. Walker?"

In the ensuing silence, Sigrun looked at her notes and quickly composed a response in case Milton, as he commonly did, choked up.

"Well ..." Milton noisily cleared his throat before he continued tentatively, "I think, uhm, I think the case held that if, uh, if both parties were mistaken about the cow being, ah, barren, there was no contract."

"Good," the professor said. "Why does it matter if both parties were mistaken?"

"Uh, well, maybe because they didn't bargain for a, uhm, pregnant cow?" Milton ventured.

"Exactly. Now, given that, Mr. Hawke, should the seller be held to the bargain if the buyer could show that he thought the cow could become pregnant at the time of the contract?"

"Yes, because he took the risk of selling," said Hawke casually.

"Mr. Teague, would you agree with Mr. Hawke's assessment?"

"Uh ... actually, no, uh" Milton sputtered, "I wouldn't."

"Why not?" Professor Acorda pressed.

"Uhm, because ... uh," he hesitated, looked down at his notes, and then continued more confidently, "well I think even then they were both mistaken. I mean, it seems to me that nobody thought they were bargaining over a pregnant cow."

"Good," she said approvingly, "in this case, there was a mutual mistake. But does the emphasis on 'mutual mistake' make sense?"

As the professor plunged into a lecture, Sigrun relaxed and let her thoughts return to her meeting with Blythe. Just before they had run to class, Blythe had suggested that they take a trip to the courthouse the next day. They had realized that their copy of the file was missing some of the exhibits that the state supposedly had filed. They were hopeful that the exhibits ... Sigrun became aware that the cadence of the professor's voice had changed. She looked up and followed the professor's gaze to the back of the lecture hall. Not her this time, but she'd better pay more attention.

><><

After departing the metro at Union Station in downtown Los Angeles, Sigrun and Blythe walked through the plaza at El Pueblo and joined a horde of tourists spilling from a bus parked at the curb. As they surged across the street, the thought struck Sigrun that she certainly was not in Burning Springs anymore. She had never before encountered such a bizarre mix of people. The business-suited men and women with briefcases were probably lawyers; they strode purposefully through the tourists, nearly all of whom were armed with cameras. No one paid the slightest attention to the wheelchair-bound man, old and unwashed, shaking a cup that clattered with change and calling out Spanish words; the rainbow-haired clown, in a striped jumpsuit dotted with stars, shuffling about in oversized shoes and hawking balloon-twisted animals; or the blanket-covered woman, sprawled untidily against a wall, pillowing her head on a bulging bag of belongings and sleeping despite the raucous crowd. Aware that she was dawdling, Sigrun hurried to catch up as they crossed a bridge spanning a traffic-clogged freeway.

At the Federal Courthouse, they found the clerk's room at the end of a granite-clad hallway, and joined a long line waiting to approach the window of the one file clerk who was working. The line moved slowly.

When it was finally their turn, Blythe said cheerfully, "Hello. We're law students working on a habeas petition that was filed here, and we checked out a case file ..."

"Yes?" the bored-looking clerk prodded.

"Well," Blythe continued at a faster pace, "we think part of the file is missing."

"Oh," the clerk said without interest, "go look in the stacks then ... Room 100." She pointed vaguely toward a closed door beyond the last of the dark filing windows.

Somewhat surprised at apparently being given unrestricted access to the file room, Sigrun followed Blythe through the indicated door and down a dimly lit interior hallway. At the end of the deserted corridor, they spied an otherwise unadorned door bearing the correct number. They stepped into a huge room, dingy and dusty and filled with row upon row of files lining floor-to-ceiling shelves. It was difficult to decipher the cryptic system, but they eventually located where the case number for their file fell; if the missing exhibits existed, they should be on the top shelf. Neither woman was tall enough to reach that shelf, however. Blythe wandered off and returned with a battered stool.

Sigrun climbed up and shoved apart the folders on either side of the spot where their file should have been. She spied a thin red folder, just barely visible, wedged at the back of the shelf. She pried it out and peered inside at two sealed envelopes, which, she was elated to see, both bore the correct case number.

They returned to the Clerk's Office to find that the line had dispersed. The file clerk finished with the last person, flicked off her light, and turned away.

"Excuse me," Blythe called as they hurried over. "We need to check this out."

"I'm closed." The clerk pointed to a large digital clock as it changed to 4:30.

"But," Blythe continued politely, "you said we could look in the stacks, and we found what we were looking for."

"Yeah?" said the surly clerk.

"Look," Blythe said, "we don't want to keep you. Just let us check this out, and we'll be out of your hair."

"Yeah, okay," muttered the clerk, shoving a register across the counter, "sign here." She jabbed at an empty line. Blythe quickly filled out the required information. The clerk grabbed the book almost before Blythe had finished and stalked away.

"Thank you," Blythe said tartly to her receding back. "Want to go filch some more files since she clearly couldn't care less what we walk off with?"

Sigrun laughed as she stuffed the red folder into her backpack. "Perhaps you shouldn't joke about committing crimes in a courthouse." They hurried out the front door and down the broad flight of granite steps.

"Come on," Blythe said, "let's see what we found."

Setting her backpack down, Sigrun retrieved the folder. She handed the larger of the envelopes in it to Blythe.

"Excellent," exclaimed Blythe. "It's the photographs. What do you have?"

Sigrun reached inside the second envelope. Her hand en-

countered several hard, cold objects, and she felt a sharp but fleeting shock that, for an instant, reminded her of the time she had accidently grabbed an electric fence as a child. "Ouch!"

"What's wrong?"

"Just static electricity, I guess." She pulled out the largest object. "**Look** at this!" Sigrun held out her hand. In her palm rested an emerald necklace – the stone a beautiful, intense but cloudy green in color – in an intricate pentagonal setting woven with thin, now-tarnished, silver wire.

"Wow!"

"There's more." She held out the envelope, and Blythe extracted two gemstones. One appeared to be a ruby, and the other looked like a rose quartz; each was cut and polished, but unset.

Blythe gasped. "Whatever are these doing in the court files?"

Sigrun shook her head in amazement. "They've just been sitting there on the shelf. I can't believe no one took them."

Blythe threw a furtive look around as she dropped the stones back into the envelope. "Well, if we flaunt them, someone is sure to suspect we stole them."

With some reluctance, Sigrun replaced the necklace.

⌒ **Chapter 5** ⌒
Gradu diverso, via una
(The same way by different steps)

Sigrun sat curled into the most comfortable of the chairs in the little common room she shared with Lupe reading a particularly long Supreme Court opinion assigned for Con Law and savoring one of the delectable hand-dipped double-chocolate truffles she had picked up at the campus store on her way back from dinner. She rationalized the indulgence as a reward for having fit in an extra workout. She was expecting a quiet weekend because Lupe had gone home. Her cell phone rang.

"Philip," she said into the phone, "you're early."

"Yeah, I guess," he said glumly. "How're things?"

"Oh, good. Hey, I finally joined Blythe for a kickboxing class today."

"And?"

"It was tough. I wish we had a tub – I suspect I'll be too sore to walk tomorrow."

"Did you like it?"

"Yeah, I did. More than I expected to; I never really envisioned myself assailing anything – even if it is only a bag. So, what have you been up to?"

"Nothing, besides studying. ... But I have a question for you. Norm was over at the Farmstead today, and he wants to know if you'd mind if we winterized the place before you're back for break?"

"Philip, did you extract more chores for use of the Mustang?"

"Nah. Actually, Norm's been doing my Saturday chores for weeks now, and I've taken over most of his after-school ones. His coach increased practice by an hour a day until basketball season starts."

"So, you **were** being generous with the car on his birthday. Why the line earlier?"

"Didn't want you feeling sorry for me."

"Still down?" she asked in a carefully casual tone.

"Well … it's mostly classes. You know, Sigrun, I look ahead, and I see four more years of this, and I wonder – do I really want to go to vet school?"

"I know," she said sympathetically. "But you **are** interested in genetics, and you don't want to end up as a farmer."

"I guess." Philip sighed. "Sometimes, though, I think I'd rather just stay with the farm and stop struggling so hard to get the grades I need in classes I detest. I probably don't stand a chance of getting in anyway."

"But like you said in August – don't do anything rash until you're positive you want to change directions. Look, you didn't flunk that quiz like you thought the other week. All you need to concentrate on right now is getting a decent grade in chemistry. And, if you do," she added encouragingly, "maybe you can come out here next year."

"Yeah, right," he harrumphed. "So, would you mind if we closed up the Farmstead? We're all so busy we're having trouble keeping up with it, and we're afraid a frost will catch us unprepared. I know you wanted to stay there, but I'd rather you stayed with us so I can keep you up late."

"Oh no, go ahead. I don't want to be a burden. And I'm happy to stay with you."

"Good – we'll go over tomorrow and start on it. So, tell me about our friend Fremont, what's the latest?"

"Well, today Blythe and I went over his claims again. Remember I've been wondering how the police heard about the murders, since there were no witnesses or gunshots or anything?"

"You said there was a 911 call."

"Yeah, but how? It turns out that the neighbor of the victims got home after a party – it must have been right after the murders – and noticed that the door of their apartment was ajar. When she didn't get a response, she stuck her head in the door and saw the bodies in the living room. She called the police and then watched the door through her peephole. It was rather dark in the hallway because the landlord hadn't fixed a broken light, but she saw a man enter the apartment."

"What!" Philip exclaimed. "But this is **after** the murders?"

"Exactly. She couldn't see his face, but she described his clothing perfectly, even though it was about 17 years later that she signed a declaration for Fremont."

"Hey, what was he wearing? You never told me."

"Oh, well, he had on a pair of tall riding boots, close-fitting pants – they don't sound like jodhpurs – and, most distinctively, a dark-colored, hooded cape that billowed around him as he slipped inside the open door. Then the police showed up. They interviewed her that night, and she said she later signed a statement that a detective brought to her apartment. But, of course, Fremont's attorney never got a copy of it."

"She never testified, and the jury didn't learn that Fremont arrived **after** the murders. But, wait a minute, why didn't she come forward during the trial?"

"She'd moved away and never heard anything about it. Turns out she's an artist and had moved to the area to be near the beach only about a month before the murders. She was so freaked out that she simply packed up and fled back to Kansas. That's why it took Fremont – or whoever's working with him – so long to track her down."

"And his attorney never attempted to find her?"

"No. There's no indication he was even aware she existed, although he had a copy of the police report listing her name."

"Wow. That's pretty persuasive."

"Except it leaves open the question of why Fremont was there. He didn't live in the building, and the police arrived pretty quickly. Exactly how did he know that he could slip inside an open door and steal the jewelry?"

"Hey," asked Philip suddenly, "did you tell me what the other jewels look like?"

"I don't think so – do you want me to?"

"Yeah. You know, I'm conjuring up an image of a scared young kid cornered in a dark apartment clutching the jewels as the police come storming in. It's extremely evocative – describe them for me."

"Okay. I have to pry myself out of my chair. Ouch! I'm getting stiff already." Sigrun stumbled into her bedroom. "You know, Philip," she said fondly, "it never ceases to amaze me how you zero in on the human element. I'm focusing on the puzzle of Fremont's claims and the problems they present, while you're picturing him as a troubled youth."

"Perhaps, but the poet in me doesn't always jibe with the demands of real life – like chemistry."

"Maybe not, but it certainly makes life more colorful."

"Why thank you."

Sigrun grabbed the envelope with the stones and settled herself on her bed. She shook the contents onto the spread. She could hear that Philip had picked up his guitar and had begun to strum it softly; he typically talked with a headset to leave his hands free for the guitar. "One looks like an extremely pale rose quartz – it's so pale it's nearly translucent – that's cut in a smooth oval. The other appears to be a ruby. It's deep red in color and brilliantly clear – it's so fine, in fact, that I wonder if it's real. It's round, with multiple facets that catch the light." She set down the ruby and fingered the emerald at the center of the necklace.

"Remind me, he was caught where?"

"He was standing by the open window, the ruby was in his hand, and the necklace and quartz stone were in an inside pocket of his cape," she said as she picked up the necklace and cradled it in her palm. "The police officers who were first on the scene testified – on cross-examination – that he didn't try to jump and didn't resist arrest."

"Did he say anything to the police?" asked Philip thoughtfully.

"Only his name and that he wanted to make a call."

"So … what's his story – what does he say happened?"

"Nothing. We can't figure it out. The claims are good, but they don't provide an alibi, point to another suspect, or explain how he came to be at the apartment."

"Do you think he just grabbed an opportunity to steal the jewels?"

"I guess so," Sigrun said slowly, looking at the necklace she held in her hand. "I mean, what the hell else was he doing standing in her bedroom with her necklace in his pocket? It's pretty clear that, at the very least, he stole the necklace …."

"Hey, you said the prosecutor made a big deal about his odd clothing; doesn't the guy at least have an explanation for that?"

"Sort of – his counsel argued in closing that the prosecutor had presented no evidence it wasn't a Halloween costume."

"But no evidence that it was?"

"Nope."

"Did you ever get a physical description of Fremont?"

"No, not really. Just the defense expert's testimony that it wouldn't have been easy for someone of his size to have thrust the knife with enough force to kill each victim with the first blow."

"And what was his size?"

"Let me get my notes." Sigrun set the necklace on her desk, pulled a notebook from her backpack, and paged through the expert's testimony, which she had marked with a tab. "Here it is. He was six foot one and weighed 151 pounds."

"That's thin – he was young and thin."

"True, but his own expert admitted that it was physically possible for him to have killed the victims – both of whom were several inches shorter."

"Hmmm."

"It's puzzling." Sigrun picked up the necklace by its chain and dangled it so that the emerald glowed in the light from her desk lamp. "You know, Philip, I'm not convinced he's innocent."

"Oh?"

"Yeah, well, it's so coincidental." She stepped over to the open window and held the necklace up in the moonlight. Interestingly, the setting did not span the back of the stone, so light passed through it. It was not transparent but, rather, was filled with tiny inclusions, bubbles, and fissures. She found it strangely captivating. Sigrun held the necklace higher. She felt a vague sort of tingly, pulsating sensation. She could see shapes in the complex cloudiness of the sharply stepped oval; she could almost detect movement. She peered closer.

"Hello?"

"What?" she asked absently while scrutinizing the stone.

"You lapsed into silence."

"Oh. ... It's the oddest thing. I'm standing in front of my window catching the moonlight with the necklace, and I swear I can see things inside the stone."

"What do you mean you're 'catching the moonlight with the necklace'?"

"Oh, well, I was just ..." Sigrun pulled the emerald up into her hand by its chain. She felt a faint echo of the shock she had felt at the courthouse. She shivered. She stared hard at the necklace.

"Sigrun, are you all right?"

"Yeah." She shook her head, returned to the bed, and set the necklace down. "I don't know; there's something ... enthralling about this necklace. It's eerie."

"Hey – that sounds like you've embraced the prosecutor's outlandish cult theory."

"Maybe I have," she said soberly.

"Come off it! You said yourself there's no evidence to support it; he cooked it up to hoodwink the jury."

"So how come Fremont was there just when the police arrived?"

"Bad luck."

On Tuesday, Sigrun carried her lunch onto the patio and spied Blythe sitting by herself reading a glossy pamphlet. Sigrun had come up with a question while reading the habeas petition on Sunday, so she headed over. "Mind if I interrupt?"

"Not at all." Blythe handed Sigrun the pamphlet. "Take a look at this. Believe it or not, I have an interview this afternoon with an actual law firm."

Sigrun belatedly noticed that, instead of her standard black jeans, Blythe was wearing a sharp black suit set off by a striking teal shirt. "You look fantastic."

"Thanks – my mother sent it. She said it was time I stopped pretending to be a teenager and started dressing like a lawyer."

"But I thought you wanted to do public interest work?"

"Yeah. Well, the last of my grant proposals was rejected. I've run out of options, so I decided I'd better start looking for a real job."

"What about the public defenders' office?"

"Hiring freeze." Blythe shrugged. "So I selected a few law firms that seem committed to public interest work, and I'll see if any of them are interested in me."

"I wish you luck. Are you in a hurry, or can I ask a quick question?"

"I've got plenty of time to get nervous, so why don't you distract me instead."

"Okay. I understand that one of the petitioner's early claims was that his counsel was ineffective because the attorney failed to object to the prosecutor's inflammatory closing argument about incipient cult activity in Cambria, but I don't understand why the petitioner didn't raise a direct claim that the prosecutor's argument was improper because it wasn't based on any evidence."

Blythe gave a thoughtful nod. "That's because he was prevented from raising such a claim. Under state law, when his attorney failed to object at the time, he effectively waived any subsequent claim that the prosecutor's conduct was improper."

Sigrun considered that. "So that's why he had to argue that the attorney's decision not to object was unreasonable?"

"Right. He can't directly attack the prosecutor, as he did with his claim that the prosecutor withheld evidence concerning the interview with the neighbor, because not objecting might have been a reasonable tactical decision by the attorney."

"And our petitioner figured that out?" Sigrun asked skeptically.

"I doubt it – that's why I'm sure someone's helping him."

"I see." Sigrun nodded. "I think I'm getting this. Thanks."

"That was a good question."

"It took a bit to get there."

"But this is all new to you. ... Like thinking about law firms is to me." She pointed to a picture in the pamphlet of several young, well-scrubbed, earnest-looking attorneys posed in a well-stocked library. "Do you think I could fit in there?"

Sigrun eyed the image dubiously. "Maybe."

Blythe sighed. "I guess I should keep an open mind." She turned her attention back to the pamphlet.

Sigrun pulled out the petition and started reading it again while she quickly ate her lunch; she wanted to make sure they hadn't missed anything. But she found her thoughts repeatedly returning to the photographs of the murder scene that they had found at the court house. Something about them didn't fit, although she couldn't figure out what. She dug out the envelope of photos and studied the two she was fixating on before shaking her head in frustration.

"Here," she said, handing them to Blythe. "What's wrong with these?"

Blythe looked from one to the other. "I don't see anything."

"Something's not right, but I can't quite put my finger on it." Sigrun took the photos back and, after one last look, returned them to their envelope.

⤚⤚

Sigrun couldn't shake the nagging feeling that she was overlooking something. After Torts class the following afternoon, she went to the library to start on Thursday's assignments, but she couldn't concentrate on the case she was supposedly reading. Once again, she painstakingly examined the photographs. Eventually she narrowed in on one of the close-up shots. She stared at it for several minutes. Suddenly, it leapt out at her: a footprint. A faint footprint was discernible in the blood puddled between the two bodies.

"Of course," she muttered to herself. Grabbing the photo, Sigrun headed to the student lounge and found Blythe at a corner table with Zvi.

"Hey, look at this," Sigrun said, thrusting the photo in front of Blythe. "Hi, Zvi."

Blythe obligingly looked at the photograph, holding it so they could both see it. "What about it?"

"Look at the footprint in the blood – it must have been made by a large, flat shoe," Sigrun said excitedly. "See, the sole must have been worn down or something because no tread pattern is visible; it's just sort of uniformly fuzzy."

Both Blythe and Zvi looked puzzled.

"Remember," she continued, "Fremont was wearing riding boots."

Blythe shook her head. "I don't get it."

"Riding boots are never flat," Sigrun said. "They always have a heel to keep your foot in the stirrup. So he couldn't have made this print."

"Wow! I never would've thought of that." Blythe looked impressed. "Let's see if Professor Ehrlich is available." She jumped to her feet and headed out of the room.

"So what?" Zvi asked as he followed. "Even if the petitioner didn't leave the footprint, that hardly points to his innocence."

"Maybe not," Blythe said, "but we just have to prove a constitutional error, not that he's innocent." She knocked on the professor's door.

"We think Sigrun spotted something important," Blythe said after opening the door in response to the professor's terse acknowledgment.

"Really? Well, come on in," said Professor Ehrlich, sounding hassled. "What did you discover?"

"Well, I've been studying the photographs we found," Sigrun said, "and I finally noticed something." Taking the photograph from Blythe, she handed it to the professor. "See, next to the man's body? The indistinct footprint? It looks too wide and flat to have been made by the riding boots the petitioner was wearing when he was arrested."

"Interesting." The professor examined the photograph closely. "Is any mention made of the footprint in the record?"

"No," Blythe said, "not at trial."

"And I don't recall anything in the police report either," Sigrun added.

"What about the petitioner – he never mentioned it?"

"Nope," said Blythe.

"So," the professor asked, "what's your theory?"

"Sigrun?" Blythe asked.

"Well, I think this is evidence that someone else was there

during the murders. Since the neighbor stated in her declaration that the petitioner arrived after she had seen the dead bodies, this supports Blythe's theory that he's only guilty of robbery."

"Okay," the professor said, "but what's the habeas claim?"

Blythe considered for a moment. "What about prosecutorial misconduct for withholding evidence of the footprint."

"But wait," asked Zvi, who had followed them into the office, "didn't you say that the photographs were introduced at trial? The prosecutor didn't withhold it if he offered it as evidence."

"Good point," said Blythe.

"How about ineffective assistance of counsel?" asked the professor. "Shouldn't petitioner's attorney have investigated evidence of a potential third party?"

"Just playing devil's advocate here," said Zvi, "but can you really say it was objectively unreasonable for his attorney to have failed to spot something so subtle?"

"He didn't have to know anything about riding boots," Sigrun argued, "to try to prove that someone else made the footprint. I mean, if the petitioner's boots had been bloody, don't you think the prosecutor would have made sure the jury knew?"

"Excellent," said the professor. "So your position is that counsel was ineffective for not investigating potentially exonerating evidence that should have been obvious?"

"Wait a minute," interjected Zvi, "are you sure that it should have been obvious? When did counsel see the photographs?"

"Do we know what evidence the prosecutor turned over to counsel before trial?"

"We only know," Blythe said, "that he gave counsel a version of the police report that didn't mention the interview of the neighbor who called 911. We don't know if or when anything else was provided."

"Maybe," suggested Professor Ehrlich, "you should ask."

"What?" exclaimed Blythe. "Ask the petitioner?"

"Yes. Why don't the two of you take a trip to San Quentin?"

"Hey," Blythe said eagerly, "I'd love to go. I've never been to a prison."

"Can we do that?" asked Sigrun.

"If he agrees to see you. We have a small budget, and I'd be happy to pay your expenses. I'll give you my contact information at the prison – see if you can set up a meeting. Of course, you're not the petitioner's counsel, so you'll need to go during regular visiting hours, which are not particularly generous, I'm afraid."

"I never expected to go to San Quentin," Sigrun said nervously.

"Good work, Sigrun." Professor Ehrlich gathered up one of the many piles of papers from her desk. "I'm afraid I'm running late for my seminar, so why don't you come back Friday afternoon, and we can work out the details."

Blythe glanced at her watch. "Zvi and I are late too. Catch you later, Sigrun."

The others hurried to class; Sigrun returned to the library, gathered her belongings, and headed for the nearest exit. She pulled out her cell phone as soon as she was outside and called Philip. The phone rang several times.

"Hold on," Philip finally said irritably over the low music in the background. The music stopped and he muttered, "Sorry, I dropped the phone trying to turn the music off – and I beg you, please speak softly."

"Oh," said Sigrun sympathetically, "you have a migraine?"

"Yeah. It's bad."

"Why don't I call you tomorrow then?"

"No, I need to stay awake to finish my damn chem lab, and I can't do anything other than lie in the dark with my eyes closed, so I might as well talk to you."

"Well, at least I rank ahead of the dreaded chem lab."

"You know I didn't mean that."

"Did you take some aspirin?"

"No. I decided I should tough it out."

"My, we are in a rotten mood, aren't we?"

"I suppose. It's been one of those days. You know how you're always after me not to wait until midnight to start the lab homework? Well, I went to school early this morning to go to the library, and I'd barely arrived before Dad called. He'd already phoned the vet – Estelle was showing signs of colic – so I rushed home. Fortunately the vet didn't find any torsion. He thinks it was the high-energy feed we've been giving her."

"How awful! How's she doing?"

"She's okay now. I stayed with her a couple of hours to walk her and monitor her response to the meds before I went to class. So, of course, I hadn't had time to study, and then we had a quiz …"

"But you didn't have chemistry today?" Sigrun interrupted.

"No. Luckily it was advanced genetics, and I think I did fine, but it wasn't fun. Then Donald called when I was almost home.

Somehow he managed to miss his ride at a 4-H Club meeting, so I had to go back to get him before starting on the chores. Then the migraine sprang up. So, yeah, I guess I'm rather out of sorts."

"I'm sorry."

"It's okay … did you call for a reason?"

"Oh yeah, I did," Sigrun exclaimed.

"Not so loud."

"Sorry," she said contritely. "I'd forgotten. I was so excited – I couldn't wait to tell you: I'm going to San Quentin!"

"San Quentin, you've been livin' hell to me," sang Philip quietly. "You've hosted me since nineteen sixty-three; I've seen 'em come and go, and I've seen 'em die."

"I sure hope that's not prophetic; I certainly don't want to watch Fremont die. Even if he is guilty."

✙

The following evening after dinner with Zvi at his favorite near-campus Middle Eastern restaurant, Blythe rooted around in her backpack and brought out a couple of pages of printed text. "Look at this, guys," she said, "I went on the California Department of Corrections' web page and found their guidelines for visitors. It's a riot."

Zvi took the sheets from Blythe and studied them. He snorted. "It seems that 'inappropriate attire will be a reason to deny a visit'."

"Read," Blythe urged, "what they consider inappropriate."

"Well, the first one may be a bit of a problem for you, Blythe – denim is prohibited, so you'll have to find something other than your typical attire."

"Ah, but they specifically mention blue denim and my jeans are black."

"And," Zvi continued, "no hats, wigs or hairpieces."

"No problem there," said Blythe.

"Oh, this is a good one – no underwire bras!"

"Well," Sigrun said, flushing slightly, "I don't have to worry about that one."

"I'll keep it in mind," Blythe said with a giggle.

"And no clothing that exposes the midriff or more than two inches above the knee – including 'slits when standing'. I wonder," Zvi added, "if the guards go around with a measuring tape. Oh, and nothing sheer or transparent."

"I'm getting the picture," Sigrun said. "Nothing my grand-

mother would have found scandalous fifteen years or so ago before she died."

"In fact," Blythe said, "I was thinking we should wear suits."

"Not a bad idea," said Zvi. "It would add gravitas."

"Oh," Sigrun said apologetically, "I don't have a suit."

"Don't worry," Blythe said. "You'll need one soon anyway – I'll take you shopping."

"I suppose," Sigrun said reluctantly, "I'll have to get one for interviews."

Zvi, who had returned to the pages of instructions, said, "By the way, you'd better pay close attention to these rules. No purses, cameras, or cell phones are allowed, and the staff must approve all writing material and books." He shook his head. "They certainly make visiting a challenge."

"Well, I'm not going to let it discourage me," said Blythe. "I think it'll be fascinating, and maybe he'll tell us what happened."

"When do you want to go?" Sigrun asked.

"How about Thanksgiving break," Blythe suggested, "do you have plans?"

"No – but don't you want to spend it with your family?"

"That's the beauty," Blythe said with a grin, "I can visit and go to the prison on the same trip, and you can come home with me."

"But, I don't want …" Sigrun began.

"Really," Blythe interrupted, "we'd love to have you. And my brother Neil will be thrilled to have someone to talk science with. He wants to be an astronaut, so when he finds out you have a physics degree, he'll bombard you with questions. It'll be great."

⤙ Chapter 6 ⤚
In tenebris
(In a state of darkness)

"Remember class," Professor Jamison said as the ending bell sounded in Con Law, "the holiday cuts into next week, and, after that, there's only a partial week left before finals. So, for those of you who haven't been keeping pace, I suggest you start putting in some extra time. Have a good weekend."

"Gee," Milton said with a grimace, "I'd better buckle down – I'm desperately behind." He ran his hand through his receding hair. "I suppose you're caught up?"

"Yeah," Sigrun said casually, packing up her things, "I've done the reading. But I need to start studying."

"Oh, but you take such amazing notes." Milton's voice squeaked. "I mean, I'm sure you'll ace the final."

Lupe called across several rows of seats, "Hey, Sigrun, got a minute?"

"Sure. See you later, Milton."

"Before class, I was talking to my mother." Lupe giggled. "So I was late, like usual. Anyway, she reminded me that I haven't invited you. I can't believe I forgot – you know, I've been meaning to ask you for ages. Can you come home with me for Thanksgiving? My mother wants to meet you, and she makes these to-die-for tamales."

"That's so kind – I would love to meet your family, but I'm afraid I have plans."

"Really," Lupe asked with interest, "are you going to Pennsylvania?"

Sigrun slung her backpack over her shoulder and started up the aisle. "No, the plane tickets were too expensive. I'm going to San Francisco with Blythe, the woman from my habeas case."

"Hey, that's great. Is her family there?"

"Yeah, and Friday, we're going to San Quentin to visit our prisoner …"

Lupe stopped in her tracks. "You're visiting that guy! But

why? I mean, really Sigrun, do you want to get into all that?"

"Well, we have some questions to ask, and, anyway, I think it'll be interesting."

"Oh, but … he's a murderer, right?"

"What are you talking about?" Chun Chang joined them in the doorway.

"Sigrun's been volunteering on this habeas case, and she's going to visit the guy in San Quentin," Lupe said with a note of repugnance. "I mean, why do you want to waste your time with him?"

"Well," Sigrun said defensively, "I don't think it's a waste of time. He may be innocent, and, even if he's not, there were some serious problems with his trial."

"San Quentin! Death row?" Chun exclaimed in horror. "Aren't you afraid?"

"Well … no," Sigrun said. "He'll be behind bars and surrounded by guards – what is there to be afraid of?"

Lupe shuddered. "I don't think you should bother, Sigrun. How likely is it that he's innocent? I mean, they all say that. And you probably don't know much about prisons – coming from a small town and all – but I have friends with relatives in prison. Let me tell you, from what they say, visiting is no picnic. So, why don't you come home with me," she coaxed, "Diego and his brother Antonio will both be there since their parents have gone down to Mexico for the holidays. It'll be a blast."

"Thank you, Lupe. I'd love to come, but I've already made these plans."

"Whatever." Lupe cracked her gum loudly. "If you, like, change your mind at the last minute, let me know. My mother always cooks for a crowd."

〜〜〜

Sigrun set her pen on her desk and stretched her stiff shoulders. She had spent all day Saturday outlining her notes for the Con Law final. Although she had kept up with the reading assignments in all of her classes, with the hours she had been spending on the habeas case – plus her three or four visits to the gym every week – she simply had not had time to start studying. Professor Jamison's reminder on Thursday had jolted her into awareness of just how few days remained. Perhaps the trip at Thanksgiving was a bad idea; she certainly could use the extra time. But she was excited about it, and they planned to return early Sunday to avoid the nightmarish traffic coming back into Los Angeles at the end of a holiday weekend. Sigrun checked her watch: nearly nine. Philip was likely to call soon, and, anyway, she was tired. She headed into the common room to pour her long-since-cold coffee in the sink.

Returning to her room, her glance fell on the stack of letters she had pulled out of the drawer in which they'd been tucked since she'd moved into the dorm. Walking back from the gym the previous evening, she had found herself thinking about her father – what must the holidays have been like for him those first few years after her mother had died, when Sigrun was too young to understand? She wished they had talked about it. Now that she had some inkling of the grief he must have experienced, she appreciated why he had preferred to leave the past behind. But in doing so, he had left her questions unanswered. Maybe her mother's letters held some clues.

Sigrun pulled out the letter with the oldest postmark, settled herself on the bed, and started reading. The ringing of her cell phone startled her.

"Hey," Philip asked, "how's the studying going?"

"Oh, I quit. I've been reading those letters we found from my mother." She noted the time. "Wait a minute, that was two hours ago. What have you been doing?"

"Well, Dad finally relented and let me go out. I went to an end-of-term party, but it was dreadfully dreary. So a few of us split and grabbed some pints at a local bar."

"Uhm, not to be too much of a stick-in-the-mud, but what about your probation? Did you drive home?"

"Lord, Sigrun, you're worse than my parents. I'm going to stop telling you things if you're going to hassle me."

"Hey, I'm just looking out for you. What if you'd been stopped?"

"Do you think I would have had less to drink at the party than I did at the bar?"

"Good point. How much time do you have left – about five weeks? Maybe you should stay home for the duration."

"I've done that," he said petulantly, "and I'm bored."

"Look – I'll be home in a month for Christmas. I promise I'll drive you to as many parties as you want if you promise to stop taking risks until then."

"But you don't like parties."

"True. But I'd like you to stay out of trouble."

He laughed. "Okay. I suppose I can stay home for another

month if you'll really agree to go out and have some fun while you're here."

"The problem with that plan," said Sigrun dryly, "is that most of the parties you want to go to are not my idea of fun."

"But you have a good time with the gang from Dickinson."

"Not when everyone is drunk."

"You're too young to be so prudish."

"Are you going to promise?"

"All right – I promise not to go out drinking again until you're home on break."

"Thank you. Speaking of going out – I'm afraid Milton is going to ask me out."

"What?"

"Yeah. Well, he keeps sitting next to me in Con Law and making comments about how good my notes are. And then he 'happens' to wander by when I'm eating lunch in the sculpture garden."

"How sweet," Philip snickered. "And what's the matter with Milton – he's not smart enough for you?"

"No! Come on! I've told you what he looks like. I'm not that desperate."

"Sooo, you're judging a potential date primarily on appearance?"

"As if you don't."

"We're not talking about me. And don't you tell me not to be blinded by beauty?"

"But," sputtered Sigrun, "that's altogether different! When confronted by a beautiful body you lose all capacity to assess character. Here … well, not to be unkind, but Milton is rather repulsive."

Philip laughed. "I'm just teasing. No, I don't think you should consider dating Milton. You can do far better."

She snorted. "Yeah, like I have a good track record."

⋇⌒⋇

On the Friday after Thanksgiving, Blythe and Sigrun arrived at San Quentin and joined a long line for first-time visitors. The line inched through a cavernous waiting room, cacophonous with the crying of children and the incessant broadcasting of a crackling public address system. Eventually, they were screened, searched, and sent to a second line, which Sigrun was grateful to see was much shorter. Then they found seats in the smaller but still noisy waiting area for the condemned prisoners. Blythe unfolded her list of questions to review yet again. Sigrun was too nervous to think. She smoothed her skirt and tugged her jacket into place, self-conscious in her new suit. She watched as other visitors were called into the partially screened booths, which terminated at a thick glass partition that separated the visitors from the prisoners and prevented any physical contact. Under the vigilant eyes of the guards on each side, conversations were conducted through the heavy metal grills set into the partitions.

At last their names were called. Sigrun followed Blythe into the booth toward which a guard brusquely gestured. She took one of the plastic chairs and leaned forward, focusing on the door through which prisoners were escorted. A tall man wearing a blue denim prison shirt, hands cuffed before him, was led toward their booth between two guards. Her first thought was that they had made a mistake – this man must be younger than their petitioner. The man carried himself with dignity, appearing nearly oblivious to his surroundings. He was thin to the point of gauntness, his light brown hair closely cropped in a prison cut. As he settled himself inside the steel cage on his side of the partition, his cool green eyes met Sigrun's in an assessing stare. His face remained expressionless as his gaze shifted to Blythe.

"Mr. Fremont," Blythe said, "I'm Blythe Jordan, and this is Sigrun Nyman. As we explained in our letter, we're law students from UCLA."

"What can I do for you?" he asked politely in a quiet, reserved voice.

"We've been reviewing your recent federal habeas petition and wondered if we could ask you some questions?"

He nodded distantly. "Certainly, but I'm sure that I won't be able to provide anything useful."

"In your new petition," Blythe began, "you raise claims concerning the ineffectiveness of your attorney. We were wondering about his trial strategy. Did you discuss your defense with him?"

"No, not personally," he said.

"Did he meet with someone on your behalf?"

"Yes, but I wasn't involved."

"Do you know what his plan was? For example, do you know if he had a reason for not interviewing the person who reported the murders?"

"Not that I know of."

"In general, what was his approach to your defense?" Blythe

asked curiously.

"He believed, as I did, that the case was ludicrous," Fremont said calmly.

"So, he didn't feel that you needed a stronger defense?"

"I can't say. Clearly, in hindsight, I did."

"But why didn't he object to the prosecutor's bizarre conjecture about cults?"

Fremont shook his head. "I can't say."

Blythe paused and then asked thoughtfully, "Mr. Fremont, of course you realize that we're not representing you, right?"

"Of course."

"Okay, so nothing you tell us is protected by any privilege, and it's certainly your right not to answer our questions. However, any information you provide might help us win a new trial for you. So, I wonder, was there a good reason not to object to the prosecutor's argument that you had some satanic motive?"

"I can't say," he said evenly.

Blythe studied her list of questions. "We think we've identified an additional claim, and we wanted to ask you about it. We've obtained the photographs from the trial, but, unfortunately, the prison won't permit us to show them to you. In examining the photographs, however, we noticed a footprint in the blood near the victims. Nothing was said about it at trial – do you know anything about it?"

"No, I'm sorry, I don't," he replied without inflection.

"Well, it looks like the footprint was made by a shoe and not your riding boots. Do you know if your attorney did any investigation of your boots or the photographs?"

"I don't believe so."

"Do you have any idea how the footprint was made?"

"I can't answer that," he said impassively.

Sigrun had been studying Fremont closely during the exchange. She watched his utter detachment with growing impatience.

"Was anyone else there while you were at the apartment?" Blythe asked.

"I can't answer ..."

"Excuse me, Mr. Fremont," Sigrun interrupted. "I'm sorry, but I thought you were claiming that you're innocent?"

In the first reaction Sigrun had yet detected, he raised an eyebrow slightly as his gaze glided back to her. "I am innocent," he said coolly, his expression impenetrable

"But you're not willing to assist us?" she challenged.

"I have no information that will be of use to you."

"But, Mr. Fremont," Blythe said, "we think you've raised good claims. We may be able to help you."

"I don't believe this petition will be any more effective than any of the others."

"Has anyone ever mentioned the footprint to you?" Sigrun asked.

"No, I don't recall ever discussing a footprint with anyone."

"Good," Blythe said encouragingly, "that's useful. Did you ever discuss the photographs from the crime scene with your attorney?"

"Not that I recall."

"But," Sigrun pressed, "you were aware the photographs existed?"

He gave her a withering look. "I was present at the trial."

Sigrun flushed and looked away to stop herself from making a sarcastic retort.

"What we want to know," Blythe asked in a controlled voice, "is whether your attorney was provided with the photographs prior to trial."

"I don't know," he said neutrally.

"Okay," Blythe said. "So, could you give us the name of the person who's been assisting you? Perhaps that person has more information."

He shook his head. "I'm sorry, I don't think that would be useful."

"But there is someone assisting you, isn't there?" Blythe probed.

"Yes, a friend filed this petition for me. I was not in favor of it."

"But," Sigrun tried again, "your friend has raised some good claims, and we might be able to work together to win a new trial."

"One cannot escape the end of one's path," he said quietly.

"Look," Sigrun said impatiently, "you **were** wearing riding boots that night, right?"

"Yes."

"A footprint was left in the blood of the murder victims by someone not wearing riding boots. If you didn't make that footprint, then we have evidence that someone else was there. Don't you think it's possible that such evidence might change things?"

"No," he said, "I don't."

"Don't you think it's worth arguing?" Blythe asked sharply.

"I'm sorry," he said in his maddeningly expressionless voice. "I do appreciate that you've given up your time to visit me, but I'm afraid I can't be of any assistance."

"I don't understand," Sigrun snapped. "How can you maintain your innocence and yet refuse to help us prove it?"

"I don't believe that you can help me."

"Why won't you let us try?" Sigrun asked, too loudly. "Do you want to die?"

Startled, he met her eyes and, just for a second, she glimpsed the terror of a young man unexpectedly condemned to death. He quickly regained his impassiveness and repeated, "One cannot escape one's path."

Sigrun was drawing breath to respond when a guard said, "It's time to go."

Blythe quickly stood. "Goodbye, Mr. Fremont. If you change your mind, you have our address."

They had to retrace their steps through the multiple layers of security to leave, but the process was rapid in reverse. Finally, they escaped into the fresh air and freedom of the parking lot.

"Well," Blythe said, shaking her head ruefully as they headed back toward the Golden Gate Bridge, "that was not what I expected."

"No, but," Sigrun said, "did you see his expression, just there at the end? I think he really might be innocent."

"You do?" Blythe sounded skeptical. "I don't know – he's way too cold."

"No, I mean, he is irritatingly remote, but maybe it's because he's frustrated."

"Does it matter?" Blythe asked. "If he refuses to help, what more can we do?"

"Well, we can try to find his friend."

"Okay, but how do you propose to do that if he won't talk to us? Officially, he filed the petition, so it doesn't have any information about this friend."

"Yeah, but maybe we can find something," Sigrun insisted.

"Why waste our time? If he doesn't want our help, then there are plenty of others on death row who do. We can switch to a different petition next semester."

"I suppose so," Sigrun said reluctantly.

Blythe took a deep breath. "I can't say I'm eager to repeat

that experience any time soon. I didn't expect it to be quite so ... well, so overwhelmingly oppressive."

"And so artificial. Can you imagine living in such a sterile environment?"

"Let's put it behind us and do something fun. After all, it is a holiday."

➤➤➤➤

"How was 'The Visit'?" Philip asked when Sigrun answered his call on Sunday.

"Frustrating. Disturbing. Useless."

Philip laughed. "I gather it went well."

"He didn't tell us anything, and he was totally uninterested in the footprint. Blythe thinks it's because he's guilty but ... I don't know, I saw something in his eyes. I think ... well, maybe he **is** innocent."

"No explanation for why he waited, waited with sirens wailing, ruby heavy in hand?"

"Hardly. He couldn't – or wouldn't – answer most of our questions. Blythe is ready to give up on him, but ... well, I keep thinking about his eyes."

Philip snorted.

"Yeah, I know. I should just forget it. I don't know why I care – I mean, it's not like it matters to me what happens to this guy."

"Because you're a compassionate, considerate, charitable, principled person."

Sigrun laughed. "It's amazing how you manage to make rubbish sound sincere."

"I'll take that as a compliment," he said. "But if you truly believe he's innocent, and you think his trial was unfair, shouldn't you at least try to fix it?"

"I think so. I mean, the petition was filed. So, it seems like we should pursue the claims if they have any potential, regardless of his attitude. ... Anyway, how's the family? How was your holiday?"

"Oh, good. It was good. But it was odd, you not being here."

"Yeah, I spent a lot of time thinking about holidays past. Hey, I nearly forgot. I wanted to tell you – I had trouble sleeping Friday night, so I got out the packet of my mother's letters I'd taken up with me. I think I may have been born in California."

"No kidding! What did you find?"

"I'm wondering if my mother wanted to keep something from my grandmother, because it's odd that she never really said how they had heard about me. But she finally mentioned a relative." Sigrun picked up a letter from the pile on her dresser. "She wrote, 'We heard from Sigrun's great aunt the other day. She's been called away from California for a while and won't be able to visit as planned. I guess I shouldn't admit it, but I'm glad because I'm afraid she might want to take the baby back'."

"Was that the first hint of a relative?"

"Pretty much. I went back and re-read the letters from right after my arrival and found one oblique reference to a woman who may have been this great aunt."

"Interesting – you reading those letters in California."

"Yeah," Sigrun said, "I had the same thought: It's like I've come full circle."

⸙⸙

As classes came to a close, Sigrun devoted all of her time – apart from visits to the gym – to studying. But, try as she might, she kept finding herself staring into space, re-living Fremont's expression in that fleeting instant and wondering if the file held some clue to the identity of the person who was helping him. Irritated at having lost her train of thought three times in the space of twenty minutes, she jumped up to fetch herself a cup of coffee from the pot in the common room. Come on, she thought to herself, get a grip; even if he didn't commit the murders, he's just some unlucky loser who got caught in the wrong place. If he didn't want their help, she had to let it go. She sat back down, resolutely put the image out of her mind, and focused her thoughts on her notes.

Then, flush with the exhilaration of finishing her first final – which by chance had been in Torts, the one she'd been most anxious about – Sigrun allowed herself the luxury of not studying for an afternoon. Instead, she gathered the habeas materials and a few chocolate truffles, intending to meticulously sort through the entire file one more time to see if she could either find the friend or finally get Fremont off her mind. Despite being mid-December, the day was sunny and pleasant, with just a slight nip from a cool ocean breeze, so she decided to head to the Sculpture Garden.

As dusk fell, Sigrun realized that she was getting cold. She had been sitting on the base of her favorite statue for hours and was just finishing the transcript of the trial when an idea finally crystallized. The only person to testify on Fremont's behalf during the penalty phase was a man who pleaded eloquently and emotionally for the jury to spare Fremont's life, arguing that he was a good kid who deserved a second chance. This witness, Gareth Malama, testified that he had known Fremont all his life. It was a long shot, but it was something.

⚘⚘

Returning to the library from lunch the following week, Sigrun heard Blythe call her name. "Hey, I'm heading to my last final! Any success finding that witness?"

"Not yet," Sigrun replied. "I've tried all the people searches and directory listings for California, but nothing's turned up."

"I can help you after my final, if you want."

"Will you still be here tomorrow?" she asked.

"Yeah, want to meet late in the afternoon?"

"That would be great. Good luck!" Sigrun continued on to the library. Her last final, in Contracts, was the following afternoon, and she was a bit nervous about it.

⚘⚘

Lupe was waiting outside the door after the Contracts final.

"Sigrun, your notes are unreal. I was blown away. I mean, I actually understood that last question! You know, I never got it when Professor Acorda explained it." She snapped her gum loudly. "Not that I came to class too often, but anyway, mucho gracias. I wouldn't have made it through the final if you hadn't let me study your notes."

"Oh, well," Sigrun said, letting her hair fall forward in her embarrassment at Lupe's enthusiastic praise, "I'm glad they helped."

"You know," Lupe gestured broadly back toward the lecture hall they had left behind on their way to the lounge, "in class, sometimes you and Tony would be having one of your exchanges – and I would be, like, totally lost – and I'd sit there thinking, whatever are they talking about? But with your notes, it all made sense. Hey, I'm leaving soon." Lupe looked at her watch and giggled. "In fact, Diego's probably already waiting for me. Merry Christmas." She hugged Sigrun warmly.

Sigrun entered the student lounge and found Blythe reading a newspaper at a corner table. "Hi, you look relaxed."

Blythe put the newspaper down with a smile. "Yeah, things are looking up. One more semester, and I'll be done with school!"

"Wish I could say the same. But it's good just to be done for a few weeks."

"So, why don't we check the property records to see if we can find that witness."

"Can you do that?"

"Of course. Here, I brought my laptop." She pulled it out of her bag. "Hey, what are you doing with the jewelry during break? You shouldn't leave it in your dorm room."

Sigrun blinked in surprise. "I hadn't given it a thought."

"I doubt anyone else knows it exists, but if we lost it, it might be awkward."

"I guess so. I suppose I'd better give it to Professor Ehrlich."

"I would," Blythe said, "then it's her responsibility. Okay, watch while I pull up the tax assessor records." She clicked away and then typed "Malama" in the box for surname. "Is that spelled right?"

"Yeah." Sigrun studied the short list that slowly scrolled onto the screen.

"Bingo!" Blythe exclaimed. "Here it is: a listing for 'G. Malama'. And it's even in Cambria. It must be the right guy."

"Wow, I'm impressed."

"You had the inspiration to look. So, what are you going to say to him?"

"Hmmm," Sigrun said thoughtfully. "I don't want to say too much in case it's not him, but I want him to be motivated to write back. I'll think about it over break."

"Good idea." Blythe scribbled his address onto a scrap of paper and handed it to Sigrun. "Call me if you want to consult. Enjoy break."

⟶⟵

Late Thursday afternoon Sigrun sat on the floor surrounded by material from the habeas case, trying to decide what she should take with her to help craft the letter. She looked at her watch and sighed; she had better head over to the Law School if she had a hope of catching Professor Ehrlich. She picked up the envelope with the jewelry. Her eye fell on the laundry piled on her bed. Right, she thought in annoyance, she had forgotten to return to the laundry room to put her other load in the dryer. She'd better do that first. She set the envelope on her dresser, grabbed some change, and hurried out.

When she returned from the laundry room, Sigrun reached for the envelope but then hesitated. It was pretty late in the afternoon, what if the professor wasn't in? Did she want to go all the way across campus for nothing? She glanced at the files on the floor. Was there anything she should ask? She sat on the bed to look through her most recent notes. What **was** she going to say to Fremont's witness – "your friend told us to get lost but his eyes have been haunting me?" She didn't think that would be particularly productive. She put down the notes.

She pulled the necklace from its envelope and cradled it in her palm. What secrets did it hold? She took the necklace over to her window and dangled it by the chain. But the sunlight was too weak; the stone only gleamed dully. She grasped the stone with her other hand and was dismayed to feel a faint jolt. She studied the emerald soberly. She leaned her forehead against the glass of the window, closed her eyes, and concentrated on bringing the image of Fremont from that one instant into the forefront of her mind. Suddenly, Fremont was looking at her as if he were sitting in the same room. Startled, her eyes flew open; she stepped back, shaking her head. She drew a deep breath. Okay. So she had an extremely clear recollection of his expression, and it was just as poignant now as it had been in person. She would write that letter, and maybe Mr. Malama would be able to help. And … perhaps Philip would like to see the stones. He seemed captivated by them. If she put them in her carry-on bag, they should be perfectly safe.

Chapter 7
Parva scintilla saepe magnam flamam excitat
(A small spark often initiates a large flame; proverb)

Sigrun took her seat for Criminal Law on the first Tuesday of the new term after Christmas break. The room was filling rather early, possibly because of the buzz about their professor. He had been a high-profile prosecutor in New York City until he had de-camped for the position at UCLA. Sigrun was a bit apprehensive. She was not particularly interested in the class, and she was afraid that his background might cause him to be even more confronta-tional than Professor Acorda. Although, in the end, she had man-aged to earn a rare "A" in Contracts – one of only three awarded that term by the notoriously stingy professor – she remained un-comfortable with the Socratic style.

"Good afternoon, class." A clean-shaven, short-haired man in a well-fitting suit strode briskly to the podium. "I'm Ronaldo Orlando. I was told that this is your first taste of criminal law, and, for better or worse, it's my first foray into teaching. So, we'll have to muddle through together."

Sigrun spotted Blythe in the corridor ahead as she left Crim Law.

Catching sight of her, Blythe asked, "Hey, do you have a minute?"

As they settled themselves in the unseasonably warm sun, Blythe said apologetically, "All the horror stories about people fail-ing the bar have gotten to me – so I've added another bar course."

"You're taking an extra class?"

"Yeah. So I'm afraid I'm going to be too busy to do anything on the habeas case. Do you think you want to stick with Fremont?"

"Well, I want to at least give it a try. But," she added with the now-familiar twinge of guilt she experienced whenever she thought about the case, "I haven't written to that witness yet."

"I really am sorry. I feel like I'm abandoning you."

"To be fair," Sigrun said, "you don't think it's worth continuing with anyway, so now it's just my time I'm wasting."

Sigrun finally forced herself to start on the letter the following Sunday afternoon. She spread the entire habeas file on her bed and sat staring at it, a fresh pad resting on her lap. Her eye fell on the envelope containing the jewelry. It was perplexing; when she had shown it to Philip, the necklace had seemed so ordinary. She shook the emerald into her hand and studied it. It was beautiful – but she felt nothing. She held it up to the light and shook her head. Nothing. How odd.

Hours later, Sigrun closed her cell phone and scrambled to her feet, stretching her stiff limbs. She had gone around in circles for a while, but she had finally written something with which she was reasonably content. She had then called Philip and read it to him. Having gained his approval, she wanted to send it off before she could have second thoughts. Seated at her desk, she carefully re-copied the letter and put it in an envelope. She changed into a less-wrinkled shirt, tucked her cell phone into her pocket, and headed out the door. Then she stopped. She shouldn't leave the necklace in plain sight. She scooped the necklace into its envelope and returned it to its spot in a dresser drawer. It was rather ironic, really, that she kept the jewels there, since Fremont had been arrested rifling dresser drawers in his quest to find them. But how had he known where they were, she wondered for the umpteenth time. She locked the door behind her, anxious to at last get the letter mailed.

As had become her nearly compulsive practice during the past few weeks, after Crim Law on Thursday Sigrun stopped in the student lounge to check her mailbox. She had gotten so used to finding it empty that she almost missed the letter it contained. Eagerly, she checked the return address. Yes! She slipped out the nearest door, perched on the edge of a patio chair, and unfolded a sheet of heavy paper.

Dear Ms. Nyman,

Please accept my apologies for the lengthy delay in responding to your letter. I regrettably was occupied with family matters and have just turned to my mail.

I was most interested to learn that you have been reviewing Zareh Fremont's habeas petition. You are correct that I am the friend who filed the petition for him. I was, however, unaware that any-one was paying the slightest attention to the petition, which I filed quite some while ago. I must thank you for taking the time to find my address and to write.

I would be delighted to discuss the case with you and to answer any questions you may have. In fact, in order to facili-tate a productive discussion, I suggest we meet in person. Because I prefer not to travel too far from San Quentin, I would like to meet near here. If that is impossi-ble, however, I can arrange to come to Los Angeles.

My cell phone number is below, and I welcome your call at any time. I truly look forward to hearing from you.

Cordially,
Gareth Malama

Sigrun read the letter a second time. Fantastic! She glanced at her watch. She only had 15 minutes before Lawyering Skills. Damn. She'd have to wait through the hour-and-fifteen-minute class, which she thought tedious at the best of times, before she could call. The response was better than she'd hoped for; Mr. Ma-lama sounded enthusiastic about her involvement. She read the let-ter a third time. Interestingly, it also sounded like Fremont had not mentioned their visit, as she had not in her letter. Tucking the enve-lope away, she reluctantly went to class.

She hurried back to the dorm as soon as class ended. She wanted both to call in private and to have the habeas file handy in case a question arose. Sigrun piled the file on her desk, got a note-pad and pen ready, and pulled the envelope out of her backpack. Cell phone in hand, she paused. What should she say? Suddenly nervous, she drew a deep breath. She read the letter again and nodded. He sounded approachable. Not allowing herself to hesitate, she called.

"Hello," a deep and friendly male voice answered.

"Hi, uhm, this is Sigrun Nyman, from UCLA Law School. I just got your letter."

"I am delighted to hear from you. I was so pleased to learn that you were working on Zareh's case."

"Uh, actually, I'm not precisely working on it, so much as reviewing it. I mean, I'm just a law student ..."

"Of course. I understand that you're not an attorney, but I am relieved that someone has at last taken an interest. I look forward to hearing your perspective."

"Oh, well ... yes," Sigrun stumbled, startled by how seriously he seemed to be taking her after she had been so unconditionally dismissed by Fremont. "I think your idea of a meeting is good. I mean, I'd be happy to meet with you."

"Splendid. Would it be possible for you to travel to Cambria?"

"Well," she said hesitantly, "I don't have a car, so ..."

"Perhaps you could take the train? We could meet at a café in San Louis Obispo, which is the closest train station to Cambria. I hear it's quite a pleasant trip."

"That might work. I'll need to check into it ... oh, there's a holiday in a couple of weeks. Would you be able to meet over the President's Day weekend?"

"Certainly," he said readily, "whenever you prefer. I generally work at a horse show that weekend, but I can arrange for someone to cover for me."

"Oh, well if you'd rather ..."

"I am at your disposal. But, I am curious, why didn't you approach Zareh?"

"Well ... we did," Sigrun said carefully, "but he was rather ... reticent."

Mr. Malama gave a bark of laughter. "Delicately put. I apologize if he was rude. Did you visit the prison?"

"Yes, over Thanksgiving."

"Ah," he said, "then you tracked me down. I admire your perseverance."

✪

⌐⊷ Chapter 8 ⌐⊷

Gutta cavat lapidem, non vi, sed saepe cadendo
(A drop hollows a stone, not by force, but by constant
dripping; Ovid)

On the Saturday of the long weekend in February, Sigrun
caught the early train to San Luis Obispo. Hours into the trip, she
realized that she was hungry. She closed the case book she had
been studying and pulled out a candy bar. She stared at the passing
scenery while savoring the chocolate. It was indeed a beautiful trip
along the coast, but she was too tense to fully appreciate it. She was
nervous; she wished Blythe had been willing to come. Sigrun was
always uncomfortable meeting strangers, but in this case, her anxiety was all the more acute because of the high expectations Mr. Malama seemed to have. Sure, she had spotted the footprint, but she
really didn't know much about habeas law. She hoped that she
wouldn't prove to be a disappointment to him – and that she wasn't
wasting his time as well as her own. Her previous trip north had
been less than productive, and it had left her plagued by the specter
of Fremont's eyes.

Sigrun checked her watch; it was nearly 2:30, their scheduled
arrival time, but she was pretty sure they weren't close. She sighed.
She'd better call and warn him.

"No problem," he said agreeably after she had explained.
"It's a beautiful day, and I am enjoying my cappuccino. Come find
me on the café's back patio – just look for a Hawaiian shirt."

"I'm so sorry to make you wait."

"Don't worry about it. Aloha entails 'ahonui', or patience."

The train pulled into the station more than an hour late.
Sigrun hurried the few blocks to the café. No employee was in
sight, so she crossed the restaurant to the patio door. She hesitated
in the doorway, scanning the sparsely occupied tables. That must be
him, she thought as she spotted a large man in his mid-40s, sitting
alone at a far table reading a newspaper. As promised, he was wearing an untucked Hawaiian shirt and jeans. With his dark and deeply

tanned complexion, long black ponytail, and shell earring in one ear, he looked Hawaiian. She approached the table and asked tentatively, "Excuse me, are you Mr. Malama?"

He looked up with a smile that warmed his friendly brown eyes. "Yes, but please call me Gareth. You must be Sigrun." He stood and offered his hand.

"Yes," she said as she clasped his hand firmly.

She felt an odd fleeting jolt.

Gareth did a rapid double-take, gave her a searching look, and said, "Greetings."

Embarrassed and confused, Sigrun ducked behind her hair. What was it? Did he feel it? If so, why didn't he say something?

"Have a seat," Gareth said in an ordinary tone of voice.

Disconcerted, she quickly sat.

"Have you had any lunch? They have good salads." He flagged down a server.

Still flustered, Sigrun studied the menu in silence for several minutes. When the server returned, she randomly selected a salad.

"So," Gareth asked genially, "you are in law school?"

"Yes, in my first year. But," she hastened to reassure him, "I'm working under the guidance of an experienced professor and, last term, another student who is quite familiar with habeas petitions also worked on the case."

"Are you from Los Angeles?"

"Uh, no … no, I'm from Pennsylvania."

"So, what brought you to UCLA?"

"Oh, well," Sigrun hesitated, startled by this turn of conversation, "that's rather a long story, and I …"

"I am in no hurry."

"Oh. Uhm … it was my father, mostly. He taught high school, but he had always dreamt of going to law school. After his father died, he had to drop out of college to help his mother run the family farm. He never did get to law school, so he transferred his dream to me."

"You used the past tense," Gareth said gently. "Did your father die?"

She nodded. "Last summer."

"I am very sorry," he said quietly. "What about your mother?"

Surprised by his interest, Sigrun shot him a questioning look, but she could discern only compassion in his expression. "My mother died when I was young."

"Did you grow up on the farm?"

"Well ... yes and no. By the time we moved back, it was too small to be functional. We just kept a few chickens and goats."

"So, how did you end up in Los Angeles?"

"Well, the professor with whom I'm now working was a student of my father's. She urged me to apply to UCLA and, so, here I am."

"And she encouraged you to get involved in Zareh's case?"

"Exactly. She thought I would be interested, and she believes that Mr. Fremont – or you, I guess – raised some good claims."

He sighed. "I can't tell you how long I have waited for someone to find merit in our claims."

"Oh, but, we don't have any official role ..."

"No, I know. Unbelievably, I have come to understand the habeas system to some degree. But I am quite interested in hearing about this new claim."

"Well, in reviewing the file, we noticed that the attorney for the State referenced exhibits we didn't have. So, we went to the courthouse and found the missing exhibits." Sigrun took a sip of iced tea. "Then we discovered ..." A phone rang.

Gareth pulled out a cell phone and glanced at the screen. "Please excuse me, I must take this call." He walked some distance from the table. She took the opportunity to get out her files and start on the salad a server had delivered.

Gareth returned several minutes later. "Coincidently, that was Zareh. Because he is permitted to make collect calls only during brief and irregular periods, I always try to take his call. He sends his regards."

"He does?" Sigrun asked skeptically.

"No, but he should have. Don't take it personally. He has disengaged from this process; he discouraged me from even embarking on a new round of petitions."

"He told us he was not in favor of filing the petition."

Gareth gave a wan smile. "The long string of disappointments has been difficult. ... Please, do tell me what you've discovered."

She picked up the envelope with the photographs. "So, the missing exhibits included photos from the crime scene. Do you remember them?"

"Yes."

Sigrun opened the envelope, pulled out the photographs, and handed Gareth the one on top. "Take a look at this."

He took the sheet and held it for a second. He then set the photo on the table; she noted that his face had gone ashen. He swallowed hard and briefly shut his eyes.

"Are you all right?" she asked with concern.

He sighed deeply. "I haven't seen these since the trial … I had forgotten." He picked up the photo again, and she was surprised to see that his hand was shaking slightly. She watched as he studied it for a long moment before returning it to the table. "Will you excuse me?"

"Of course," Sigrun said uneasily as she watched him walk quickly into the restaurant. She shoved the rest of her salad aside, her appetite having vanished in the suddenly somber atmosphere. She picked up the photo. If you weren't studying it for clues, it really was rather grisly. She set it down and opened her notebook to her list of questions. She wondered what it was about the photo that had so affected Gareth. She was struck by the thought that Fremont had been Norm's age when he was arrested. She shuddered to think of Norm being sentenced to death. Obviously Gareth had known Fremont well; the trial must have been a terrible ordeal for him.

"I apologize," Gareth said when he returned, looking drawn. "I had forgotten how gruesome those photographs are. What is it you wanted me to look at?"

"No, I'm sorry," Sigrun said, "I was too abrupt – I should have realized how difficult it would be for you to revisit the trial."

He gave her an inquiring look. "Why do you say that?"

"Well, I mean, it must be hard for you to think about what Mr. Fremont's life would have been like had the trial gone differently."

"Yes … of course," he said softly. "Zareh is like a little brother to me. I remember the day he was born; I taught him to ride." He paused. "Zareh is innocent, you know."

Sigrun started. "Uh … I'm not …" She stopped. Gareth was looking at her with an intensity that staggered her. She met his eyes and read his absolute certainty. "I believe that he is."

"Good." He nodded. "Good. Maybe you can help us then."

⚡⚡⚡

On Tuesday afternoon, Sigrun impatiently shifted in her seat during Crim Law. That morning she had arranged a meeting with Professor Ehrlich for 2:30, which was immediately after Sigrun's class. Fortunately, her inattentiveness would not cause her embarrassment since, contrary to her expectations, Professor Orlando had proven to be her most easygoing professor, calling only on volunteers.

"In that case, would the accomplice be guilty of murder for the security guard's death?" the professor asked, catching her attention.

"Doesn't it depend," Quentin asked, "on the mens rea? I mean, even if the accomplice could be said to have assisted in the burglary, he can't be guilty of murder without an intent to commit murder."

"Is that correct?" asked the professor.

"No," Tony asserted. "He's guilty of all foreseeable crimes, right? The murder flows from the burglary, and it's certainly likely that someone will end up dead in an armed robbery."

"But," Quentin insisted, "he only intended to break into the warehouse to spend the night; he thought it was empty, and he didn't know his friend was armed."

"So," the professor asked, "what if the crime partner was surprised by the security guard, picked up a pipe, and killed the guard with a blow to the head? Is the accomplice in the other room guilty of murder?"

"I still think," Quentin insisted, "that, at the most, he's only guilty as an accomplice to burglary. Even if he's guilty of foreseeable crimes, it seems to me that his only intent was to trespass or something trivial. I mean, what did he do to assist in the murder?"

"Since we haven't discussed the various degrees of murder yet," the professor said, "maybe it would be easier if we used an example …"

So, Sigrun mused, maybe Zvi was right – even if the footprint belonged to the murderer, Fremont could still be guilty as an accomplice. It seemed clear that he'd had an intent to commit burglary. Maybe he had acted as a lookout and then joined the murderer in the apartment? But no, the neighbor hadn't seen anyone leave after she had gotten home – so what happened to the other guy if they were working together? She jotted a note to herself to make sure she argued that Fremont couldn't have been present in the apartment at the same time as the person who had made the footprint.

Finally, the class ended, and she hurried up the aisle.

"Sigrun," Lupe called from across the room. Sigrun waited for her and said, "I'm kinda in a hurry."

"I'll walk with you," Lupe said cheerily. "What's up?"

"Oh, just a meeting on my habeas case. Did you need something?"

"You know," Lupe cracked her gum loudly, "you really should stop wasting your time on that guy – I mean, it's not like you're learning anything useful and …"

"I know," she interjected before Lupe could finish, "he's probably guilty anyway. What was it you wanted?"

"Oh yeah – I was wondering – are you free Saturday? Diego called and Antonio – you remember, he's Diego's younger brother – is coming up for the weekend. So, Diego and I thought, wouldn't it be great if you'd go out with us? Maybe we could, like, catch a movie?"

"Oh, well, uh …" Sigrun tried in vain to concoct an excuse as they arrived at Professor Ehrlich's office. "Okay, yeah, sure."

"Outstanding!"

"Excuse me, Professor," she said, knocking on the partially open office door.

"Sigrun, come on in." The professor pushed aside a pile of papers and pulled a pad from the clutter that covered the desk. "So, you were right about the witness?"

"Yeah, and he filed the petition – well, he not only filed it, he also found the missing neighbor, got her declaration, and researched the claim." Sigrun smiled. "Actually, I'm quite sure he understands habeas jurisprudence better than I do."

"Good work. Was he able to shed any light on your questions?"

"Some. Apparently the petitioner was more or less right when he said they thought the prosecutor's case was preposterous. Mr. Malama said the attorney convinced them that it was best to let the prosecutor present whatever evidence he unearthed without objection and then ridicule it in closing. What's interesting though," Sigrun added, "is that Mr. Malama said he asked the attorney several times how it was that the police had arrived so quickly in the middle of the night when there'd been no gunshots or anything, but the attorney just shrugged it off."

"That's good. Is the attorney still practicing?"

"No, in fact, Mr. Malama said he died some time ago."

"Fine – we don't need a declaration from him if we have one from Mr. Malama. His testimony together with that notation in the police report about a 911 call establishes that a reasonable attorney should have looked into what alerted the police. The declaration from the neighbor, I believe, is adequate to demonstrate a reasonable probability that, but for his counsel's failure to investigate, the petitioner would not have been convicted. At least, it is if we take into account the footprint."

"Right," Sigrun broke in eagerly, "Mr. Malama said they first saw the photos at the preliminary hearing – months before the trial. So, since he had time, I think we can argue that it was unreasonable for counsel not to investigate the footprint."

"Slow down," the professor said with a smile, while jotting a note. "You're skipping several steps. First, we need evidence that the footprint could not have been made by a riding boot. Then we have to raise the claim. Which brings up other issues." She glanced at her watch and continued writing. "Which we can address later, since I have to run to class. So, your next task is to locate an expert willing to examine the photograph and the boots – which we have to obtain – and to render an opinion. But, in order to do that, we need two things."

The professor paused and looked at Sigrun. "Because you're not yet an attorney, you can't represent the petitioner, but I can. Could you please contact him, and get his agreement to have me represent him pro bono? I'll need to have him sign something, but we can start with a verbal agreement. Second, could you ask Mr. Malama if they can pay for an expert? If not, I'll need to write a justification and get approval for funds."

"Okay," Sigrun said, taking notes on her tasks. "I'll work on getting his agreement right away. But I'm afraid I'll need some help in finding an expert."

"Of course," the professor said. "You're doing an amazing job for a first-year. Let's see," she pushed aside a pile on her desk and pulled out a calendar, "what about Thursday at the same time?"

"No, I've got Lawyering Skills," she said with a grimace.

"Well," Professor Ehrlich said dryly, "I can't condone cutting class, so how about Friday, say at 4:00?"

Sigrun left the office, notepad in hand. She stopped at the student lounge because it was closer than the library, dropped into a chair, and attempted to capture everything the professor had said. She was reviewing what she had written when she became aware that someone was watching her.

"Uh, hi," Milton said from across the room. He came closer, wearing his typical deer-caught-in-the headlights expression. "Uhm, I didn't want to disturb you, but, uh, is it okay if I join you?"

"Well ..." She hesitated, thinking with a sinking feeling that he seemed even more nervous than usual. "I have to run."

"Oh," he said with disappointment. "You seem like you're always busy lately."

"Uh, well," she said with a pang of guilt because she had, in fact, been avoiding him this term, "I've been putting a lot of time into my habeas case."

"So, uh, I guess you don't have time to eat in the sculpture garden anymore?"

"Well, you know, the weather hasn't always been that nice ..."

"Yeah, I guess ..." Milton ran his hand through his hair. "Hey, I was wondering, maybe, if you don't have any plans," his voice rose as he rushed on, "do you think you might want to catch a movie on Saturday?"

"I'm sorry," she said, thanking her lucky stars, "but I already have plans."

"Oh." He sounded dejected. "Okay. Maybe another time?"

"Sure," she said gently, getting to her feet. "I really do have to go – I need to make a phone call on this case. See you later." As she hurried out of the lounge, she felt both remorseful for blowing him off and relieved that he had managed to select the one Saturday in the foreseeable future for which she had a real excuse.

Sigrun spent the walk to her dorm debating whether she could just ask Gareth to contact Fremont, or if she had to talk to him herself. Professor Ehrlich had specifically said that she should ask the petitioner, but maybe that wasn't strictly necessary. On the other hand, what if he ultimately refused to sign the agreement and she had to confess that she had never spoken to him directly? Sigrun sighed. It seemed she had two options: either go back to the professor and clarify whether it was necessary for her to speak with Fremont personally, or just get up the courage and do it. She was tempted to call Philip, but she knew what he would say. Why was it, she wondered, that since coming to law school she kept putting herself in situations that required her to do things she found loathsome? Perhaps it was an indication that she was ill suited to the law? Or maybe she was just an idiot.

She let herself into the suite and dumped her backpack on the floor. She pulled out her notes from the meeting that afternoon and extracted Gareth's letter from the file on her desk. She set her cell phone next to the letter and stood in front of the desk composing a message in case Gareth didn't answer. She paced across the room and back. Gareth was easy to talk to and she had dealt with Fremont once already. Why then, she thought with frustration, was she so nervous? She grabbed her phone and punched in a call. It rang several times.

"Sorry," Philip said over the loud music in the background, "what's up?"

"Do you have time for a reality check?"

"Yeah, hold on." The music quieted. "What don't you want to do?"

"Well, I just met with the professor, and she wants to represent Fremont to raise the new claim."

"Cool."

"Yeah … but she asked me to contact him to get his agreement to proceed. So, do you think I can ask Mr. Malama to talk to him, or do I have to call him myself?"

"But you've met Fremont."

"Yeah, but, I mean, I'd have to call San Quentin and …"

"Have him call you."

"Oh. That's a good idea. But, what if he doesn't want to do it? You know, he was against filing the petition, so I don't expect he'll be keen for us to take over."

"So persuade him."

"Yeah, well, you know me – I'll probably get angry again and yell at him."

Philip snorted. "You can be plenty manipulative if you want to be."

"Hey, I don't think …"

"Sigrun, you're the most stubborn person I've ever met – if you want something enough, I'm completely confident you can achieve it."

"Really?"

He laughed. "Absolutely. You're just perversely shy. Hang up, call this Malama guy, and arrange for him to have Fremont call you."

"Okay. Thanks."

"Don't mention it. Keep me posted."

She immediately dialed Gareth and, when he answered, said, "Hi, uhm, this is Sigrun Nyman …"

"Sigrun, I didn't expect to hear from you so soon – good news, I hope?"

"Yes. I spoke with my professor this afternoon, and she'd like to represent Mr. Fremont on a volunteer basis to raise the new claim. Do you think he'll agree to that?"

"Are you suggesting that she become his attorney?"

"Right – at no cost to him."

"Cost is not an issue," he said dismissively, "but Zareh is … wary of lawyers."

"Well, I can't say I blame him, after his trial, but this is different. We think he has solid claims. We need to develop them a bit, but my professor's optimistic."

"I can promise you that Zareh will not be. If you believe we have a chance at success, however, I will attempt to persuade him."

"I personally don't have enough experience to know," she said carefully, wanting to be clear, "but my professor believes that he does."

"Well, any chance is an improvement over our record. I'll speak to Zareh."

"Good. Uhm, would it be possible, then, to have him call me?"

Gareth laughed. "Certainly, if you're willing to talk to him again."

"Oh, well," Sigrun found herself admitting, "I don't want to, but I think I should."

"I will ask him to be more considerate. It is, however, impossible to know when he might have access to a telephone. When would be best for him to call?"

"I can talk to him whenever I'm not in class. So, Thursday after 4:30, Friday after 10:30, or anytime on the weekend would work. Is that good?"

"That should be sufficient. I generally visit at the end of the week, so I'll let you know by Friday if there is a problem."

"Oh, one other thing, we need to hire an expert to examine the footprint and the boots. I was wondering, uhm, would it be possible for you to pay for the expert?"

"Certainly. Please, don't hesitate to ask if you need any funds. Believe me, any costs are inconsequential balanced against the hope that you offer. In addition, please don't hesitate to call if you have any questions. Unlike Zareh," he added dryly, "I am most eager to assist you."

〜 Chapter 9 〜

Altissima quaeque flumina minimo sono labi
(The deepest rivers flow with the least sound;
Q. Curtius)

Sigrun was in the library Friday afternoon when her phone vibrated. She answered in the sparsely occupied hallway.

"Hello, this is Gareth. I've just left Zareh, and he has agreed to your proposal."

"Oh good. Was he at all ... interested?"

"Suffice it to say that he acquiesced."

"So, I shouldn't expect much cooperation?"

"No. I suggest you use me as your contact; I now and then have some small success at influencing him."

"Okay, that's fine. But ... will he call me – just to confirm the agreement?"

"Well," Gareth said apologetically, "he has agreed to, but a recent disturbance has caused his cell block to be placed in a state of indefinite lock-down, suspending all phone privileges. Will that pose a problem?"

"I don't think so, I'm pretty sure we can go ahead and retain an expert. And thank you," she added gratefully, "for approaching Mr. Fremont for me ..."

"Please," he interrupted amicably, "no one ever calls Zareh 'Mr. Fremont', and I always think of his father whenever you do. Would you mind calling him 'Zareh'?"

"Uh, well, no, I guess not."

"So, please do proceed, and please keep me apprised of any funds you require."

Sigrun hung up with a sense of anticipation. "Fantastic!" she exclaimed, garnering an odd look from a passing student. So, now she needed to find out how to retain an expert and get the boots – as well as figure out how to raise the new claim. She returned to the library to record the call in her notes and review her list of questions in preparation for her 4:00 meeting.

Sigrun had just taken her seat in Property the following Friday morning when her cell phone vibrated. She jumped to her feet and brushed by Milton on her way up the aisle. She answered the call as she exited the lecture hall.

"Sorry to disturb you," Gareth said, "but I am driving up to visit Zareh, and I realized I forgot to ask you when you might be available on Mondays through Wednesdays; I have your schedule for the rest of the week."

"Oh, sure. Let's see ... uhm, he can call me after 3:00 any of those days."

"Thank you. Is there anything you'd like me to tell Zareh?"

"Well, I'm afraid we're still looking for an expert – apparently this is a pretty unusual specialty, and, so far, I haven't found anyone interested. But," she hastened to add, "I have plenty left to try."

"Good. Please do not feel pressured by my call; I just wanted to let you know that I will be out of town for the next week working a horse show. But I'll check my messages as frequently as I can, if you need anything."

"Thanks for telling me." She hesitated – ordinarily she tried not to pry, but her curiosity was piqued. "Uhm, you mentioned a horse show? What is it you do, if you don't mind my asking?"

"Not at all. I have a rather esoteric job – I work as a braider at horse shows."

Sigrun tried to puzzle that out, but failed. "I'm sorry?"

"People who show horses hire me to make their horses' manes and tails attractive."

"Wow," she said.

Gareth laughed. "It keeps me outside and leaves me free during most weekdays to visit Zareh. The show that starts tomorrow and lasts through the following weekend is a rather large one that requires more of my time than usual."

"By the way, do you know if conditions have changed at the prison?"

"Not yet. I was there Tuesday, and the guards I spoke with thought the restrictions were likely to remain in force for several more weeks."

"Okay. I need to get to class."

"I will check with you sometime during the week, if I may."

Sigrun squinted at her mailbox as she dashed through the

lounge on her way to grab a quick lunch before Crim Law; she heard her name called from a corner of the lounge where Blythe sat with Zvi.

"Have a seat," Zvi said as Sigrun approached. "I haven't seen you for weeks. How are you?"

"Busy," she replied. "But I'm so excited – we just found an expert for the habeas case. Remember, we need the expert for …"

"The footprint. Yes, of course, I recall," Zvi said. "Blythe told me you've persuaded the petitioner to push forward with the claim."

"Well, it wasn't me, exactly. But, regardless, I've been contacting experts for a couple of weeks, and one finally agreed to conduct the analysis."

"Great," Blythe said. "But were you able to get the boots released?"

"Professor Ehrlich's a marvel – she has contacts everywhere. She called someone in the prosecutor's office here who put her in touch with someone in San Louis Obispo who knew a person in the crime lab. Anyway, she finally got permission for our expert to examine the boots. You know, interestingly, the petitioner's clothing was lost. Our contact said there's an entry noting that the clothing was released by the trial court, but it never showed up in storage."

"Then I guess it's not too surprising," Blythe said, "that the stolen jewelry ended up stuck in an envelope in the habeas file. Hey, did you turn it over to the professor?"

"Uh, no," she said guiltily. "I ran out of time at the end of last term, and I haven't gotten around to it since."

"Really, Sigrun," chided Blythe, "don't you think it would be better if you didn't have responsibility for those gems?"

"Yeah, well," she said uncomfortably, ducking behind her hair, "I just never seem to remember them when I'm going to be seeing the professor."

Zvi's eyebrows shot up. "Do they have any possible relevance to the case?"

"None."

"I'd have to agree with Blythe – you must turn them over. And I think Professor Ehrlich should notify her contact that she has some trial evidence. It's probably listed as missing as well."

"I never thought of that," Sigrun said. "I guess you're right, I'd better talk to her." She noticed Regan and Quentin leave the lounge. "Oops, I've got to run."

⌒⌖⌒⌖

"Hey, Sigrun, isn't this your phone?" Blythe called from the front of the gym, holding up Sigrun's ringing cell phone.

"Thanks," she said as she took the phone.

"Hello, Sigrun," Gareth said. "I apologize for calling so late but I had a dinner engagement with my cousin. Are you free?"

"Sure – but I'm at the gym, so it's a bit noisy."

"I won't keep you. I wanted to let you know that I visited Zareh today, and his telephone privileges have been restored. He should be calling you shortly."

"Okay, thanks. Oh, I heard from our expert. She made an appointment to examine the boots, and she expects to have her report finished early next week."

"Splendid. Could I trouble you to call me as soon as you hear from her?"

"Of course. And I'll send you a copy of the report as well."

"Thank you. And I truly appreciate how much time you've taken with Zareh's case. I trust that it's not adversely impacting your schooling."

"Uh, well ... we're on spring break next week, so I can catch up."

"Please," he said seriously, "you must not jeopardize your future on our account."

"No, really, I'm just a bit behind – nothing I can't rectify next week."

"I'll take you at your word. But, please do not take umbrage when I inquire after your progress."

"Oh," she murmured, "that's so kind of you."

"Not at all," he said sternly. "Sigrun, you've taken it upon yourself to advocate on behalf of my kaikaina. It is my responsibility to stand behind you. Now, I have interrupted you long enough. Aloha and I will talk to you soon."

Sigrun surreptitiously wiped her eyes as she returned to her workout.

⤙⤚

Friday afternoon, Sigrun knocked at the professor's office door at what had become their regular time.

"Come on in, Sigrun. Have you heard from our petitioner yet?"

She took a seat before an atypically bare desk. "No, but I expect I will soon."

"Okay, but I need his express agreement before we can take

any official action on his behalf. By the way, you'd better ask him where we should send the written agreement ..." she said as she looked absently around the clean desk, "which I had right here. Now, where did I put that? That's why I rarely clean up. Here it is." She pulled a multiple-page document from an open drawer and handed it to Sigrun.

"Should I mail it to him, then, after I talk to him?" Sigrun asked.

"Yes. It's mostly a form agreement, but why don't you read it over first and make sure I haven't misrepresented anything. If you find any problems, it can wait until I get back from break. So, where are we otherwise?"

"The expert's report should be ready early next week. Assuming she finds what we're anticipating, I thought I'd start outlining our arguments."

"Good idea. Keep in mind two points: First, we have to present the claim from the perspective that any reasonable attorney would have pursued a lead with the potential to produce evidence that someone besides his client was in the apartment. Second, the state is going to scream that he should have raised this claim years ago – so see if we can support an argument that actions by the petitioner's counsel prevented him from learning about the basis for the claim – in this case, the footprint. Following?"

Sigrun looked up from the notes she was jotting. "I think so. But just so I'm clear – this claim is for the state court, right?"

"Yes. We'll need to seek a stay of the federal case and file a new petition in state court. But we can outline the scope of the petition later – for now, focus on this claim. Oh, and you might ask the petitioner if he's willing to provide a declaration about his attorney's failure to investigate who called the police. Maybe he has something to add."

"I doubt it," Sigrun said dryly, "but I'll try to ask."

"Well, you can always have his friend ask him, I suppose. Anything else?"

"Not at the moment."

"Okay. So, Sigrun, I've been thinking about our conversation last semester, and I wanted to tell you that I'm going to be visiting my mother. Would you like me to see if she recalls anything about your adoption?"

"That would be great. I've been reading some letters from my mother that I found – or, I was when I had some spare time – but I haven't learned anything much. So, I'd really appreciate it if you could ask. Thanks."

"Of course. I mentioned it to the one high-school classmate I keep in touch with a few weeks ago in an e-mail, but she didn't recall anything either."

"Thanks so much for taking the time …"

"Not at all, it's no trouble. I'd love to be able to track down some information for you. Maybe my mother knows a mutual friend." She stood. "Well, have a good break, and leave me a copy of the report to read when I get back."

Sigrun left the office and slowly strolled through the nearly deserted corridors to the library. She couldn't afford to succumb to the jubilant mood that had been bubbling all day. Not only did she hope to make significant progress on the footprint claim, but she also was behind in her assignments in both Crim Law and Property. She planned to catch up on her course work first so that she would be free to devote her full attention to the habeas case after she heard from the expert. Fortunately, the forecast called for rain continuing at least through the weekend, so she wouldn't be lured outside. Sigrun thought sadly that she'd be far happier to be heading home for a week in Pennsylvania.

The past few assignments in Crim Law had dealt with the various degrees of murder, and Sigrun had been lost for the duration. She settled into her favorite corner of the library and flipped back through her notes until she reached the last lecture she had understood. She opened the case book with a sigh and set to reading. Her cell phone vibrated. She jumped to her feet and headed out of the library while she attempted to extricate the apparently entangled phone from her pocket. She was in the hallway before she got the phone out and, afraid it was going to switch to voicemail, answered without checking the screen.

"Hey, how's things?" Philip asked.

"Oh, it's you."

"Why thanks. I'm glad you're happy to hear from me."

Sigrun laughed. "Well, actually I'm not – I'm expecting that call from Fremont, and I was hoping you were him."

"Well," he said in mock indignation, "fine. If you'd rather wait for his call, I'll just hang up and not share with you the tidings brought by today's mail."

"Oh. The mail! Tell me!"

"Nope." Philip gave an exaggerated sigh. "I can tell that I've been supplanted in your affections by Fremont. So, I'll just go write a song to drown my sorrows."

"Philip! Tell me!"

"But why should I if you no longer care?"

"I care, I care. Tell me."

"Perhaps I will later," he said languidly, "if I feel like it."

"I'd strangle you if I could reach you. It must be good news or you wouldn't be so cheerful."

"Who says I'm cheerful?"

"I'm going to hang up," she threatened.

"Okay, okay," he said, laughing. "Are you sitting down?"

"No! I'm standing in the hallway outside the library – so tell me already."

"It's from Davis."

"And?" She closed her eyes and held her breath in anticipation.

"I got in."

"YOU DID IT!!"

"Yep. Sure surprised the hell out of me."

"Fantastic! Congratulations. I'm so happy."

"I can't believe it; I keep re-reading it, and it keeps saying the same thing."

"Did you tell your folks yet?"

"No, I waited to open it in my room so I could mope in private. Then I called you."

"Oh, go tell them – they've got to be wondering."

"Okay. Call me later – I expect I'll be up late tonight."

"I expect you will. Wow. That's really wonderful, Philip."

"Yeah it is, isn't it."

She carried the phone back into the library and set it on her carrel. She had to admit she'd been doubtful that Philip would get into Davis. After all, it was one of the best vet schools in the country. But he had composed what (after her edits) she had thought was an elegant essay expounding on his goal of using selective breeding to improve a horse's ability to recover from a broken leg. She knew he'd been preparing himself for rejection letters from all five schools he'd applied to. To have the first – and in her mind the most important – be an acceptance was incredible.

Sigrun felt even less like studying. She sighed and pulled her case book closer. After several false starts, she managed to get her mind back to malice aforethought and the case she had begun before Philip's call. Her cell phone vibrated on the desk. She grabbed it and checked the screen on her way out. It was Gareth.

"Hi, Gareth," she said with a questioning note. She had not

expected to hear from him until the following week.

"I hope I am not disturbing you, Sigrun. I was wondering if you had spoken with Zareh?"

"Uh ... no, he hasn't called."

"Oh, I had hoped he would have. I've just returned home from a visit, and he promised he would try to call after I left. But," he added, "one never knows what obstacles prison life will cast in one's path."

"I suppose," she said skeptically. "I do need to talk to him, though."

"He will call," Gareth said, "he promised he would."

"Okay, if you say so. It's not a problem – I've plenty to do before I talk to him."

"And your school work as well, I trust."

"Yes, and my course work too," she agreed.

"Good. I'll let you get back to work then."

Sigrun hung up and returned to the library. It was lucky, she thought as the librarian gave her a suspicious look, that hardly anyone was around to be disturbed by her comings and goings. She started over again on the same case. At this rate, she thought glumly, she wouldn't finish even one assignment before the library closed – early tonight because of break.

Her phone vibrated. She leapt to her feet, checking the phone as she walked. It was an oddly formatted number, unlike any she'd ever seen. Her stomach clenched.

In the corridor, she drew a deep breath and answered hesitantly.

"Will you accept a collect call from San Quentin State Prison from a Mr. Fremont?"

"Yes, yes I will."

"Please hold." The officious-sounding voice was replaced by a series of clicks.

"Ms. Nyman? This is Zareh Fremont."

"Yes, hello ... uh, thank you for calling."

"Gareth asked me to," he said evenly. "What can I do for you?"

"Well," Sigrun said as she paced the now-deserted hallway nervously. "First, uh, I need you to confirm that you would like to have Professor Ehrlich represent you as counsel on your pending habeas petition."

"Gareth already advised you that I have agreed."

"Uh... yes, he did, but we need to verify that it's your wish to substitute the professor as your attorney."

"It is not my wish," he said without inflection, "but I did so agree."

"Okay. Well, I'll settle for that. So, we have a written agreement that we need you to sign. Should I send it to you at the prison?"

"No," he said with a slight edge. "Please do not send anything to me here. If I must look at something, simply send it to Gareth, and he'll ensure that I see it."

"Okay. That's fine – I'll do that. Will you sign it?"

"Yes."

"Good. Uhm, I have some questions I'd like to ask – if you have time, that is."

"No. I was allowed a call now only because I said it would be brief."

"Oh, well, would it be possible for you to call back? We're on spring break next week, so you can call me any time."

"By that do you mean that you have no classes?"

"Yeah, not next week."

"I'll try. But, as I said when you were here, I don't have any useful information."

"Maybe so, but," she said, attempting to be persuasive, "would you mind taking the time to let me ask?"

"It's not easy for me to call."

"Yes I know, Gareth explained that. But," she coaxed, "you have all week, and I'll be available whenever you get a chance."

"Why don't you ask Gareth?" he said with a note approaching annoyance.

"Oh I plan to," she said, keeping her voice pleasant with an effort, "but I'm hoping you might recall something relevant."

"I expect not," he said with a return to his expressionless voice.

"Okay, fine," she said tartly, abandoning the gently persuasive approach. "But, really, what else do you have to do?"

In the ensuing silence, Sigrun waited for him to hang up.

"So," he said, sounding amused, "you're the one who accosted me last time."

"Yeah, that would be me."

"Two things you should know about me – I place a high value on honesty, and I never go back on my word. I'll call you next week."

"Thank you," she said with relief, "I look forward to it."

"I too," he said before hanging up.

She stared with bemusement at the phone in her hand. Surely she had not heard that last comment correctly. But maybe he would talk to her. She checked her watch; the library was closing in less than an hour. All right, at this rate she definitely was not going to figure out how it could be that malice aforethought required neither malice nor forethought – so, she'd capitulate, head to her dorm, and call Philip in comfort.

She returned to her carrel, the librarian at the front desk glaring at her as she passed by yet again. She bundled her things into her backpack, grabbed her umbrella, and nodded politely to the librarian on her way out. Perhaps she should call Gareth; otherwise he would be left wondering until he next heard from Fremont. And, she thought as she stepped out into the rain, she'd better pick up some dinner on the way because she wasn't going to want to get wet again. She detoured to the nearest cafeteria. With a bit of searching, she found a packaged salad that still looked edible. She added a bag of chocolate cookies – after all, it was a holiday.

Naturally, Lupe had long since left for San Diego, so Sigrun settled herself comfortably in a chair in the common room. Yeah, she decided, she should let Gareth know. She punched in his number.

"Greetings, Sigrun," he said, sounding surprised.

"I hope I'm not bothering you."

"Not at all. Well, you are interrupting my chores, but I am more than happy not to do them."

"I wanted to let you know that Mr. Fremont …"

"Zareh, please."

"Right, sorry, Zareh called me shortly after you and I spoke."

"Splendid. Did you resolve your concerns?"

"Yeah, although he stated most precisely that he'd merely **agreed** to the plan."

"Yes, well," Gareth said with amusement, "that should be sufficient."

"Oh certainly – that's fine. I have a form that he needs to sign, and he asked me to send it through you."

"Yes, please," he said quickly. "I am sorry, I should have made that clear. Please don't send anything to the prison. It is far better if I deliver it."

"Okay, I'll get it sent tomorrow. Also," she added, still marveling, "he agreed to call me next week to answer some questions."

"He did?"

"Yeah. I'm not exactly sure what happened, but, anyway, he promised to call."

"Once again," Gareth said, "I commend your tenacity."

"Thanks. I'll let you know if he actually answers anything. And I'll call you with the results from the expert."

Sigrun disconnected and immediately called Philip.

"Hey," she said when he answered, "have you returned to Earth?"

"Nope – I'm still in shock. Can you believe it?"

"I assume you're planning on accepting?"

He laughed. "I haven't gotten that far. All I care about right now is that I wasn't rejected."

"Well I care – I want you to come out here."

"I know," he sighed. "But I need to think about the farm and the family and everything. Let's wait to see what happens with the other schools and what Norm decides to do. Someone has to take care of the horses."

"I understand," she said, trying not to sound too disappointed. "But regardless, it's remarkably great news."

"Yeah, fabulous. Weird though. I can't quite wrap my mind around it."

"It's been a weird night. I finally heard from Fremont."

"You did! How'd it go?"

"Uh, it went rather well, I think."

"He didn't blow you off?"

"No, no, he didn't. I'll tell you about it later …"

"No, I want to hear. But hold on – let me grab my guitar. I still need inspiration."

⁓⁓

⮞⮜ Chapter 10 ⮞⮜
Res mihi integra est
(I am still undecided)

By Tuesday afternoon, Sigrun had made sufficient progress on her backlog of class assignments that she had started on the habeas research and was impatiently checking the mail every few hours. She was pretty sure the report would support the footprint claim, but she didn't want to do too much work on it, just in case.

On her way from the library to lunch on Wednesday, she ducked into the deserted lounge to check yet again. A large envelope was stuffed into her box. She yanked it out and tore it open. The envelope held several copies of a thin, spiral-bound report. Sigrun dropped into the nearest chair and opened one. Yes! There it was – clearly stated in black and white: It was the opinion of the expert that the size, shape, and pattern of the impression of the shoe left in the blood by the male victim's chest could not have been made by the riding boots the petitioner was wearing at the time of his arrest. She was right. She flipped to the end of the report to ...

"Hi, Sigrun," a tentative voice said.

"Oh!" She looked up to see Milton hovering nearby. "I didn't hear you."

"Sorry to startle you." He cleared his throat. "Uhm ... I noticed you in here ..."

"It's been pretty empty around here this week – I'm surprised you're here."

"Oh ... uhm, well, my father 'suggested' I might do better this term if I spent more time in the library. So, I thought I'd at least give it a try."

"It's not a bad idea. There are fewer distractions in the library, so I do generally get more done."

"Yeah, well, I'm my own distraction, so it doesn't much matter where I am. But ... I was wondering if ... uh, maybe you have time for lunch?"

"Yeah, sure," she yielded to his woebegone expression. It

wouldn't hurt to spend a little time with Milton. Then she could read the report and call Gareth. "Just give me 15 minutes to drop one of these reports in a mailbox. I'll meet you back here."

~~~~~

Sigrun sat cross-legged on her bed, the contents of the habeas case strewn across it and around the room. She tore off the top sheet of her notepad, crumpled it into a ball, and tossed it at the wastebasket by her desk. It missed and joined several other crumpled sheets on the floor. She chewed thoughtfully on the end of her pen. It had seemed so clear when she had discussed it with the professor – but now she wasn't able to articulate why Fremont's attorney was unreasonable in ignoring the footprint. Of course, he probably had never noticed it. But, if he had been making a reasonable effort to defend his client, shouldn't he have examined the photos? What exactly did the cases say constituted an adequate investigation?

She carefully got off the bed without disturbing her piles and pulled out from under her backpack a folder with the stack of cases she had copied. Okay, so, she should be able to argue that the attorney failed to investigate sufficiently to make a tactical decision as to whether another defense strategy was preferable. But, she thought as she stared unseeingly out the window, as Zvi had said, just because someone else was there, it didn't exonerate Fremont. Well true, but taken together with the testimony of the neighbor, wasn't it enough to undermine confidence in the guilty verdict? She returned to the bed and resumed her position, beginning anew on a fresh sheet of paper. Her cell phone rang. Sigrun looked around the room; where had she left it? She scrambled off the bed, lunged across the room, and pushed aside the folder on her desk to grab the phone.

"Will you accept a collect call from San Quentin State Prison from a Mr. Fremont?"

"Yes."

"Greetings, this is Zareh Fremont."

"Hello. Uh, thanks for calling ... do you have time today for some questions?"

"That is why I called."

"Yes, of course. I mean, do I have to worry that you'll run out of time?"

"No. Patience perhaps."

Sigrun blinked. Was that a joke or a warning? "Okay, I'll try to be concise." She sat at her desk and pulled over her list of questions. "First, I have a quick question about the claim that Gareth has already raised – that your attorney should have found and interviewed the woman who called the police. I was wondering, did you talk to your attorney about the arrival of the police?"

"I don't believe so."

"Did you ever discuss with your attorney how the police knew about the murders?"

"No."

"Do you recall your attorney ever asking you about how they arrived at the apartment?"

"I don't think I understand – are you asking whether the attorney questioned me about the circumstances under which the police entered the apartment?"

"Yes. Did he ask you whether there were sirens, did the police come running up the stairs, those type of questions?"

"No, I don't believe so."

"Okay. So, did you volunteer any information about the arrival of the police?"

"No."

"Did you answer any of his questions?"

"Not many."

"Okay, then. Moving on – I wanted to ask you about the new claim that we plan to raise concerning the footprint. Do you recall examining the photographs prior to trial?"

"I never examined the photographs," he said without inflection.

"Oh!" Sigrun was surprised by both the directness of the response and the fact that he apparently had not been sufficiently curious about the photographs to study them. "Uhm, okay. Do you recall your attorney telling you that he had looked at them?"

"No."

"Did you ever see your attorney examine the photographs?"

Zareh paused. "I'm sure that he did during the trial."

Sigrun thought she detected a note of uncertainty. "But you're not confident?"

"I don't recall anything specific."

"But you think he did?"

"The prosecutor handed him the photographs during the trial. I imagine he looked at them."

"You were sitting next to him?"

"Yes."

"I'm sorry, I don't mean to be rude, but this is important. I need you to support our argument that your attorney studied the photographs and ignored an obvious clue."

"I don't recall."

"I don't believe you," she responded quickly, then instantly regretted it.

"That is your prerogative," he said coldly.

"Please, Mr. Fremont, I'm trying to help you. It simply is not plausible that you don't recall what your lawyer did during such a pivotal moment at your trial."

"I was not watching him."

Again, she was startled at his apparent disinterest in his own trial. She rubbed her eyes. This was not proving to be useful. "So, did your attorney show them to you?"

"No."

"Why not?"

"I asked him not to."

"Did he offer to show them to you?"

"Yes."

"Okay, so we'll have to come up with another argument there. Let's try a different approach. Did your attorney ever ask you whether you saw anyone else near the apartment that night?"

"Yes."

"And what did you say?"

"I did not answer."

"Mr. Fremont, I ..."

"Please call me Zareh."

"What?"

"If you're going to continue to question me, I would rather you addressed me by my first name."

"Uh ..." Sigrun was momentarily at a loss for words. "Sure, whatever you prefer. I was just going to say that I can't help you if you won't answer my questions."

"As I explained to you when we met, I don't believe that you can help me."

"I realize that. But Gareth does."

"Yes, he is ever hopeful."

"So ... maybe you could answer my questions based on his hope."

"I'm speaking with you at his behest – I can do no more."

"All right. I'm sure you won't answer these either, but for the sake of completeness, I'll ask. Did you ever discuss with your attorney the possibility that he might discover evidence that someone else was in the apartment that night?"

"No."

"Did you tell your attorney that the door of the apartment was open when you arrived?"

"No."

"Do you know that the expert we retained unequivocally stated that the footprint in the blood could not have been made by your boots?"

"Yes, I spoke with Gareth yesterday."

"So, now we have strong evidence that someone else was present in the apartment before the police appeared. But, since the police arrived no more than an hour after the murders, and you had already been there some time at that point, isn't it likely that you know something about the other person?"

"That is a logical conclusion."

"But one that you won't discuss?"

"Correct."

"Look, Zareh." Sigrun jumped to her feet and began to pace the bedroom in frustration. "I don't **need** to know what happened that night. I can't deny that I want to know – but the argument we're trying to make doesn't depend on it. All I need from you is some basis to support that your attorney should have attempted to raise a defense that someone other than you committed the murders."

"I'm afraid I can't help you."

"But why not?" she snapped impatiently.

"Why do you care?"

The impassive question stopped her up short. "I don't know," she responded honestly. "I've been trying to answer that question for months. But we're not discussing me. I'm struggling to get you to assist Gareth in his heroic efforts to stop the State from killing you. And I'm beginning to wonder why he even bothers."

"You'll have to ask him."

"So you're unwilling to be of any assistance?"

"I can't help you."

"Okay then. I guess that's it." Sigrun was reluctant to end the conversation, thinking that there must be a way to break through his reserve, but she had to concede defeat. "Thank you for calling."

"Thank you for caring."

Sigrun tossed the phone onto her desk and resumed pacing. Did any of it make sense? He had so much as admitted that he knew something about whoever had made that footprint, but she didn't think she was ever going to get him to tell her anything. She'd have to argue that the defense was self-evident. After all, what defense counsel would have failed to explore the possibility that someone else had committed the crime? Someone who knew his client to be guilty? Of course, but … was that the answer? Was he guilty? Gareth seemed so sure. But how could he know, really? The only person who knew for sure was Zareh. And the murderer, if it wasn't Zareh. She had put so much effort into the case; she was loath to consider quitting. But, really, did she want to stick with it if she didn't have faith in his innocence? Even if someone else had been there, Zareh could still be guilty of murder. Maybe the attorney did the best he could without admitting his client's guilt.

Her cell phone rang. Sigrun checked the screen; it was Gareth. For a fleeting instant, she debated not answering. "Hello," she said warily.

"Zareh suggested that I might want to smooth things over."

"Did he?" she said dryly. "I can't imagine why."

"He seemed to think you were angry."

"Well, I didn't yell at him this time."

"Oh? I guess I never heard the details of your first exchange."

"I must admit I'm extremely frustrated." Sigrun sighed. "Actually, when you called, I was debating whether I want to put any more time into this. Look – I realize you think that Zareh is innocent …"

"No, Sigrun: I **know** he is innocent."

"But, Gareth, you weren't there. You knew the boy he was, but he **is** hiding something. How can you be so sure he wasn't involved in the murders?"

"At the risk of alienating you completely, I must say that I can't discuss that. But I know with absolute certainty that Zareh did not participate in any way in committing the murders."

Sigrun considered that for a moment. It made sense that Zareh would have told Gareth whatever it was he refused to discuss with her. But it didn't satisfy her. "I'm sorry. I know it shouldn't matter whether he's guilty – he still deserves a fair trial. But, if he is guilty, I'm not sure I can raise the arguments we want to raise."

"What made you go to the effort of tracking me down?"

"Uh … I thought he might be innocent."

"Isn't that enough?"

Sigrun readily recalled the emotion written in Zareh's eyes. It could have been a reflection of his fear of death. But … what if her instincts were right? What if he were innocent? Could she live with that possibility, even if remote, after his execution? "I suppose so," she said reluctantly.

"Maybe I can help. Why don't you try asking me the questions that Zareh would not answer."

"Sure …" she said absently while considering how she would feel if she quit now. She knew it would nag at her, and she would never stop wondering what might have happened had she stuck with it. "Will you promise to answer one question truthfully?"

"I can't promise that I will answer. But I can promise that, if I do answer, it will be truthfully."

"Did Zareh's attorney have good reason to believe that it would have been futile to pursue a defense that someone else committed the murders?"

"No," Gareth responded immediately. "Positively not."

"Okay, then," she said, feeling a weight lift.

⤙ ⤚

"Ah, Sigrun, come in," said Professor Ehrlich as Sigrun stuck her head in the open office door the Wednesday after break. "I've been reading the expert's report. It's exactly what we wanted – good work."

"Thanks. I thought she made a compelling case."

"I did too. And I see that you managed to secure the petitioner's signature on the agreement. Did you get any information from him?"

"No. I did manage to talk to him, but he essentially refused to answer my questions. So I don't think I'm going to get anything more."

"That's okay – we have plenty to work with. So, we need to discuss the format of our claims for a state court petition. But first, just to make sure we don't run out of time, I have one piece of news I want to share with you. My mother thinks she met the woman who brought you to your parents."

"Oh." Sigrun sat forward in her chair.

"You see, for many years my mother was a housekeeper for a wealthy family, and she used to drop off the family's clothing at the dry cleaners where your mother worked as a seamstress. They got to be friends, and my mother would stay and chat. A few times while she was there, one of your mother's regular clients, a middle-aged woman – very dignified, my mother said – stopped by for fittings. My mother would never have remembered her except for the fact that, shortly after your arrival, your mother told her that it was that client who had brought them the baby. My mother recalls that your mother seemed to regret having said anything because she asked my mother not to tell anyone, and they never discussed it again."

"How interesting. I don't suppose your mother knew who the client was?"

"No, she said she didn't know the woman's name. Nor could she recall anyone who might know anything else."

"That must be the great aunt my mother mentioned in a letter."

"That would make sense. I'm sorry I don't have anything more concrete."

"Oh, no, this is more than I've been able to discover. Thank you."

"No problem. So, here," she offered a stack of papers to Sigrun, "I found a few sample petitions that might be helpful, and I'll keep looking. I'll also draft a request for a stay in federal court. It will be quicker for me to do it. Did you have specific questions?"

"Yeah. I think I've got a good grip on what we need for the footprint claim, but I don't understand how it fits into a new petition."

"Good question. We need to decide if there are other claims we can raise. Did you happen to bring his past petitions?"

Sigrun waved a thick folder that she pulled from her backpack. "And I have a list that Blythe compiled of what claims were raised in which petition."

"Wonderful." The professor pushed aside several piles to clear a space on her desk, which had regained its standard state of clutter in the few short days since break. "Let me see that list."

⟿⟿

On Friday of the following week, when Sigrun's cell phone vibrated, she immediately headed out of the library. As she expected, it was Gareth; he had taken to calling her on the way to his regular Friday visit with Zareh.

"Good morning, Sigrun. I wanted to check to see if you needed anything."

"Actually, I do. You remember last week, I mentioned that

we were considering raising a separate claim concerning the cumulative effect of the errors?"

"Yes."

"Well, Professor Ehrlich wants to include all of the claimed trial errors, even those that were rejected in the earlier petitions. She explained that it isn't really permitted, but she wants to put forth the best case we can, despite the fact that the other errors can't be considered separately in this petition."

"I see. That's an interesting idea ... but don't we risk having the entire petition rejected for violating the procedural rules?"

"Yeah, I think you may be right, but the professor is convinced that our strongest argument is to show how each error, even if not terribly significant when considered individually, points to the fact that Zareh is not the murderer. She thinks we should make it clear to the judge that the prosecutor's erroneous closing argument was exacerbated by his failure to turn over the interview of the neighbor as well as by the various errors made by Zareh's attorney."

"Maybe," Gareth said. "But I am exceedingly cautious by nature, and I will not agree to any approach that might result in the forfeiture of the new claim."

"That's a good point." Sigrun reached the end of the hallway in her pacing. As she pivoted, she caught a glimpse of Zvi down the connecting corridor and waved. "But truthfully, I don't know how much of a risk it is. I'll discuss it with the professor this afternoon and let you know. On another topic, I was wondering ... we've talked about the attorney's reasons for not objecting to the prosecutor's cult theory, but I never did get an answer about Zareh's clothing."

"What was the question?"

"Oh, well, you argued in the first set of petitions that Zareh's 'odd clothing' was no stranger than a Halloween costume, and I'd like to add something."

"I am not responsible for that assertion. It was raised in the first state petition and was based on counsel's closing argument at trial. But how can I help?"

"Uh, well, was he wearing a Halloween costume?"

"No. It was a riding outfit."

"Oh ... but it was midnight."

"Yes."

"Had he been riding?"

"I truly do not know."

"Uhm ... perhaps you could ask him?"

"Is it important?"

"Well ... I suppose I could argue that his clothing wasn't particularly odd, and the prosecutor offered no evidence to support that it had any cult characteristics. And, since it's disappeared, they can't prove anything now."

"Oh?"

"Yeah, we discovered that none of his clothing apart from the boots made it back to storage after the trial."

"Interesting."

"Okay, so don't bother to ask him. I don't imagine he'd answer anyway. You know," she added impulsively, "it would be great if I could explain how he happened upon the apartment just then."

"You know he won't answer that question."

"I guess not." Sigrun debated whether she should push Gareth or if she risked angering him. He didn't seem prone to anger. "It's just that – I'm trying to paint a picture of a young guy who was in the wrong place at the wrong time. It would be helpful if I could say something specific about how he ended up getting caught in the apartment."

"I see your point, but I don't have anything to offer."

"Maybe something about what he had been doing, or where he was going, or why he entered the building. Anything."

"But none of that is relevant to the claims you're raising."

"No, I know. But the problem is – once you've read the claims and the transcript – it's still a mystery why he was there."

"I am sorry," Gareth said simply.

"This is so frustrating," she said irritably as she spun on her heel to change direction in her pacing. "Excuse me," she muttered to the student who had been behind her, who had to sidestep quickly to avoid a collision.

"I am sorry," Gareth repeated, sounding sincere. "But I think your legal arguments are compelling; I am confident you can craft a persuasive claim."

"It would be a better story if I had something to work with."

"That's not possible."

"Yeah, okay," she said with a sigh. "I just thought I'd try one more time."

"I truly appreciate the effort you're making on our behalf."

"Thanks," she said grumpily, irked that they both knew something they refused to share with her.

"And how are you doing with your school work?"

"Oh, uh, fine."

"You are not particularly good at lying."

"Oh. Yeah, well, I'm a bit behind. But not too bad."

"Sigrun," he said sternly, "you must put your course work first."

"No, really," she protested, "I can catch up."

"You should set aside the petition until after classes have concluded."

"I don't think it should wait. I mean, it's been so long and …"

"Exactly. It can wait a bit longer. What are you doing after school is over?"

"Uh … I'm going home."

"Perhaps you could work on the petition during the summer?"

"Well, I suppose I could. But, I need a library, and I don't know how …"

"Could you stay in Los Angeles?"

"No, not really. I mean, I won't have a room, and I … well, I need a job."

"But you are working on behalf of Zareh, and I am more than happy to provide for your needs."

"No. Really, I couldn't take …"

"Why not? I can think of nothing more valuable to me than winning Zareh's release. If you can help us toward that goal, I will do anything I can to assist you."

"Thank you, that's very considerate," Sigrun said awkwardly, uncomfortable with the turn of conversation, "but I couldn't."

"If you were an attorney, you would take money from a client."

"Well … yes, but this is different."

"I think you should concentrate on your classes now, but I would like the petition to be filed as soon as possible. The most practical solution is to have you work full time on the petition once the term is over."

"I don't know, I just …"

"Sigrun," Gareth said seriously, "money is not a problem for me. Why don't you discuss it with your professor? If you prefer, I can give her the funds, and she can use it to support your work."

"Well … okay, I'll talk to her about it."

"Happy Birthday!" Sigrun said when Philip answered her call

that afternoon.

"Thanks. Hey, you called early."

"Yeah, I wanted to be sure to catch you. What did you decide to do?"

"You remember Eric – he was my old group's lead guitarist my first year?"

"Didn't he go off to New York after high school?"

"Uh-huh, and formed a band that's doing pretty well. So, I heard they're playing tonight at a club in Harrisburg and got a group together to go."

"Oh, sounds like fun … hey, don't get any ideas!"

Philip laughed. "No. Now that I've been accepted, I've gotten excited about school."

"And about California?"

"Sigrun…"

"I know, I know; we're not discussing it yet. But that doesn't stop me from grabbing every opportunity to promote my position."

"You're turning into an attorney."

"Yeah," she said slowly, "that brings up something I wanted to discuss. This morning, while I was talking to Gareth, he offered to support me to stay here and work on the petition this summer instead of doing it now."

"Oh. … What do you think about that?"

"I'm opposed to taking his money, and I'd miss being home, but, on the other hand, I don't see how I can possibly finish it before finals and …"

"You don't want to leave it hanging over the summer."

"Exactly. But, I don't know, how can I not come home?"

"It won't take you all summer, will it?"

"I shouldn't think so. And, once I get it filed, I don't imagine anything will happen right away. So, maybe I could come home at the end of summer."

"Yeah. You know I've been worried that you're putting way too much time into that habeas case and not enough into your classes."

"I know. But I was really looking forward to coming home. And, there is the money thing."

"I don't see your problem there – you're working on Fremont's case. If Gareth wants to support you, why should that upset you?"

"Yeah, that's what he said."

"I assume you'd still come home for my graduation?"

"Absolutely! I wouldn't miss it. So ... you're in favor of the idea?"

"Well ... not exactly. I'm in favor of you being here as long as possible. And I had wanted you to work with Arabella – she's not responding, and I thought you might have more success in training her. But I don't think it's good that you've been neglecting your classes ... so, yeah, it seems like a good way to get the petition done without compromising your degree."

"I think that's a bit melodramatic."

"Yeah, but how are you gonna feel when you get bad grades this term?"

"I'm not worried about my classes."

"You should be; you've never not studied before."

"Maybe you're right," Sigrun agreed reluctantly. "I do have a lot of catching up to do, and it's taking far more time than I ever imagined to figure out these claims."

"Think about it and we can discuss it again this weekend."

"Okay. Have fun tonight; I wish I could be there. And behave yourself."

He laughed. "The only good thing about you being away is that I get to drink more – and don't worry, I'm not driving."

🙰 🙰

After Lawyering Skills on Monday, Sigrun peered into her empty mailbox. She had fallen into the practice of checking it after every class, just in case Professor Ehrlich wanted something. But, she thought with some regret, that was no longer necessary since they had decided earlier that morning to postpone work on the petition until the summer. When she had presented Gareth's offer, the professor had been strongly in favor of the plan.

"Hey, Sigrun," said Lupe. "I just heard from my sister, Rose, and she's arranged an internship for me with the Insurance Commissioner. Isn't that great? I mean, you know, I'll be in Sacramento, and I'm not sure what Diego will do, but still."

"Congratulations," Sigrun said warmly. "Will you be able to stay with her?"

"Yeah, so I won't have any expenses. Of course, I won't make any money either." She giggled. "Maybe I'll have to relent and let Diego drop out of school."

"Does he want to?"

"For years." Lupe cracked her gum loudly. "But I keep telling him I won't marry him unless he graduates from college, and so, like, he's stuck with it."

Sigrun's cell phone vibrated in her pocket. She pulled it out –
the prison. "Oh, excuse me, I have to take this call." She headed
outside.

"Will you accept a collect call from San Quentin State Prison
from a Mr. Fremont?" asked the same officious voice.

"Yes, yes."

"Greetings, Sigrun. I hope I'm not disturbing you."

"Oh no, this is fine," she said while searching for an empty
table on the crowded patio. "I wasn't expecting to hear from you."

"Upon further reflection, I've thought of something that I
believe you would like to know."

"You did?" she said, dropping into a chair.

"Yes." Zareh sounded amused. "You're surprised?"

"Uh … yeah. I mean, you haven't exactly been forthcoming
up to now."

"True. But Gareth is impressed by your efforts, and so – because I do not wish to die – I have given some consideration to
your questions."

"Oh! Well, what did you recall?"

"I told you that I don't know if the attorney ever examined
the photographs. And I don't know what he did at the trial. However, I now remember that he visited me in jail shortly before the
trial. I … well, shall we say that I was not happy to see him. He
attempted to show me the photographs then."

"Really!" Sigrun sat upright in her chair, pulled her backpack
closer, and dug around for a notepad. "Tell me what happened."

"Please keep in mind that I was quite young. It was probably
two days before the trial, I'm not sure. He arrived unexpectedly,
and I had no time to contact Gareth."

"Oh – had Gareth always been there before when you met
with him?"

"Yes. I'd asked him not to meet with me alone. He set a pile
of photographs on the table between us and told me to look at
them. I refused."

"All right. Hold on. Do you remember his reason for coming?"

"No – he said something about his opening statement, but I
don't recall what."

"Can you think of any specific question that he asked?"

There was a pause. "No, I don't believe so."

"Did he talk to you about testifying?"

"No."

"Did he say he had just received something from the prosecutor?"

"Not that I recall."

"What about the newspaper stories? Did he mention the news coverage?"

"Yes … I believe he did. Would that have been at this meeting, though?"

"Well, I don't have my notes with me, so I can't be sure, but my recollection is that the first interview with the prosecutor was published a few days before the trial."

"Maybe," Zareh said thoughtfully, "he did mention something. I remember that he was upset – perhaps that was the reason."

"Okay. So, he mentioned the article in the paper. Was there some connection between that and the photographs?"

"I … don't believe so."

"Did he say something about what was in the photographs?"

"The necklace," Zareh exclaimed softly. "That was it. He wanted to tell the jury that I had never seen the necklace."

"Good," Sigrun said encouragingly. "So, he asked you to look at the photographs, which included one of the necklace?"

"Yes."

"Okay. Did you look at them?"

"No," he said flatly.

"Okay," she said gently, afraid he would retreat. "That's okay. Do you recall anything specific he said about the photographs?"

"I only recall him pushing a pile of photographs toward me and telling me to look at them."

"Well, if he knew there was a photograph of the necklace, then he had clearly studied them before meeting with you, so we can state with certainty that he examined the photographs before trial."

"I hope that's useful."

"Yes, enormously. That's exactly what I needed. But … will you sign a declaration setting forth what occurred at the meeting?"

"If you wish."

"Thank you," she said with relief, "I think it will make the claim much stronger."

"No, thank you. You're extremely good, you know."

"I'm sorry?"

"You're good at getting information – do you come from a

family of attorneys?"

"Oh, no. Not at all. My father was a history teacher."

"And your mother?"

"Uh … she was a seamstress."

"Are they deceased, then?"

"Uh …" she was confounded by his interest, but saw no reason not to answer. "Yes, they are."

"They must have died young," he probed.

"No, well, yes, I suppose my mother was young, but my father was 74."

"So, they had you rather late in life, then?"

"Uh … well, I was adopted."

"Adopted! As an infant?" he added sharply.

Confused, she hesitated. But, what was the harm in telling him? "Uh, yeah."

"Hupo o na hupo!" he said in a harsh undertone.

"I'm sorry?"

"I must go. Please let Gareth know if you have any additional questions."

"Okay … thanks for calling."

"Please take care of yourself."

Sigrun found she was holding the phone to her ear after Zareh had hung up. She set it on the table and stared at the notes she had taken. She could not fathom what had triggered his transformation. She was still sitting staring blankly at her notes when she heard her name; she looked up to find Blythe approaching.

"I'm on my way to class but I spotted you and wanted to apologize for missing the gym so much lately. I guess I was a bit optimistic about that extra class."

"I don't mind working out alone," Sigrun said.

"I mind missing! But anyway, what's happening on the habeas?"

"Actually, I've put it aside until summer. I've realized I can't possibly finish it …"

"Hey," Blythe exclaimed, "why don't you stay with me? My apartmentmate is taking the bar exam in San Francisco. She's leaving right after graduation, and her room will be empty all summer."

"But won't I disturb your studying?"

Blythe laughed. "Don't be ridiculous. You work so hard you'll help keep me honest. I've gotta run, but I won't take no for an answer. Catch you later."

Sigrun, a bit dazed by recent events, decided to head back to the dorm to call Gareth and let him know she'd decided to take him up on his offer. At least, she thought with relief, if she stayed with Blythe, it would be less expensive for him.

Exiting the classroom after her final in Crim Law, Sigrun was filled with a rising sense of elation; a feeling clearly shared by the swarm of students flooding noisily out of nearby classrooms as the last final of the year finished.

"We're done, dude!" Hawke exclaimed as he pounded Tony on the back.

"Sigrun," Lupe called from across the hall, "are you leaving?"

"My flight's tomorrow morning," Sigrun explained, "but I'm meeting Blythe to move my things over to her apartment."

"I'm going as soon as Diego gets here." Lupe giggled. "You know, turns out he's really excited about spending the summer in Sacramento." She clasped Sigrun in a warm hug. "Have a great summer!"

"Hi, Sigrun. Uhm, what are you doing this summer?" Milton asked.

"Oh, well," Sigrun said, "I'll be here part of the time working on my habeas case."

"Really," he squeaked. "Uh, maybe, can I call you?"

"Uh … yeah, sure. Did you manage to find a job?"

"Yeah, sort of. My father arranged a judicial externship with a friend of his."

"Oh, well, that should be interesting."

"I suppose so." He brightened. "Maybe we could catch a movie sometime?"

"Yeah, okay. Well, I've got to finish packing," she added as she left.

⌢ Chapter 11 ⌢
Periculum in mora
(There is danger in delay; Livy)

Feeling stiff from the long flight to Philadelphia, Sigrun took the stairs rather than the escalator down to the baggage claim area. As she descended, she scanned the waiting crowd for Norm, who Philip had said would pick her up. She was surprised and pleased to instead spot Philip leaning against a wall, watching people being deposited by the adjacent escalator. Sigrun headed toward him; he caught sight of her, stepped forward, and swept her into a hug so enthusiastic her feet left the floor. Laughing, she said, "I didn't expect to see you!"

"I missed you," he responded. "You're looking fit – all those visits to the gym have been good for you."

"Thanks. What's with this?" She rubbed her hand over his days-old stubble.

"Oh," he said ruefully, "I used the excuse of being too busy studying for finals to try a beard. But Mom hates it and is threatening to boycott graduation. So, I'll shave tomorrow. What do you think?"

Sigrun stepped back to get a better look. "I agree with your mother – it makes you look slightly scruffy."

"Scruffy!" he exclaimed in dismay. "That's certainly not what I was aiming for. How about dashing?"

She cocked her head appraisingly. "If you let it grow, you might get there."

Philip laughed. "Maybe another time."

After they had finally retrieved Sigrun's luggage and had successfully navigated their way onto the highway, she asked, "But shouldn't you be studying?"

"Nope, I'm done for the day, and, anyway, my last final isn't until Wednesday, so I've got plenty of time. And," he added, "I wanted to warn you – Ted's invited us to an almost-graduation party tonight. That is, if you're interested and not too tired."

"Sure," Sigrun said, "it sounds like fun – I haven't been anywhere for weeks."

"Excellent. So, what would you like to eat?"

"Pizza," she responded without hesitation.

"What, don't you get good pizza?"

"Yeah, but it's all California style."

"Ah hah! There is something about California you don't like."

"No – I've just been craving good, crusty, New York style pizza."

"Pizza it is, then. And speaking of California, I'm pretty definite about Davis."

"Oh," she said noncommittally, "how come?"

Philip shot her an amused look. "Well, it's a better school, and I don't think it'll cost that much more than Maryland. I mean, with the loans, it shouldn't make much difference. And Norm seems set on Dickinson."

"What did he say?"

"He knows he's never going to make pro, so he doesn't want to waste time chasing a fantasy. And he really wants to live at home."

"That's pretty level-headed for 18. But will they be able to manage without you?"

"Well, we talked it over with Dad, and he thinks we can afford to hire a part-timer to do some of the heaviest chores. So, yeah, I think they'll be okay."

"Uhm."

"And then there's you."

"Oh, that was a factor?"

"Yeah, well," he said lightly, "I thought it'd be good if we could get together for the occasional weekend."

"Well, you know Davis has my vote."

"I figured."

"I've never hidden my bias."

"I know. I'm just, well … I feel guilty dumping my projects on Dad."

"But he's thrilled at the thought of you becoming a vet."

"That's true. Hey," Philip pointed at a billboard, "what about that place?"

"Sounds good to me. By the way, am I staying with you again?"

"'Fraid so. We kept hoping we'd get the Farmstead open, but we've been too busy. And then I thought, with you only being here for three weeks, it didn't make sense to waste the effort. We can still pack. But, if you'd rather, we can work on it tomorrow."

"Oh no, I'm perfectly happy at your place. You know, maybe I should try to rent the Farmstead next year. That would make it easier for your dad and the boys."

"Let's talk it over with Dad. Right now, the only serious topic I want to think about is pizza – I skipped lunch."

After a protracted stop at the pizza place, which was packed on a Saturday night, it was nearly ten by the time they pulled into the driveway.

Philip got Sigrun's luggage out of the trunk and held out her backpack. "Hey, that's heavy! What's in there?"

"I brought all my research notes and stuff from the habeas case. I thought, if nothing else, I'd spend the return flight re-familiarizing myself with them."

"That reminds me," Philip said as he held the side door for her, "I want to play you Fremont's song. I'm still not satisfied with it – maybe you'll inspire me."

"Inspire you to get out of bed before noon?" Norman said cheekily from the kitchen.

"Unless you're being a slacker, how would you know when I get up?" Philip retorted.

"Good point. Yo, Sigrun," Norm said from the sink, where he was washing dishes. "I'd give you a hug, but I figure you'd rather not get wet." He gestured toward a young woman with short wavy hair coming into the kitchen from the dining room carrying a linen towel. "You remember Amanda?"

"Of course," she said warmly.

"How was your trip?" Amanda asked with a shy smile.

"Good," Sigrun said. "Philip managed not to get lost even once."

"Watch it, or I'll make you drive on the way back."

Sigrun laughed. "You never let me drive the Mustang unless you're drunk."

"I won't dignify that with a response," Philip said airily as he joined Amanda. "Here, let me – you shouldn't be stuck with the dishes."

"Oh," Amanda said softly, "I don't mind."

"I'll help you put these away, anyway," he said, gathering an armload of glasses before following her back into the dining room.

"So," Sigrun said quietly to Norm, joining him at the sink, "looks like things are going well with Amanda?"

"Yeah," he said happily, "they are."

"Philip said you're really set on Dickinson. Might she be part of the reason?"

"Yeah, part."

"So," Sigrun probed, "you'd rather live at home than stay with basketball?"

"Yeah. You and Philip – well, you've got wanderlust or something. Me, I like it here; I'm happy on the farm, and, well, I like Amanda."

Sigrun patted him on the back. "Good. I just don't want you to sacrifice your dreams so that Philip can come out to California."

"Nah." Norm shook his head. "I mean, it'd be great to go pro – but, you know, I'm just not good enough."

"Hey, Sigrun, you still want to go to that party?" Philip asked as he returned to the kitchen, trailed by Amanda.

"Sure, just give me a minute to put on something less travel-worn."

"Good idea. I'll change my shirt and grab my guitar."

"Guys," Norman said, "keep it down upstairs – Mom and Dad are in bed."

"No problem," Philip said. "But don't you need to get up early tomorrow?"

"Mom decided not to go to market tomorrow – she didn't think we had enough for both Sunday and Monday. So," Norm added with a wide grin, "Amanda and I thought we'd hang out for a while."

"Well," said Philip sternly, "behave yourselves."

Norm punched Philip's arm. "Come off it. We're not parking at Furnace Hill."

Philip turned beet red.

Sigrun laughed. "You deserved that. Come on, let's go change."

"But," Philip protested, "I'm four years older! And, anyway, you should learn from my mistakes."

"We did," Norm said cheerfully. "We stay home."

"Okay, okay, I've been put in my place." He handed Sigrun her backpack and picked up her suitcase. "You keep him in line, Amanda."

☙☙☙

On Tuesday morning, Sigrun rose at daybreak, but found that everyone, apart from Philip, who was taking a rare opportunity to sleep in the day before his last final, was up before she was.

"Morning," murmured a sleepy Norm over his breakfast cereal when Sigrun entered the otherwise-empty kitchen.

She poured herself a cup of coffee. "Did I miss your mother?"

"Nope – I think she's waiting for the eggs."

"I'll see if I can help." She stepped outside, sipping her coffee. The truck for market was still parked in the driveway, so Sigrun headed to the chicken coop. "Hey, Donald," she called softly as she slipped carefully into the chicken-filled yard.

"Morning." Donald stuck his head out the door. "Checking on their welfare?"

Sigrun laughed. "No, I trust you're taking great care of them. Want help?"

"Sure, there seems to be a bumper crop this morning."

Sigrun set her mug high on a small shelf near the door and grabbed a box. They quickly gathered the remaining eggs, and Donald stacked the boxes on his cart. Sigrun held the door for him, remembering to grab her now-cold mug of coffee.

"There you are," Ernestine Schlichter called. "Morning, Sigrun. I was just coming for the eggs."

"Are you sure you don't want me to come along?" Sigrun asked as she helped load the eggs onto the truck.

"No, dear," she said, "it's a small market, and I'm fine by myself. You go on over to the Farmstead – we're going to keep you so busy you won't have time to pack."

"Bye, Mom," Norm called from the side door.

"Don't forget to pick up your cap and gown." Mrs. Schlichter climbed into the driver's seat.

Sigrun ate breakfast and cleaned up the kitchen, knowing that Philip wouldn't want anything other than coffee. She put together some lunch, found the keys to her father's old truck and the Farmstead on the key rack in the mud room, and drove next door. She hadn't been there since early January. She pulled to a stop in the driveway, and sat in the pickup studying the house. She had accompanied Mrs. Schlichter to market the previous day, and they'd had a long talk. They had agreed that, regardless of what the others thought, it would be best if she rented the place to someone who could take over the routine maintenance. Sigrun had mixed emotions about the idea, but since she didn't know when she'd be able to live there in the foreseeable future, it made sense. She sighed. She loved the Farmstead, but maybe she should just sell it. She couldn't face that thought at the moment.

As she always had, she rounded the corner and let herself in the kitchen door. Although someone had been inside regularly, the place had a closed-up sense that made Sigrun uneasy; she went around opening windows throughout the lower level. She'd already worked out a plan of action – she wanted to go through her things and pack an extra suitcase of books and clothing to take back to California with her. Blythe had said it would be fine if she left stuff at the apartment during the last weeks of summer, when she would be back here again. She also wanted to put everything from her room that she wasn't going to need at school into the attic; if she were going to be staying over at the farm, she needn't keep a room ready here.

Sigrun had emptied the bookcase in her bedroom and had just tucked her baby box into a carton of things to save when she heard the crunch of tires on the gravel driveway. She looked out the window; it was the Mustang. She glanced at her watch – a quarter past four – maybe Philip had time for a ride. She ran down the stairs and arrived on the front porch as he was getting out of the car. "How's the studying?"

Philip groaned. "I need a break before I can face any more. I thought I'd come see how you're doing."

"Good timing – I've packed a box that I want to take back to school with me. Maybe you could carry it out to the truck."

"Sure. So," he said as he followed her back into the house, "am I right in thinking I could convince you to go for a ride?"

"You could."

"Fabulous."

"Hey," she said as she joined Philip in the kitchen after closing the windows, "did you check on Arabella's leg this morning?"

"Yeah, it's worse, so I put her in a stall. I guess her training will have to wait."

"So which one do you want me to ride then?"

"Do you mind taking Ellie out again? I've been neglecting her."

"No, she's a sweet girl."

"Yeah, but way too tame for you."

"Oh, I'm out of practice."

"Well, practice today and then tomorrow, after my final when we have more time, you can have Nolan."

"Really! You are feeling generous."

"Come off it, you've ridden him any number of times."

"Well, maybe a countable number."

"Hey, I'm man enough to admit that you're a better rider than I am."

Sigrun laughed. "Can I write that down and get you to sign it?"

"Okay, so it's taken me some time to get there, but I think I still deserve points."

"You do. But," she tossed over her shoulder as she got into the pickup, "it won't stop me beating you in a race – even on little Ellie."

⌐☜☞⌐

Late the following Monday afternoon, Sigrun stood up with a sigh and looked around the now barren room that had been her father's. She pushed her hair away from her sweaty face. "Too bad it had to get hot today. Why don't we take a break?"

"Just let me finish this box," Philip said.

Sigrun went downstairs and paused in the shade of the front porch to catch a breeze. It was the first truly hot day of her visit. Fortunately, it had remained cool the day before for Philip's graduation ceremony, which had gone flawlessly. She pulled two sodas from the cooler they had brought with them and headed inside. She heard Philip's phone ring. He must have left it in the truck. She hurried back. It was Philip's father. "Hi, it's Sigrun," she answered as she headed toward the house.

"How are you doing over there?"

"We're getting lots done. Here's Philip," she added as Philip appeared at the front door. "It's your dad."

"How's Estelle?" Philip asked into the phone.

Sigrun perched on the wide porch railing where she had both shade and a breeze. She leaned back against a post and took a long drink of her soda. She was tired because she and Philip had been up most of the previous night with Estelle, who had been due to foal a week earlier. Philip and his father were becoming concerned; this pregnancy had been troubled from the start, and Estelle had never been this late. After the family had returned home from a celebratory dinner out following graduation, they had checked on her and it appeared that she might give birth that night. So Philip had skipped his graduation parties to stay with her, and Sigrun had kept him company. Consequently, they hadn't made it over to the Farmstead until after lunch. Between graduation events and helping at the markets, it was the first time Sigrun had managed to get back since the day she'd started on her room. Philip closed his phone, and Sigrun tossed him the other can of soda. "How is she?"

"Maybe tonight."

"Do you want to head home?"

"Nope. Dad said she's looking good, and there's nothing I can do, so no reason to. Unless you're tired."

"No, I'd like to pack more."

"Are you set on getting a renter?" Philip asked unexpectedly.

"Yeah … I mean, what else can I do? I can't live here – there are no jobs."

"I guess you're right." He stared off into the distance, sipping his soda.

After several minutes of silence, Sigrun asked, "What are you contemplating?"

"The future. I'm wondering where we'll both end up."

"Well, you've got four years at Davis, so I've been thinking, I could try to get a job in San Francisco next summer and maybe after I graduate too."

"Really? You never mentioned that."

"I've been mulling it over. What do you think?"

"I like it … for the short term anyway."

"What's troubling you?"

"Oh … just the usual. I pushed Dad into investing in the horses, and he's sunk a lot of time and money into it. I feel like I'm abandoning him."

"I know," she said with a sigh, "but you can't stay here and go to vet school."

"Right. So, I keep circling back to maybe I shouldn't go to vet school."

"Oh, but no steps backward – remember? You've worked so hard to get this far, and," she added in a teasing tone, "maybe you just want to think you're indispensable."

He smiled wanly. "Maybe." He finished his soda and crushed the can in his fist. "But … did you ever think, maybe I won't want to come back?"

Sigrun studied him sympathetically as he carefully examined the crushed can. "Yes," she said gently, "I've thought of that."

He looked up at her with a troubled expression. "It's … hard to live here."

"I know, but, you know, I think Norm really wants the farm."

"Yeah, I think so too." He sighed, looking thoughtful. "Want to pack more?" he asked after a minute.

"You know," she said slowly, "what you need to think about is whether you still want to go to vet school if you don't want to live here."

"What?"

"Vet school started as a way to stay on the farm without being a farmer, right?"

"Yeah, but I ..."

"You're a poet at heart, Philip, not a doctor."

He shrugged. "So what? There's no way I can even consider pursuing music. You know that."

"Yeah. Okay, it was just a thought." She paused. "So, here we are then – both being swept along in the wake of our fathers' dreams."

Philip got to his feet and dusted off his jeans. "Maybe – but you're doing well."

Sigrun slid off the railing. "So far."

⟶⟵

It was just after midnight when Sigrun slipped quietly back into Estelle's stall, having taken a bathroom break, and re-joined Philip and his father.

"I don't think it's going to be tonight," Mr. Schlichter said.

"Yeah, maybe you're right," said Philip. "But I want to stay with her just in case."

"That's probably a good idea. I'm off to bed, but call if anything changes. You have your cell phones?"

"Yeah," they both responded. "But," Philip added, "I'll only wake you if I think she's really going through with it."

"Okay, I trust your judgment. Goodnight kids." Mr. Schlichter hesitated at the stall door and turned back. "You know, you two should go off and do something fun while Sigrun is here – you both work hard, and you deserve some time off."

"Oh," Sigrun said, surprised, "we don't ..."

"Thanks, Dad," Philip said, "maybe we will."

Mr. Schlichter let himself out of the stall. Sigrun stroked the white star on Estelle's forehead before gently rubbing her ears. "How are you doing, girl?" she murmured as the horse shifted her weight restlessly. "Do you think she's all right?"

"I think so – why?"

"I don't know ... she seems ... tense."

"Just uncomfortable, I imagine."

"Maybe," Sigrun said, unconvinced. She leaned against Estelle's side and stroked her. She could feel Estelle's taut muscles just beneath the surface as the horse continued to make small adjustments with her hooves. "Come and see – she's anxious."

Philip looked skeptical, but exchanged places with Sigrun and gently stroked Estelle's neck. He then carefully felt her extended belly. "I can feel the foal moving. She's probably just tired of the long pregnancy."

"Maybe you should get the vet to see her in the morning, if she hasn't changed."

"You think?"

"Yeah, I mean, I was here when Ellie was born, and Estelle was unfazed. This is what – her fourth foal?"

"Yes, but she's never been late before."

"Exactly. She's late and she's nervous."

"Okay. Your instincts are good, so yeah, it won't hurt to have the vet take a look at her. But come and sit down, we've a long night to get through first."

"I hope the coffee's still hot." Sigrun sat in one of the folding chairs they had brought into the stall and pulled over the one that Mr. Schlichter had been using to put up her feet. She poured herself some coffee and sipped it carefully – it was adequately warm. "Good," she said with satisfaction, "I do hate cold coffee. Want some?"

"Sure."

"I've been thinking," said Sigrun.

"Uh-oh."

"Yeah, well, I think maybe it would be better if I just sold the Farmstead."

"You don't want to do that."

"I don't want to – but don't you think it would be best for everyone?"

"No," Philip said adamantly, "I don't. Why would you sell?"

"Because it's just a burden for you guys – I mean, when am I going to live there? After all, I really need to get a legal job next summer, the summer after that I have to study for the bar in California if I'm going to work there at all, and after that – well, who knows – but there aren't any job prospects here."

"So, we rent it."

"But it's still a burden for your folks."

Philip shook his head. "No it's not. Your father had it rented out all those years that he and your mother lived in Lancaster after his mother died. It wasn't a problem. I mean, the property has been in your family for generations. My grandparents bought this place from them."

"Yeah, I know, but ..."

"If you sell, you sever your only tie to your family."

"No. Your family is my family. Your mother said I could take over the guest room and consider it my own, so I'll always have a place to come back to."

"That's true – but ... family is important, and I just don't think you should sell."

"Okay, if you feel so strongly about it. But let's work on getting it ready, and maybe we can get a renter in there before the end of the summer."

"What about when you come home in August?"

"I'm perfectly happy here."

"All right then. Donald probably has time to help – let's see if we can get everything packed up before you leave."

"Okay." Sigrun settled back in her chair, sipping her coffee. She heard what sounded like tires on gravel. "Hey, isn't that a car in the drive?"

They both listened intently. Philip shook his head. "I don't hear anything."

"Probably just someone hitting the shoulder of the road, I guess."

Philip went over and checked out Estelle. "You are being stubborn," he murmured to the horse. "How are you feeling?" She continued to shift restlessly. "Yeah, maybe getting the vet is a good idea – she does seem uncomfortable."

Sigrun watched Estelle for a moment. "I think she's worse."

"But I don't see anything wrong – the foal is where he should be and he's moving." Philip returned to his seat. "I think we should stay with her though."

"Yeah, me too." She sipped her coffee and shuddered; it had grown cold.

"Too bad the guitar bothers Estelle," he said, "I'd love to spend time ..."

Sigrun heard the squeal of tires rapidly accelerating on gravel.

"What the hell?" Philip leapt to his feet. "I'd better check that out."

"Wait," she said, jumping up, "I want to come." She latched the stall door behind them and hurried after him.

Sigrun was nearly thrown off her feet as a deafening percussive explosion passed through the barn. She stumbled, caught her balance, and took off at a run. Philip was several yards ahead of her. She emerged into the oddly bright yard and gasped in horror. The side of the house closest to the barn was engulfed in flames. Philip was running toward the side door, but she could see that he wouldn't be able to get near.

"PHILIP," she shrieked, "THE FRONT!"

He either heard her or came to the same conclusion, because he changed course. By the time she got there, he was tugging on the front door, but it didn't move.

"It's locked!" Sigrun yelled into his ear.

Philip continued to wrench at the door handle. The long narrow window to the right of the door blew out, and they both were enclosed in a thick cloud of smoke that set them coughing. She clutched Philip's arm as he jumped toward the broken window and yanked back sharply. "NO! You won't make it!"

Philip hesitated briefly before he backed off, coughing hard. Then, lurching forward, he yelled, "I have to try."

"No – you can't!" Heart pounding, Sigrun hauled frantically on his arm. "We need help!" She tugged with all her strength, and he finally yielded. They stumbled a few steps off the porch. Sigrun fumbled in her pocket for her phone while watching Philip – worried he would dash forward again. She needed both of her shaking hands to get her phone open and punch in 911.

"Fire," she croaked to the operator who answered. "It's huge. The Schlichter farm – out on ..."

"I know it," the operator interrupted. "Stay on the line."

Sigrun waited, mesmerized by the flames. She coughed harshly.

"Where are you?" the operator asked urgently.

"In front." She gasped in disbelief as the flames shot still higher. "I can't see anything but flames."

"Back away," the operator said sharply. "Is anyone inside?"

"The whole family. Four ..." She was racked with coughs as the wind shifted and they were engulfed in smoke. "NO!"

Philip shot forward. Sigrun dropped the phone and grabbed his arm.

"The back," he cried, "maybe I can get in a window."

"NO!" she screamed, struggling with him. She heard the wail of approaching sirens. "They're almost here."

He dragged Sigrun a couple of steps closer, but stopped when he was overcome by violent coughing. "I can't ... just ... watch them die," he wheezed between coughs.

"Back up!" she yelled frantically. "COME ON!" She kept

pulling until, still coughing, he took a few reluctant steps backwards. She heard a truck in the driveway. "MOVE!" she screeched. "Out of the way!"

The first truck neared; a firefighter jumped out and ran over. He grabbed each of them by a shoulder and dragged them back before he gestured the truck forward. It crossed the yard and stopped in front of the house. "Do you live here?"

"I do," Philip rasped.

"Who's inside and where are they?" the firefighter demanded.

"My parents and my ... brothers ..." Philip gave a racking cough, "two brothers."

"On the second floor," Sigrun added quickly.

"Stay here." He ran back to the trucks.

Sigrun watched in horror as the firefighters doused the house with water from numerous hoses. But the flames were already shooting through the roof, and she knew with a dreadful sinking certainty that no one could have survived. She looked at Philip – he was standing transfixed watching the flames, coughing sporadically. She hugged his arm close. He glanced down at her but didn't say anything. They stood silent in the tumult for what seemed to Sigrun to be an eternity; she was lost in a sense of unreality, unable to comprehend the scene unfolding in front of her eyes.

A uniformed firefighter whom Sigrun recognized vaguely as having been a couple years ahead of her at school grabbed her arm and said something incomprehensible.

"The barn," he shouted. "Are there horses in the barn?"

Sigrun blinked at him and then clasped her hand over her mouth as the meaning of his words sunk in. "My god! Yes. Yes." She started toward the barn.

He clutched her shoulders. "NO! How many and where?"

"Uh ... Estelle – she's in labor. That's why, uh, in the large stall at the far end." Sigrun gestured. "I should go ..." She tried to step around him.

"Stay here." He held her firmly in place. "I'll get help. Who else?"

"Arabella – on the left as you go in, part way down. She's lame. And Nolan – same side, but further – he's got his own pad-dock."

"That's all?"

Sigrun fought to focus. "I think so."

"Okay. Don't come closer – it's too dangerous." He turned and ran toward the barn. "Joe," he hollered, "get on the radio and get us a vet pronto."

Sigrun heard more vehicles arrive, but she didn't pay any attention. Someone threw a blanket over each of them and thrust a cup of coffee at her. It immediately spilled in her shaking hand. She steadied the cup with her other hand and turned to give it to Philip, who had not taken his eyes off the burning house.

"Here," she said to him, holding the cup toward him, "take this." She saw his hands. "Oh no." She gasped and looked around. A young woman was standing nearby who must have handed her the coffee. "His hands," she shouted at the woman.

A few minutes later, a medic arrived carrying a bag and said to Philip, "Let me see your hands." He ignored her. The medic picked up Philip's hands one by one. He never acknowledged her presence. She turned to Sigrun and said, "He's in shock. Stay with him while I get a doctor."

Sigrun took Philip's arm again. The fire was beginning to die down – the house was nothing more than a skeleton. The firefighters appeared to be concentrating on watering down the barn and nearby outbuildings. Sigrun felt someone touch her shoulder; she turned to find Amanda, tears streaming down her face, standing next to her with an older woman.

"My father heard – on his police radio. Is it true? Are they all …"

Sigrun could only shake her head. The woman pulled Amanda close as she burst into uncontrollable sobs.

Someone else tapped Sigrun on the shoulder from behind, and the young firefighter beckoned her. She stepped away from the group. He leaned close and said, "I have more bad news – the dark bay mare in the side stall?"

"Arabella." She suspected what was coming.

"Apparently she panicked, tried to kick her way out of the stall, and broke her leg badly – the vet says she needs to be put down right away. Will you tell Philip?"

She swallowed several times and managed to say, "What about the others?"

"We got them out – the vet thinks they're okay. The foal hasn't come yet."

Sigrun looked at Philip and back at the firefighter helplessly. "He's in shock."

"The vet said it had to be now."

"Okay," she said heavily, "I'll tell him." She tugged on Philip's arm. He looked blankly at her. "Philip?" He didn't seem to hear and looked back at the house.

"Philip," she repeated louder. He continued to watch the house.

"Let me," a voice said.

Sigrun turned to find a casually dressed man carrying a doctor's bag standing next to her. She got out of his way. He stepped in front of Philip and said firmly. "Okay, Philip, I'm a doctor and I want to check you out. Come with me."

Philip seemed to focus on the man. "I'm fine."

"I'm afraid not," the doctor said sternly. "I want to look at your burns. Step over here." He took Philip's arm and turned him around; Philip didn't resist.

Sigrun watched them walk to an ambulance. "Could you get the vet to sedate her?" she asked the firefighter. "I don't want to do anything without Philip knowing."

Sigrun felt sick. She wanted to know for sure – but whom could she ask? She looked about in confusion for several minutes. The scene was still chaotic with people going in all directions. She retreated to the ambulance. Philip was standing next to the vehicle, still staring at the house. His hands were bandaged. The doctor was leaning on the hood, a few feet away, writing.

She approached the doctor. "Excuse me. Do you know – I mean, I assume …" She looked back at the house.

He looked at her sympathetically. "The family?"

"I wanted to know …"

"They haven't found the bodies yet as far as I know," he said too softly for Philip to hear, "but no one survived."

She nodded and turned away; it wasn't as if she hadn't known that. A gentle hand was placed on her shoulder.

"How about you," the doctor asked, "are you injured?"

"I didn't touch anything. Just the smoke."

"Okay. Keep your eyes on him; he refused to be sedated and he refused to leave. He doesn't need any further treatment at the moment, so the medic's going to take him to the Medical Center when he's ready to leave. Why don't you go with him and have someone look you over as well."

"Okay," she murmured. She went to join Philip.

"They're gone," he wheezed brokenly in utter disbelief. "They're just gone …"

ᴧᴧᴧᴧᴧ

⤙⤚ Chapter 12 ⤚⤙
Principiis obsta
(Resist the beginning; Ovid)

On the 31st of May – the Saturday after what would have been Norman's high school graduation – Sigrun awoke with the realization that she had a ticket to return to Los Angeles the following day. She had lost track of time and had failed to take in that it was almost June. She sat up in bed, feeling dreadful and panicky. She had not been sleeping well since the fire, but last night had been the worst. She and Philip had accompanied Amanda and her parents to the graduation ceremony. The entire graduating class and a large portion of the audience had worn black armbands. Philip had barely been steady enough to cross the stage to accept his brother's diploma. Sigrun and Amanda had cried the entire time. It had been heart wrenching to watch the basketball team standing stoically together during a moment of silence.

Sigrun got out of bed and rummaged around in the pile of items she had accumulated in the room she had been using at the family home of their friend Brian until she found her cell phone. It twice failed to turn on before it sunk in that, of course, the battery had died. And both her battery charger and Philip's had been in the house. She sighed. She stood there staring blankly at the dead phone for a few minutes before the thought crystallized that she should add buying new chargers to her seemingly never-ending to-do list. Then she dressed and went downstairs to use her hosts' phone to contact the airline and explain the situation. It took her over an hour of discussions with a series of agents and supervisors before she had secured a new reservation for nearly three weeks later – the longest delay they would permit without charging her a huge fee to issue a new ticket. While on hold, she had the thought to leave a message for Professor Ehrlich to let her know her new arrival date. But first, Sigrun thought while jotting a note on her list, she'd have to call directory assistance to get the number. And Blythe, she realized – she must call Blythe.

⤙⤚

The following Friday, Philip and Sigrun were on their way to yet another appointment with Philip's lawyer, Ray Reinhardt, at his office in Carlisle. She was driving because Philip's hands were still bandaged. And, in any case, he wasn't interested in driving anything other than the Mustang, which had been thoroughly trashed in the fire. Philip was conflicted about the Mustang because his father had cherished it so, but he had decided that he had neither the time nor the skill to repair it. Thus he was reconciling himself with the idea of selling it to someone who did. They were silent as she drove through town – Philip sunk deep into sadness, Sigrun nervous because they were running late. While stopped at a red light, she glanced over at a bank sign displaying the date and time. "June 6th," she murmured.

"What?" asked Philip.

"Oh, nothing. We're almost there."

"No, what did you say?"

"It's just … I had forgotten that today is the 6th of June."

After a moment, Philip said, "It's been a hell of a year since your father died."

By the time they arrived at Ray's office, they were more than 30 minutes late. The warm and supportive woman who ran the place – whose name Sigrun didn't know, having failed to catch it the first couple of times they had met – assured them that Ray would fit them in shortly. Philip, uncharacteristically restless, paced while they waited. As soon as they had been ushered into Ray's office, Philip blurted out, "I want to get the farm sold as quickly as possible."

"What makes you say that?" Ray asked calmly.

"The sooner I sell," Philip said vehemently, leaning forward, "the sooner I can move on."

"But, as we've discussed, you may regret decisions you've made in haste."

Philip shook his head adamantly. "I'm not being rash. It's been nearly three weeks – do you think I've been thinking about anything else?"

"I know you've been giving it a lot of consideration these past weeks," Ray said carefully, "but my concern is that you may feel differently in a year or so."

"Let's focus on the facts," he said irritably. "I'm in school for the next four years, and then I'll need a job. I can't take care of the horses, the farm, or any part of it. And there's no possibility of Sigrun getting a job near here – so why would I hold on to it?"

"Because," Sigrun said quietly, "it's your family's land."

"Less so than the Farmstead is yours."

"It's true," said Ray, "that you can't use the land now, but there's no reason you can't pursue your dream of breeding horses there at some point in the future."

Philip shook his head violently, jumped to his feet, and crossed to the window. "I couldn't live there without being haunted by images of the house burning."

Sigrun threw Ray a helpless look.

He sighed and said gently, "I understand how you feel. But over time ..."

"No!" Philip cut him off in an intense voice. "I stood there and watched them die. I can never again set foot on that property free of that knowledge."

Sigrun took out a tissue and tried to stem the tears streaming down her face.

"All right," Ray said, "here's what I suggest. During the next week, I'll look for ways for you to retain ownership but transfer responsibility for the property to someone else." He put up a hand to stop Philip, who had returned to his chair, from interrupting. "But I'll also pursue preparations for putting it on the market. In the meantime, Philip, I want you to think about what you might want to do – say in 20 years or so."

"Yeah, well ..." Philip said skeptically, "I can try, but I can tell you right now that I won't feel any differently next week than I do now. Look, Sigrun's going back to California, and," he gave a humorless laugh, "there's certainly no reason for her to return at the end of the summer. Maybe," he said, turning to Sigrun, "we could do something with that time – take a trip, see something different?"

"Yeah," she said, her spirits lifting marginally, "yeah, maybe we could. You can definitely come and stay with me as soon as you get done here and then, when I'm finished, maybe we could go somewhere."

"So," Philip said to Ray, "like I said, the sooner I sell, the better."

"Okay. But I promise you that taking a week to think about it won't delay things. We can't put it on the market until I work through the legal issues. Speaking of which," he picked up a pile of documents and handed it to Philip, "we need to discuss these."

🐾〜🐾

That night, Sigrun got out one of the new chargers they had

bought after the meeting with Ray and plugged in her phone. She didn't expect any messages since Philip, obviously, had not been calling her. To her surprise, she found she had three, all from Gareth. It simply hadn't occurred to her to call him. He had first tried to reach her on June 1st, the day she had been scheduled to return. In his last message, from earlier that same day, he sounded quite concerned and said he was going to contact Professor Ehrlich. Good, she thought with a sigh, the professor would have let him know when she'd be back – so she didn't have to call him right now. She left the phone on to charge and went about packing the things she had accumulated in the preceding weeks. Ray had assured them during their meeting that the smell of smoke that had permeated her Farmstead had dissipated. She and Philip had discussed it on the drive back, and he thought he would be okay now being so close to the scene of the fire. He really wanted to stay there while he wrapped up the sale of the farm, and they were both tired of imposing on the hospitality of people they didn't know well – despite Brian's repeated assurances that his family was happy to host them as long as they liked.

⚬⚬⚬ ⚬⚬⚬

On Monday afternoon, Sigrun and Philip were sitting on the front porch of the Farmstead, having recently returned from an appointment at the Medical Center during which the last of his bandages had been removed. His hands were healing well. The doctor had told him even earlier that he could play a guitar as long as it didn't hurt too much. But, although one of Philip's old bandmates had lent him a guitar weeks ago, this was the first time he had even looked at it. Sigrun silently sipped a soda while he contemplated the guitar sitting near him.

"It's interesting that you don't miss what you think you will," he said eventually. "If I had been told a few weeks ago that I could never play the guitar or sing again, I would have been devastated. Now, well, I don't know that I want to any longer."

Sigrun pondered that. "I wish you would. I miss it – and it might help you heal."

"I suppose," he said half-heartedly, "but I seem to have lost my … oh, I don't know, my compulsion to express myself in music."

"I think you're depressed. But that doesn't mean you can't give voice to your grief."

"Maybe." He picked up his soda. "Do we have any more

appointments today?"

She shook her head. Most days it seemed as though they had an endless stream of things to do. Today, however, the doctor's appointment had been the last.

"I was wondering if you wanted to take a ride?"

Sigrun started: She had not expected that. They had been visiting the horses nearly every day – especially Estelle and her new colt, Otto, who had been born healthy the day after the fire – and had been helping to care for them, but they hadn't been riding since before the fire. "Do you?" she asked uncertainly.

"I'm not sure," he admitted. "But you know, I had the thought that, if I'm gonna sell the horses, it seems like we should take a goodbye ride for each of them."

She turned away to hide her tears. "I don't think I'm ready for that."

"Yeah, maybe you're right."

They lapsed back into silence. Sigrun got her emotions under control and suggested, "Maybe we should get back to packing things here."

"No. I've told you I don't want you to rent it, so I don't see why we should pack anything else."

"But I don't see why it shouldn't be rented if we're both out in California."

Philip didn't say anything for several minutes, and then he suddenly picked up the guitar and started tuning it. "Because," he said quietly, "we both need to have a place to come back to. And this is all we have."

That started Sigrun's tears flowing again. She sat and watched as Philip, occasionally wincing in pain, tuned the guitar. It was true that they would have no place to call home if he persisted in his plan to sell the farm. So, maybe keeping the Farmstead … her phone rang. She jumped to her feet, wiping her wet eyes on her sleeve as she went, and ducked through the front door into the foyer where she had left the phone on a table. Damn, it was the prison – she definitely had not expected to hear from Zareh. "It's the prison," she called as she headed toward the kitchen.

"Will you accept a collect call from San Quentin State Prison from a Mr. Fremont?" said what sounded like the same officious voice.

Didn't they have more than one person handling these calls, Sigrun wondered distractedly as she agreed.

"Greetings, Sigrun," Zareh said, "Gareth and I have been

worried about you."

"I'm sorry," she said, trying not to sound defensive. "In his last message, Gareth said he would contact Professor Ehrlich, so I thought he'd hear that I've been delayed."

"Yes, he did, but we were still worried."

"Oh," Sigrun said in confusion, feeling too fragile to deal with the ambiguities Zareh always presented.

"Are you well?"

"Uh, yeah, I'm fine. I ... well, something came up, and I ... I've been busy."

"So, you are expecting to return ... when?"

"Oh, uhm, June 20th – what is that – about two weeks."

"I would like to meet with you when you have time."

"Oh. Uh ... sure. But, I haven't been working on the case for a while now, and I ... I'm sorry, but I'm not up to speed on things at the moment."

"That's fine. Would you be willing to register as my legal representative so that we can talk freely when you do come?"

Sigrun felt as if she had missed something. What did he want to talk about? "Uh – I'm not a lawyer."

"But you are over 21, correct?"

"No, I'm not. I mean, I'll be 21 later this summer, but no."

There was silence on the other end of the phone, and, after a minute, Sigrun asked, "Are you still there?"

"Excuse me," he said, "I must go. Will you answer if Gareth calls?"

"Yes. I'm sorry I didn't call ..."

"It's not a problem," he said shortly. "Please take care."

Sigrun shook her head as she closed her phone. Why was it that talking to Zareh always left her disconcerted? She had not given the habeas case a thought since she had arrived in Pennsylvania. At the moment, she simply wasn't able to reconcile that part of her life with the present. She tucked the phone into her pocket and headed back to the porch. She paused at the front door. Philip was pensively strumming the guitar. She lingered, unwilling to interrupt him, but he must have heard her because he looked up.

"What's up?" he asked, continuing to strum.

"That was Zareh." She resumed her seat. "I gather that my continued absence has upset him." She sipped her soda. "I guess it's understandable that he's impatient."

"Not really," he said thoughtfully. "If he doesn't think anything will come of your claim – what does he care when it gets filed?"

"You're right. I hadn't thought of that. I don't know – he wants to talk to me."

"Oh?" Philip looked up from his guitar. "Maybe he's finally going to tell you what happened."

"I don't think so – I mean, why would he? But I guess I'll see what he has to say."

Lingering over a take-out dinner that night, they were drinking beer in the sitting room and debating, yet again, Philip's plan to sell the farm when Sigrun's phone rang. She pulled it out and grimaced. "It's Gareth – I promised I'd talk to him." She answered.

"Hello, Sigrun. Thank you for taking my call."

"I'm sorry – things have been rather unsettled here, and I ..."

"No, do not apologize. I have no right to your time. Are you well?"

"I'm fine," she said a bit sharply, sure that he had talked to Zareh.

"Obviously," Gareth said wryly, "you failed to convince Zareh of that."

"Yeah. So, anyway, what is it that Zareh wants to discuss with me?"

"I too would like to talk to you, but it would be best done in person. Would you consider coming up here after your return to California?"

"Well ... I haven't worked on the case for so long that I'm not really connected ..."

"Please, we must talk."

"Well ... okay, if you think so, but I need time ..."

"We can review where you are when you visit. I would rather that it not wait."

"But," she protested, feeling pressured, "I'm not ready to discuss anything."

"I am sorry," he said, sounding strained, "but it's extremely important that we talk as soon as possible."

"I don't understand," she said, sounding petulant even to herself.

"I'll explain when you visit, but there is something you must know."

"Oh ... okay. My flight gets in late on Friday the 20th, so maybe I could come the following Monday or Tuesday ..."

"Could you come on Saturday?"

"The next day?"

"Yes. I will pick you up in San Luis Obispo."

"Well ..."

"Please," he pressed.

"Okay," she conceded with a sigh, "but I'll have to catch the later train because I'll need time to gather my things that morning. I'll let you know the time."

"Thank you. Perhaps we might drive up to San Quentin while you are here."

"Oh," Sigrun said, "yeah, I suppose we could."

"Good. And please **do** call me if your plans change."

"I'm sorry. I didn't realize you'd be worried."

"Yes," he said softly, "we were. Aloha and I will see you shortly."

Sigrun hung up and said to Philip, "I don't get it – he says there's something I need to know, and he seems to think it's urgent."

"Ah, like I thought, I suspect Fremont is going to share his secrets with you."

She smiled, happy to hear Philip sounding almost like his old self. "Well, if you're right, I'll be sure to let you know so you can revise his song."

⤙ Chapter 13 ⤚

Fata viam invenient
(The fates will find a way; Virgil, Aeneid)

Sigrun descended the steps onto the platform and spotted Gareth, once again wearing a Hawaiian shirt and blue jeans, waiting some distance from the train. She waved and walked over. As she neared, she thought he looked anxious, and he appeared to give her a searching look. But he said pleasantly, "Greetings Sigrun, I am delighted to see you." He took her bag and headed to the parking lot. Once there, he put her bag into the front luggage compartment of a sleek silver Porsche convertible.

Well, she thought, he clearly had meant it when he said that money was not an issue.

As they left the parking lot, he asked, "Are you in good health – you appear to have lost weight?"

"Uh … yeah." She pushed her hair back from her face. "I have. I'm amazed you noticed."

"You'll find that I am quite observant."

She was a bit taken aback by the implication that she would have the opportunity to get to know him that well.

"Is something wrong at home?"

"Yes," she admitted with relief. "Yes – actually, it's horrible. My friend Philip – his family was killed in a fire while I was home."

"What!" Gareth gave her a concerned look. "What happened?"

"We don't know for sure, but the fire inspector thinks it was a gas leak. The house was destroyed, and his parents and his two brothers were killed."

"I am so sorry. So you stayed to help him?"

"Yes. I'm sorry for not returning your calls – I was …"

"Please," he said, with a wave of his hand. "That is not important. How is your friend coping?"

"He's doing okay. Well, most of the time, anyway. He's coming to stay with me as soon as he finishes making arrangements to sell the farm."

"You're close friends, aren't you?"

She caught an odd note in his voice that made her uncomfortable. "Yes, we are," she replied quietly. Now that she thought about it, Gareth seemed reserved and edgy. It seemed out of character for someone she had, to date, found to be extremely relaxed and easygoing. But then, she didn't really know him. Several minutes passed in silence. Sigrun felt that she needed to explain her distance from the case. "I wanted to ..."

At the same time, Gareth said, "Would you mind ..."

"Sorry," he continued when she ceased talking. "You were saying?"

"Oh, I was going to say that my research notes and other files for the habeas case were at the farm, and ... well, they were destroyed in the fire."

"I see. But you can replace them, can't you?"

"Yeah, sure, but it will delay me. And ... well," she added apologetically, "it's just ... I haven't been able to concentrate on the case at all."

"Of course," he said. "Once you take it up again, I am sure you'll be able to regain your momentum."

"I suppose. ... Well, you said you wanted to talk to me about something – maybe that will help me get back on track."

"Yes," he said slowly, "I do. But, if you don't mind, I would like to take advantage of the long hours of daylight today and take a walk on the beach."

"Uh, no, I don't mind."

"Thank you. Montana de Oro Park is near. It's rarely crowded and quite lovely."

They soon turned off the road into a parking lot. Only a few others were about as they strolled across the wide, sandy beach.

"Have you been to the beach much since you've been in California?" he asked.

"No. A couple of times – but I really haven't had much free time."

"Please forgive me for occupying your recreational time."

"No," she said with a shake of her head, "I didn't have time even before I started on the habeas case. ... I guess I study too much."

They walked for several minutes in silence – keeping just far enough above the waves to not get wet. Gareth seemed preoccupied and kept picking up and discarding stones. "Do you like living in California?" he asked eventually.

"Yes, I do. … Do you?"

"Ah, that is an interesting question. In some respects." He did not elaborate, and Sigrun was too shy to ask.

It was quiet except for the calls of gulls, the crashing of waves, and the murmur of distant voices drifting across the beach. As the silence grew, Sigrun began to feel more uncomfortable; perhaps she should suggest they turn back.

Gareth picked up a particularly large and smooth stone. After fingering it for a time, he sent it skipping far out onto the water. "May I ask you a personal question?"

"Uh … yeah, I suppose."

"Is Sigrun the name you were given at birth?"

She was astounded; why on earth would he think to ask such a question? But she could see no harm in answering him. "Well … no … it's not. Why do you ask?"

"Was your name Firinne?"

She stumbled and gasped, "How did you know?" This was getting just too weird.

He nodded and sighed and said slowly, "I'll tell you. But it is a long story – let's sit at that picnic table over there."

As they crossed the sand toward the redwood table, Sigrun wondered uneasily how he could possibly have known her birth name. What was going on? Bewildered and perturbed, she perched on the picnic bench.

"I don't know where to start, and I am not the person who should be telling you this," he said, sounding flustered. He drew a deep breath and continued in a calmer voice. "Sigrun, you don't know me well, and you have no reason to trust me, but will you please give me a chance to tell you my story before you decide that I am a lunatic?"

She shifted on the bench to look over the ocean. She leaned forward to let her hair shield her face and, with a nervous laugh, asked, "Are you a lunatic?"

When he replied, quite seriously, "No," she grew even more nervous.

"No," he repeated, "but I am certain that you will think I must be."

She wondered if she should ask to leave. Gareth was acting oddly. It was true – she didn't know him well, and they were more or less in the middle of nowhere. But it seemed safe enough. She said nothing.

After a lengthy pause, he said, "Let me start by saying that, although you told me you came to law school because of your father's dream that you become a lawyer, I believe there is another reason that your father's aspirations brought you to California. As you might say – it was fate's way of bringing us together."

Sigrun waited for him to continue with growing alarm. Had she totally misjudged him?

"You have not told me, but I know, that you were raised by adoptive parents after your birth parents were killed."

Feeling that the conversation had gotten altogether too personal, she jumped to her feet. "I think I should be getting back."

"No, wait," he pleaded. "I realize I am making you uncomfortable, but please give me a chance to explain before you judge me."

Sigrun hesitated and looked around. Several clusters of people had come within shouting distance, and she supposed nothing much could happen in such a public spot. She sat back down.

Gareth started again, staring out to sea while he spoke. "When you were a small baby, your parents were assassinated."

Sigrun flinched.

"You were their only child. Your mother had a younger brother who, of course, is your uncle. He heard a rumor that your parents were going to be killed that night, and he came to Cambria to warn them. Unfortunately, he arrived too late. He was at their apartment when they were killed. Unbeknownst to the killer, you were there as well. Your mother knew that those who had wanted her dead would seek your death if they learned of your existence."

Gareth paused and looked at Sigrun. She gaped at him, too dumbfounded to form a question. He continued in a gentle voice, "It was your mother's dying request that you be protected. Your uncle was able to take you safely from the apartment before he returned to destroy the evidence that you had ever existed. He didn't have time to finish before the police found him."

She gasped and, feeling as if she had been punched in the stomach, murmured, "Zareh! You're talking about Zareh."

"Yes," he said, "yes, I am."

Before he could continue, Sigrun protested, "But he didn't know the victims."

"Zareh kept his identity secret to protect you."

"Yeah, but ..."

"Wait, it will become clear. Zareh turned you over to a trusted relative and asked her to hide you. Your existence was so well concealed that he didn't even tell me until quite recently. I've told you that I've known Zareh since he was born. What I have **not** told you is that ... Eireen, your mother, was my closest friend." Gareth sighed deeply. "Even after all these years, I have trouble believing that she is gone."

"But," she said slowly, "that means you – at the trial – you knew the victims too?"

"Yes."

"But then ..." she shook her head in confusion. "I don't understand – why didn't you tell me?"

"That is rather complicated. I'll get to it later. So, about a year before the murders, Eireen came to live in Cambria. Zareh stayed with her and your father the summer you were born, and then he returned home to finish school. Zareh said you were not quite three months old at the time your parents were killed, which was 20 years ago, last October. So, you must have been born that prior August."

"I turned 20 in August," Sigrun said faintly, feeling acutely nauseated.

"That fits," he said, with a knowing nod.

"Wait a minute." She drew a shaky breath. "You're telling me that by some ... uncanny coincidence – to put it mildly – I just happen to be handed the habeas case of the one death-row inmate I'm ... related to? Get real!!"

Gareth shrugged. "I can't explain that. But one's path takes the turns necessary to reach one's end."

Sigrun blinked at him. "What?"

"Anyway, I also can't explain how you arrived at your adoptive parents. Zareh will have to supply that part of the story. In truth, he wanted to tell you the entire story, but, because you are not his legal representative, it's not possible for you to have a private conversation. So, he asked me ..."

"Stop," she interjected. "This doesn't make any sense. If Zareh was there – why didn't he tell the police what happened?"

"Ah, yes ..." he said, becoming agitated again. "Well, there is a lot more to the story." He looked at the people on the beach, several of whom were now close enough to hear their conversation. "Please believe me, I'll understand if you refuse; however, I would prefer to go somewhere more private. Of course," he added dryly, "you probably **have** decided by now that I am crazy."

Sigrun's thoughts were churning. Why should she trust him? His story was ludicrous. But ... unless it was true ... how could he know her birth name or when she was born? She had told neither fact to anyone in California. She stole a sideways glance at Gareth; he was gazing into the distance with a distracted expression. Somehow – even though she didn't know what to believe – she inexplicably felt secure with him. Well, her father had always said she had good instincts about people. And she wasn't about to leave his story hanging.

"I want to hear the rest of the story," she said more calmly than she felt. "To be honest, I'm not sure I believe you – but I'll listen."

"Good," Gareth said with obvious relief. "Why don't we go sit in my car?"

"No," she said with growing assurance, "I trust you, let's go somewhere private."

Getting up from the picnic bench, he gave a nervous laugh. "I must be more persuasive than I thought if you place any confidence in me."

When they reached the car, he asked, "It's such a pleasant evening, would you mind if I put the top down?"

"No, I like the breeze." Sigrun rummaged in her pocket for a tie for her hair.

As they left the park, he said, "I live about 20 minutes north of here. I'll head that way because I want to show you something at my place. But you must promise me that, if you decide you want to leave, you'll ask me to turn around. I give you my word that I'll take you back to the train station any time you wish."

"I will," she said and waited for him to continue.

After a few moments, Gareth said, "Well ... that was the easy part."

"Come off it! My real parents were assassinated and my uncle, whom I didn't know I had, sits on death row, falsely convicted of murdering them after spiriting me away from the murder scene to be raised in obscurity. To top it all off, I just stumbled onto his habeas case. That's the easy part?"

"When you put it that way, it does sound incredible but, trust me, it is nothing compared to the rest of the story." He nervously cleared his throat. "So ... where to begin?" After another lengthy pause, he said, "Well then, let's start with something easy. Do you remember when we first met?"

"Of course – what do you mean?"

"Do you recall feeling a small shock when we shook hands?"

"So you did feel it! What was it?"

"Hold up your hand."

Sigrun held out her hand, and he grasped it. She felt a sharp jolt, milder this time. "Yes! Like that. What is it?"

"That shock indicates that you have Power."

She laughed. "Yeah, right. Whatever that means."

"Please hear me out. ... This is extremely difficult to explain because you were raised by a family unaware of your history." He cleared his throat again. "I can think of no other way to say this: Sigrun, you do not belong in this world."

So ... had he waited until they were driving before getting to this part because he thought she wouldn't jump out of a moving vehicle? But, she could consider it.

"I know it sounds insane, but please bear with me. You, your parents, Zareh, and I, are all from another world – a place we call Kaia. It lies in a parallel plane with Earth. We know much about this world, but hardly anyone here knows that we exist."

"Of course," she said sarcastically. He had to be certifiable. So, where exactly was he taking her? Maybe she **should** consider jumping.

"On Kaia, Power – what you would call 'magic' – is pervasive. We can use our Power to move between worlds. When they were killed, your parents were secretly working for the Orbis Concilium – the entity that governs our world."

Sigrun laughed humorlessly.

Gareth gave her probing look. "You look queasy, do you want to turn around?"

After a moment she found her voice and said, "No ... no, I'm fine. Please do continue."

"The reason I asked you about the shock you experienced when we shook hands is because that's what told me that you were from Kaia. We all feel it on Earth if we touch within reach of something we call the Grid."

"The Grid?" she echoed.

"It's rather complicated, but the Grid acts as an infrastructure; when we use Power, we interact with the Grid and cause a disruption in its current. Think of it as a vast interconnected electrical system covering Kaia. Here, if you need electricity, you put a plug in an outlet and connect to the power system. In the same manner, when I use my Power, I connect mentally with the Grid."

"Okay," she faltered, "but you're ... here?"

"We also can use Power on Earth; but here the Grid is 'stretched', in a manner of speaking. It's not important for our purposes, but the Grid is only accessible in limited areas here.

Where it is, anyone with Power brushes against it when they touch someone else with Power. That doesn't happen on Kaia because the Grid is interwoven into the fabric of everything."

Too flabbergasted to follow his explanation, Sigrun asked, "Why didn't you say something when we shook hands?"

"Based on your reaction at the time, I thought you seemed unaware of Kaia. So, I assumed you would not have believed me had I said anything. And, anyway, I had no idea who you were."

"How did you figure it out?" she asked suspiciously.

"After our first meeting, I told Zareh that you had Power – but he had no reason to suspect your identity. And, at that time, I didn't know you existed. I did wonder who you might be, but I thought if you were ignorant, questions would be too awkward. Later ..."

"Hold on," she interrupted. "So ... you didn't know who I was. But you felt this shock thing, and – you just ignored it? Does it happen that often?"

Gareth laughed. "No. I see now that I was remiss in not pursuing it at the time. But there are people from Kaia living on Earth – particularly in Pennsylvania, where you said you were from. I imagine some of them must have children who are ignorant of their heritage. I confess that, at the time, I was more interested in Zareh's case than in who your parents might be."

"Yeah, sure," she said dubiously.

"But later Zareh discovered that you had been adopted. He realized, once he thought about it, that you bear a striking resemblance to your birth father. I didn't know Ed well, and I didn't detect the resemblance until after Zareh had mentioned it."

Of course, he would have known her real father too. So, she looked like her father. She had always wondered. But wait ... she wasn't buying his story.

"Then, you may recall, during your last phone conversation Zareh asked you how old you were. Prior to that, we had thought we must be wrong because we believed you had to be several years too old if you were in law school. But when you confirmed that you were the right age, Zareh asked me to talk to you. He said you should know your birth name; if it was 'Firinne', then you are Eireen's daughter."

Gareth paused, and Sigrun broke in. "I'm so confused. Correct me if I'm wrong ... but, you're telling me that you and Zareh can perform magic, right?"

"I would not put it quite that way, but," he said with a note of amusement in his voice, "yes, that is essentially correct."

"Then why has Zareh been sitting in prison waiting to be executed for the past 20 years?" she asked with incredulity.

Gareth sighed. "That too is a bit complicated. However, the short answer is that it's forbidden for anyone to use Power to rescue him as long as he has been convicted of a crime. And, regardless, as long as Zareh is confined within a steel prison, neither he nor anyone else has the ability to assist him. You see, steel interferes with our access to the Grid and prevents the use of Power."

"Right! So you wouldn't be able to demonstrate this 'Power' now because of the car?" Sigrun asked sardonically.

He laughed. "That was quick. You're correct that my access to the Grid is limited while I am in the car, even with the top down. You're also right to be skeptical, but I **can** show you as soon as we arrive at my house. That is, unless you've changed your mind and would rather turn around."

She hesitated and then said truthfully, "I have no idea what I think."

"I understand that this is difficult for you to accept on my word alone. We're nearly at my home. Let me show you something that will assist you in believing me."

They stopped at a red light in town, and he asked, "Would you like to pick up something to eat?"

"No. I can't say I feel much like eating."

After a few blocks, they pulled into the driveway of a deep lot. A tiny wooden house was set back from the street in the shade of several large pine trees. He parked by a bed of exuberantly colorful flowers. "Please come inside."

Sigrun slowly climbed out of the car and stopped, giving Gareth a wary look. His car was one thing, but his house?

He nodded. "You should be cautious. I promise you that I will **never** harm you. But you have no reason to believe me." He unlocked the front door. "Do you drive?"

"Uh … yeah."

"Here." He tossed her his keys. "The car is unlocked. You have the keys. If you feel you are in danger – take my car and leave."

Sigrun eyed the keys. That plan, of course, was premised on the assumption that she would be able to escape and get to the car. She shot him a questioning look. He was waiting patiently at the open front door. He didn't **look** like a lunatic, not that she would know. Of course he didn't look in the slightest like a space alien either. But … the bottom line was: There was no way she was going to walk away from this and spend the rest of her life wondering. She put the keys in her pocket with a shrug. "Okay."

He breathed a sigh of relief and indicated that she should precede him. "Go on through the kitchen." He closed, but did not lock, the front door. "I want to go outside."

Sigrun looked around curiously as she crossed first the short hallway and then a minuscule kitchen; it seemed entirely normal and earth-like. She stepped out the back door onto a brick patio that substantially filled the small back yard, which ended at a low cinder block wall abutting a vast open field that stretched to the horizon. In the distance, she could just make out the crests of breaking waves; she could hear the distant pounding of the surf and the calls of seagulls. Apart from the open field, the yard was completely screened from the view of the neighboring yards by tall, thick pine trees.

"Please, sit." He motioned toward a solid redwood table surrounded by four matching chairs. "I'll make us some tea and bring out what I wish to show you."

Sigrun sat and stared blankly at the table, her thoughts spinning about chaotically in her head. She felt too numb to compose a coherent question. This was beyond belief! He simply must be delusional. A parallel world!? That was the stuff of bad science fiction. And how could Zareh be her uncle?

Soon, Gareth returned bearing a tray with steaming mugs of tea and a plate of chocolate-dipped tea biscuits. He placed the tray on the table. "I know you said you weren't hungry, but I find that chocolate helps me focus my thoughts."

"Thank you." She wavered but, feeling rather weak, she took a sip of tea and reached for a biscuit. Then she drew her hand back – if he did have nefarious motives, he might be attempting to poison her. She decided to stick with the tea. Only after a second sip did the thought present itself that, of course, the tea was just as likely to be spiked as were the biscuits.

Gareth settled into the chair facing the open field and set something on the table. "This is a drawing from your parents' nuptials. You should recognize Zareh – he has changed remarkably little. And," he added as she picked up the framed picture, "you do look a lot like your father."

Sigrun scrutinized the drawing suspiciously. The lines were so fine and detailed that it looked almost like a color photograph. She stared at the oddly dressed group of men and women arrayed on a black-sand beach with a deep blue ocean behind them. Gareth was right; she did recognize Zareh. And, could that possibly be her birth mother standing next to him? She touched the face of the woman with a tentative finger. It was … inconceivable. She examined the picture for an extremely long time. The surroundings fit her mental image of Hawaii. Beyond that, it was like no wedding picture she had ever seen. The bride and groom stood at the center of the group with their hands bound together with a cord of green leaves. Everyone wore leis of white flowers, and the bride had a lei woven into her dark brown hair. With a start, she spotted a much younger Gareth at the edge of the group. Looking closely at the groom, she did discern some resemblance to herself – he was somewhat short, with the same thick, wavy, brown hair and brown eyes. But really, what did that prove?

After a time, her brain seemingly incapable of forming words, she returned the picture to the table. Reeling with shock and feeling wobbly, she picked up her tea and reached for a biscuit. So … was she hallucinating? Or was this some complex plot, and Gareth had produced the drawing as a prop? That struck her as preposterous – and for what purpose? At a loss, she mechanically ate her biscuit while gazing unseeingly into her tea. Then, finally latching onto a practical thought, she remembered that he had offered to demonstrate his "magic." She looked up to find him watching her closely.

"How are you doing?" he asked.

She ignored the question. "Back in the car, you said you could show me your … uh, Power once we got here?"

"I can. But, you must first promise that you will keep my secret. I asked you to trust me by coming here; but if I show you my Power, I am trusting you with knowledge you could use to force me to leave Earth. You must agree not to reveal a word about Kaia to anyone."

"I hadn't thought of that," said Sigrun. So, in the unlikely event his story was true, he was risking something in telling her. But, even so, was she willing to keep this quiet? On the other hand, she remained intensely curious. "Okay, I promise not to tell anyone." Of course, she thought wryly, they'd probably lock her up if she tried.

"All right then," he said, suddenly sounding rather jovial as he reached into the front pocket of his jeans. He withdrew an unset gemstone – rectangular in shape and a transparent golden-yellow in color – and held it toward her on the palm of his large hand. "This is my focus stone. We use such stones to concentrate the Power of the Grid to perform complex tasks." Gareth placed the stone on the table.

Sigrun gasped. "The necklace," she said with dawning realization. She reached out a finger and cautiously touched the stone. She felt nothing. "Her necklace – it's …" She looked up to find him regarding her with a pleased expression.

"Yes," he said, "Eireen's necklace was a focus stone."

"So, that's why Zareh …" Sigrun suddenly recalled the other gemstones. "Wait – the ruby and the quartz – are they also?"

"That's right. Everyone on Kaia has at least one focus stone. But a stone isn't necessary for something simple, like sending my empty mug back to the kitchen." He pointed to his mug, which lifted smoothly into the air and, following his point, headed through the open back door.

He looked back at Sigrun, who was studying him with bemusement.

"How about something more impressive?" He turned toward the other side of the patio, where an open firepit was stacked neatly with several logs. With a wave of his hand, the logs burst into flames.

Startled, she said, "I'm sure there's a perfectly logical explanation for those tricks. After all, lots of magicians make a good living performing similar feats."

"Right you are," he said with a laugh. "I can see you are not going to be easy to convince. Trouble is, I don't want to draw attention to myself by doing anything unusual." He looked around briefly and then said, "So, come inside, I can show you something I do frequently enough."

Gareth picked up the stone and headed inside without checking to see whether Sigrun was following. After a few seconds, she stood up; well, she thought with a shrug, no reason not to see more before she ran screaming from the house.

Gareth led the way down the hall to a small bedroom, where he stopped next to a pile of dirty clothing on the floor.

"I don't usually share my untidy habits with my guests, but," he said, "I think this 'trick' might convince you. Because this is more complex, I need to use my topaz." As he spoke, he held the stone in front of the pile of laundry. He then studied the stone in his hand for several seconds. She watched in open-mouthed amazement as, after a long flash of deep magenta light, each piece of clothing picked itself off the floor, shook itself briskly, folded itself neatly, and flew off to land on various shelves and in drawers that slid open as the items approached.

Sigrun looked back and forth between Gareth, who stood, still and silent, concentrating on the stone he held in front of the rapidly dwindling pile of laundry, and the clothing that flew in several directions at once. Feeling weak-kneed, she leaned against the door frame behind her. "You do this often?"

"Yes," said Gareth cheerfully. "Why wash clothing when the Grid can do it for me? If I haven't frightened you off for good, you will find that I hate household chores and never do anything myself that my Power can accomplish."

"Oh!" Sigrun murmured. "Maybe I could sit down?"

"My apologies." He gave her a worried look as the clothing in the air fell limply to the floor. "I did not intend to upset you. Let's go back outside." He took her elbow.

Unnerved by the jolt that accompanied his touch, she jerked her arm away and said testily, "Don't worry, I won't faint."

"I am sorry. I know this has been a terrible shock for you."

Sigrun perched on a patio chair and gazed vacantly across the field. What **was** going on? She attempted to marshal her muddled thoughts, but she could think of no even remotely plausible explanation. Yet, somehow, she didn't believe that he was nuts. And even if he was, that couldn't account for what she had just seen. She stared hard at Gareth's back as he stood at the wall looking out over the distant ocean. He appeared so ... ordinary. Well, perhaps not ordinary, but surely nothing like someone from another planet should look.

Finally, without turning, Gareth asked, "I haven't grown two heads, have I?"

"It wouldn't surprise me," she said, abandoning her attempt to square his innocuous facade with the absurdity of his story. "Are you **sure** you're not crazy?"

"I am not crazy," he said, turning toward her, "and neither are you. How about doing something familiar, like going out to dinner?"

"Dinner?" Sigrun said blankly, as if the word were new to her.

"Yes, dinner. I could conjure up something here, but I thought you might prefer something less challenging."

She realized that she was staring at Gareth again as she wondered what, exactly, he meant by "conjure up" dinner. Intrigued, she said, "No, actually, I'd rather stay here and see more of your 'magic'."

"Splendid. What do you eat? How about linguini with peas and broccoli fresh from the Farmers' Market in a white wine sauce?"

"You ... shop," she asked with astonishment, "at a Farmers' Market?"

"I do. Unfortunately, our 'magic' does not encompass producing food with a wave of a hand, or a focus stone for that matter! Although I can create this," Gareth said as he rapidly moved his left hand – in which he still held his focus stone – through a complicated series of motions. In a burst of bright green light, a long-stemmed yellow rose appeared in his right hand.

Sigrun gasped.

"For you." He handed her the rose with a small flourish.

"Oh!" She took the rose gingerly. As she touched it, she felt a slight tingling sensation in her fingers.

"It looks and feels real – but smell it."

She did so; it had no scent. "It's not ... real?"

"No, it is merely a vessel to hold Power that I shaped like a rose. It will vanish once it has consumed its small reserve of Power."

Sigrun studied the rose and stroked its soft petals – it seemed pretty much like a rose. "So, is everything you do an illusion?"

"No, not at all. I realize I keep saying this, but utilizing Power is rather complicated, and there are many types of gifts. I happen to be able to create small objects – like that," he added with a gesture to the rose, which was fading.

She looked at her now empty hand as the rose disappeared. Her fingers ceased tingling. "Well, in that case," she said dryly, "I guess it's good you can't create food."

"I promise that what I prepare will not vanish as you eat. In truth, I am not a bad cook. Come, I'll show you."

They went into the kitchen. "The washroom is down the hall if you'd care to wash up while I get started."

Grateful for a moment alone, Sigrun went off to the bathroom. When she returned, she found Gareth in the middle of a bustling scene. A bowl of peas on the table was shelling itself as an onion was being rapidly chopped on a large wooden chopping block under his watchful eye. Just then, he turned the water off in the sink, where a large copper pot had been filling. He waved toward the stove, and the pot floated over to land gently on a burner. Gareth followed it, turned on the burner, and added some salt to the water. "Do you drink wine?"

"Not legally," she responded absently, watching the whirl of activity with some consternation.

"Right. I forgot how young you are. No wine."

Dinner was ready in a surprisingly short time, and they ate on the patio with a fire crackling in the firepit while watching the sun set over the ocean. It was not until Gareth had gone inside to make coffee that it occurred to her that she was not at all uneasy in his company. Was she being an utter fool, she wondered? But he was so … likable.

"The coffee," he said as he returned carrying two tall mugs, "is from my home island – what you would call the Big Island of Hawaii. I hope you enjoy it."

"Thank you." Sigrun picked up a mug and inhaled the rich aroma of strong coffee. Then she drew back and eyed it warily. "You … brought it with you?"

"Yes. I am afraid I am rather partisan about some things Kaian – like coffee."

She set the mug down assertively. "So why are you living here?"

He smiled. "If by 'here' you mean Earth, the answer is to assist Zareh."

"Really?" She sat back, leaving her coffee untouched. "But why Cambria then?"

"I moved here about ten years ago. At first, I lived close to San Quentin so I could visit Zareh more often. But I found living in such a dense urban area too claustrophobic. I need open space and the ocean. I was familiar with Cambria because … well, because Eireen was living here when she was killed."

"How did they end up in Cambria?"

"The portal is near here." He gestured across the field. "Above the beach."

"What's a portal?"

"That is a bit too complicated for so late in the day – just think of it as a means to travel between the two worlds."

"Right." He must be a psychopath. But, even accepting that he was deranged … how could that account for what she had seen tonight? No – it must be that **she** was losing her mind.

"By the way," he asked after a lengthy silence, "would you be willing to drive up to San Quentin tomorrow to see Zareh? He is anxious to talk to you."

"I don't think so." Sigrun was quite taken aback at the thought of dealing with Zareh in her present emotional state.

"Anyway, tomorrow is Sunday – we couldn't get there before the end of visiting hours."

"After all these years, I have contacts at the prison; we would not have a problem gaining admission."

"I don't know," she said defensively, "I'm not sure I want to see him."

"That's fine," Gareth said easily. "You can decide in the morning. But perhaps we should call it a night now."

Instantly wary again, she got to her feet. "I don't want to stay …"

"Don't worry," he said calmly, "I have reserved a room for you at a small inn near here. You can even drive yourself if you prefer."

Chagrined at her unfounded suspicion, she pulled his keys from her pocket and set them on the table. "I wouldn't drive your car."

"I trust you."

"Oh, but I …" she trailed off in bewilderment.

"Perhaps I have given you too much to absorb at one time. Try to get some sleep, and we can revisit things tomorrow."

⚓

Chapter 14
Actus secundus
(Second act)

The next morning, Sigrun awoke exceedingly early, judging by the quality of the light edging past the drawn curtains. She surveyed the strange room in some surprise. She had been certain that she was dreaming and would wake in her dorm room. But, she realized with nearly crushing disappointment, she appeared to be in a motel room. Clutching at the faint possibility that she was somewhere – **anywhere** – other than where she feared she was, she jumped out of bed and pulled back the curtain on the window. Yep – that was the ocean; it must be Cambria. So, then, it was not a dream.

Feeling an acute need for air, she dressed quickly and went outside. She crossed the street to a path leading down to a boardwalk at the edge of a sandy beach, randomly turned right, and started walking. Despite the beauty, Sigrun was filled with an oppressive foreboding. As she strolled slowly along the empty boardwalk in the early morning light, she struggled to make sense of the previous day's events.

She stopped to watch a boy tossing a stick into the waves for his dog to fetch. Standing there by herself on a beach in California, she was staggered by the total transformation that had taken place in her life in the short time since her father had died. After nearly 20 years of feeling loved and secure in familiar surroundings, how was it that she had come to be alone on the other side of the country having a conversation about parallel worlds, Power, portals, and her parents with a man she barely knew? Then again, bizarre as it seemed, Gareth apparently knew more about her than just about anyone.

She needed to call Philip; she should have called the night before, but she had been too discombobulated after Gareth had dropped her at the motel to figure out what to say. Should she tell him? She desperately wanted to get his reaction. Since her father's death and the fire, the only person in the world she had any real ties to was Philip. She just had to tell him. How could she not? But, she thought bleakly, she'd promised not to. And it was hardly a topic that lent itself easily to abridgment – especially in a phone call. Overwhelmed, she sat down on the edge of the boardwalk. The boy and the dog moved on; she had the beach to herself.

She pulled out her phone. "How are you?" she asked when Philip answered grumpily.

"Oh, you know, pretty much the same. How about you?"

"Depressed. Lonely. Missing you."

"Well, that makes me feel a bit better. But are things not going well with your visit? I was kinda surprised you didn't call last night."

"Yeah, well, I planned to. But I … I was feeling … oh, I don't know, I was … disconnected. So I just went to bed. Not that I slept much." She pushed her hair back as it was swept into her face by the breeze, still debating saying something. "I'm staying in a motel across from the beach, and I came out for a walk."

"So, what did they want to talk to you about?"

"Oh, well, we didn't really get into the habeas case much yesterday. Gareth wants to drive up to San Quentin today."

"You're staying up there another night?"

"I guess so. I hadn't given it a thought. What are your plans?"

"Brian should be here soon. Like we talked about, we're going over to the farm and start an inventory of what's salvageable."

"I hope it's not too tough on you."

"I've got to do it. Having Brian will help – you know he's not the sentimental type."

"I should have stayed."

"No! You made a commitment, and you've got to live up to it. I'll get by."

"I know." Sigrun hesitated, sorely tempted … to say what? He'd think she'd gone off the deep end. And she had promised. "I'm just feeling … well, have you ever stopped to think about the fact that you're the only person in the world I really know?"

"Yeah," he said wryly, "actually, I have. Why do you think I want to sell everything and come to California?"

"Oh! Well, you're a step ahead of me. It just hit me this morning."

"Chin up – at least you've got a network started at school. And there's Gareth – it seems like he cares about you?"

If ever there was a slippery slope! She simply couldn't go

there, so she moved on. "Anyway, I don't mean to weigh you down. It's something about being out in nature – it makes me feel insignificant."

"Hey, a little insignificance isn't bad. Remember, you're but a grain of sand. It prevents you from getting puffed up."

"Yeah, right. Anyway, I suppose I should let Gareth know I'm up – I think he wants to get an early start."

"Okay. Let me know how it goes."

"Yeah. I'll be sure to call tonight. You keep your chin up too."

So, she thought with a heavy sigh, she had lied to Philip. And it seemed that she was going to see Zareh after all. But, she thought with a flicker of anticipation, maybe now he'd tell her the real story. Before she could change her mind and call Philip back, she phoned Gareth.

"Hello." He sounded as if he had been asleep.

"Oh, I'm sorry, it's Sigrun. Did I wake you?"

"No problem," said Gareth, "I don't mind answering the phone before 7:00 in the morning as long as you're calling to tell me that we should take a drive up the coast."

"I think we should take a drive up the coast."

"Good. I'll get dressed and pick you up in half an hour. We can stop for some coffee and a pastry in town."

❧❧

Despite Gareth's confidence that they would have no problem getting in, they encountered a long wait once they arrived at San Quentin. They maintained an awkward silence most of the time, constrained from engaging in anything apart from small talk by both the close proximity of other visitors and the incessant din of the processing room. Finally, they passed through the second security screening and were left to wait again in the small visiting room for condemned prisoners, which, Sigrun was relieved to see, was otherwise empty.

She was agitated as they waited for Zareh's arrival. Could he possibly be her uncle? It was ridiculous. Yet, somehow it seemed … almost self-evident. She could not reconcile her incredulity with the inexplicable connection she'd always felt to the case. But, if she **were** related to Zareh, then didn't the rest of it have to be true as well? She flatly rejected that idea. And she simply couldn't accept the mind-boggling coincidence of stumbling onto his case. So … there must be another explanation; she just hadn't thought of it yet.

Gareth reached over and placed his hand on top of the ones she was twisting in her lap. Startled, she looked up.

"Don't worry," he said gently, "Zareh is a generous and thoughtful person once you get past his reserve. You have not had a chance to get to know him."

"Mr. Malama," called a guard in the doorway.

As they took their seats in one of the booths, Zareh was led into the steel cage on his side of the partition. His sharp gaze immediately fell on Sigrun. She saw his usually impassive expression slip into uncertainty before he quickly regained his control. They remained silent while the guards retreated slightly.

"Greetings," Zareh said evenly. "I wasn't expecting both of you."

"We thought we would surprise you," Gareth said cheerfully. "Sigrun and I had a lovely long chat yesterday."

"Really," Zareh said, sounding guarded. "And?"

"She wanted to see her uncle today," he responded softly.

Zareh, who had been watching Gareth closely, turned his eyes to Sigrun. He examined her in silence for what felt like a long time. "Please," he asked tersely, "hold your hair away from your face."

She did as he asked, flushing slightly under his close scrutiny.

Finally he nodded and his expression relaxed into a slight smile. "Yes," he said in a barely audible voice, "I should have seen it immediately, but I wasn't looking. Sigrun, you look a great deal like your father."

"As soon as you told me," Gareth said, "I detected the resemblance."

"I'm sorry, Kako," Zareh said. "I always wanted you to know, but the others thought it was best if you didn't."

"That is not important now," Gareth said dismissively. "I've told her the truth about her situation to the extent that I know it."

"Do you believe him?" Zareh asked Sigrun bluntly.

Meeting his eyes, Sigrun responded honestly, "I don't know what to believe. I have a hard time ..."

Before she could continue, Gareth placed his hand on her arm and made a small gesture toward a watchful guard.

"I'm not sure that I do," she concluded.

Holding her gaze, Zareh asked in his usual expressionless manner, "Do you believe that I did not kill Eireen and Ed?"

"Yes! **That** I knew long before yesterday. But the rest of the story is ... difficult."

"Do you have something that came with you as an infant?"

Zareh asked.

"Why ... yes, I do."

"It's a small wooden box that is carved on top with the name 'Firinne', and it's lined with soft emerald-green cloth," Zareh said, so quietly that she had to listen intently to catch his words.

Sigrun gasped. "How did you know?"

"Because your mother gave it to you shortly after you were born, and I carved your name on it," Zareh responded, still speaking softly and sounding sorrowful. He paused and looked away. She thought she saw the glint of tears in his eyes. "It's the only thing you have that she gave you."

Throwing a quick look at the guard, she said inadequately, "I had no idea."

"We needed to conceal your identity from you for your own safety." Turning to Gareth, Zareh said, "Kako, I must, as always, depend on you. You need to contact Greer immediately; she believes they have learned that a child exists. Sigrun must be protected."

"Protected from what?" she asked.

"Not here," Gareth replied firmly. To Zareh he said cryptically, "I could take her for a visit."

"No," said Zareh, too loudly. "Absolutely not! It's far too dangerous."

At the raised voice, the guard stepped closer and gestured to Zareh to go.

Zareh leaned forward and said quickly to Sigrun, "Be extremely cautious; don't trust **anyone** other than Gareth or Greer. No one!" he added as the guard grabbed his arm.

Gareth grabbed Sigrun's arm in turn and said, "Let's get out of here."

They did not talk while exiting. Once at the car, he said, "Would you mind if I put the top down? Being in the prison always leaves me with a need for air."

As soon as they were underway, Sigrun asked, "Who is Greer?"

"Greer is the woman with whom Zareh left you that night," Gareth explained. "I assume she is the one who took you to Pennsylvania, but I am not certain. All I know is that she returned home to Kaia shortly after the murders. She is also a first cousin to Zareh and Eireen's mother, Firinne, for whom you were named."

"Will I be meeting her?" she asked curiously. Somehow, she had yet to consider the possibility of other "new" relatives.

"Soon, I hope. Greer," he continued, "has always been at the core of the opposition – a group that we call the Kestää – that is battling to protect Kaia's veridictrices, maintain the equilibrium of the Grid, and, ultimately, preserve Kaia."

"Very whats?"

"A veridictrix is a woman who has the gift of seeing and interpreting a person's prospective paths."

"What do you mean by 'paths'?"

"It is an extraordinarily complex concept, but a path is a possible future."

"Like a fortune-teller?"

Gareth laughed. "Not at all. A veridictrix does not make predictions, she sees possibilities. It is a gift of precognition."

"I don't think I understand."

"I do not believe that I am the appropriate person to expound on that topic. Perhaps you could ask Greer. I plan to contact her after our return to Cambria, and, if she thinks it safe, I would like her to come and meet you."

"Why wouldn't it be safe?"

"I do not mean to be evasive, but I could not possibly explain the situation in one conversation, even if I knew all the details, which I do not."

"But ..." Sigrun interrupted, only to be cut off by Gareth's upheld hand.

"Wait. I will answer your questions to the best of my abilities, but I am not equipped to describe the political upheavals on Kaia over the past few decades. You must keep in mind that I've been living here for 20 years – Greer is much more knowledgeable than I. She is, and always has been, central to our struggle. Suffice it to say that you will face grave danger from the people responsible for killing your parents. Once they have confirmed your existence, they will take steps to eliminate you."

Taken aback both by the unexpected sternness of the statement and the uncomfortable thought that someone might want to "eliminate" her, Sigrun changed the subject. "Okay, then tell me how you contact Greer if she's on Kaia."

"That I can answer," he said readily. "Greer is uncommonly gifted. One of her gifts is loquansmente, or the ability to converse mind-to-mind. The ability is not itself rare – I share it with her as, I am confident, you do as well – but to have the ability to communicate between worlds is less common. Once we have returned to my house, where we have erected shields that obstruct others from monitoring certain of my connections to the Grid, I can alert Greer that I wish to talk to her and, when she too is shielded, she will contact me. We can then 'talk' mind-to-mind."

"Really?" The thought was not as unsettling as it should have been; she must be growing numb. "Can others hear this … talk?"

"Yes, in general. In our case, however, the special shields we both have in place prevent others from listening. In addition, Greer has an unusual gift of being able to 'hide' her access to the Grid. As I told you yesterday, whenever we connect to the Grid, we cause a disruption that is detectable. Greer, however, is able to access it without a discernible disruption, which enables her to use the portals without leaving a record."

Feeling immensely intimidated at the thought of meeting this impressive-sounding woman, Sigrun decided to shift the focus to something a bit more approachable. "So, apart from this 'loquans-mente', what else can you do?"

"Oh, I am not particularly gifted."

"That's not true!"

Gareth shot her a quizzical look. "Why do you say that?"

"I don't know," she said impatiently, "why does anyone ever think someone's not being completely truthful?"

"But you had no reason to think my statement false," he said logically. "What about this, is this a true statement: Most of the males in my family share an ability to communicate with animals?"

Nonplussed, she hesitated for a long moment. "Yeah … that's true."

"You had no facts on which to judge the truth of that statement. Why do you, correctly I might add, think that it's true?"

Flustered, Sigrun thought hard – what had prompted her response? Before she could formulate a guess, he continued.

"Think about what you see when I say this: Your mother was a joyful, exuberant, headstrong individual."

"Was she?"

"Yes she was, but what did you see?"

"Oh yeah … uhm, I'm not sure what you mean."

"Close your eyes and think about the difference in your response to these: One, I prefer to live in a city because I thrive on the stimulus of an urban environment; and two, I love this portion of the drive because the coast is so beautiful and wild."

"The color?" Opening her eyes, she ventured, "I kind of see different … colors."

"Good," said Gareth approvingly. "Now, what do you see in

response to my saying: Once you have been taught how to access the Grid, you too will be able to communicate with animals?"

Sigrun considered for a moment with closed eyes. "I don't know. ... I didn't really see a color – it's sort of ... mingled?"

"Splendid. That is because I do not know whether my last statement is true or false since we do not yet know what gifts you have."

"I don't understand – what do the colors mean, and how did you know?"

"You see colors because you have a gift for judging the truth. It's a gift that your mother shared. And, because I grew up with her, I recognize how it manifests."

"Really! Do I have other of these, uh, 'gifts'?"

"Yes," he said without hesitation, "I am certain that you do."

Sigrun realized that, in the tumult of the past two days, she had not spared a thought for the idea that – if she bought his story – **she** too had the ability to use this so-called "Power." The concept was so intriguing that it pushed her trepidation to the background. "Can you teach me how to use them?" she asked eagerly.

Unexpectedly, Gareth laughed heartily. "Now you sound just like your mother. I was older than Eireen, so I started school a year ahead of her. Each time I saw her during my first year at the Academy, she wanted me to show her everything I had learned. Eireen was always more ambitious than I – not to mention considerably more talented! Yes, I can teach you. But," he added, "not before I speak with Greer."

Deciding not to push things, she said, "Okay, but could I watch while you communicate with her?"

"Certainly." Gareth seemed pleased. "I have been trying to determine how best to tell you that I'd prefer that you not return to the inn. We suspect that Zareh's visitors are being monitored. By accompanying me, it is possible that you've drawn attention to yourself. And, if you wish to watch, which, I am afraid, will be most boring, you'll have to stay with me because I don't know how long it will take Greer to respond to my hail."

Sigrun was torn between lingering apprehension that he was luring her into a false sense of complacency and anticipation at seeing another of Gareth's demonstrations. Maybe, she thought hopefully, she could start making sense of things if she had more information. "Okay, but I'm getting hungry. We didn't have any lunch."

"Right! I had forgotten. How unlike me to overlook a meal. You have good timing – I know a place just ahead that shouldn't be crowded so early."

In a few miles, they turned off the highway and, a short while later, pulled into the parking lot of an uninspiring little place at the end of a rundown-looking block across the street from the beach. After they had ordered, Sigrun asked, "I was wondering, what was that word Zareh used for you?"

"Oh, he calls me 'Kako'. It's an endearment based on a Hawaiian word that loosely means to provide support," he answered, sounding embarrassed. "He persists in believing that he would not survive without me, but, in reality, he is an amazingly strong person."

Gareth leaned forward, his face taking on a somber expression. "Sigrun, I know you've found Zareh's emotionless facade difficult and off-putting, but you must remember that he was only 18 when he saw his sister, to whom he was extremely close, brutally killed in front of his eyes. And he has spent the last 19 or so years believing that he will be executed for her murder. It might not appear so now, but he was utterly devastated when he was sentenced to death. I believe he had not even understood that it was a possibility – on Kaia, there is no capital punishment."

"I'm ashamed," she admitted. "I never tried to see the situation from his point of view. It never occurred to me to think about why he was so uncommunicative."

"It is his armor," said Gareth soberly. "He had to learn to withdraw emotionally from his surroundings in order to retain a sense of his inner self – and, I believe, his sanity. If he does not allow himself to feel, he can hold his hopelessness at bay. But," he added in his typically cheerful tone as the server approached with their dinners, "Zareh would not thank me for discussing his emotions with you."

∞ Chapter 15 ∞
Certis rebus certa signa praecurrunt
(Certain signs precede certain events;
Marcus Tullius Cicero)

"I have a very small guest room that you are very welcome to use." Gareth opened the first door on the short hallway at his house and set Sigrun's suitcase in the sparsely furnished room.

"Do you mind if I change?" she asked, gesturing at the skirt she had put on for the prison visit.

"Go ahead – I'll be on the patio."

After changing into jeans and a T-shirt, she found Gareth seated in one of the two chairs he had brought over to the firepit, where a fire blazed. Two tall mugs sat on a small table between them. It was a lovely, balmy evening; the sun had not yet set.

"I made you some coffee," Gareth said when he caught sight of her, "but I should have asked first, do you drink coffee this late in the day?"

She took the other chair. "Too often."

"I assumed so – it seems to be a weakness in your family. Zareh frequently says he misses good coffee more than decent food."

"Really," she murmured absently, contemplating the conundrum of the coffee. If it had originated in a world whose physical properties were unknown to her, then perhaps it was not safe to drink. But if she were sufficiently leery of the coffee not to drink it, then she was necessarily conceding that this … world existed. Oh, what the hell, she thought as she picked up the mug and took a sip of hot coffee.

"So," he said, "I'll contact Greer now and let her know that I need to speak with her when she has the time and is secure. Then we can talk while I wait."

Sigrun kicked off her sandals and tucked one leg under herself as she settled into her chair to watch. Gareth cradled his focus stone in the hands he held cupped in his lap. He stared at it intently

– silently and without expression – for several minutes. She considered him curiously while sipping her coffee, wondering how the stone helped. She shook her head. That was altogether inadequate: She wondered what it was that he was doing, what it felt like to engage in this "loquansmente", how one could communicate between two worlds – a whole host of things. Now that she stopped to think about it, how was it even physically possible to have parallel planets; did they occupy the same space? But that just wasn't feasible. So ... was this proof that the multiple universe proponents were right? But in that case ...

"I am done." Gareth's voice shook Sigrun out of her reverie. "I caught Greer in a free moment, but she has several things she needs to address immediately. I assured her that I wasn't in a hurry, so she's going to take care of her other commitments before contacting me. Then I will ask her if she can come and meet you."

Sigrun studied Gareth apprehensively. It was altogether incredible, yet he seemed honest. And sane. "So," she asked uncertainly, "you were ... communicating with this woman, Greer?"

"Yes."

She nodded. "And she's on ... Kaia?"

"Yes." He sounded amused. "In Hawaii."

"Oh. You hadn't mentioned that. Greer lives in Hawaii too?"

"Yes, the capital of Kaia – Maluhia – is in Hawaii, roughly where Honolulu is."

For some reason, this detail struck Sigrun as even more outlandish than others he had told her. She gave up with a shake of her head. "I'm afraid my skepticism is getting the best of me."

Gareth nodded. "All right. Let me tell you a story while I wait for Greer." He gave a wry smile. "Trust me, it will be difficult to deny the reality of Greer."

"Okay. But, would you mind if I make a quick call to Philip first? I told him I'd call tonight, and he'll worry if he doesn't hear from me."

"Please do. I'll go inside; come find me when you're through."

"Oh, no, I don't want ..."

"You're my guest," he said, picking up his mug, "I want you to be comfortable."

"I won't be long." Sigrun pulled her phone out of her pocket, took a deep breath, and called. "How did your day go?" she asked.

"Not bad," Philip replied evenly. "I managed to get through with only one total breakdown. It was the basketball, of all things – I just lost it. … Anyway, Brian was a saint; he ignored my tears and kept me focused. But I'm afraid it's a lot more tedious than I thought – I've loads left to do."

"But are you up to being over there by yourself?"

He sighed. "I guess I have to be. Ray said he could help next weekend, and Brian's free again on Sunday. I could probably find someone else during the week, but I really don't want to be there with someone I don't know well."

"Are you sure you don't want me to come back?"

"Yes. Thanks for offering, but you've got to finish that petition."

"Yeah, but …" Sigrun trailed off, suddenly realizing that it seemed as though she did have a vested interest in the case after all.

"No 'buts', I'll manage. So tell me, what did they want to talk to you about?"

"Oh," she said, ready for the question, having spent part of the drive from San Quentin composing her response and bolstering her resolve not to say anything to Philip just yet, "it's just that Zareh did know the victims after all. You know how I've been wondering how he happened by just at the right moment?"

"He knew them?"

"He'd been living in Cambria since that summer and had run into them around town – it's a pretty small place. They had taken pity on him because he was so young and was on his own, so they'd invited him over a couple of times. That night, he says, he stopped by and found the door open."

"So," he asked slowly, "he stops by at midnight, finds his friends dead, and rifles their place rather than calling the police?"

"Yeah, well, I guess that's why he was reluctant to tell me. It doesn't exactly make him a sympathetic character." What a lame story, Sigrun thought – she had never been any good at lying. Luckily, Philip seemed too preoccupied to notice.

"Not exactly! So why now?"

"No clue. It's been a weird weekend. I'm feeling kind of … adrift."

"Where are you, at the motel?"

"Yeah." She felt a sharp stab of guilt at yet another lie. "I'm planning to go back to school tomorrow, but I don't know what time. Maybe I can call you on the train? I don't feel much like talking now."

"Are you all right?"

"Yeah. You know my funk from this morning – well it's worse, and I'm ... oh, I don't know. I wish you were here."

"I wish you were here, but we both have stuff we've got to get done."

"Yeah. Well ... do you mind if we just talk tomorrow?"

"No, that's okay. Call anytime."

Sigrun sat staring sadly at the glorious sunset, mired in confusion and remorse over her lies. But, despite herself, she was soon buoyed by the sheer beauty of the scene. With an almost grudging anticipation at the thought of Gareth's promise to tell her more about Kaia, she went inside. She found him seated at a substantial desk crowded into a corner of the front room, reading an odd-looking newspaper.

"How is your friend?" he asked.

"He's getting by, but it wasn't a good day."

"Have a seat," Gareth said. He swiveled his chair to face her as she settled in a corner of the couch. "I gather you've known Philip a long time?"

"Since I was four."

"Does he have anyone to help him get through this apart from you?"

"Oh, well, he has other friends, but no, I mean ... he's not in a relationship, if that's what you're asking."

"I was merely wondering if you felt you needed to go back to assist him."

"Oh." She ducked behind her hair. "Yeah, I do. But, well, I can't, can I?"

"Was that rhetorical," he asked neutrally, "or are you soliciting my opinion?"

Startled, she looked up to meet his concerned eyes. "No, I mean, I know I need to finish the petition ... but, what is your opinion?"

He drew a deep breath. "I think it's important that you trust me," he said slowly, "so I'll admit that I am in a difficult position. I know you are doubtful, to say the least, about everything I've told you, and yet it's not safe for me to take you to Kaia to convince you. Unfortunately, I must also tell you that I believe it's no longer safe for you to travel by yourself."

She sat up straight. "What! You mean I can't go back to Pennsylvania?"

"I know you are having trouble accepting it, but we believe

that your life is, or soon will be, in extreme jeopardy. If Greer is correct and your existence has become known, it is inevitable that you will be targeted."

Sigrun shook her head with a shrug. "Yeah, well, I just don't buy that."

"So, let me work on convincing you. Shall we return to the patio, and I will tell you what we believe was the beginning of this saga."

Sigrun settled herself in one of the chairs by the fire as Gareth added more logs. It was now fully dark and stars were blanketing the clear sky.

Gareth set his topaz on the table between them. "So, we must go back about 30 years to the August when I was 17 and Eireen was 16. At that time, we were all living at Palepouli – which is the name of my family's estate on what you know as the Big Island of Hawaii. Firinne – Eireen's mother and your grandmother – had just returned home for the break that the Concilium takes for most of August and September each year. The evening of August 8th was dark and moonless. I was walking Eireen and Zareh, who was almost 8 then, back from dinner at the hale nui – the main house on the estate – when we heard Firinne arguing with your grandfather, Zeroun Fremont, on the lanai of their bungalow. We crept close to listen."

>[∼]⚭

"No, it's too dark," said Zeroun, a thin and stooped man, appearing older than his 54 years, "you mustn't go out tonight."

"Please, dear," Firinne said in a quiet and intense voice, "we've gone over this endlessly. I'm perfectly capable of protecting myself, and if I want to go riding, I'm going to go."

"Firinne, you're the veridictrix – you **know** that your path has become perilous."

She waved a dismissive hand. "That's the future. I've ridden these hills and cliffs for 25 years – I think I'm able to handle anything that's likely to come my way."

"But you told me that you saw movement in the paths last night."

"So?" Firinne tossed her thick auburn hair. "I didn't see anything specific. Zed, I've been working hard, and I want to feel the ocean breeze on my face. I won't be long, but I am going."

Zeroun laughed. "I guess I have only myself to blame."

"For what?"

"When I allowed you to convince me to marry you. I should have known that someone who was so obstinate at 18 would only grow more willful as she got older."

Firinne closed the distance between them. "Do you regret giving in to me?"

"Never for a moment," he murmured as he hugged her close.

She gave him a quick kiss and then pulled out of the embrace. "Good. Tell Zareh I'll be back to put him to bed, will you, please?"

She bounded energetically down the stairs from the lanai and threw a wave over her shoulder.

The three children shrank deeper into the shadows as Firinne strode quickly by on her way to the stables.

Eireen put a finger to her lips and pointed back the way they had come. They scurried across the space that separated the Fremont bungalow from the adjacent one, which was empty that night.

"I don't like it," Eireen said quietly.

"Why?" asked Gareth, a tall, pony-tailed youth.

"Mother saw something new in the paths. Remember Gareth, when I last checked, I told you things were cloudy and confused and nothing looked right?"

"Yeah," Gareth said slowly, "I do – do you think …"

"I don't know," she broke in, "I didn't see anything specific either, but I'm worried. You know Mother doesn't always think before she acts."

"What do you mean?" asked Zareh fearfully.

Eireen put her arm around the brown-haired

boy's thin shoulders. "Don't you worry – I'm probably imagining things, but here's what I want to do. Zareh, you go home and tell Father that I stayed at the hale nui to listen to Gavin and Gareth sing. Keep him from looking for me. Gareth, you come with me, and we'll follow Mother."

Gareth raised his eyebrows. "You're not supposed to go out alone after dark."

"I won't be alone!" she scoffed. "Can you do that?" she asked Zareh gently.

"Do you think it's a good idea?" he asked hesitantly.

"I'm sure Mother's right and she's perfectly safe, but it can't hurt if Gareth and I take a look, can it?"

"All right," he said. "I'll go and get Father to spin a story."

"Good idea, Zareh," she said warmly. "Thanks for your help. Run off now, and we'll wait until you're on the lanai before we leave."

Zareh scampered toward the Fremont bungalow and his young voice could be heard saying, "Greetings, Father."

Eireen pulled on Gareth's arm. They slipped into the shadows of the next building and stole stealthily toward the stables. Of course, Firinne had already left by the time Gareth had asked their horses to meet them at the edge of the corral, where they mounted bareback.

"So," Gareth asked quietly after they had opened the shield, slipped through the gate at the far side of the corral, and walked their horses carefully away from the stables, keeping to the darkest shadows, "where should we go?"

"Ask Argus to contact Mother's horse. She couldn't detect that, and we can find out where they are."

Gareth placed his hand on the side of his horse's neck. After a couple of minutes, he said, "They're crossing Pa'a Naele Flats pretty fast."

"Let's go." Eireen broke into a gallop, not

waiting to see if Gareth would follow, but follow
he did, catching her easily on his larger and more
powerful mount.

"Slow down," he called urgently. "Mr. Fremont's right – it's too dark to ride so fast."

"Don't come then."

"How will it help your mother if you cata-
pult into a crater?"

She slowed slightly. "And we're making too
much noise. Let's go quietly – they can't be that
far ahead."

The pair rode in silence until the edge of a
cliff came indistinctly into view. They slowed
and paralleled the cliff from a distance.

"Do you see anything?" Eireen whispered.

"It's too dark. Let me have Argus check
again." After a minute, he said with a note of
alarm, "Her horse didn't respond. Let's get
closer."

They quickly but cautiously rode to the edge
of the low sea cliffs and dismounted. They led
their horses along the bluff, searching for any
sign of Firinne. They didn't see anything until
they rounded a bend and confronted a gaping
hole in the ground just ahead of them.

"What! That wasn't here a couple of days
ago. Contact your father, and get some help."

Eireen pulled a green gemstone from her
pocket and cradled it.

Gareth left his horse with Eireen and
crawled toward the hole. He peered over the jag-
ged and unstable new edge and caught sight of
something where the waves were breaking on the
beach below. With a muttered exclamation, he
pulled out his topaz. Lying prone on the ground
so that he could cradle the gemstone in both
hands, he called forth a beam of pale yellow light
and sent it plunging over the edge of the cliff. In
the dim glow it cast when it neared the shore, he
could discern the bodies of a horse and a woman
lying at the water's edge. He closed his eyes
briefly in grief before squirming backwards until

he could safely stand.

Eireen watched him apprehensively.

He waited until he was close enough to grab her left arm firmly before he said, "They went over the cliff."

Eireen lunged toward the cliff with a wail, only to be stopped up short by his hold. "Let go of me!" She turned on him with fury.

"Is someone coming?"

"Yes. Let me go," she demanded, struggling against him. She still held her stone in her left hand, and she studied it briefly before drawing back her right arm and casting a thin bolt of amber light at Gareth's arm. He ducked and the bolt passed harmlessly by to fizzle out against a rock behind him. She drew back her arm to repeat the motion but Gareth yanked her closer and grabbed her other arm.

"Stop it! You can't get down that way. But if you stop fighting me, we can make our way around over there." He jerked his head to the side, where the cliff sloped more gradually toward the ocean.

"Let go!" She jerked against his hold.

"Do you promise not to bolt?"

"You're wasting time!"

"Look," he snapped, "I am not going to let you follow your mother over the cliff, so if you can't act reasonably, we'll have to wait for the others to get here."

"All right, we can go your way."

Gareth released her; she immediately raced by him.

"Haka! Slow down!" He followed a bit more slowly while drawing a new column of light from the gem in his left hand. He sent it forward so that it hovered just in front of Eireen, lighting her way. The two of them scrambled down the steep slope, slipping and sliding painfully on the eroding old lava. Reaching the narrow black sand beach, Eireen sprinted toward the body visible only as a lump in the distance. Gareth stopped to renew his light column. Once it gleamed brightly, he waved it forward until it illuminated the gruesome scene. He heard Eireen's wordless cry as the light fell on her mother's clearly lifeless body.

He then called up a vibrant red strip and stretched it from where he stood on the sand to as high in the sky as he could while holding it stable. As soon as it was steady, he rushed after Eireen, who had collapsed in the water in a crying heap next to her mother's head, which rested on what appeared to be a broken neck.

Gareth knelt down and felt for a pulse, but he knew it was hopeless. He stood and painstakingly scanned the surroundings in the dim light. Nothing appeared amiss apart from the newly fallen chunks of cliff that were scattered about the two bodies. He kicked at the sand in frustration – he didn't have the gifts to determine if anyone was nearby. He checked Firinne's horse; her neck also appeared to have been broken in the fall, and she too was dead.

He returned to wait silently with the sobbing Eireen. Eventually, they heard a hail from a distance. They looked up to see a crew clambering down the cliff where Gareth's marker still shone. He stood and waved his arms slowly in the air. "No need to hurry," he yelled.

It took them several hours to get both bodies back to Palepouli. While they were still at the beach, Greer Fortes, Firinne's cousin and friend, arrived from the capital, grim-faced and silent. She rigorously inspected the bodies, the beach, and the fallen pieces of cliff. When Gareth and Eireen left with the bodies, she was still there with Gavin, Gareth's older brother, examining the cliff top and the surrounding area. Gareth and Eireen told their story first to the rescuers, then to Greer, then to Zeroun back at Palepouli, and again to Alaric O'Suaird, Firinne's other cousin and the head of the Concilium, who arrived at first light the next morning from his home in Britannia, accompanied by the Concilium's Minister of Justice.   Firinne had been a prominent Conciltor, and her sudden death aroused instant suspicion.

But, despite repeated examination of the site, no sign was found that anyone had harmed either Firinne or her horse, or had been in the vicinity before the cliff had collapsed. Nor had anyone who didn't have a good reason to be there traveled through any of the three portals on the island within a week prior to the incident. The only odd finding was the evidence that Fir inne's horse had been sweating profusely before she died, indicating that she had been running hard.   In the end, the official investigation concluded that it had been a freak accident.

As soon as Zeroun told her early the following evening about the determination, Eireen, who hadn't slept since the incident, went tearing into the hale nui to find Gareth.

"Did you hear?" Eireen exclaimed scornfully as she burst without warning into Gareth's bedroom. "**They** think it was an accident."

"Yeah, they said they found nothing conclusive."

"They're wrong!" Eireen threw herself onto the middle of his bed and tucked her legs under her. She reached inside her tunic and pulled out an unset emerald and a small wooden box and set them on the bed. "I'm going to check the paths – will you watch my back?"

"Of course, but you know you're safe here."

"My mother wasn't."

"But she was out ... sure, go ahead." He settled himself on the floor with his back against the door so that he could keep an eye on Eireen as well as the window. He set his left hand, palm up, on his knee; rested his topaz in his hand; and established a deep link with the Grid.   He watched Eireen as she opened the box in front of her and pinched some of the grey-green powder it contained. She inserted the substance into a nostril and inhaled sharply. She repeated the process with her other nostril, and then shut her eyes, taking several slow, deep breaths. After a couple of minutes, she opened her eyes and picked up her stone. She sat, silent and still, for an exceedingly long time, concentrating on the emerald cradled in her cupped hands.

Finally, Eireen severed her link to the grid, sighed heavily, and rubbed her eyes. Her deeply suntanned face was pale and her eyes looked haunted when she met Gareth's gaze where he still sat on the floor. "I want to talk to Father, Aunt Greer, and Uncle Alaric in private. Would you gather them discreetly while I recover?"

"Are you all right?" Gareth broke his own link before getting stiffly to his feet.

"No, but I want to tell everyone at once."

"But ..."

Eireen gave a wan smile. "I'm fine. Go on, and let me know where we'll meet."

"All right," he said reluctantly. He glanced back as he left the room – she had rested her head in her hands.

Gareth returned shortly, knocking lightly before opening the door. "Are you ready?"

Eireen looked up from the same spot on the bed. "You didn't have to fetch me."

"I know, but I thought you might need help."

She stood and stretched her stiff legs. "I'm pretty spent."

"By the way," he asked nervously as they descended the deserted staircase, "is it all right if Gavin joins us? He saw me leaving Aunt Greer's and asked what I was doing, so I told him. I didn't think you would mind."

She was thoughtful while they managed an unobserved exit. "No one else. And can you shield us so no one can listen?"

"Uh ..." he said in surprise, "sure, if you want."

"Yes," she said, sounding suddenly far more mature than her years.

They entered the bungalow set on the out-
ermost edge of the estate. Greer, Alaric, Zeroun,
and Gavin, who looked nearly identical to Gareth
apart from the extra bulk he carried, being almost
five years older, were gathered in front of the
fireplace that dominated one wall of the spacious
parlour. The murmur of their voices ceased as
Eireen stepped inside; all eyes swung to her.

Gavin leapt to his feet and solicitously ushered her to a chair positioned so as to be in view
of everyone. "Would you like a drink?"

"Some water, thanks."

Gareth approached Greer and leaned down
so that he could speak softly. "Excuse me, Aunt
Greer, but she wants us to be shielded from
eavesdroppers – do you mind?"

"Does she?" Greer threw a puzzled glance
at Eireen. "No, we'll do it." She pulled a clear
gem from her tunic and cupped it in her left
hand, and then looked to Alaric who, in turn,
cradled a honey-colored oval.

Gavin returned carrying a glass of water and
a cup of coffee for Zeroun, who broke off his
quiet conversation with Eireen to give Gavin a
grateful smile.

Alaric and Greer took up positions facing
opposite sides of the room. In what clearly was a
well-practiced routine, they each extended a
hand. After the barest delay, a wide beam of
navy blue light burst from both jewels. They
made identical broad sweeping motions with
their stone-holding hands; a nearly translucent
band, tinged with a pearly blue glow, formed
across either end of the room. The two turned
in unison and stretched the bands up and over
until they merged in the center of the room.
Greer's stone then projected a narrow beam of
silver light into the center of the gabled ceiling.
As soon as it contacted the translucent bubble
that now spanned the room, it diffused throughout, adding a shimmer of silver to the pearly
glow. Greer nodded, and she and Alaric dropped

their arms and took their seats, never having spoken a word.

"We're shielded, Eireen," Greer said, "go ahead when you're ready."

Eireen appraised those assembled with a look containing equal amounts of anxiety, accusation, and grief. She hesitated and then began in a rush, "I know without doubt that my mother was killed, and I don't see how any of you can believe otherwise." She confronted Zeroun, who was seated close to her side. "What did Mother see that was different on the paths the night before the homicide?"

"Oh," he said in a soft and sad voice, "she said the paths were changing, and she saw lots of shadows, but nothing distinct. In fact," he added, even more softly, "she said it was so hazy that she wasn't confident she could distinguish her own path."

Eireen closed her eyes and clenched her fists. She shook her head and opened her eyes to give her father an anguished look. "And you let her go? It was her death – that's what was changing!"

"But why," Alaric asked, "do you think it was homicide?"

She turned on him with a defiant glare. "Because I saw the shadows. And the changing paths. And the havoc. Mother just looked too soon. It's not clear – not yet. But I saw darkness where her path ended, and I saw darkness at the end for nearly every veridictrix I could think of to check." She paused to draw breath and brushed her hand across her eyes, which had taken on a haunted look again. Zeroun put a hand on her arm, but she shook it off. She resumed in a flat voice, utterly unlike her usual ebullient lilt. "I saw many wrong paths – they all end in chaos and devastation. It's murky, but I could still see the true path, and it's my path. I saw my assassination, but the true path continued, and on it was a baby, and the baby was bathed in moonlight." She came to an abrupt stop and swept the group with a challenging gaze.

Alaric was the first to speak. "When? Do you know when it was that you saw your death?"

She shook her head. "Soon, but not too soon."

Zeroun wordlessly drew her into an embrace and pressed her hard against his chest. She let him hold her for a moment, but then pulled away, leaving a hand resting on his knee.

"You know it was homicide and not just your death?" Greer asked.

"Yes! He's on my path – like all the others. That part's clear."

"He?" Greer asked, leaning forward.

"He's vile!" She shuddered. "Vicious and powerful – so strong his presence is everywhere."

"Do you know anything about his identity?" Greer pressed.

"No … no," she said. "I don't know if it's because I don't know him, or because I couldn't see."

Greer nodded thoughtfully as Alaric asked, "Is he alone?"

"No!" she said with sudden realization. "No, he isn't, at least," she paused, looking thoughtful, "not later on. He's surrounded by others. And," her eyes widened in shock as she appeared to recall the detail, "they too are bathed in moonlight."

Greer threw a startled glance at Alaric, who shrugged.

"You said," Zeroun asked, "that you saw darkness on the paths of all the veridictrices you checked?"

"I don't know why – I can't explain – I just wondered if it was because she was a veridictrix, so I checked. They all die."

∼∽∽∼

"And," Gareth said to Sigrun in a somber voice, "she was right about that as well. Most of the veridictrices in prominent positions or in prominent families on Kaia have been killed or have died unexpectedly in the years since that night. ... Eireen's assassination was ten years later."

"So it was murder? Did you catch the man Eireen saw?" Sigrun asked, mesmerized by the story.

"Yes, we are certain that Firinne was murdered but, although we know who the 'vile man' is, no, he has not been caught."

"But how did he do it?"

Gareth opened his mouth, but then paused and listened for a second before saying, "That's Greer getting back to me. I likely will speak with her for some while. You are welcome to watch, or wander the house, as you wish." As he spoke, he picked up his topaz and cradled it in his cupped hands.

"Okay," Sigrun said as he turned his eyes to his stone. She sat and watched him for a couple of minutes but, as he had said, it was decidedly dull. He simply sat there, studying his topaz, looking serious. She fished around under her chair for her sandals and, slipping them onto her feet, got up quietly. Gareth gave her a quick smile as she stepped around the firepit. Uncomfortable about prowling around in the house, she headed to the back wall by the wooden gate into the field.

It was too dark to see the ocean, but she could hear the distant crashing of the waves – which brought to mind an image of Firinne lying broken and bloody in the surf. She shivered. Gareth was a skillful story-teller, and Sigrun had easily visualized the scene on the beach with him as a young man and Eireen ... Eireen who also had ended up dead, lying in a pool of her own blood, not far from here and not that long after that night on the beach. Well, she knew for a fact that Eireen had been murdered and when it had happened. Otherwise – of what was she certain? Gareth had known her birth name, and Zareh had known about her baby box. Gareth also had that odd drawing, but only her chance resemblance to the groom connected that to her. And of course, there was the shock thing when she touched Gareth ... and the emerald. She spun about to look at Gareth. A focus stone! Her ... mother's focus stone? Could it be true?

🐾〜🐾

⟶ Chapter 16 ⟵
Nosce te ipsum
(Know thyself; Ancient Greek proverb)

Sigrun peered across the dark field, but she could see nothing apart from stars. Feeling claustrophobic in the cramped yard, she contemplated the small wooden gate set into the wall. She threw a quick glance over her shoulder at Gareth. He remained engrossed – ostensibly deep in mental communication with Greer. Maybe she could take a walk; if she stayed within sight of the house, she couldn't get lost, and the field looked empty. Perhaps she could get close enough to see the ocean. She reached for the latch and jumped back when she received a shock significantly stronger than any she had yet experienced. So, no walk, she thought ruefully, rubbing her tingling fingers. She turned to go inside instead and found that Gareth was watching her. She shrugged and headed toward the house. He pointed to the chair she had vacated, so she returned to her seat.

"Sorry," he said moments later, looking up from his gemstone. "I forgot to tell you that the yard is shielded – you can't go out by yourself."

"Shielded?! ... Right. ... No problem. I just thought it would be nice to take a walk. But, are you finished?"

"Yes." He got to his feet and stretched. "Since you've been expressing considerable skepticism about Kaia, we've decided that a demonstration is in order. Would you care to go for that walk?"

"Uh ... sure." She followed him back to the wall. "What demonstration?"

"You'll see." Gareth made a quick movement with his left hand; Sigrun drew back as bursts of neon light briefly outlined the gate. He opened it and signaled her to pass through. She did so – throwing a watchful glance at the gate as she warily stepped into the field. Gareth followed, swinging the gate shut behind him. "Be careful where you step," he said, "cows use this field too. Head toward the ocean, and then we'll walk along the bluff."

"So, what did Greer ... say?"

"She is delighted that we've made contact and were correct about your identity but terribly troubled by the thought of you remaining unprotected."

"Okay." After a moment's reflection, she added, "So, the idea is that I'm a – what do you call it – a, a veri ... dictrix?"

"Yes."

"And you believe that because ...?"

"I definitely am not the most appropriate person to explain that to you. In general, it is a gift passed from mother to daughter."

Sigrun digested that while they crossed to the top of the bluff and began walking on a path that paralleled the beach. "So, based on Eireen's ... vision, you think I'm in danger because of this ... ability?"

"Yes, of course, you would be at risk as a veridictrix regardless of who you were. You, however, will be targeted in particular because you're Eireen's daughter."

"Why is that?"

"I think I will leave that to Greer."

"Oh! Am I meeting her?"

"Shortly," he said with amusement.

"The portal!" She stopped in her tracks. "You said there's a portal out here."

"Stonycliff." He continued walking, and she hurried to catch up. He pointed at a crumbling old stone bench not far ahead. "Come over here where you can watch." He stepped inland from the path.

"Watch what?"

"Greer's arrival."

"Oh!" Sigrun joined him in facing the bench. "Now?"

"Well, perhaps we should have waited because she has to walk to Poholo – the primary portal in Maluhia. But she was planning to leave soon, so it should not be long."

"Really! So ... she arrives here directly from ... Kaia?"

"Not exactly, but if she leaves from Poholo, it's more or less direct."

"Oh? What does that mean?"

Gareth laughed. "Later. Just watch."

Sigrun eyed the bench, feeling more than slightly foolish to be standing on a bluff late at night scrutinizing an old stone bench. It was so easy, she thought, to get caught up in Gareth's imperturbable calmness and lose sight of the fact that his story was punctuated with preposterous details like portals. Nothing happened. Of course. She looked around. They were too far back from the cliff to see down to the beach. The black ocean merged seamlessly with the dark horizon. "You're sure she's arriving ... here?"

Gareth merely smiled and pointed at the bench.

Sigrun turned back to the bench, which hadn't changed. She put her hands in her pockets and encountered her cell phone. What would Philip think if he could see her now, she wondered with a wry smile? He would think she was being an idiot. She shifted her weight between her feet. She heard the rumble of a distant plane overhead and looked up, but it was too far for her to spot in the darkness. She jumped at the jolt Gareth's hand on her shoulder generated.

"Sorry. You're exhausting me. Stand still and sharpen your senses. If I am correct, you'll perceive the opening of the portal before you see the burst of Power."

"What?"

"Pretend you're listening hard to hear something just beyond your range – a sound that is too high-pitched to truly be heard, but yet is still discernible."

Unconvinced, she stood and tried to do as he suggested. She stared fixedly at the bench, and strained to listen past the night sounds of insects and the surf. Apart from that, it was quiet. She imagined a band playing far in the distance – could she detect the upper reaches of a female vocalist? But in that case, the thought intruded, she would feel the bass long before she would hear the singer. Not a good example. Abruptly she was bathed in a prickly sensation that passed almost before she perceived it. A pillar of intense white light erupted alongside the bench, precisely where she was staring. The sudden light in the darkness hurt her eyes, and she swiftly shut them.

She opened her eyes to see a stately woman with a gleaming cap of short grey hair standing where the light had been. Sigrun swallowed hard and stumbled backward. The woman surveyed the area fleetingly before stepping forward. She stood straight and moved with confidence. In the dim light of the waning moon, Sigrun could make out that she was wearing tall close-fitting boots, pants that ended just above the boots and flared out slightly at the thighs, and a cape that swirled as she moved. The clothing was of a pale, bluish-grey color that complemented her hair. As she approached, Sigrun could see that the woman was not young – probably in her late 60s.

"Greetings, Gareth," the woman said in a low, gravelly voice,

"I didn't expect a welcoming committee."

"Greetings, Greer," he replied, sounding jovial. "I thought the demonstration would be more potent with proximity. I am delighted to introduce you two." He motioned Sigrun forward. "Sigrun, I'd like you to meet Greer Fortes. Greer, Sigrun Firinne Nyman."

Sigrun, feeling utterly intimidated by the woman's mere presence, took a small step forward and hesitantly offered her hand.

Greer clasped Sigrun's hand firmly and raised her eyebrows slightly at the accompanying jolt. She brought her other hand up to hold Sigrun's hand between hers as she studied Sigrun's face intently. Greer smiled slowly. "Greetings. Words are inadequate to express my feelings at seeing you again after 20 years."

"Perhaps," Gareth suggested, "we should be shielded before anything more is said."

"Excellent point." Greer indicated that Sigrun should join her as she strolled across the bluff. "Gareth tells me that your adoptive father died last summer. And I recently learned of your adoptive mother's death several years earlier. I'm so sorry to hear the news. I didn't know William well, but I was close to your mother for a couple of years. My condolences."

"Thank you," Sigrun murmured, absorbing the fact that Greer indeed must be the "great aunt" who had not visited as planned.

"As I recall, there were no other children, so you are alone now on Earth?"

"Well, yes."

Greer nodded thoughtfully.

"Greer, did you eat," Gareth asked, "or would you like something?"

"Thank you for asking, but I managed to find time for a cursory dinner. I would, however, love some coffee, if you don't mind."

"Don't worry," Gareth said as they reached the wall at his yard, "I know you too well not to have offered." He performed a quick movement with his stone-holding hand and opened the gate as the resulting bursts of light dissipated. "Why don't you two have a seat by the fire while I fetch the coffee."

Greer took one of the chairs by the fire and pointed Sigrun to the other. She turned in the brighter light to study Sigrun again; her eyes were a grey that matched her cape. "You do resemble Edoardo," she said after a moment, "but I detect Eireen in the shape of your face."

The scrutiny embarrassed Sigrun, and she looked down, hair falling forward.

"So," Greer said, "Gareth tells me that you are dubious about the concept of Kaia, not to mention your connection to it. Is that a fair statement?"

She nodded, still at a loss for words.

Gareth appeared in the doorway of the house, following a tray with three mugs. He waved a hand at one of the chairs that remained at the table, and it floated over to join the others at the firepit. Greer gratefully took one of the mugs.

"So, Sigrun," Gareth asked, "did you detect the opening of the portal?"

"Yeah," she said reluctantly, "I did."

"Interesting." Greer cast an appraising look at Sigrun before asking, "You suspected she would?"

"Yes. And she's already judging the truth."

Sigrun, annoyed at being evaluated as if she were not present, asked, "Excuse me, but I'm afraid I don't understand: Where exactly did you come from?"

"Yes," Greer said, sounding amused, "back to addressing your doubts. In Maluhia I stepped through Poholo Portal into the multi-dimensional intersection that links Kaia with Earth and, after an intermediate course adjustment, stepped out onto the bluff here. Although the total transit took only a moment, the distance that I traversed was vast. You see, we say that Kaia and Earth are parallel, but that's not really a good physical analogy because you expect them to be adjacent."

As Greer paused for coffee, Sigrun tried to absorb the concept of stepping into a "multi-dimensional intersection" in space as if it were a revolving door.

"I prefer to think," Greer continued, "of the two worlds as 'alternative'. We occupy an identical space and time – if it's a summer night in California on Earth, it's a summer night in the corresponding area on Kaia. The planets are, for the most part, the same physically, and we've followed comparable evolutionary paths."

"But," Sigrun protested, "genetically, you're not the same?"

"Well, to the extent of my limited understanding of the concept, we are," Greer replied. "People from Kaia quite successfully have children with people from Earth."

"They do!" She had not contemplated that possibility.

"The differences that exist," Greer continued, "arise from the fact that those born to Kaia have an ability to perceive and manipulate the energy of our planet that flows along what we call the Grid. It's a component of Kaia – like oxygen or iron. We have those as Earth does but, in addition, we have the Grid. It sustains us and our society in ways that those not born to a Kaian parent cannot experience. Because of it, we can do all manner of things that you perceive as 'magic'. They're not: they are merely skills that we are able to develop and use. And abuse. Which takes me where I must go."

Greer gave Sigrun a thoughtful look while draining her coffee. "I gather you don't believe that you were born the child of Eireen and Edoardo?"

"Uh … well, I guess you brought me to Pennsylvania as an infant, so …"

"Yes, I did. I also watched you being born. I know who your parents were and how you came to be raised in Pennsylvania. Let me turn the question around – who were your birth parents if not Eireen and Edoardo?"

Sigrun shrugged. "I don't know because my adoptive parents never told me."

"They did not know because I did not tell them."

"What did you tell them?"

"That your parents, my niece and her husband, had been killed in an accident, and that you were unharmed because you were with me. I said I traveled too much to care for an infant and asked them to look after you. Then I never came back."

It fit too well to be mere coincidence. "How did you meet my adoptive mother?"

"I was living outside Lancaster – near a portal – and I needed clothing that passed for Earth wear. I can't abide most of what is sold here, so I had your mother sew a few things for me."

Sigrun nodded. That too fit.

"And of course you are aware of how Eireen and Edoardo died?"

"Well, no, I mean, I know the story from trial – but that's not what happened."

"But you accept that they were killed when you were three months old?"

"Well … yes."

"The reason they were killed then, which, I might add, was quite a difficult feat, as I'll explain some other time, was to prevent your birth."

"Oh!" breathed Sigrun.

"Eireen hid the fact that she was with child – Gareth can confirm that, I'm sorry to say – because she knew that she would not live to give birth if it became known."

"So," Gareth exclaimed softly, "she did see a change in the paths that she didn't tell me about!"

"Yes, she had seen the time of her assassination growing nearer, and she had seen her unborn baby killed. So, we secreted her on Earth, and you were born, Sigrun. Only six people apart from your parents knew of the birth. As far as we know, no one has been searching for her child until quite recently."

Sigrun gazed into the fire and tried to find holes in Greer's story. It made sense, however, and she could come up with nothing to counter it.

"Now, I'm afraid, it's no longer safe for you here."

"Okay – you lose me there."

"Yes," Greer said with a nod. "Again, I can't explain now, but I've been watching for you for the past 20 years. After you came to California, you started sending me signals by brushing against the Grid. At least once was when you met Gareth, but I didn't know that at the time."

"I did not think it important enough to mention to you," Gareth added apologetically.

"Well, I needed to find out why Eireen's child had appeared in California. So I traveled to Lancaster to find your adoptive parents. I learned that your mother had died and that William had moved away with you. I tracked you to Burning Springs, but once there I became aware that I had been followed. I had unfortunately blundered into a spy who was curious about what I was looking for. So I disappeared without learning your name or whereabouts. They can only suspect that you exist, but I'm certain that they do suspect."

"'They' being?" Sigrun asked.

"The vile man on Eireen's paths," Gareth interjected.

Greer shot him a surprised look. "She knows about that?"

"I told her the story of Firinne's death tonight while we waited for you."

"Good," said Greer. "So, Sigrun, what do you think?"

"I still don't see how you get to the fact that I'm suddenly in mortal danger. If they don't know for sure that Eireen's daughter exists, or who I am, how can I be?"

"Never underestimate your enemy," Greer said. "We do not

know what information they have – or will soon have. You've had multiple contacts with Zareh and Gareth, and they may make a connection through either."

"So, I'm in grave danger," Sigrun said doubtfully. "What do you propose I do about it?"

"You must come to Kaia as soon as possible."

"No way!"

"We can't protect you here."

"I don't care," Sigrun said. "First, I need to draft the petition to try to get Zareh out of prison. And second, I don't know that I want to go to Kaia."

Greer raised her eyebrows. "You must – it's your heritage."

"No." Sigrun shook her head adamantly. "I'm from Earth. That's what I know, and that's where I want to live."

"You can't know that," Greer said impatiently. "I've lived on Earth, and I can tell you that the advantages of living here over living on Kaia are extremely limited."

"But it's my choice," said Sigrun defensively.

"I don't think you understand. The only reason we left you here all these years was for your protection – you're **not** born to Earth, and you're no longer safe here."

"I'm an adult," she asserted, "and I can live where I like."

"Perhaps," Gareth suggested, "you could work on the petition here so that I could keep an eye on you."

"No, I can't," Sigrun said. "I need the law library, and, anyway, I can't do it without Professor Ehrlich."

"Is this action likely to make a difference?" Greer asked Gareth irritably.

"We have a chance," he said, "and I must try."

"Yes, of course. I want Zareh to be freed as well – but we cannot endanger Sigrun to do so."

"I'm sorry you feel that way," said Sigrun, "but I made a commitment, and I'm going to file that petition."

"Surely that should not take long. As soon as it's done, you must come to live on Kaia."

"No. Look, I don't mean to be argumentative, but I don't know you, and yet you seem to think I'll do whatever you like."

Greer look startled and turned to Gareth.

"Sigrun," Gareth said calmly, "we are trying to explain the situation to you so that you understand why we want you to go to Kaia. I know you well enough not to expect you to do something without understanding it."

"Then you should know that I'm not going anywhere until I've finished Zareh's case – which could take years."

"Years!" Greer exclaimed.

"Yes. He might win at federal court, but we have to get there first. And anyway, I have law school to finish, and I have plans with Philip. So I'm ..."

"Who is Philip?" Greer interrupted sharply.

"My best friend. He's coming out to visit me later this summer, and then he'll be in vet school. I'm not going anywhere until he's done ..."

Greer asked Gareth, "Did you know about this?"

"Yes. I am not sure how much of a problem it's going to be."

"I'm sorry," Sigrun said, "but I don't perceive Philip to be a 'problem'."

"Have you told him about Kaia?" demanded Greer.

"No! I promised Gareth I wouldn't."

"Good. You must not tell him anything."

"Yes, yes. Look, you've charged into my life without asking, and now you're trying to control ..."

Greer held up a hand. "Excuse me," she said with a sigh as she pulled a clear gemstone from a pocket of her cape, which she had draped over the back of her chair to reveal a simple but elegant short-sleeved black tunic.

"Can I talk to you?" Sigrun asked Gareth quietly.

"Certainly." He got to his feet and they crossed the yard.

"I'm sorry," she said, "but I'm not going to meekly do as she wishes."

"Sigrun, Greer wants above all to keep you safe – it's difficult for you to fully appreciate ..."

"No, it's more than that. Regardless of motive, I can't accept someone I don't know unilaterally making decisions about my life."

"I am sympathetic to your position, but you cannot possibly understand the situation thoroughly enough to make a decision."

"Well, I can't argue with that, but it's still my life."

"Greer is exceedingly busy, and she doesn't have the time to explain things to the extent you would like."

"Why can't I just visit?"

Gareth shook his head. "Once you appear on Kaia, your identity could be confirmed. If so, it would become too dangerous for you to live here without protection."

"Come off it," she said impatiently. "How would anyone even know?"

"Of course you could come for a brief stay," Gareth conceded, "but that would not give us time to teach you what you must learn."

"I'm done," Greer called.

They returned to their chairs, and Sigrun said, only slightly testily, "I was telling Gareth that, although I realize that you're concerned for my welfare, I'm simply not willing to live on Kaia now."

"Something has arisen that requires my immediate attention," Greer said. "So I suggest we agree that you will return to school and finish what needs to be done as soon as possible. If you promise to keep in close contact with Gareth and promise not to touch anyone you don't know …"

"I'm sorry?"

"If someone from Kaia wants to know if you are who they suspect you are, they will simply touch you."

"Of course!" Sigrun exclaimed. "I didn't think of that. It's pretty hard not to touch people … but I'll try."

"And I will call her daily," Gareth added.

Greer sighed and rubbed her eyes tiredly. "Please get this … document filed quickly, and we will talk again."

Sigrun nodded after considering the suggestion. "I have no problem with that."

"So," Greer said, "Gareth, would you mind walking me back to Stonycliff – I want to discuss a few things with you."

"Of course. Sigrun, why don't you go inside? The house is completely shielded as well, so you are perfectly safe alone."

Sigrun stood, and Greer clasped her on the shoulder; Sigrun didn't even start at the now-expected shock.

"I regret that we've had some disagreements, but please believe that I am truly delighted to meet you, and I look forward to getting to know you."

"Thank you," Sigrun said. "I hope our next conversation can be more relaxed."

"I find that I am rarely relaxed," Greer said ruefully. "But we shall see. Please be extremely circumspect in your interactions; don't trust **anyone** you don't know. And call Gareth if you have even the slightest concern."

As Gareth and Greer left, Sigrun retreated to the front room of the house, which appeared to be a joint living room and office. She curled into a corner of its generous couch and tried to contemplate the day's events. But so much had happened since that morning's walk on the beach that she couldn't concentrate. Instead, she was deluged with images: the opening of the portal, Zareh's expression when describing her box, a young Eireen racing toward the bodies of Firinne and her horse in the pounding surf, Gareth explaining this ... so-called gift she seemed to have, Greer's puissant presence. After a time, exhausted and emotionally drained, her eyes fell on a guitar propped on a stand. She got up to examine it. She had never seen such a carefully crafted instrument – it must be an antique. She wished fiercely that Philip could see it. Unexpectedly, she felt tears well up in her eyes. She brushed them away impatiently.

"Do you play?" Gareth said behind her.

She spun around; she hadn't heard him enter. She shook her head and retreated to the couch. "No, but Philip does. It's beautiful."

Gareth took the other end of the couch. "You're upset."

"No. Yes. I mean, shouldn't I be?"

"I imagine it must be truly disquieting to learn that you are not who you thought you were."

She kicked off her sandals and pulled her legs close to her chest. "But that's just it! I don't **feel** any different than I did before – you're just telling me that I am."

"Sigrun, you must not think we're trying to force you to relinquish your past or any part of yourself. Kaia **is** a part of you and always has been – it was merely hidden from you until yesterday."

She mulled that over. "Okay. But, now that you've revealed my ... 'true identity', shouldn't I have an epiphany or something? You know, like a frog turning into a prince."

"I am sorry," he said with a smile, "I don't know that story. But no, I don't think you should expect to intuitively grasp the nuances of being a veridictrix or having Power. I am afraid you will need to learn all that it means over time."

"Of course. I don't expect to be able to do any of the things you and Greer seem to do so effortlessly. But ..." She struggled to find words to express her ambivalence. "Look – Greer's explanation for my birth and arrival in Pennsylvania is unassailable, so I should accept it. And I can't dispute your reality – you believe in Kaia and your experiences growing up there. You know Eireen to have been the person you described to me. But that leaves me feeling ... well, like a nobody who was raised on a farm in middle America with no distinguishing skills or abilities who is supposed to be this ... this predestined child of powerful and special people. ... Does that make sense?"

"Ah, I think I see. It's not so much that you question the existence of Kaia, it's more that it is clearly impossible that **you** are the daughter of Eireen."

"Exactly!"

"So, how do you explain this?" Gareth touched her arm.

She recoiled from the resulting shock and shook her head. "I don't know."

"Why don't we call it a night? Things are always at their darkest before dawn. In the morning, I will try to address your questions."

"Okay," she agreed with a shrug, thinking that sleep was pretty improbable.

⟿ Chapter 17 ⟿
Infixum est mihi
(I have firmly resolved)

Back at UCLA, as Sigrun struggled to draft the habeas petition, each day dawned grey and cloudy – what locals referred to as
"June gloom," although it lingered into July – a perfect mirror for
her mood. She alternated between interludes of intense grief that
caused her to call Philip at all hours to check on his well-being and
episodes during which she was consumed by the sheer surrealism of
her conversations with Gareth and Greer. She repeatedly had to
restrain herself from blurting out something revealing to Philip.
Her concentration was fragmentary at best. Fortunately, she had
left a copy of her most recent draft of the petition with Professor
Ehrlich, but she had lost her notes in the fire, so she had to dupli-
cate much of her research. She could tell that the professor was
concerned about her mental state by the searching looks she gave
her at their every meeting. Gareth called her at least once a day.
She found herself clinging to his voice as the only stability, apart
from Philip, in her shaky world – which, if she thought about it,
was ludicrous since it was Gareth who had launched her into this
whole fantasy of parallel universes. In fact, if she reflected too long
on anything, she began to doubt her sanity. Her solution was to
force herself to work as many hours as she was physically able and
to go to the gym without fail every day. She ducked anyone she saw
on campus that she knew, didn't return Milton's calls, and confined
her contact with Blythe to passing in the kitchen or hallway.

Finally, one day in mid-July, she felt the petition pull together.
She had been closeted in her room at Blythe's apartment most of
the day because the law library wasn't open on Sundays in the
summer. She had been struggling for days to compose the narrative
setting forth their theory behind the cumulative error claim. She
had discussed it repeatedly with the professor, and she knew what
they wanted to say, but each time she attempted it her words were
wooden and, she thought, unpersuasive. Then, that morning, she
had been trying to explain to Gareth why she was still dissatisfied

with her efforts, and he had said, "But you've eviscerated the prosecution's case; I don't see why you're not pleased." She had hung up quickly, discarded her latest attempt, and crafted what, after much tightening, she felt was a powerful argument. Gareth's words had helped her crystallize their theory – how the errors, if considered individually, might not be sufficiently prejudicial to merit habeas relief, but their combined impact tore the guts from the prosecutor's case.

She read through her section and sat back with a satisfied sigh. Not bad – maybe she **could** get this finished. She checked the time – a quarter to nine! She grabbed her phone and called Philip. She had promised to call early tonight so that he could get to bed in preparation for what he anticipated was going to be an emotionally taxing meeting with the lawyer to finalize the documents for the sale of the farm.

"I'm sorry," Sigrun said when he answered, "I was supposed to call earlier."

"It's okay, I would have called if I'd wanted to go to bed. But I'm feeling more … upbeat than I expected."

"How come?"

"Well, partly because that guy from Texas sounds serious about the Mustang. I sent him some pictures, and he's sufficiently excited that he's driving all the way up here to take a look at it. If he likes it, he's planning to take it home with him."

"That's fantastic! You like the sound of him, right?"

"Yeah. He's a collector, and he seems to know what he's talking about, to the extent that I can tell. Anyway, I think he'll restore it, and that's what I want."

"Hey, things are really falling into place quickly now."

"Seems like it. What about you?"

"I'm good. I finally found the words that have been eluding me for days. I'm too close to it to tell, but I'm beginning to think it works."

"Really! You haven't sounded that optimistic in weeks."

"No, longer. But … I don't know, today's the first day I think I can see the end. Maybe you were sending me positive thoughts."

"Fabulous. When do you want me to come out? Everything's pretty much under control here, and I really should buy a ticket."

"Excellent! How about two weeks? Blythe will be done with the bar exam by then, and she'll be leaving on vacation, so your sleeping on the couch won't bother her. And maybe I'll have gotten this thing filed."

"Let me grab a calendar – I have one in the kitchen that I've been using to track my appointments now that I'm forced to function without my appointment secretary."

"Sorry, I've been a bit busy."

"Yeah, always an excuse. So, two weeks – how about the 26th?"

"Perfect."

"Okay. I'll see about a ticket tomorrow. And you should start thinking about where we might want to go."

"Oh, well, I wasn't planning ..."

"Hey, you promised me we could take a break, and, well ... I have some money now. So I want to go somewhere fun."

"I'll think about it. Buy the ticket, and I'll try to finish this before you get here."

After hanging up, she wandered over to the bedroom window, which, being on an upper floor of a high-rise building, had a city-lights view. Over the cityscape hung a beautiful full moon in a deepening cerulean sky. Gorgeous, she thought with a sigh. So, what was she going to tell Philip? She had promised him, but she had also agreed to talk to Greer after the petition was filed. She felt torn – as she had ever since that morning on the beach in Cambria when she had kept her promise to Gareth by lying to Philip. Well, she resolved as she headed in search of something to eat, Greer would just have to wait.

It took her another week of intensive work, but she finally was sufficiently satisfied with the petition to give a final draft to Professor Ehrlich. It took several more days of meetings and revisions before the professor deemed it done during a late-afternoon meeting just two days before Philip was due to arrive.

"Wonderful. This is excellent work." Professor Ehrlich closed the copy of the petition she had been reading and set it on her desk with a satisfied whack. "I'm so impressed, Sigrun; this reads like it was drafted by a team of experienced lawyers."

"Thank you. For a long time, I thought I wasn't going to be able to do it, but now I'm happy with it. Do you think we have a chance?"

"I do." She rummaged around on her desk and unearthed a calendar. "We have what – almost four weeks before classes start. Here's what I want to do. You take the petition up to San Luis Obispo and hand-carry it through. Then I'll give the judge a quick call to let him or her know the situation before I alert the media.

As long as I keep the State's attorney abreast of our plans, it should be fine."

"I'm sorry," Sigrun interrupted. "You want me to file it in San Luis Obispo?"

"It has to be filed in the county where the trial was held. You don't mind traveling up there again, do you?"

"Well, my friend Philip will be here, but I'm sure he'll be happy to come along."

"Good. So, we need to get enough copies made – talk to the secretary for the habeas clinic about that. Be sure to get an extra copy for each of us as well as one to send over to the State's attorney. And a couple for petitioner, of course." She handed Sigrun a multi-page form. "You'll need to fill this out to be filed with the petition – just reference the attached petition where it asks you to list the claims. You should have the rest of the information about his earlier cases. Then, I'll see if we can get an expedited hearing – it would be great if we could get things moving before classes interfere."

"Really! I didn't think anything would happen for ages once it was filed."

"Oh, but," the professor said with a wide smile, "the suggestion of unwelcome media attention can be very persuasive – and I'm very good at suggesting."

It was too late that afternoon to talk to the secretary, so Sigrun spent the rest of the evening and part of the next morning puzzling through the confusing form. Once she had finished it, she made arrangements for the requisite number of copies; but they wouldn't be done until Monday afternoon. She dropped by Professor Ehrlich's office.

"Excuse me, professor," Sigrun said as she knocked on the open door.

"Come on in. I'm nearly done."

While the professor finished her phone conversation, Sigrun thought about the discussion that she needed to have with Gareth. Philip was arriving the following day, and she had yet to tell Gareth about their travel plans, or the fact that she was going to file the petition in person. She was certain that he would insist on meeting them at the train station so he and Philip ...

"Sorry, Sigrun, what did you need?"

"Oh, I just wanted to let you know that the copies won't be done until noon on Monday. So, I guess we'll go up on Tuesday."

"Well, why not take the late train on Monday? If you catch

that, you can file the petition first thing Tuesday. Don't worry about the hotel costs, the program will cover them. And I'll have a copy delivered to the State's attorney Monday afternoon."

"Uh, well ..."

"I don't want to waste any of our few days, and August is a bad time to schedule things – with vacations and all. I think we should get it filed as soon as possible."

"Sure, we can go Monday, and I'll get to the courthouse when it opens Tuesday."

"Perfect. Be sure that you insist on getting the petition file-stamped and processed while you wait. They may want you to drop it off. Don't let them push you around – it's perfectly acceptable to walk the documents through and hand them to the judge's secretary. Then call me when you're done."

"Okay. Is there anything else I need to know?"

"I was just going over my notes," the professor said. "We need to be ready with our arguments about timeliness. I have your research memo, but do you have copies of the cases you cited? I want to review them."

"No, they were lost in the fire. But if you give me the memo – I'll make new ones."

"Good. I also wanted your thoughts on a potential evidentiary hearing. Before I talk to the judge, I want to be prepared to discuss what additional discovery we think might be needed to develop any of the claims."

When she had finally finished discussing strategy with Professor Ehrlich and copying the relevant cases, Sigrun headed to the gym, feeling the need to work out some of her anxiety. She had never dreamt that the professor would want her to file the petition in person, or that a hearing might be imminent. She had been hoping to take a break from the habeas case as well as the corresponding complications of Kaia during the few weeks before school started. Of course, she thought with a rueful shake of her head, why she expected that Gareth was going to let her go anywhere unescorted, she wasn't sure. But now – well, she'd better give him a call and get his reaction before she ramped up into indignation.

Sigrun tossed her backpack and her gym bag on the cluttered floor of her room and looked around with a sigh. Stacks of papers were piled everywhere, not to mention dirty laundry. She'd better get things cleaned up before Philip arrived. She had been planning to take her notes and research materials with her if they did have a hearing. So, if it might be soon, she should get everything organized now. In fact, maybe she should take it along when they went to file the petition; they didn't necessarily want to come back to Los Angeles right away. But first she'd better call Gareth. When he had called as usual that morning, she had brushed him off with a plea of needing to finish the paperwork. She took her shoes off and settled herself on the bed. As she punched in his number, she vowed not to let herself get angry.

"Greetings, Sigrun," Gareth answered her call. "Did everything go well?"

"It's finished! The petition is being copied – it'll be ready Monday."

"Splendid! When will it be filed, then?"

"Oh. Well, I wanted to let you know ... the professor wants me to file it in person so, well, I'm coming up there Monday."

"Really! I am delighted! But you sound ambivalent?"

"Oh ... well, it's just that ... well, Philip will be here."

"I see. And what are your plans?"

"I don't know. I assume he'll come with me, and we'll get the petition filed. Then, well, I thought I'd better check with you."

Gareth laughed. "I appreciate that. I will, of course, pick you up at the train station. I would prefer to extend my hospitality, but I am afraid my place is rather small for two guests. Would it be acceptable to you if I made arrangements at the inn where you stayed last time?"

"That's fine," she said cautiously, "but I wasn't planning on staying more than a night or two."

"And after that," Gareth replied equally cautiously, "are you intending to return to Los Angeles?"

"Well, we want to travel some ... maybe up along the coast."

"I see. Have you given any thought to when you might like to resume your conversation with Greer?"

"Uh, actually, I have. I think I should wait until Philip's in school – his classes start before mine – so I can spend a day or so with you then without him wondering."

"And when would that be?"

"Uh – at the end of August."

"I will consult with Greer and see what her thoughts are."

"That's it?"

"You were expecting?"

"Well ... I didn't think my plan would go over terribly well."

"I don't anticipate that it will," said Gareth easily.

"But you're not going to argue with me?" she ventured.

"No, I will leave that to Greer."

"Oh, good. Then I don't have to worry about getting mad at you."

"Were you?"

"Worried? Yes, but I'd rather not. So, we'll be taking the late train on Monday – it gets in at 8:30. And then I need to come back into San Luis Obispo first thing Tuesday to file the petition. Would you mind …"

"Of course I will drive you," he said readily. "In that case, I will visit Zareh on Monday and share your news."

"Good. Tell him that Professor Ehrlich is going to try to arrange an expedited hearing in August – but we won't know if it'll work until after she contacts the judge."

"I was not expecting any progress so soon."

"Well, we don't know, but she wants to see if she can push it along."

"That would be much appreciated."

"Anyway, I need to get my room cleaned up. I guess I'll see you on Monday."

"I will call you tomorrow as usual. Aloha, and please do be cautious around strangers."

᠁

"It is **so** good to see you," Sigrun said earnestly to Philip, who was sprawled in her desk chair. They had returned significantly later than planned from dinner because Philip's plane had been delayed, and then they had joined Zvi and Blythe at Zvi's favorite Middle Eastern restaurant, which had been mobbed. "You must be exhausted."

"Yeah, rather. But it doesn't matter – I'm done."

"Did you really get everything finished up before you left?"

"We did. The farm's sold, the stuff that survived the fire has been sold or given away, the Mustang's on its way to Texas, and … well, the horses are all taken care of."

"Amazing. So, did you … were you able to say goodbye to Estelle and Otto?"

Philip sat up straighter and looked away. "No," he said softly. "I wanted to but … in the end, I couldn't."

After a moment, Sigrun said, "I miss them. I miss your family … I miss being there." She snorted. "Hell, I even miss picking vegetables."

"**Don't** get me started," he said reproachfully. "I need some distance."

"I know; I'm sorry ..." she said contritely. "You're looking good."

"Am I? Thank you. You, on the other hand, are even thinner than you were when you left Pennsylvania."

"Oh, well, I've been working too much."

"True – but you look drawn."

"That's from not sleeping well – I'll be better once I get the petition filed." She sighed heavily. "It's turned into an albatross around my neck." And not only that, she thought, once again teetering on the edge of telling him ... what exactly? That she was from a parallel world? Right. She shook her head doubtfully. "I hope it was worth it."

"Does it really matter what happens?" Philip asked soberly. "You had to try."

"Yeah, I know, but, at the moment, I almost wish I'd never heard of the case."

"But it was the right thing to do."

"I know that," she said testily. "And now that I'm involved, I'm going to see it through. It's just that ... well, let's not go there right now."

Philip gave her a perplexed look. "So, you said we're going to be taking the train on Monday to get the petition filed?"

"Yeah, the trip up the coast is pretty, and Gareth offered to meet us at the station. We can stay at the little motel in Cambria where I stayed before."

"Couldn't we just stay in town if we have to be back there in the morning to go to the courthouse anyway?"

"Yeah, well," Sigrun said with a grimace, "you don't know Gareth. He has a keenly developed sense of hospitality, not to mention duty. He simply wouldn't hear of it. Anyway – you'll like him."

"Oh?"

"Uh-huh. Did I mention his guitar?"

Philip looked confused. "Not that I recall."

"You'll see. So, what should we do tomorrow? We have the entire day free."

⤙⤚

⁓ Chapter 18 ⁓
Amicus est tanquam alter idem
(A friend is, as it were, a second self;
Marcus Tullius Cicero)

The train arrived in San Luis Obispo as darkness fell. Grabbing her bag, Sigrun followed Philip down the steps to the platform, wondering yet again exactly how she was going to explain Gareth's protective attitude toward her to Philip. He knew that she spoke frequently with Gareth, but if Gareth were just her contact on the habeas case, he'd be … someone bumped rather forcefully against her back. Sigrun jerked away as she realized that she had felt a mild version of the sharp shock she experienced whenever she touched Gareth. Startled, she turned to find that the person – a woman – was already walking rapidly away with her face averted. Suspecting that it had not been an accident, she scanned the crowd on the platform to locate Gareth's large figure. Spying him nearby, she unceremoniously dropped her bag, pushed past Philip, and threw herself into Gareth's arms, thinking that this was not going to improve the situation.

As Gareth instinctively hugged her, she leaned up and whispered urgently into his ear, "See that plump, middle-aged woman in the green flowery dress with a small bag? She just bumped into me pretty hard, and I felt that shock."

Gareth quickly surveyed the crowd. "Brown curly hair?"

At her nod, Gareth strode rapidly toward the woman and called, "Excuse me, ma'am, I believe you dropped something." As the woman slowed and turned back, he grabbed her arm with his right hand. Only someone watching intently, as Sigrun was, would have seen the brief flash of amber light emanating from his left hand.

The woman sagged and collapsed against Gareth's side. Sigrun hurried over. "What happened?"

"I believe she is simply feeling faint," Gareth replied calmly. "Here, take her bag while I help her over to that bench." He virtually carried the woman to a nearby wrought iron bench and set her gently down. Sigrun suddenly remembered Philip and looked around. He was standing by their luggage near the train steps, watching them with an expression of utter perplexity. She beckoned him over.

As Philip approached, carrying both his and Sigrun's bags, Gareth said in a confident and friendly tone, "Ah, you must be Philip."

"Yes," Philip responded flatly.

"Good. Please sit next to this woman; hold her upright, and fan her gently." Gareth handed Philip a folded newspaper he had picked up from the bench. "Don't answer any questions, and brush off any offers of assistance. She'll be fine."

Without waiting for a response, he turned to Sigrun and said, "Come with me, I must move away from the train."

Sigrun called, "Don't worry," over her shoulder to Philip as she followed Gareth around the corner of the station.

"Did you have any contact with that woman earlier?" Gareth asked.

"No, that was the first time I felt the jolt."

"Good. Stand here." He took Sigrun firmly by the shoulder and placed her next to him. "Block anyone from having a view of my hands. Pretend to be studying the schedule on the wall there."

She did as he asked. In the dim glow cast by the overhead lights shining on the posted schedule, she watched covertly as Gareth cradled his focus stone in both hands and stared down at it with great concentration. Sigrun glanced around – no one was paying them any attention, and Philip was still sitting on the bench fanning the woman. Gareth soon looked up. "All right, Greer and I agree. I need to do something a bit risky, and I need you to keep watch. First, I must move the woman away from that bench. Do you think you and Philip can get her over there?" he asked, indicating a wooden fence that stretched along the edge of the parking lot.

Sigrun looked around again; no one appeared to have noticed anything amiss. "I think so. But how do I keep watch?"

"Just keep your eyes and your mind open. As when you perceived the opening of the portal, you should be able to detect any significant overt use of Power in the vicinity. Oh, and please ask Philip to keep quiet for now."

Sigrun walked casually back to Philip. "I'll explain later, but could you help me get her over there? Please don't ask any questions right now, okay?"

He gave her a hard stare but merely said, "Lead on."

The two of them supported the woman on either side and mostly dragged her over to the nearest unlit portion of the fence. After leaning her against the fence, Sigrun asked Gareth, "Do you want Philip to hold her up?"

Gareth said, with a hint of humor in his voice, "At this point I don't see why he shouldn't watch!" He turned to Philip. "Would you mind supporting her?"

"Anything to be of assistance," Philip said dryly.

Sigrun released the woman and stepped away, scanning the area in the growing darkness. She attempted to "listen" alertly with her mind ... having no clue as to what she was listening for. No one was near; everyone around appeared to be in too much of a hurry to notice the group's odd activities. In the tension-filled silence, she continuously surveyed the surroundings, but they were not attracting any attention. She glanced at Gareth and saw a thin beam of vivid violet light radiating from the gem he held close to the woman's forehead as he murmured quietly. A flash of the amber light was followed by an even briefer flash of pale green.

Gareth moved away from the woman. "Do you feel better?"

"What happened?" asked the woman, confusion in her eyes as she studied the small group around her.

"Oh, I believe you felt lightheaded stepping off the train," Gareth replied. "I saw you collapse and caught you before you fell. We brought you over here away from the crowd, and you recovered quickly. How do you feel?"

"I think I'm fine," the woman responded unsteadily. "Thank you for your help ... sorry to delay you." She looked around suspiciously.

"Uh, here's your bag," Philip offered, sounding shaky.

"Thank you." She reached out to take her bag from Philip, touching his hand as she did so. She gave each of them a curious look. Sigrun pasted a pleasant smile on her face. "Well," the woman said uncertainly, "I guess I'll be on my way then."

The trio wordlessly watched the woman walk toward the station, then looked at each other awkwardly. Gareth briskly took control. "So, shall we go to the car before we get into things that are best not discussed in public?" Without waiting for a response, he walked over and picked up Sigrun's bag. Philip grabbed his own bag, and he and Sigrun followed Gareth to his car.

After stowing the luggage, Gareth said, "My back seat is too small for someone as tall as Philip. Sigrun, would you mind sitting in back?"

"No, that's fine." She climbed into the cramped space.

Nothing else was said until they were on their way. Then Gareth threw a glance at Philip, and said, "I am terribly sorry, I am usually not this rude to strangers. I am Gareth Malama, as you must have gathered. I suspect all of that came as a total shock to you." He caught Sigrun's eyes in the rearview mirror with an inquiring raise of his eyebrow. She nodded in return. "I can't explain at the moment, but let me assure you that the woman at the station was not harmed."

Sigrun interjected, "What did you do to her?"

Gareth responded vaguely, "I just altered her memories. She'll only remember what I told her: that she bumped into Sigrun uneventfully, stumbled on the steps, and felt faint for a few minutes. Other than feeling a little light-headed, she should suffer no consequences."

Sigrun hesitated, but decided not to say anything about the Grid in front of Philip. If that woman **had** bumped into her deliberately – and Sigrun was pretty sure she had – then they were right: Someone else did suspect that she was from Kaia. That thought was so unsettling that she shoved it to the back of her mind.

Gareth continued addressing Philip. "I have asked Greer, a close friend of mine, whom Sigrun has already met, to join us at my house. She should be there by the time we arrive. What I did at the station was not necessarily wise, and I need to consult with Greer."

Philip said nothing, but his barely contained curiosity was plain. Sigrun asked obliquely, "Will Greer be able to explain to Philip what happened?"

Gareth threw her a cautious glance in the mirror. "I do not think so."

"Philip is my best friend," she said fiercely, "**and** all the family I have left. I don't intend to keep this secret from him any longer."

Gareth paused before he said in a measured tone, "I can't tell you what to do, but you know how Greer will feel about that."

"I don't care how Greer feels! I want you to know that I intend to tell Philip the truth to the extent that I know it."

"As you wish. But be aware that you may cause serious problems by doing so."

"Doesn't that depend on your point of view? From my perspective, you caused serious problems in my friendship with Philip by your actions at the station."

Gareth's laughter defused the growing tension. "I am sorry," he said playfully, "but as I recall the incident, you were the one who threw herself into my arms on the platform. How exactly were you planning to explain that to your friend?"

"Yes, well ..." she said, feeling her face warm with a blush, "I did wonder about that at the time – but it seemed like the best way to get your attention quickly without causing a scene."

"I could tell that you both were being careful not to cause a scene," Philip deadpanned.

Gareth laughed again. "And I thought we were being so discreet! But seriously, Philip, I do want to thank you for providing such calm and unquestioning assistance – you clearly are someone to have at hand in an emergency."

"I generally find that I remain calm when confronted by irrational behavior."

"Good, we may need that," said Gareth with unexpected seriousness. "We'll be at my house shortly. Sigrun, I suggest that you let me talk to Greer alone before you challenge her about Philip. She can be just as stubborn as you are."

"That's fine." Then she added casually, "You could drop us off at the motel first to give you two a chance to talk."

"Nice try! You know that Greer won't permit you to stay at the motel now."

Sigrun sighed. "No, I didn't think so."

"You know," Philip broke in, "this is almost as entertaining as a movie; I just wish I knew the plot!"

"Oh, it'll get better! Trust me, it's a **lot** more riveting than a movie! And, if we ask nicely, I bet we can even get Gareth to perform some magic tricks for you."

"Why do I get the feeling that you're going to hold it against **me** that Greer will come down hard on you?" Gareth asked with barely suppressed amusement.

"Right, and who called Greer?" she asked mockingly.

"You didn't believe me when I told you I wasn't particularly gifted."

"I stand by my total disbelief of that claim; you appear plenty gifted to me!"

"Why, I believe that was a compliment. Thank you."

"Yes, it was," Sigrun responded seriously. "I was quite impressed by how quickly you swung into action based solely on my instinct."

Gareth glanced back at her in surprise. "I'll always trust your instinct."

She once again felt her face warming. "But you hardly know me!"

"On the contrary," he replied quietly, "I believe I know you quite well."

Startled by the feeling detectable behind his words, Sigrun lapsed into silence. It was true – she did feel that she knew him through their phone conversations even though she hadn't spent much time in his company. And, as irrational as it seemed, she trusted him completely. Maybe he would be able to smooth things over with Greer. She was not going to be dissuaded from telling Philip. Anyway, what else could they do now? Well, she mused, they probably could make him forget the incident, as Gareth apparently had done with the woman from the train. ... But then she'd have to continue lying to him, and that simply wasn't an option.

Sigrun's thoughts were interrupted by their arrival at Gareth's house. As Philip helped her extract herself from the back seat, she said quietly, "Don't be put off by Greer. She's gruff, but I think she's just concerned. I'll explain later."

"Leave the luggage," Gareth said, shepherding them toward the front door.

As they entered the house, Greer appeared in the kitchen doorway. "Sigrun, I'm exceedingly glad to see you."

Sigrun approached with the vague thought of shaking her hand, but Greer unexpectedly reached out and, ignoring the shock that resulted from their contact, pulled her close in a hug. Thrown off balance by the warmth of the greeting, Sigrun returned the hug. "I'm happy to see you too." As she said it, Sigrun realized it was true. Embarrassed by her emotion, Sigrun pulled away. "Let me introduce my friend, Philip."

Whether Greer had expected to see him or not, Sigrun couldn't tell. Her voice held no hint of surprise as Greer grasped his hand firmly and said cordially, "Greetings. Sigrun has told me how much you mean to her." Greer held Philip's hand and his gaze. "I hope that we will be friends."

"I won't lie and say that Sigrun has told me anything about you, but if you care for her as much as you appear to, I too hope that we will be friends," Philip replied gallantly with a slight bow.

"Well," Gareth said, "I hate to disrupt the pleasantries when things are going ever so much better than I had feared. But I suggest that Philip and Sigrun go out back. I'll bring you two some refreshments before Greer and I talk."

Sigrun noted that Greer threw a sharp glance at Gareth, although she remained silent. Sigrun led the way out back and Philip followed her over to the wall. It was a moonless night; she could see nothing apart from the stars that were beginning to blanket the sky.

They stood without speaking for a few minutes before Gareth appeared, bearing a tray of tea and biscuits. "Please help yourself," he said, placing the tray on the redwood table. "We shouldn't be long."

Sigrun became aware that Philip was regarding her with consternation. She drew a deep breath and leaned back against the wall. "I don't know where to start."

"I guess the beginning would be too obvious?"

Sigrun snorted. "I wish it were that easy. But I don't think I know the beginning. I don't even know what part of the story we're in at the moment. I do know that I've been longing to talk to you for weeks." She pondered how much to say and decided that it would be best to at least wait to see what Greer said before raising the issue of Kaia. "Let me start by saying that Greer really does care about me. And I admit that I'm embarrassed I underestimated her. I didn't expect her to show any affection in her greeting. ... It's kind of convoluted, but it turns out that Greer is my cousin, a couple of times removed." At Philip's start of surprise she added, "Yes, this all involves my birth parents. You might recall that I'd begun to suspect that I was born in California?"

He nodded.

"Greer, if I have this right, is a first cousin to the mother of my birth mother." Sigrun paused and looked questioningly at Philip.

"I'm with you so far – but you're clearly avoiding the more 'delicate' topics."

"Yeah, I am." She looked at the house and saw no sign that they were about to be disturbed. "Okay," she said resolutely and drew a deep breath. "One of the more 'delicate' topics, as you so aptly put it, is that, well, Zareh is ... my uncle."

"**What!** Come off it – you're making this up!"

Sigrun laughed. "That was pretty much my response when Gareth told me. No, I'm serious. To make things even more interesting, uh ... he was convicted – wrongfully, I emphasize – of murdering my birth parents."

"Get real!" he exclaimed weakly. "That's too far-fetched even for the movies!"

"I know, and I'm having trouble believing it. But, well, it's rather complicated."

"I don't get it. How did this … extraordinary coincidence come to light?"

She glanced again at the kitchen door, but Gareth still was not in sight. Should she launch into the rest of the story? "Gareth said Zareh eventually realized that I look like my birth father and …"

"Wait a minute," he interrupted. "If he's your uncle, why didn't Zareh recognize your name?"

Sigrun looked away. "It's a long story. I've been wanting to tell you, but I promised Gareth I wouldn't tell anyone. So …"

"Oh!" Philip exclaimed softly. "You've been so … reticent since you left and I … well, I thought you'd gotten tired of my whining."

"Oh, no! No, not at all. I just … well, I couldn't tell you about it and I … I've felt this tremendous urgency to get this petition filed before something goes horribly wrong and Zareh is executed. He really is innocent, you know."

"No wonder you look frazzled."

"I'm so sorry I couldn't come back to Pennsylvania. I felt so bad abandoning you to deal with everything by yourself. I can't imagine how you've been coping."

Philip said carefully, "Sigrun, I know how much you hurt. I wouldn't know what to do if I didn't have you. … And I can't tell you how much I appreciate what you told Gareth in the car. It means more than I can say that I'm still important enough that you want to share your secrets."

"Oh, Philip! I love you dearly, you know that!"

He turned away as he quickly dabbed at his eyes with a tissue he pulled out of his jeans' pocket and gave a tremulous laugh. "Now you've gone and made me cry! I'll look a mess for your new relatives, whom I want to impress."

Sigrun hugged him. "I don't care what you look like. And you don't have to impress anyone."

"May I interrupt?" Gareth said quietly from the back door.

Stepping away from Philip with a start, she asked, "Yeah, are you ready?"

"Yes. But, Sigrun, could we talk to you alone first?" he asked in a neutral tone.

"Sure," she replied as they joined him.

"Philip, could you please wait inside?" Gareth held the door open.

Greer came out and stepped aside to let Philip pass. Gareth

closed the door behind him while saying to Sigrun, "Please have some tea."

Sigrun settled in a chair and reached for a mug of tea, surprised to find that it was still warm. She braced herself for the inevitable confrontation.

Greer didn't bother with any tea or any formalities. "Sigrun, you know you cannot tell your friend about Kaia. It's far too dangerous and absolutely prohibited. I'll do what Gareth did to the woman from the train and alter his memories."

Sigrun bristled with anger. The unexpected warmth she had been feeling toward Greer evaporated. "No," she interrupted. "I'm sorry, but that's not acceptable."

"I'm sorry too, but it doesn't matter whether you find it acceptable or not," Greer said firmly. "You may not disclose the existence of Kaia to anyone without Power."

"You forget," she said just as firmly, "that I don't live in your world, and I'm not bound by your rules."

Greer raised her eyebrows slightly as she gave Sigrun an appraising look. "No, you don't – at the moment. But as I understand the situation, you hope that Zareh will soon be released, correct?"

"Yes," she said, seeing where Greer was going, but not inclined to help.

"After Zareh is free, he will return to Kaia, and, I assume, so will Gareth." She looked at him, but he remained non-committal.

"All right, Gareth, I don't need your assistance. Zareh gave up his freedom to protect you, Sigrun. Knowing that he risked capture, he returned to the apartment to remove all traces of your birth to prevent your parents' enemies from discovering your existence. After he was arrested – and even when faced with death – he remained silent. He did this so that you could eventually return to Kaia and fulfill your potential. Sigrun, you are so young, and you don't know our history – you can't possibly understand the importance your mother ..."

"If you would stop telling me that I can't understand," she interrupted rudely, "and just explain the situation to me, we might get somewhere."

"I haven't the time," Greer snarled, "nor, frankly, the desire, to explain 30 years of history to you at the moment."

"Look, I didn't ask to get involved!"

"No. And Eireen didn't ask to be killed – no more did your grandmother. Or your father's mother and sister, for that matter.

But it **is** your heritage, and you **are** involved whether you are willing to face it or not."

"I think," interjected Gareth, "that Sigrun and I should take a walk. Greer, didn't you tell me you needed to get back to my brother?"

"Yes. Yes, I did," said Greer with a tired sigh, looking tense. "All right. Let's take a break, and I'll see if I can reach Gavin. Maybe you can reason with her."

Gareth turned to Sigrun, who was sitting in chilly silence, and gestured toward the field. "Come for a walk."

They strolled along the path in the darkness. Despite her ill temper, Sigrun noted the profusion of stars in the now fully dark sky. Soon, the beauty of the setting worked its usual magic, and she began to feel calm enough to become ashamed of her anger. "I'm sorry, I can't seem to keep my temper in check with Greer."

Gareth placed a comforting arm around her shoulders; she found that she was adjusting to the accompanying shock. "I know you don't want to hear this, but Greer is right. At the moment, you do not have the knowledge to understand the situation that you've been drawn into. But," he continued before she could protest, "I promise that we will tell you everything as soon as we have suffi-cient time. It is unfortunate that this incident happened now. I think that if we had had the opportunity to talk things over, this confrontation could have been avoided."

"She doesn't seem to care about my feelings at all."

"No, never believe that. She cares deeply. You must under-stand, Greer is not only just as stubborn as you are," he chuckled, "that trait certainly runs true in your family, but she is under tre-mendous pressure as well. She simply does not have the luxury of being considerate of your feelings."

"Fine," said Sigrun irritably, "but how am I supposed to make important decisions about my life without any context?"

"Fair point," he conceded. "But it does not matter to Greer. The problem is that this is far more important than either one of you. Greer understands that perhaps better than anyone alive."

"But I don't!"

"Sorry, I guess I am not doing much better than Greer. Let's take a different tack. We're not really arguing about telling Philip here, but whether you will come to Kaia after Zareh's release. Why don't we accept that you're not ready to make that decision?"

"That's true."

"So you must stop challenging Greer. Focus on Philip and

convince her why she should allow you to share this with him."

"I'm never going to agree that wiping Philip's mind is acceptable."

"That is not what Greer is suggesting."

"What harm could it possibly do to tell Philip? He's not going to tell anyone, and even if he did, no one would believe him!"

"It is prohibited."

"Yeah, right! And it's not like you don't bend the rules when it suits you!"

"Touché! Look, I understand how important it is for you to maintain your relationship with Philip; Greer doesn't. If you trust Philip, I accept that, but you need to persuade Greer. And, Sigrun, you should not be so hard on her – she is inordinately concerned for your safety considering tonight's events."

"I suppose so," she said reluctantly.

"Let's not keep her waiting, and, please, try not to give way to anger."

Upon their return to the yard, they found Greer still sitting at the table staring at her focus stone. Gareth gestured to Sigrun to wait.

She leaned against the back wall and absently watched Greer. Try as she might, she could not quell her resentment at Greer's uncompromising expectation that she acquiesce to their plans for her future without discussion. Even if she were in danger – or maybe, especially if she were in danger – she **had** to share this new world with Philip. It was too confusing and far too frightening to consider facing alone. She watched as Greer slowly wiped her forearm across her brow. Even from a distance, Sigrun could tell that she was weary. Greer sat still for a moment and then waved them forward.

"Were you able to resolve the situation with Gavin?" Gareth asked.

"For the moment." She took a deep breath. "Sigrun, I didn't mean to attack you. I can't expect you to understand what's at stake here. But I hope that the thought of not seeing Zareh – or Gareth, for that matter – again is a sufficiently powerful inducement that you will accede to my wishes. In addition, I don't know if you're aware of it, but your grandfather is still alive. Just barely, and he's not likely to live much longer. I told him that we found you; he asked me to tell you that he's anxiously waiting to meet you."

Sigrun studied Greer with what she hoped was an expressionless face as she tried to absorb this unexpected information. Feeling a tightening of her insides she identified as pain at the thought that she had a dying grandfather she might never meet, she said quietly, "You certainly play hardball, if you understand that analogy."

Over Gareth's muffled laughter, Greer replied evenly, "Yes, I do." And waited.

Sigrun took a sip of the still-warm tea, trying to think quickly. "All right, for the sake of argument, let's accept that I'll visit your world. But I don't see why I must move there and abandon my life here. After all, Gareth has lived here for 20 years."

"Sigrun," Gareth interjected soberly, "you must understand that I **will** return to Kaia if you succeed in freeing Zareh. And, I know, so will he."

Feeling rather adrift at Gareth's words, Sigrun cast about for the threads of her argument. "But I am from **this** world, and Philip is an important part of my life. I would be an ignorant stranger in your world. I have a life here ... and I can't abandon Philip!" Sigrun paused, but Greer's expression remained resolute. "Look," she pleaded, "we both have only each other left. Philip's entire family was killed in a terrible fire two months ago. I'm his best friend. I can't just lie to ..."

"Wait," Greer interrupted, an expression that Sigrun could not interpret coming over her face. "What did you say about a fire? When was it?"

"While I was visiting Pennsylvania for Philip's graduation in May."

"Where was the fire?" Greer pressed.

"At Philip's place – next door to the farm where I grew up. Why?"

"Where were you during the fire?"

"Philip and I were in the barn with a horse in foal – why do you want to know?" she asked with growing impatience.

"Gilda!" Greer spit in a voice laden with hatred.

"What!" exclaimed Gareth, leaning forward in his chair so quickly he almost lost his balance. "What do you mean?"

"It must have been Gilda," Greer said, speaking rapidly to Gareth. "I recorded an odd disruption on the Lancaster Grid a couple of months ago. At the time, I thought it was a deflagration taika. I didn't see anything to connect it to Sigrun, and she showed on my sentinel the following day, so I never mentioned it to you."

"What are you talking about?" demanded Sigrun.

Greer contemplated Sigrun with narrowed eyes. "You are

your mother's daughter, whether you credit it or not. I knew Eireen extremely well, and I know how passionate she was about Kaia. So, I'm going to assume that you will soon understand the importance of joining what is **your** world as well as ours. Gilda Gleipnir is a principal in a group – which we call the Ødeleggers – whose present course of action will bring about the destruction of Kaia. Eireen passed on to you the gifts that are vital to preventing the havoc that will otherwise devastate all of our paths."

Greer paused and placed her hand over Sigrun's on the table. "I'm afraid that your friend Philip's family was killed on Gilda's orders."

"What!"

"Yes," Greer said heavily. "She acted so quickly because she discovered that I was searching for someone. I'm guessing that – fearful that Eireen had in fact borne a daughter – she wanted to thwart my efforts to find you. It seems that she knows, or at least suspects, that she failed to kill you. Because of your quick thinking today, she does not yet know your whereabouts, but that soon will change."

"You're saying this woman murdered Philip's family? In Pennsylvania?"

"Yes. She, or rather, someone following her orders, unleashed a burst of Power to set fire to the house, believing you were inside. I'm afraid, as I explained earlier, that I inadvertently led a spy to your father's house. She must have placed a sensor there, which you later triggered; my sentinel showed that you brushed against the Grid three times in that area. Someone must have followed you to Philip's home and destroyed it without verifying your whereabouts. Fortunately for us, it was not on your path. But I'm afraid Philip's family fell victim to her zealotry."

Sigrun was shaking as she jumped to her feet. She headed into the house without a word. "Philip?"

"Here," he responded from the direction of the living room and appeared in the doorway. Upon seeing Sigrun, he quickly asked, "What's wrong?"

"You must come outside. Greer has something to tell you."

Sigrun returned to the table and demanded in a carefully controlled voice, "Greer, please tell Philip what you just told me."

Greer gave her a long and thoughtful look. Then she sighed. "You win. Philip, sit down, this is going to be difficult for you."

⋙ Chapter 19 ⋘
Magni nominis umbra
(The shadow of a great name; Lucan)

As Greer concluded her account, Philip sat unmoving at the table, staring fixedly at the hands he held clasped tightly in front of him. Then, without looking at anyone, he murmured, "Excuse me." He got to his feet and walked rapidly inside.

Sigrun stared after him, troubled. Should she follow? Or would he rather be alone? But he couldn't possibly take everything in ...

"I'm sorry," Greer said gently.

"What?" Sigrun asked.

"I'm responsible for their deaths."

"Oh, I don't ..." Sigrun said in confusion, "I mean, I don't think ..."

"No, I vastly underestimated Gilda. I thought I knew her tactics, but I failed to consider that she might have maintained a contact all these years in Lancaster. I certainly could have anticipated that she would act in haste, but I had no idea her intelligence was so good."

"You were, however, correct that Sigrun is in grave danger," Gareth said soberly. "I must confess that, until tonight, I had perceived the threat to be rather remote."

"And now she's been followed here," Greer said grimly. "They'll realize soon enough what happened. We must re-assess the situation, and quickly."

Gareth nodded. "I agree, but I need her here while the habeas case is proceeding."

Greer started to say something, then shook her head. "No, too much has happened tonight. I want to go home and look into this further. Sigrun, I understand that you're taking care of this legal matter tomorrow, correct?"

"I'm going to file the petition tomorrow, but ..."

"Yes," Greer interrupted impatiently. "Then we can discuss your future?"

"Well ..." Sigrun threw a beseeching look at Gareth.

"Why don't we put that off until tomorrow as well," said Gareth.

Greer sighed. "Fine. When do you anticipate finishing your ... tasks?"

"Oh," Sigrun said quickly, "it should only take a couple of hours."

"All right. Before I go, Gareth, I think it prudent to strengthen your shields."

"An excellent idea," he agreed.

"Sigrun," Greer instructed, "please go inside and see that you and Philip don't move about. You may talk, but you must not move or you'll interfere with our work."

Philip was slumped in the far corner of the couch when Sigrun entered the living room. He looked up warily. Mindful of her instructions, she quickly sat in the opposite corner. He watched her with an inscrutable expression.

"I'm sorry," she said miserably. "I've been wanting to tell you for weeks, but I promised Gareth ..." she trailed off, thinking it sounded like such an inadequate reason for lying to him.

"How long have you known?" he asked flatly.

"About your family? Just now – I happened to mention the fire ..."

"No," he cut her off brusquely. "About this alternate world stuff?"

"That weekend in June – that's what Gareth wanted to tell me. But I promised." She shrugged helplessly. "I didn't know what to do ... I had no idea about the fire."

"I've always wondered about the gas leak theory – the fire moved so fast."

Sigrun watched Philip absently stroke the scars on his hand.

"I can't believe they were murdered," he muttered.

"Greer said it was her fault."

"I suppose," he said disinterestedly, "but she didn't kill them. I wonder ..."

"What?"

"Do you think anyone will be punished?"

"Uh ... I have no idea. I don't know if they have any sort of justice system."

"Even if they do ... I guess no one would bother. I mean, it happened here."

"Do you ... believe there is a there?" she asked dubiously.

Philip stared at her. "Don't you?"

"I don't know," she admitted.

Gareth entered and sat in his desk chair, turning it to face them. "I am so sorry, Philip. I am terribly troubled that we must add your family to the unbearably long list of innocent victims of our conflict. I know that it will not give you much comfort, but you are not alone in your grief."

"Thank you ... it does help. It's good to know that others share the pain of their lives cut short for no reason at all."

"Oh, there was a reason – it was just an irrational, reckless, abhorrent reason. But I grieve with you, as do Greer and Zareh, and far too many others. Someday, perhaps, I'll have the opportunity to tell you the entire story. In the interim, may I address any specific questions?"

"Will anyone be charged?" Philip asked.

"I wish that I could answer otherwise but, in truth, probably not. It is possible – and Greer will do all that she can to bring it about – but those responsible are too highly placed for us to win many legal skirmishes."

"So you do have a legal system?" Sigrun asked.

"Oh yes; not as influential or as multi-layered as here, but we do."

"But why would someone want to kill Sigrun?" Philip asked. "I mean, it sounds like a pretty involved plan?"

"Yes. Even more than you realize – it's not easy to travel between worlds." He paused and looked thoughtfully at Sigrun before saying to Philip. "Sigrun is having difficulty accepting the fact that she is essential to the survival of Kaia." He sighed. "I know that sounds melodramatic; it is, however, literally true."

Sigrun shook her head in denial. "I'm not. I mean, I can't be; it's ridiculous." She shrugged. "How could I be ..."

Philip looked between Sigrun and Gareth. "I don't understand."

"No, of course not. Let me put it this way. Regardless of what **you** believe, Sigrun, because you are Eireen's daughter, Gilda – who, by the way, is the head of the central government of Kaia – believes your existence endangers her vision of what Kaia should become. And we – Greer, Zareh and I – know unequivocally that Gilda's path will result in the devastation of our civilization, if not the very planet on which we live."

Philip again looked between Sigrun and Gareth. "Wow."

Sigrun jumped up and paced nervously in the small space.

"So this woman believes this … fantasy. But if she's so powerful, how could I be safer there?"

"Because we can protect you."

"Who?"

"Greer, me, my brother, and others who work with us."

Struck by a sudden realization, she turned on Gareth. "You could have stopped that – whatever Greer called it – that fire thing?"

"Yes. Had we known you were in danger."

"It could have been prevented?" asked Philip slowly.

"Yes, I am distressed to admit. But we did not know who Sigrun was until she had already returned to Pennsylvania, and we had no reason to suspect that she was in any danger during her visit. To the contrary, we believed that the risk would arise from her contacts with Zareh or with me."

Both Sigrun and Philip stared at Gareth. Sigrun was trying to piece together what Greer had said about the spy. "Greer said something about me having been followed here. Did she mean from Pennsylvania?"

"Greer believes that the woman on the train was the spy she ran into in Pennsylvania."

Philip sat forward. "Wait a minute! I thought she seemed familiar – but, well, I was focused on other things at the time, and I didn't place her. But … I'm pretty sure I saw her at the airport in Philadelphia."

"What!" Sigrun exclaimed.

"Yeah … " Philip said hesitantly. "I think it was her. A woman ran into me as I was getting my luggage out of Ted's car – outside the terminal. She bumped into me; I turned, and she apologized and left. I didn't think anything of it."

Feeling wobbly, Sigrun sat back down.

"Interesting," Gareth said with a thoughtful nod. "When she bumped you, she must have applied a … substance that enabled her to track you at a distance. She then apparently watched to see what flight you were taking, found you again at the airport in Los Angeles, followed you to Sigrun's place, and finally followed you onto the train. Quite impressive."

Sigrun swallowed. "So I guess she's not likely to give up and go home?"

"No, I don't expect she will," Gareth said gently. "Well, I think everyone has been exposed to rather too much information tonight for productive thought. Philip, do you mind sleeping on the couch here? I only have one extra room, and I cannot allow either of you to leave the house."

Sigrun blinked at him, thinking she must not have heard correctly.

"I don't mind," Philip said. "But I'm afraid I'm a bit slow – didn't you say you altered that woman's memories?"

"Yes, I did. But she did not forget her mission. Did you notice that she touched your hand when she took her bag?"

"I saw that," Sigrun said, nodding. "So she was checking to see if Philip was from Kaia?"

"Yes. She also got her first good look at you, Sigrun. If I had been thinking clearly, I would have kept you out of her sight."

"But she didn't follow us here," Sigrun said.

"As soon as she reports to Gilda, I will be recognized, and, trust me, they know where I live." Gareth stood. "We should be off to bed. In the morning, we must file the petition, and then we can return to these issues."

"But I don't ..." Sigrun persisted.

"I am tired, and I think we all could benefit from some sleep. And don't worry – my shields are strong enough to ward off things more deadly than a deflagration taika."

Philip held out a hand to haul Sigrun to her feet, and they followed Gareth into the hall.

"What time does the courthouse open?" Gareth asked.

"Uh ..." she struggled to shift her mind from its fixation on the idea that someone capable of setting the kind of fire that destroyed the farm was out there watching her. "Uhm ... 8:30."

"We should plan to leave around 7:30 to arrive when it opens." Gareth picked up her suitcase and headed toward the guest room.

⤚⤚

They arrived at the courthouse just past 8:30. Sigrun climbed out of the backseat and took the backpack Gareth handed her. "I'm supposed to walk the petition through the process. Should I call when I'm done?"

"No," Gareth said, "I'll accompany you."

"Yeah," Philip agreed, "I've nothing better to do."

"Let's go in then," she said absently, eager to get it done. She was impatient while they waited in a lengthy line for security screening. Then they found another long line at the clerk's office. "I feel bad, making you guys wait with me – why don't you go get some coffee or something?"

"No, thank you," Gareth said pleasantly.

Philip shot him a look and said, "I'm fine."

She shrugged. "Up to you. So, did you let Zareh know we were filing it today?"

"Yes," Gareth said, "I saw him yesterday. And he asked me to call him after we finish here – please remind me to do so."

"I wonder," Philip said, "which version of the story makes a better song?"

"Pardon me?" Gareth asked.

"Oh, well, I wrote a song about Zareh – or more accurately, I've been writing it. I was never quite happy with it ... so now I'm wondering if I should incorporate the relationship stuff."

"Do you sing?"

"Yeah. And I noodle with composing. But nothing serious."

"Don't listen to him," Sigrun interjected, "he's terrific."

"Oh? Did you notice my guitar?"

Philip snorted. "Did I notice? Before my world – no pun intended – came crashing about my ears, I was gawking at it."

"You are welcome to play it," Gareth offered.

"No way. I'm not good enough to even touch that instrument! What is it? I could see the Martin mark, but I didn't recognize it."

"It's one of their gut-string models from the early twentieth century."

"Of course," Sigrun said, "you wouldn't want to play a steel-string guitar."

"What?" Philip asked.

"I'll explain later," Gareth said. "I had a hard time finding this one; it plays beautifully. You must give it a try. And I would love to hear the song you wrote."

"I can sing you the song, but I'm not sure I can play that guitar."

Sigrun finally reached the front of the line and became engaged in a discussion with the apathetic clerk, who wanted to process the petition later.

"No," Sigrun insisted politely. "I want to walk it through myself."

"We don't do that here," the clerk said.

"I believe that you do. Would you rather I spoke with your supervisor?"

"I don't think my supervisor is around," she said indifferently, reaching for the pile of petitions. "I'll just stamp it, and you don't have to wait."

"No," Sigrun said firmly, keeping her hold on the stack of papers. "I'll wait for your supervisor to return."

"Fine," the clerk snapped. "Let me see that."

Sigrun handed her the top copy. The clerk took it and typed the name into a computer. She clicked away for several minutes, sighing frequently. "This is really old," she muttered. "I have to go look this up. Hold on." She disappeared into the back of the large room behind the filing windows.

Sigrun turned to check on Gareth and Philip; they were watching from the side of the room. She shrugged. The clerk took so long that she was contemplating asking someone to go look for her, but she had neglected to read the woman's name badge.

Finally, the clerk flounced back, looking annoyed. "I found it. Here's the case number. I have to stamp all of the copies." Sigrun handed the clerk the petitions, and she methodically stamped each one. "Okay. You need to take it to the judge's clerk."

"Who is the judge?" Sigrun asked, maintaining her temper with difficulty.

"The initials." The clerk jabbed at the end of the case number. "That's Judge Deemer."

Sigrun joined Gareth and Philip and stuffed several of the file-stamped copies into her backpack. "Now we have to find the judge's clerk. Let's check the directory."

"Who is the judge?" asked Gareth.

"Deemer," Sigrun said.

"Oh," Gareth said with dismay.

"I think state court habeas cases are typically given back to the same judge who tried the case originally."

Philip frowned. "But doesn't that mean you're asking the judge to admit that he made a mistake?"

"Yeah, essentially, I suppose," Sigrun said. "Here's the directory. Okay – so I have to go up to the second floor. Do you want to stay here?"

"No," Gareth said firmly.

Sigrun finally perceived that Gareth was not going to let her out of his sight. "Sorry, guess I'm being slow. Fine, come along then."

The group found the judge's clerk, and Sigrun convinced her to process the papers while they waited. Then they proceeded to the judge's chambers, and Sigrun pressed the buzzer. "Yes," an irritated voice responded.

"I have a new case I want to hand to you."

"Just leave it in the box by the door," the voice said.

"Is it possible to hand it to you? I want to make sure the judge sees it today."

"He's very busy."

"Yes, I'm sure he is, but this case may attract media attention once it becomes known that it was filed, and I want to make sure he has a chance to see it first."

"Yeah, sure. All right, I'll come and get it. Hold on."

They waited, and the door opened after a few minutes. An older woman appeared in the opening and held out her hand. "What is it?"

"A habeas petition from a 1982 capital case."

"Well, that is interesting." She took the copies and disappeared.

"So, now I have to call the professor."

"Shall we go outside," Gareth suggested.

They found some tables on a small patio behind the courthouse, and Sigrun called Professor Ehrlich.

"Did you get it filed?" the professor asked.

"Just finished. It was assigned to the trial judge – Judge Deemer." Sigrun read her the case number.

"Interesting. I thought he'd been appointed to the Court of Appeal."

"Evidently not. I handed it to his secretary."

"Well that's good news, actually. I know him slightly from some moot court competitions he participated in a couple of years ago. I'll give him a call and have a chat. I already informed the State's attorney that we were filing it. I'll let you know. Thanks for being so prompt."

Sigrun tucked her phone back in her pocket. "So, what now?"

"If you are finished, let's return to Cambria. Once we hear back from your professor, I want to contact Greer from my house."

They were nearly back in Cambria when Sigrun's phone rang. She extracted it from her pocket and answered.

"This is Emma Ehrlich. Great news – Judge Deemer, who, in fact, is expecting a hearing on his nomination to the higher court soon, wants at all cost to avoid negative publicity. So, he cleared his calendar and set a status conference at 10 on Monday."

"What?!"

"He's determined to get the case resolved before he leaves the lower court. I've already checked with the State's attorney, and they grudgingly agreed to send someone. This is amazing. I never expected him to move so fast. He said Monday was the soonest he could set it because he has to have the petitioner transferred to the county jail."

"The petitioner's going to be present?"

"Yes. The judge is committed to moving this forward. So, here's what I want you to do: Go over the petition and think through what you feel I should focus on in my introductory remarks. I'll call you – or wait, are you going to be in Los Angeles?"

"Uh ..." she caught Gareth's eye in the rear-view mirror; he looked curious. "I don't know, maybe not."

"No problem. Let's set up a time – say Thursday – for a call to discuss strategy. Maybe 2:00 in the afternoon?"

"Fine. I don't have to say anything, do I?"

"No. I need you for support, but I'll do the talking."

"Good," Sigrun said with relief.

The professor laughed. "Don't worry, I'll do my part. You've done a wonderful job, now it's my turn to contribute."

Sigrun hung up feeling dazed.

"What did she say?" Philip asked.

"Monday," Sigrun said faintly. "There's a status conference Monday morning."

"Next week?" Gareth asked incredulously.

"Yes. And he's arranging for Zareh to be brought down here."

"Why?" Gareth asked.

"According to the professor, the judge is afraid of messing up his pending appointment to the higher court."

"So fortune favors us," Gareth said quietly.

"Seems like it. You should let Zareh know."

"Yes," Gareth said, "I will call as soon as we get home. I am simply stunned."

⤙⤚

"All right," Gareth said late that afternoon from the back doorway, "I am finally finished with Greer. Do you two mind if I make dinner for you?"

"No," Sigrun said uncertainly, looking up from the research material she had been organizing on the patio table. "I mean, as opposed to?"

"I don't want to go out," he explained.

"Oh." Sigrun looked over at Philip, who was studying some musical scores from Kaia that Gareth had given him. "I don't mind, do you?"

"Me?" Philip asked. "I never mind if someone else wants to cook."

"Good." Gareth disappeared into the kitchen.

Sigrun gathered her papers together and joined him; Philip followed. "Do you want some help?" she asked.

"No, the kitchen is too small for more than one. And," he added apologetically, "I am afraid neither of you could keep pace with me."

Sigrun sat down at the kitchen table. "And I'm not much of a cook."

"I'm no better." Philip took the other chair at the table.

"Yeah, Philip's mother is — was — such a superb cook that we never were motivated to learn."

"So," Gareth asked, "would either of you care for a glass of wine?"

"Yes, thank you," Sigrun said.

"Philip?" Gareth asked as he poured a glass of white wine.

"Uh, I don't suppose you have any beer?" Philip asked apologetically.

Gareth grimaced. "No, sorry. Beer is one thing here I've never been able to develop an appreciation for."

"Oh, well, wine's fine, then."

Gareth poured him a glass; Philip gingerly took a sip.

"Did you ever get through to Zareh?" Sigrun asked.

"No. First the prison experienced a problem with the phones, and then no one was available to escort him, so I'll have to try again tomorrow." While he was talking, Gareth had been pulling food from the refrigerator. He got a loaf of bread out of the freezer and turned on the oven.

"What about Greer?"

Gareth sent a large copper pot full of water floating over to the stove and turned on the burner. "She's afraid that news of the hearing will reach Gilda from her contacts — which we are aware of — at the prison; they'll be able to deduce that Sigrun is involved and, consequently, will be waiting for her at the courthouse."

"Oh." Sigrun took a swallow of wine.

Gareth turned back to his tasks and set a couple of knives chopping vegetables on a nearby chopping block while he washed something at the sink. "So," he said in a conversational tone, "we've decided that it would be best if the two of you stayed here until after the hearing."

Sigrun studied the table. It wasn't a bad idea. The thought of traveling about on their own with this – spy, or whatever – in the vicinity was not terribly attractive. And she needed to spend time getting ready for the hearing anyway. She gave Philip a questioning look. He shrugged.

"Yeah, maybe that's okay," she said equivocally, "I need to work on the professor's arguments, and I guess I can do that here …"

"Splendid," Gareth said. "So, I hope that you both like shrimp – I don't have much at hand, because the farmers' market I go to is tomorrow."

"Yeah, we do," Sigrun answered after Philip failed to respond. She realized that he had been extremely quiet. She looked over to find him avidly watching the activity in the kitchen. "Are you okay?"

He shook his head, looking dazed. "So it's really true, then?"

Gareth turned. "What, Kaia?"

"No. Well, yes, I suppose ultimately, but I'm not there yet. I mean – you really can do, well, magic?"

"Yes," Gareth responded simply, "I can."

"Wow."

"And so can Sigrun," Gareth added gently.

Philip took a gulp of his wine and turned to study her doubtfully. With an emphatic shake of his head he said, "Yeah, well, I'm not there yet either."

Sigrun smiled weakly. "I'm having a little trouble with that too."

"Unfortunately," Gareth said, while tossing a colander full of shrimp into the boiling water, "given recent events, I cannot show you how to access the Grid until we are on Kaia."

"Uh …" Philip looked at Sigrun in surprise. "I think I missed something – what's this about going to Kaia?"

"Oh," she said, looking down. "They want me to go … there."

"Oh!" Philip sat back in his chair.

"I refused," Sigrun added, still not looking at Philip.

"Of course! That's why you were talking about protection – I should have realized."

"I don't want to," she said miserably.

"Look," Gareth said calmly, "we have agreed that you're staying here until Monday. Why don't we take this one step at a time?"

"But ..." Sigrun stopped when Gareth held up his hand. She watched as he pulled his stone out of his pocket and concentrated on it. He listened, cocked his head slightly, and then smiled broadly before returning his topaz to his pocket. "That was my cousin. It appears that we are having company. I hope you don't mind."

"No, not at all," Sigrun said, cautiously curious to meet someone else from Kaia.

"She's nearly here," Gareth said, returning his attention to dinner preparations.

"Does she live ... here?" asked Philip hesitantly.

"Yes, she lives on Earth, but in Hawaii."

"How exactly is she arriving?" Sigrun asked with consternation.

"In a rented car," Gareth replied with a smile.

A few minutes later, Sigrun noticed that a tube-shaped light on a peculiar board mounted on the wall in the tiny hallway had begun flashing.

"Excuse me," Gareth said, "while I go meet her."

Sigrun followed him and stopped before the large and intricate-looking board. She was studying it with complete incomprehension when she heard a car in the driveway. So, she thought, the flashing light must have warned him that someone was nearing the house – it must be linked to his so-called "shields." She returned to the kitchen but continued to watch the board. Gareth escorted an older, dark-haired woman, impeccably attired in a pilot's uniform, through the hallway. As he passed, he gestured at the board, and the light stopped flashing.

They entered the kitchen, and Gareth tossed out casually, "Kila, this is Sigrun and Philip. This is my cousin, Kila."

"Greetings," said Kila cheerfully as she gave each in turn a searching look.

"Would you care for a glass of wine, Kila?" Gareth asked.

"Oh, I don't think so," Kila said, "I can't stay too late; I have a long drive back to San Francisco tonight. I'm sorry to be so rude as to invite myself to dinner."

"You are never rude," Gareth said, "and I always welcome your company."

"Thanks, Cousin." Kila crossed the kitchen to give him a peck on the cheek. She turned to Sigrun and Philip and explained, "I'm based in Honolulu, and I had a flight into San Francisco today with an overnight layover. Generally, if I have time, I try to visit my friend …" She broke off and asked Gareth, "Do they know about Zareh?"

"Oh, yes!" said Gareth.

"Well, I try to visit him whenever I can, but today's flight was too late. So, I decided to drive down here instead." She threw Gareth a mischievous grin. "After we landed, I contacted Greer, who happened to mention that you had visitors."

"Did she?" Gareth asked. "And what exactly did she say?"

"Oh, not much," Kila said lightly. "Just that I might like to meet them."

"Well, meet them you shall. Sigrun, would you please shake Kila's hand."

Sigrun gave Gareth an uneasy look but, without a word, offered her hand. Kila clasped it firmly. Sigrun felt the now familiar shock. Kila raised her eyebrows and continued to hold Sigrun's hand as she studied her face intently.

Uncomfortable from the extended scrutiny, Sigrun let her hair fall forward.

Kila shook her head and gave Gareth a baffled look. "I'm stumped."

"Sigrun was born Firinne Durante."

"No!" Kila gasped, eyes flicking back to Sigrun in disbelief. "Nullo modo! That's not possible!"

"Yes," Gareth said firmly, "it is. I gather, then, that you were as much in the dark as I was?"

Kila dropped Sigrun's hand and clutched at her chest. "Perhaps I could have that glass of wine after all? I suspect I'll be staying rather longer than I had planned."

"Certainly," Gareth said pleasantly. "Philip, would you mind pouring a glass for Kila while I finish here? Kila, dinner is nearly done, would you care to wash up?"

"Yes, thanks." She shot Sigrun an incredulous look before heading down the hallway.

"Uhm," Sigrun faltered, "I guess I should get used to that kind of reaction?"

"I am afraid so," Gareth said. "And Kila's firmly on your side. You'll need to be prepared for far worse from those who are not."

"My side?" she echoed faintly, a sense of having lost her script washing over her.

"Those of us fighting against Gilda Gleipnir and the others

who killed your parents ... and Philip's family."

Sigrun took a too-large swallow of wine. She choked.

Philip took her glass out of her hand. "Are you okay?"

Sigrun nodded as she tried to catch her breath.

"Why don't you two go outside? Kila and I will bring dinner out shortly."

In the yard, Sigrun wandered over to the back wall and leaned against it. Philip followed. "Can we do a reality check here? Did he just tell me that a group of people is 'fighting' on my behalf?"

"Yeah, he did. But I'm not at all sure about the 'reality' part."

"Do you think he meant 'fighting', exactly," she asked, "or do you take it to be more figurative – like 'campaigning', maybe?"

"Uhm ... well, judging by the fact that they seem pretty convinced that the 'other side' killed my family, I'd have to say I think he meant it literally."

Sigrun reflected on that. "Yeah ... I guess you're right." She looked at him helplessly. "So what do I do now?"

"Haven't a clue."

"Philip, please, promise me you won't leave. I'm afraid I'm going mad."

"Since I sincerely doubt that we both went loony at the same time, I think you must be sane," he said soberly.

"Really?"

"Well ... I heard Greer's story, and I watched Gareth's performance at the train station and in the kitchen. And I saw how this woman reacted to your mere existence."

"That's true," Sigrun said, feeling relieved. "So ..."

The kitchen door opened, and a large wooden tray upon which was balanced food, plates, bowls, and glasses floated into the yard; it was followed by Gareth and Kila, each carrying two wine glasses. Sigrun and Philip stood as if frozen while the tray glided gracefully over to the redwood table and set itself down gently.

"Dinner's served," Gareth said cheerfully.

"Of course," Philip murmured, "why carry a heavy tray if you don't have to?"

Sigrun managed a weak smile before heading to the table.

"I'm sorry, Sigrun," Kila said. "I hope I didn't upset you. It's just that I'm ... shocked, and I'm afraid I don't understand ..."

"Before I attempt to address everyone's doubts," Gareth interjected, "I'd like to propose a toast to new-found friends and family."

⤙ **Chapter 20** ⤚
Inter spem et metum
(Between hope and fear)

Sigrun awoke early and was flooded with recollections from the previous night's conversation with Gareth and Kila. Kila had called a fellow pilot and had switched to a later flight, enabling her to stay in Cambria much later than she had planned. They had entertained Sigrun and Philip with stories of Kaia and their reminiscences of Eireen and Zareh as children. Sigrun had had a bit too much wine, and it had left her with a headache. Groaning, she got up and dressed, longing for some coffee. She quietly stuck her head out her bedroom to find that Gareth's door was open. Good – he was up. Finding a fresh pot of coffee in the empty kitchen, she poured herself a mug before heading outside. Gareth was seated at the table with coffee at his side and topaz in hand. He glanced up and gave her a quick smile before returning his attention to his gemstone. Not wanting to intrude, she retreated to the back wall and admired the view while drinking her coffee.

"Good morning," Gareth called some while later.

As he crossed the yard, it occurred to Sigrun that she had never seen him in any other attire. "So," she asked curiously, "do you always wear Hawaiian shirts?"

He smiled. "It's become my personal quirk. Years ago, I grew tired of changing my clothing each time I went between worlds. Now, I just wear this – nothing has steel – and don't worry about it."

"Of course," she said, feeling exceedingly stupid, "Zareh's clothing! It was from Kaia – like what Greer was wearing. I knew you weren't being truthful about his clothes, but I never could figure out what it might mean."

"I don't believe I lied to you."

Sigrun laughed. "You wouldn't be responsible for it going missing at the courthouse, would you?"

"I think I should not answer that."

"Well, good thing you didn't make the boots disappear as

well."

"I've had that thought. In truth, I was aiming for the focus stones, but I only had one opportunity, and I picked the wrong package."

"The jewels!"

"What?"

"Oh, well I ..."

"Morning," murmured Philip from the doorway. "Do you have an aspirin?"

Sigrun turned to find Philip standing with one hand pressing against his temple and the other clutching the frame of the back door while he carefully looked at the ground. "Do you have a migraine?" she asked.

"Just starting. I can't seem to find my aspirin."

"I've got some," she said. "Go lay down and I'll get it for you."

"A migraine, I gather, is some form of headache?" Gareth asked.

"Yeah," Philip muttered as Sigrun headed down the hall, "a bad one."

She quickly grabbed her bottle of aspirin and hurried to the living room.

"Well," Gareth said, "I need to go to the market and pick up some food. Philip obviously must stay here. Sigrun, I assume you would prefer to stay with him?"

"Yeah," she said, watching as Philip lay down and draped his arm across his closed eyes, "I think so."

"Come," Gareth motioned for Sigrun to follow him into the kitchen. "You are of course aware of the shielding at the back gate. When I leave, I will erect a shield over the front door that will block access there as well. I trust that will not be a problem."

"Can I assume," she asked with a rueful smile, "that the object is to prevent anyone from entering and not me from leaving?"

A smile twitched at the corner of his mouth. "Yes, you can assume that."

"But it's not necessarily the truth?"

"I only want to protect you," Gareth said easily.

"Right. So, I shouldn't expect anyone?"

"No. Unfortunately, this is the end of the school term in Maluhia, and Greer is too busy to get away at the moment. I will be gone for several hours because I have some errands to run as well. Do you need anything?"

"No," she replied, wondering what connection Greer had with school terms, but deciding not to delay him by asking.

After he had left, Sigrun poured fresh coffee and went to check on Philip.

"How are you?" she asked quietly.

"Not too bad," he said without moving his arm.

"Do you want to be alone, or would you rather talk?"

"Keep me company."

Sigrun settled herself cross-legged on the floor where she could see Philip and still talk quietly. "Did you sleep?"

"Not really," he said. "I'm obsessing about the fire … I'm absolutely filled with rage. It's just so unfair! I mean, they didn't do anything; they weren't connected to this fight, or to … that place."

"It's my fault," she said miserably. "I wish I hadn't been staying with you. If I hadn't been followed …"

"Sigrun!" Philip sat part way up and then collapsed with a groan. "Stop that! I didn't mean that at all. It wasn't even your choice to stay with us – it was mine."

"Yeah but," she insisted, "it **is** my fault. I mean, I got involved with the habeas case in the first place; then I tracked Gareth down, and my contact with him sent Greer to Pennsylvania; and that caused the spy to follow me. So, yeah, it's my fault."

"You're clueless – you're just a pawn. How is it your fault when you were utterly unaware of what was going on, and you couldn't have done anything to stop it?"

"I guess, but I certainly set it in motion."

"No, Greer did."

"Yeah, but … well, I wish I had never heard of Zareh's case."

"Don't say that." Philip gingerly sat up and opened his eyes. He cringed a bit, but he stayed upright, rubbing his temples. "Look, they're your family. You've got this heritage you've discovered. I mean, it's a bit tough to swallow, but can you honestly say you wish you'd never met any of these people?"

Sigrun considered that statement, trying hard to be honest with herself. She sighed and shook her head slowly. "No, I suppose not."

"I have to confess, though," he said quietly, "that this talk of you going to Kaia scares me. I'm pretty sure I'm not going to be invited."

Sigrun studied him soberly for several seconds. "Would you come?"

"Yes," he said without hesitation.

"Really?"

"I told you!" He flinched in pain. "I'm consumed with rage. I would ... give just about anything to have a chance to bring whoever killed my family to justice. It's my responsibility."

"But, Philip," she said cautiously, "I get the idea that it's fairly unlikely that anyone will even be charged."

"Yeah, but it's a lot less likely if I'm not there and can't do anything."

"Probably true."

"Look. If you go – would you come back?"

"Of course I would."

"How do you know you'd be able to?"

"Oh! I never thought of that. I guess they could prevent me ..."

"I think they could prevent you from doing anything they didn't want you to do."

"I'm scared too," Sigrun admitted.

"Tell me about it. I'm scared about what happens if you stay and that woman really wants to kill you, and I'm scared for you if you go. ... And what do I have if you leave?"

"Would you really want to come with me? I mean – it would be even harder for you. You can't ..."

"Yeah, I know, I can't do magic. But, yes, I would. Think about it – if that woman had come to the farm even a few hours later, we'd both have been in bed, and we'd be dead now too."

"I've thought of that. I guess it was just one of life's random quirks ..."

"Or it's fate."

"What?"

"We both have something we need to do."

"I don't know," Sigrun said uncertainly, "I'm not sure ..."

"I'm not sure about much of anything right now, except – I'm alive and they're gone. And I want to make someone pay."

⤜⤛

Sigrun was sitting at the patio table reviewing her habeas notes when Gareth appeared in the kitchen doorway bearing a couple of bags.

"Philip appears to be asleep, but I brought some sandwiches and espresso brownies for lunch. I hope that is acceptable."

"Espresso brownies." Her eyes lit up. "A perfect combination of my two favorite foods."

"A good guess, then." He settled into his usual chair and started on a sandwich. "I need to try again to call Zareh, but, before I do, I wanted to ask you something."

Sigrun carefully swallowed the bite of sandwich she was chewing and sat back in her chair. "Go ahead."

"I would like you to stay with me until your school term starts. The habeas case appears to be moving more rapidly than anticipated, and I would prefer that you remain nearby."

"What about Philip?"

"He is welcome to stay as long as he likes."

"But we were planning to travel."

"I am sorry, but I don't think that's a good idea at the moment. Do you?"

"No," she said, "I suppose not. I mean, if that woman really followed Philip …"

"I think it is clear that she did."

"Maybe so, but I don't see how my staying here until school starts addresses the issue."

"Meaning?"

"What happens when I go back to school?"

"Yes, well," Gareth said lightly, "I thought we would consider that later."

Sigrun studied him suspiciously. He was not being truthful, she realized slowly. She just knew. Well, how useful! "You don't want me to go back."

"No, I do not," he admitted.

She shook her head. "I'm not ready to think about that."

"We don't need to discuss it now," he said. "How is Philip faring?"

"Not bad – we talked for a time and his headache improved so he decided to try napping. I guess it worked if he was asleep when you passed."

"I can call Zareh from inside," Gareth offered as he finished his sandwich.

"I don't mind – I'm not really concentrating." She picked up a brownie, pulled her notes over, and studied them while he began the slow process of contacting Zareh. But she found herself fixating on his suggestion; she did want to finish school, didn't she?

⤙⤚

After the sun had sunk completely into the sea that evening, Gareth turned to Philip and asked, "Are you fully recovered?"

"Yeah, once it's gone, I'm fine. And getting some sleep helped."

"In that case, would you care to see my guitar?"

Philip leaned forward in the chair he was lounging in near the fire. "Definitely!"

"Shall we go inside, then?" Gareth dampened the fire with a downward motion.

As they entered the living room, Gareth pointed to a straight-backed chair beside the guitar. "Have a seat." He removed the guitar from its stand and handed it to Philip. "You'll notice that it's smaller and quieter than a steel-string model."

Philip studied the guitar reverently. "Amazing. How did you find it?"

"I attempted to have one made on Kaia based on an unstrung sample that I brought back with me, but I wasn't happy with the results. So I found an agent who approached collectors until he located this one."

"So," Sigrun asked curiously, "can you play a guitar with steel strings?"

"Yes I can. I do have an electric guitar, but I prefer playing this one if I am somewhere, like here, where I can access the Grid."

"You said steel prevents you from using your Power, right?" asked Philip.

"Correct," Gareth said.

"So, that means you use your Power when you play?" he ventured tentatively.

"To a degree. Musical ability is as much a gift as any other. I certainly use my gift to learn new pieces – it's a form of pattern recognition – but also to increase my dexterity. Please, go ahead and try it," Gareth added.

Philip was cradling the guitar, but he had made no attempt to play it. He fingered the instrument cautiously and then hesitantly tried a few chords. "Sweet," he muttered softly to himself.

"Did you lose a lot of music in the fire?" asked Gareth.

"Yeah, hundreds of discs. But what I regret most is my guitar," he said sadly. "It was nothing much – it didn't even have very good sound – but my parents bought it …"

"Will you sing something for me?" Gareth asked.

"No," Philip said, shaking his head. "No, I'm not up to it."

"Please," Gareth said gently, "I would really love to hear you sing."

"I'm not nearly good enough for this." He stroked the guitar.

"I don't care. Please sing for me – anything you like."

"Well ..." Philip strummed a tentative chord and then absently started to tune the guitar. He stopped and looked at Gareth. "Do you mind?"

"Go ahead," Gareth said easily.

Philip nodded and continued tuning for several minutes in silence. Then he said slowly, "Okay ... but I've only had one song in my head for weeks now." He paused, started a line of melody, stopped, shook his head in annoyance, and started over again. After a couple of measures, he closed his eyes and sang with quiet intensity.

His pain was palpable; watching him made Sigrun feel as if she were touching his soul. She pulled her legs close to her chest and leaned her forehead on her knees while she listened. As the last strains of music faded, she drew a deep breath and looked up. Philip appeared drained.

"That was extraordinary," Gareth said softly.

Philip handed the guitar to Gareth with an unsteady laugh. "Maybe you could play something less morose?"

Gareth took the guitar and tuned it thoughtfully. "That was REM, wasn't it?"

"Yeah," Philip said, "'Try Not to Breathe'."

Gareth nodded. "I thought I recognized it. The only song of theirs I know comes from that same disc. I learned it for a friend of mine, but I think it's equally applicable here – it's called 'Everybody Hurts'." He sang in a deep, resonating voice.

"You're awesome!" Philip exclaimed as he finished. "Did you do the arrangement?"

"Thank you," Gareth said. "Yes, I play in a local band, and I've been arranging our pieces for several years now."

"You do!" Philip exclaimed. "Wow, I wouldn't have thought ..."

"That I would play with ferravaccae?" Gareth suggested as Philip trailed off.

"Is that what you call us?"

"I do not. It's derogatory."

"So," Sigrun broke in, "people from Earth **are** viewed with derision."

"Yes, by some," Gareth said apologetically.

"Well," she snapped, "I'd expect so."

"Perhaps here. But on Kaia, we are taught to respect differences."

"Differences are one thing," Sigrun said with a shrug, "inferiority is another."

Gareth raised his eyebrows. "You should not feel that way," he chided gently. "If you view people of Earth as inferior, where does that leave Philip?"

"Maybe, but that's how I'd feel if I came to Kaia."

"Is that your primary concern?" Gareth asked.

"No," she responded querulously, "I've loads."

"Would you care to share them?" Gareth asked calmly.

"Well, what would I do?"

"Initially, you must learn to use your gifts."

"Oh. And how would I do that?"

"You will have to attend school."

"What, start over? That would be fun!" she said sarcastically. "And then what?"

Gareth smiled and shook his head. "I cannot say – it would, of course, depend on your gifts."

"But," she asked testily, "aren't I supposedly at the crux of some grand plan?"

"I have no plans for you, other than to do my best to ensure your safety."

"All right, maybe not you, but you can't tell me that Greer doesn't."

"We only hope," Gareth said soothingly, "that your gifts will allow you to assist in defending Kaia – if you wish to do so."

"Yeah, right! In the first place, I don't believe you. And in the second, that tells me nothing about what I'd be doing." Sigrun got to her feet and headed out of the room, tossing over her shoulder. "I want some water."

As she entered the kitchen, she heard Philip say softly, "You might want to know that she hates being coddled."

Sigrun poured herself a glass of water and stood looking out the open back door while drinking it. To be honest, she thought, the inferiority issue was a major problem for her. She couldn't imagine putting herself in a situation where everyone knew things she didn't and could do things she couldn't – and, on top of that, she wouldn't know anyone. She sighed and returned to the living room. Philip had taken the guitar back and was experimenting with chords; Gareth had moved to the other end of the couch.

"Sigrun," Gareth said as she resumed her seat, "I am not hiding anything from you. We believe that you are a veridictrix, and we know that a veridictrix is vital to our struggle. But we do not know what part you must play in protecting Kaia."

"Oh," she said peevishly, "so I'm expected not only to perform some fantastic feat, but I've got to figure out what it is first?"

"You're being infantile," Philip said amicably.

"Thanks."

"Do you think, Gareth," Philip asked, "that I would be allowed to come?"

"I think," Gareth said neutrally, "that would be extremely problematic."

"Yeah," Philip said with a sigh, "I thought so."

"Do you wish to?" Gareth asked.

"Yes, I do."

Gareth nodded thoughtfully.

"But, Philip," Sigrun said fretfully, "we don't really know anything about the place or how we'd be received. I mean, it's all pretty nebulous."

"That's true," said Philip. "And I won't pretend that the idea doesn't frighten me, but ..." he played a discordant chord and continued in a firm voice, "I find I have no greater goal than avenging my family."

"But I would not," Gareth said seriously, "anticipate that you could achieve that goal even if you were on Kaia."

"Maybe," Philip said with a shrug, "but I certainly can't here."

"What about school?" Sigrun asked.

Philip waved dismissively. "You've always insisted that I don't really want to go to vet school. And don't pretend that you're all that committed to law school either."

"Oh?" Gareth gave Sigrun a questioning look.

"I don't know," she said, turning away. "I just don't know."

"If you agree to stay with me until the start of term," Gareth suggested, "you could continue to think about it."

"But I left stuff in Blythe's apartment."

"Why don't we drive down and pick it up?" Gareth suggested. "You have your telephone conference tomorrow, so we can go on Friday."

"No, I ..." Sigrun started.

"Yeah," Philip interrupted, "that's a good idea. Why don't we go get your stuff, and then we don't have any constraints."

"Fine," Sigrun said crossly. "Okay, fine."

Later that night, after tossing and turning for what seemed

like hours, Sigrun got up and crept carefully out her room, thinking she could make herself some warm milk. Her father had always insisted on giving her warm milk when she had trouble sleeping as a child, and she found that the idea held nostalgic appeal. She glided quietly past the living room, where Philip appeared to be asleep, and into the kitchen. She poured some milk into a mug and looked around in vain for a microwave. She heard a footfall and turned to find Philip coming into the kitchen, stifling a yawn.

"Couldn't sleep?" he asked quietly.

"No. Sorry to wake you."

"I was sleeping restlessly. What's the matter?" He nodded at the mug she held.

"Of course," she said ruefully, "he wouldn't have a micro-wave."

"Use the stove."

"I don't want to wake him."

"Just be quiet."

Sigrun found a small pan in a cabinet and poured the milk into it. "Want some?"

"Nah." He sat at the kitchen table. "I never liked it."

"I don't either, really. But ... well, it's familiar. And, on that note – when did you become so ... so comfortable with the idea of Kaia?"

"I'm not ..." he said slowly. "I'm quite conflicted. But it's intriguing, isn't it?"

"Intriguing? I suppose so." She poured the warm milk back into the mug and sipped cautiously. "Mostly, it terrifies me."

"Me too. But think about it – it's like ... space exploration. We could go where few ever have a chance to go."

Sigrun snorted. "I'm not Captain Kirk."

"Why not?" he asked earnestly. "We wanted to do something different. Like Emerson said: 'Always do what you are afraid to do'. We could both take a leave and give it a try. School will wait."

"But, Philip, Gareth said you can't go."

He shrugged. "You're stubborn – get them to change their minds."

𝄇 Chapter 21 𝄇
Tu ne cede malis sed contra audentior ito
(Yield not to misfortunes but advance all the more
boldly against them; Virgil)

"Here we are then." Gareth pulled into a parking spot at the rear of the bar on Saturday evening. "We generally don't play too late," he added as he extracted from the luggage compartment the electric guitar he had retrieved from a closet at his house. "But if you wish to leave, please let me know."

Philip laughed. "There's no **way** I'm leaving before you're done playing. Don't worry, we're thrilled to get to hear your band."

"Good evening, Gareth," a rather husky woman's voice said from the back door of the bar. "You've brought guests."

"Hello Judith. Yes I have." As Gareth neared the 40ish woman standing in the doorway, she reached up and gave him a kiss that appeared to Sigrun to be something more than casual. "I'd like you to meet my friends, Sigrun and Philip. This is Judith – the lead singer and force behind our band."

"Delighted to meet you," Judith said warmly as the group filed past her into the tiny backstage area. "Would you let me buy you drinks?"

"I'll take care of it." Gareth set his guitar case in a corner. "Come around front," he said to Sigrun and Philip.

Sigrun took a seat at the table Gareth led them to near the stage in the moderately full room. "I'll have a cappuccino."

"I'll have a beer," Philip said, "whatever they have on tap."

As Gareth headed to the bar, Philip observed quietly, "It's odd – being out."

"I suppose," Sigrun agreed slowly. "But then – with things so bizarre – this seems comparatively normal."

"I'm not sure that I recognize normal anymore."

"Here you are." Gareth set their drinks on the table. "Do you need anything?"

"No," she said, "we're fine. I promise not to bolt while you're not watching."

Gareth laughed. "I hope we're not that bad! Please do stay inside, however; the building contains sufficient steel to block all Grid access."

Soon the four musicians strolled on stage and promptly launched into a spirited rendition of "Me & Bobby McGee." Judith had, Sigrun thought, a pleasing, if slightly sultry, voice.

"Thank you so much," Judith said as the applause abated. "We're going to take a break, but I've been told that a friend of Gareth's who's here tonight is a marvelous singer. So, would you like to hear from Philip when we return?" Philip shook his head adamantly. "I'll see what I can do," she promised.

As the band left the stage, Gareth immediately approached their table.

Philip jumped up and shook his hand vigorously. "You're fabulous!"

"Thank you," Gareth said. "But Philip, Judith has a rather forceful personality – don't let her push you into doing something you would rather not do."

"Well," said Philip tentatively, "I wouldn't mind, really ..."

"Isn't he terrific?" Judith arrived rather breathlessly at their table, a glass of white wine in hand. "So, Philip, Gareth said I really should hear your voice; would you please sing something for me?"

"But," Philip protested, "I doubt you guys know anything I can sing; I don't do many female vocalists."

Sigrun offered, "You do a wicked Janis Joplin."

"I don't think that would be ..." Philip began, flushing.

"Does he really?" Judith interrupted to ask Sigrun.

"Yeah," Sigrun said with a grin, "he's outstanding on 'Move Over'."

Judith laughed. Philip pointedly ignored Sigrun's comment.

"What about U2?" Gareth asked.

"Are you kidding? But I wouldn't have expected Judith to ..."

"I convinced her that she would shine on 'Love is Blindness'. Do you know it?"

Philip reflected briefly. "Yeah, I guess I could sing that – if I go over it a bit."

"Would it help if I played it for you?" asked Gareth.

"That would be great."

"Shall we go backstage, then?" Gareth asked. "Sigrun, will you be all right here?"

"Yeah," Sigrun said readily, "I'm good."

"Go on," Judith said, shooing them away, "I'll stay and chat. So, Sigrun, how did you meet Gareth?"

"Through a friend."

"Oh?" Judith asked with interest. "I know several of his friends – who?"

"Do you know Zareh?"

Judith appeared taken aback. "Why no, I haven't met him, but I certainly know of him. You know him?"

"Yeah, I'm a law student, and I'm working on his habeas case. We have a hearing next week."

"How wonderful." Judith sounded genuinely pleased. "Such a sad story. I'm so glad someone is finally taking an interest."

"We think he might have a chance this time."

"I do hope so." Judith swirled the dregs of her wine. "It's taken such a toll on Gareth – he's invested so much emotional energy in Zareh over the years. For his sake, I hope that it gets resolved in Zareh's favor."

"How did you meet him?" Sigrun asked, equally curious.

"Serendipity. Shortly after he moved down here, he dropped in on a show. By chance, it was our former guitarist's last night, and I jokingly said from stage that, if anyone in the audience wanted to join us on guitar, they should come see me afterwards. He did and … here we are. I still can't believe he stumbled on us that night," she added with a shake of her head, "he is **so** good." Judith drained her wine and set the glass on the table. "Well, I'd best go see where we're at."

As Judith headed backstage, Sigrun wondered how much emotional energy she had invested in Gareth over the years.

⤞⤝

Gareth began the opening measures of the song; he was soon joined by the percussion and bass. Sigrun could see Philip relax as he gave himself to the music. He picked up his cue and made a flawless entry.

As Philip's voice faded and the band followed, Judith stepped onto the stage, applauding along with the audience. "That was wonderful! Thank you, Philip. So, guys, let's use some of that energy and do Stevie Nicks' 'Talk to Me'."

"Not bad," Sigrun said with a wide smile as Philip returned to the table, "you know, for being out of practice and all."

"Think so?" he asked quietly as the band struck up the next song. "I forgot that line in the last verse, and I missed …"

"I'm joking," she said softly. "You were great!"

Toward the end of the song, Sigrun noticed Gareth glance at the cell phone he had placed on a small table at his side. As soon as they finished, he grabbed the phone, whispered something in Judith's ear, and hastened backstage.

"The next song we'd like to do," Judith said, "harks back to my Irish heritage. It's a traditional little tune, called 'Lish Young Buy-A-Broom'." She threw a look backstage. "It has its origins in the Lake District and has been recorded by the group Clannad."

Gareth reappeared, whispered in Judith's ear again, and stepped down from the stage. As he approached their table, Judith said, "I'm dreadfully sorry, but there's been an emergency in Gareth's family, and he has to leave. We'll continue as best we can."

"We must go," Gareth said urgently, then ushered them through the crowded room toward the back door, thanking the many patrons who wished him luck.

They piled into the car and were on the highway before Gareth spoke. "The call was from Kila," he said in a controlled voice. "Apparently Greer contacted her when she couldn't reach me. There was a terrible incident at Festival in which my brother Gavin was seriously injured."

"What happened?" Sigrun asked.

"Kila said Greer had no time for details but was quite explicit that I was to keep a close eye on you, Sigrun."

"Oh?" she asked in puzzlement.

"I assume," Gareth said soberly, "that a veridictrix was attacked. It has happened before. Kila said Greer instructed us to wait to hear from her. While we wait," he said as he pulled into his driveway, "I want to try to contact my sister, Malie."

Gareth closed the front door behind them and turned to face it. He raised his topaz high before him and stared at it for several seconds before he moved the gemstone slowly and deliberately through a rectangular pattern. Sigrun heard Philip gasp behind her as she watched a luminous line of midnight blue stream from the stone and then radiate from the rectangle he had traced until it enveloped the entire wall.

Gareth hurried through the house. "I prefer to be on the patio, and, I hope you don't mind, I prefer that you both stay where I can see you."

"That's fine," said Sigrun swiftly, discomforted by his unmistakable distress. She and Philip, in unspoken agreement, proceeded to the back wall as Gareth concentrated on his gemstone.

"I wonder what happened," Sigrun said, watching Gareth.

"Do you know what 'Festival' is?" asked Philip.

"No idea." Gareth remained engaged, so Sigrun turned to join Philip in gazing at the vista in the dim light cast by a sliver of moon. "He's really rattled ..."

"What's that?" Philip exclaimed at a brief flash of bright light in the distance.

Sigrun spun to look at Gareth, who was already on his feet. He peered inside the open back door and then called, "It's Kila."

"Oh!" She turned back to Philip.

"What's going on?"

"It's the portal," she explained. "Did you notice that decrepit stone bench we passed today on our walk along the bluff? It's something they call a 'portal'; somehow it permits instantaneous travel."

"Really!?"

"Yeah. I saw it the first time I met Greer." Sigrun gave a weak smile. "You'll have to see it up close and personal sometime, it's pretty impressive. Anyway – I'm guessing Kila used the portal to join us."

"You're kidding, right?"

"No, I'm not. Watch for her along the path."

"So," Philip said cautiously, "that explains how they go between worlds. ... Do you know why it's difficult?"

"No. I mean, apart from the obvious obstacles intrinsic in using an old stone bench on a bluff overlooking the ocean as a mode of transportation."

"Yeah, well, of course, I was referring to the additional ... whoa!" Kila, casually attired in shorts and an over-sized T-shirt, came into view. "You weren't kidding."

"Greetings," Kila called softly as she neared. "Is Gareth around?"

"Yeah," Sigrun said, "he's right here, but he's ... communicating with someone."

Kila stopped at the gate. "He knows I'm here; he'll be over."

"How did he know it was you?" Sigrun asked.

"Oh," Kila said distractedly, "it's Greer's watch taika – that board in the hall."

"Right," Sigrun said uncomprehendingly.

"Sorry," Gareth said as he joined them and opened the shields.

"Did you get any news?" Kila asked.

Gareth shook his head. "I finally reached Malie. She's seen Gavin, and he's still unconscious. But she doesn't know what happened because everyone's too busy to talk, and she wasn't at Festival. All Greer told her was to go to Paola – that's the Sanatorium – and that someone was killed."

"Oh no!" Kila gasped. "Greer was unsecured when she contacted me and she only mentioned Gavin. I wonder who …"

"No idea," Gareth said grimly. "So, we wait. I asked Malie to let me know if she learns anything – but since she plans to stay with Gavin, I don't expect to hear back from her for some while."

"What about Makoa – we could try contacting him?"

Gareth shook his head. "I don't want to meddle. We'll wait for Greer. Would anyone else like something to drink?"

"Coffee would be welcome," Kila said.

They had long lapsed into strained silence when Sigrun finally glimpsed a flare of light across the field.

Kila jumped up and glanced into the hallway. "I'll go meet her."

Gareth escorted her to the gate and raised the shields. When he returned, he said, "I want to make fresh coffee. Please come inside, Sigrun."

Sigrun followed him into the kitchen. "Is it okay if I use the bathroom?"

He studied the board in the hallway and darkened it with a wave. "Go ahead."

As she returned to the kitchen, Gareth motioned at a tray of mugs. While it floated outside, he carried one of the kitchen chairs. He then headed to the back wall, waving at the firepit as he passed. The logs set at the ready burst into flame.

Philip shuddered and muttered under his breath, "I just can't get used to that."

Gareth waited until Greer and Kila had reached the gate before he lifted the shields. No one spoke as Greer, looking drawn and weary with her clothing in disarray, crossed the yard and dropped into a chair. "First, I want you to know that I believe Gavin will recover completely, although I didn't have a chance to check on him prior to my transit. But, before I continue, may I have a moment alone?"

"Certainly." Gareth motioned the others toward the house.

Sigrun, Philip, and Kila filed past him and he followed, closing the door behind him. It was too crowded for everyone to comfortably stand in the kitchen, so Sigrun stepped into the hallway and peered at the tube-laden board.

"A sentinel; it's surprisingly sophisticated," Gareth said at her shoulder. "I'll show you sometime."

"It tells you," she asked, "not only that someone's coming, but who it is?"

"Only if it is a person for whom I am watching."

"So … you need to know the identity of your enemies?"

"Exactly."

"She's ready," Kila called.

They joined Greer outside, where she sat cradling a mug of coffee. "Thank you, I really needed this."

Greer surveyed her anxious audience. "For the benefit of Sigrun and Philip, Festival is an annual four-day celebration held in the streets of Maluhia around the Kholm – the common name for the town center – to commemorate the end of the Orbis Concilium's session and to induct any newly elected Conciltors. It's the largest and most prestigious gala on the planet, and it attracts a crush of people from every corner of the world. In recent times, it's also proven to be an ideal setting for homicide; this year was no exception. The oath-taking ceremony was yesterday evening. Tonight was the end of the second day, which is typically the quietest." She sighed and took a sip of coffee before asking Gareth, "Have you told Sigrun about the Concilium yet?"

"No," he said, "I thought I should wait until we could provide the full context."

Greer nodded. "Sigrun, this will be confusing for you because I've collected only part of the story as of yet, and you don't have the background to understand. But, regardless, our small group was stretched too thinly tonight. I accompanied Conciltor O'Dougherty and her children at her request."

"Really!" exclaimed Gareth.

"I warned her that attending in my company would be interpreted as insurrectionary, but she insisted." Greer shrugged. "We need her support, so I agreed. Consequently, I requested that Gavin forbid Mwanakweli from coming after she resisted all efforts to persuade her to stay home, but Gavin decided that it was not in our interests to antagonize her to that extent."

Greer paused for coffee, and Gareth added, "Mwanakweli Sithembile – or Kweli – is one of the few veridictrices on the planet we've managed to protect."

"Yes," Greer said flatly. "She was quite instrumental this past year in campaigning for Africana's new Conciltor, Imhotep Nassor, who was just inducted. Mwanakweli lived in isolation in Africana much of her life, and she desperately wished to attend her first Festival as an adult. She was escorted by Gavin and his partner, Aoede Guarani. We decided Jebediah Hicks should accompany me so that he could be dispatched quickly should his services as a healer be needed. Jebediah joined us at the Academy, where I had secured rooms for Gavin's party for the duration of Festival."

"Greer is a professor at the Academy," Gareth explained.

"The main events of the day began at sunset," Greer continued. "So, it was approximately one and nine bells – what you would call 7:00 in the evening – when Jebediah arrived at my door."

⌒⌒

"Greetings, Jebediah," Greer said, sounding hassled, as she opened the door of her suite to a tall bearded redhead in his mid-20s, sturdy-looking and plainly dressed.

"Greetings, Greer," he said. "Are things still calm?"

"Seemingly," she said brusquely as they strode down a short hallway. "Would you let Gavin know that you're here and we're ready?"

"Will do," Jeb said as he entered the sitting room. Greer returned to the adjacent office. Two people were seated at the large cluttered oval table that crowded the small room, the walls of which were lined with brightly lit sentinels.

"Any questions?" Greer asked, plucking a steel blue cape from a chair back. "You should strive to cover the entire Kholm every hour or so."

"Should we report to you or Gavin, or both?" asked Morgan O'Sheridan, a fair-skinned, black-haired woman in her mid-30s.

"Both for routine reports, I think. But if either of you encounters anything urgent, contact Makoa first. He's backup on Conciltor Nassor, but he's the designated first responder if anyone needs assistance."

"Got it." Morgan stood, slipping the large pearl that had rested on the table in front of her into a pocket of her breeches.

"Humphrey?" Greer inquired of Humphrey Haldir, a slightly younger man with the sinewy build of a distance runner.

"I'm good." He too got to his feet.

"May fortune favor our paths tonight," Greer said as they entered the sitting room where Jeb sat staring at a reddish amethyst cradled in his large, cupped hands. He looked up and nodded.

Greer pulled on her cape and threw Jeb an irked look. "You two go on ahead," she said to Morgan and Haldir and headed down the hallway before raising the shield on the door.

"Gavin said they'll meet us outside," Jeb reported as he joined Greer, waiting impatiently in the hall. "They're moving rather slowly."

Greer shook her head irritably. "I should have put a stop to this."

They stepped outside, and Jeb scrutinized their surroundings while they waited. Meticulously groomed paths meandered from where they stood in front of the staff housing throughout the expansive grounds of the school. A gaily attired bunch of revelers ambled toward the grand baroque building that anchored the grounds. Someone waved and called out greetings to Greer; she responded tersely.

After awhile Greer asked testily, "When did he say they'd be here?"

"Do you want me to contact him again?"

The door behind them opened, and a large dark-haired man in his early 50s held it for the two women who followed. One was in her late 30s, tall and statuesque, her shaved head gleaming darkly in the lights that were just beginning to come on. She wore a vivid, multi-colored, sleeveless garment that floated softly about her knees; long slits in its sides parted when she moved to reveal flamboyantly orange, skin-tight leggings underneath.

"Greetings, Madam Fortes," she said in a mellifluous voice as she glided over to Greer, "I'm delighted to be able to share such a joyous occasion with you."

"Greetings, Mwanakweli," Greer said, with a slight edge, "I'm glad you're enjoying yourself. Greetings, Aoede," she added as the second woman joined them.

"Sorry to keep you waiting," said Aoede. In her mid-40s, she was muscular and compact and moved with a coiled energy. Her close-fitting attire contrasted sharply with that of her companion, being uniformly of a hard-to-distinguish color that shimmered and shifted and seemed to disappear against the darkening sky.

While the others exchanged pleasantries, Gavin enclosed the group in a semi-rigid, but barely visible, bubble shield that floated a foot or so away from them. "Shall we be off then," he said, giving a nod to Jeb.

They fell in behind Jeb as he set off down the broad gravel path, amethyst in hand. Jeb led the way through the center of the grounds toward a pair of imposing wooden gates set in the tall stone wall that surrounded the Academy.

"Mwanakweli, I understand that you wish to savor the experience of Festival," said Greer. "But do keep in mind that we are **extremely** worried about your safety. You **know** that your path ends in violence."

"At some point," Kweli said nonchalantly. "But I've been well-drilled in what I can and can't do tonight, and I've promised Aoede," she took the other woman's arm, "to stay close."

Greer gave a long-suffering sigh.

Jeb came to a sudden stop and made a small motion behind his back. Gavin halted Kweli with a hand on her shoulder. "What?" Gavin asked softly, sweeping their surroundings with a searching gaze.

"I caught something," Jeb said, staring intently at the amethyst he now held high in front of him. He shook his head. "It's gone. I felt a fierce and focused malevolence. I'm certain that whoever passed," he gestured to the nearby wall, "is plotting violence directly."

Gavin nodded and looked at Greer, who shrugged and said, "No more than we expected."

"Stay alert," Gavin said and gestured for Jeb to proceed.

Leaving the Academy grounds, they merged with the flow of people in the wide, palm-tree-lined avenue, all traveling – some walking; some on horseback; some riding the slow-moving ver-voeder, the ground-level conveyance that ran down the middle of the street – toward the Kholm. Soon, the cacophonous sounds of multiple musical ensembles, intermixed with the yells of street vendors, wafted down the hill. In the deepening darkness, the tiny twinkling lights that blanketed the Festival site flickered into view. Gavin and Aoede walked with a buoyant Kweli close between.

"Jebediah and I need to stop at Conciltor O'Dougherty's residence," Greer said as the group reached the intersection with the Ring Road that encircled the Kholm. "Gavin, I'll check with you after we collect her. Please remain alert."

Morgan O'Sheridan threaded her way along the margin of the rapidly growing mob in the vast, eleven-sided, paved open space that was the town center's piazza, her left hand in her pocket clutching her pearl as she scrutinized those in her vicinity. She ducked into a tiny, nearly deserted alley, now jammed with empty hand carts stashed there by street performers, and pressed herself into a dark corner where she speedily but unobtrusively strengthened and anchored the virtually transparent shield that clung to her. *"Greer,"* she called mentally, *"Greer, are you free?"*

"Yes, Morgan?" Greer's crisp reply came after a moment's delay.

"I've circled the Kholm and so far no turbulence. I checked with Gavin a few minutes ago, and he also reported calm."

"Good," Greer responded, *"keep in touch."*

Staying closely shielded, Morgan cast her senses in as expansive a sweep of the packed piazza as she could from her confined vantage point. An "umbra," she had the gift of perceiving the reflection of soon-to-occur events in her close vicinity. She paused and reviewed a portion of the Grid approximately opposite her present position. Just at the periphery of her range, she discerned a troubling disruption. She cast loose the grounding on her shield and plunged into the center of the crowd. Her movement was significantly hindered by the horde of people, not to mention the various vendors and street performers scattered about the space. She skirted the edge of the central fountain.

At the top of the piazza, a company of identically attired children was assembling on the imposing granite steps of the Conciliabulum. Morgan spared them no attention as she sought to place the pending perturbation in physical space. When she reached what she believed was the corresponding spot on the piazza, she paused and shifted her attention to her internal view of the Grid. The fluctuation had stabilized – she could now pinpoint where the taika was being set – but she was not yet there. She stepped up her pace, rudely brushing aside a mime who skipped into her path.

Finally, she reached what she felt was the fulcrum of the fluctuation. She joined the fringe of the throng gaping at a group of jugglers furiously tossing flaming torches far into the air. She unobtrusively grounded her shield, brought her pearl-holding hand out of her pocket, and gazed at the gem as inconspicuously as possible. The scene in front of her receded as she focused on the events that were about to unfold. She "saw" the perturbation run toward a pair of young girls – about 16 or 17 – whom she did not know. One was tall, with blond braids bound tightly around her head; the other – the target – was slight, with long, fine, copper-colored hair loose about her shoulders. She traced the disturbance in the other direction and found two men she did know – Vihtori and Hakon – moving deliberately toward the girls; she recognized the garment shop they were striding past as being quite near.

Morgan let go her link and shifted her focus, urgently searching for the targeted girl. After a moment, she located the unmistakable copper-colored hair. She pushed her way through the press of people as the ethereal sound of the children's choir washed over her.

"Barriss, let's go," the blond-haired girl said anxiously, "my father said to meet him at the choir performance, and they've started."

"Just a minute," the redhead responded, inching closer to an artist who was skillfully sketching a portrait of a young couple posing for her. "She's really good."

"I'm going to get in trouble," the other girl pleaded.

Morgan squeezed through the spectators until she stood behind the girls. She edged herself into a position between them and where she knew Vihtori and Hakon soon would be before she sent out a loquansmente hail. *"Makoa,"* she thought, *"Makoa, it's Morgan."*

"Yes, Morgan," came the almost-instant response. *"Having fun?"*

"Loads," Morgan thought in reply. *"In fact, I just spotted two interesting fish I think I recognize, and I wondered if you'd come and see if you know what species they are."*

"On my way," Makoa responded. *"Are they alive?"*

"And active." She adjusted her position to stay close to the girls before hastily scanning the

portion of the perimeter of the piazza she could see. *"I'm in Octavus Sector, opposite Brigitte's shop. I'll meet you 15 passus in from Harbor Weg."*

"Got it."

Morgan inched closer to the girls and dissolved her shield. The blond-haired one grabbed the other girl's arm and tugged her back, stepping on Morgan's foot as she did so.

"Sorry," the girl muttered an apology to Morgan.

"No problem," said Morgan. "I was about to give my greetings to Barriss."

"You know Barriss?" the blond-haired girl asked suspiciously.

"Oh, yes," Morgan said. "We met a couple of Festivals ago at a concert."

Barriss hesitantly shook her head, a blank look on her pale, guileless face. "I'm sorry, I don't recall."

"Barriss," the blond-haired girl insisted, "we've got to go. Aloha," she said dismissively to Morgan.

"I won't hold you up," Morgan said without retreating. "Where are you heading?"

"I'm meeting my father at the choir performance," said the blond girl.

Morgan looked at her closely. "Would your father be Clovis Skalbaggen perhaps?"

"Do I know you?"

"No. But I know your father. You'd best be off then, enjoy the Festival." Morgan moved aside, and the girls brushed by her.

Morgan jostled through the crowd, heading toward her rendezvous. She repeatedly scanned the space in front of Brigitte's Vetements, near which Vihtori and Hakon had passed in her image. Finally, she found them hovering by a gem vendor loudly hawking his wares. At the appointed site, 25-year-old Makoa Malama stood waiting, idly watching the crowd with a nearly imperceptible shield in place. Morgan stopped at his side. She then moved her eyes slowly and deliberately to her left, where Vihtori had detached himself from the gem vendor's audience and was striding purposefully toward the Conciliabulum.

"Vihtori!" Mak muttered in a barely audible voice. "And?"

Morgan shifted her gaze back to the point where the men had been standing, where Hakon was walking, rather more casually, in the same direction as Vihtori.

"Got it. Who do you want?"

She leaned close and whispered in Makoa's ear, "I'll take Hakon. Vihtori's on point tonight. Their target is a redheaded girl, about 16, named Barriss, walking with Sorren Skalbaggen toward the choir performance to meet Sorren's father."

Mak started in surprise but only nodded. "Let me take Vihtori first so I don't lose him in the confusion."

Morgan turned on her heel and headed after Hakon. He was moving slowly so she swiftly closed the distance between them. She enhanced her shield, but only to the point where it became discernible, and held her pearl at the ready. Hunting ahead, she spied Vihtori's back. She kept half an eye on him while she cautiously followed Hakon. Then she heard a cry, followed closely by a scream. She threw a glance where Vihtori had been and caught a glimpse of Makoa's cape. She returned her attention to Hakon, who had picked up his pace and changed course to head toward the commotion. She too quickened her pace while briskly moving her gem-holding hand through a pattern close against her body. A shimmering translucent mound of nearly corporeal energy took shape in her right hand, which was cupped and ready. She gathered herself and jumped high at Hakon, catching him solidly with her foot in the back of his knee. His shield flared, then faded. People dodged as he dropped. He tried to scramble to his feet, but she tossed the shimmering field of energy over him; it clung to his body, temporarily immobilizing him where it touched.

Morgan then made her way to where she had last seen Makoa. She found Vihtori on the ground, spewing epithets, while Mak — a knee pressed firmly into Vihtori's back — twisted a glowing coil of Power around Vihtori's hands. A small crowd had amassed to watch, but no one interfered. Mak hauled the younger man roughly to his feet.

"Hele haka!" Vihtori bit out furiously. "I'll get you for this, Malama."

Makoa snorted. "In your dreams." Makoa cocked his head and held up his hand as Morgan began to speak. "Forget this hupo," he said to Morgan, "we've got trouble."

They tore off.

JT Clark shoved people from his path as he shouldered his way through the crowds.

"HELP!"

JT clearly caught the wide mental hail he identified as Gavin's. Picking up his pace, he heard a sharp explosion to his left, followed by a puff of smoke and screams. He dodged the people rushing recklessly at him. He pushed past the remnants of the crowd, now mostly having fled, and ducked under the branches of an ancient banyan tree at the edge of the piazza. Gavin lay prone and motionless on the ground, the last vestige of his shield fading. JT promptly pulled his own shield up and over his head and flung it onto Gavin. Then he sprinted toward the two women who huddled, nearly hidden, beneath an almost-opaque shield being pounded by bolts of Power hurling at it from two directions.

"I've got the one to your left," an unseen Humphrey Haldir called.

JT turned his attention to a dense cluster of the tangled aerial roots of the banyan tree, from which soared a steady stream of blasts. As he drew close to the downed women, he flung a quick bolt at the attacker's apparent location. Then he hastily erected a new shield before stepping in front of the women and grounding his shield. He ducked the incoming bolt as his shield wobbled precariously.

JT redoubled his shielding before shaping a second bolt. He hurled it toward the hidden attacker and edged aside, looking for a clear line of fire, only to be rebuffed by a barrage of small but damaging blasts. He dropped to the ground and crawled closer, dragging his shield with him.

"I'm at your right." It was Makoa. *"But I can't see the guy."*

"He's hiding in that clump of roots – I'll keep him pinned. Circle around and come behind him."

From beneath a sturdy shield, JT furiously fired off a series of small bolts until the outbound bolts ceased. JT leapt forward and lunged around the roots. Makoa had crept exceedingly close before drawing the fire of the heavily shielded man squatting deep in the roots.

JT diminished his shield so that he could pull enough Power to form a crippling bolt. He glanced over at Makoa; Mak's shield had weakened, and it wobbled dangerously under the unflagging attack. JT drew a deep breath, and yelled, "NOW," just before he let fly a crimson-colored bolt.

Mak's own bolt, also deep crimson, followed mere seconds later.

The potent and practically simultaneous blasts collapsed the attacker's shield. Before he could recover and re-shield, Mak and JT each pelted him with another round. Then JT scurried over the roots to reach the man, who had collapsed forward in a heap. JT kicked him onto his back, prepared to strike again should the man still be capable of attacking. The body fell lifelessly to the ground, a face coming into view.

"Ua'upiki! It's Egil!" Mak exclaimed. "He's not dead, is he?"

"'Fraid so," said JT grimly after searching for a pulse. "Come on."

The two men raced around the roots. Jeb was tending to the still-prone Gavin. Greer was crouched next to a weeping Aoede, who cradled Kweli's head in her lap.

"His first blast," Aoede said faintly in a strained voice, "took me by surprise. My shield collapsed."

"Yeah, well," JT said as he joined them, "the first one I took just about got through my shield, and I was ready. It was Egil – he's dead."

"Haka!" Greer snarled. "JT, see if you can help Humphrey – he was pursuing someone in Quartus Sector."

As JT ran, he sent a mental hail, *'Haldir, whereabouts?"*

"She got away. Wait, I see you."

While JT waited, two long tones of a deep, sonorous bell rang over the Kholm.

⚲⚲⚲

"From what I've pieced together," Greer said to her listeners, "it was a three-pronged plan. Morgan and Makoa foiled the first part. The second prong was then thwarted when Conciltor Nassor's aide – he's an umbra like Morgan – perceived another impending attack and called for assistance from Gavin. The third prong was against Mwanakweli. Egil Gleipnir …"

"Oh!" Sigrun exclaimed at hearing the surname.

"Yes, he was Gilda's elder son. Egil was set to attack Mwanakweli as soon as Gavin left to assist with Nassor. Then, because Nassor had already retreated at that point, his intended attacker doubled back and caught up to Gavin as Gavin returned to aid Aoede. One of the attackers shot a toxic dart under Gavin's shield." Greer turned to Gareth and added, "I spotted Tiergan Lloyd slipping into the crowd as I arrived."

Gareth nodded, appearing unsurprised at this news.

"When Gavin left to help Nassor, Aoede contacted me," Greer continued. "She said they were joining us, so I sent Jebediah to meet them. But by the time he found them, Gavin was down."

"What happened to Kweli?" Sigrun asked with trepidation.

"She died," Greer said bleakly. "When Aoede lost her shield, it left them momentarily exposed. Mwanakweli must have taken a hit then. Aoede's in the sanatorium also, but she sustained only moderate blast wounds – nothing that won't heal soon."

"Did Gavin suffer muscular paralysis, then?" asked Kila.

"Yes. Apparently it started in his legs and spread swiftly – it must have been a highly concentrated dose. Fortunately, Jebediah not only arrived quickly, but he also recognized the symptoms. He was able to stabilize Gavin until we got him to the sanatorium, where they administered an antidote. If he hadn't been near at hand, Gavin may have died."

"What followed from Egil's death?" Gareth asked.

Greer sighed deeply. "That's primarily what has occupied me in the intervening hours. I immediately contacted Iason Medici. He's Second Ali'i for the Pacifica Region's government and formerly was married to Kila's sister," Greer informed Sigrun and Philip. "As soon as he arrived, he took control of the confused local constables while we took care of the injured. Then I returned to thwart Gilda's fierce attempts to have JT and Makoa arrested. Ultimately, I had to call on JT's father."

"Oh, no." Gareth shook his head. "JT's father is a Concilitor," he explained, "and JT is strongly opposed to seeking favors from him."

"I know," Greer said with another sigh. "Particularly in this case since he was thoroughly incensed at JT's involvement. But I believe I would have failed without the weight of his position. Gilda was livid – bellicose and vengeful – and intent on holding the Kestää accountable. In the end, however, even as creative a story-spinner as she is, she found it impossible to come up with a credible innocent explanation for Egil hiding in a tangle of Banyan roots precisely where a woman was killed and a man was almost killed. Eventually, she backed down."

"No charges were brought against anyone?" asked Gareth.

"No. I decided that any effort to establish Egil's role would stir up a storm and ultimately cause trouble for JT and Makoa. And Concilitor Clark wanted it kept quiet." Greer sat back and slowly sipped her coffee.

"Why target Barriss?" Kila asked after several minutes of silence. "Isn't she a student of yours, Greer?"

Greer sighed again. "She's a veridictrix."

"Nullo modo!" Kila exclaimed. "I didn't know that."

"No," Greer said heavily, "hardly anyone does. I'm fairly certain, but, although she seems to trust me, I haven't succeeded in prying an admission out of her. That's why I became concerned for Sigrun's safety. Not only do the Ødeleggers appear to be aware of Barriss' gift, but their staging of a simultaneous attack on two of the few genuine veridictrices at the Festival is unsettling to say the least." Greer rubbed her temples, looking drained. "I never should have allowed Mwanakweli to attend."

"You could not prevent her if she was determined to go," Gareth said gently.

"I suppose not," Greer murmured, shaking her head. "Yet another one lost."

"It was her decision," said Gareth. "You made her aware of the risks."

"That doesn't make it any easier. Sigrun, I would have preferred a less-deadly introduction to Kaia's turmoil for you. However, perhaps you now have some appreciation for the vicious determination of your enemies."

"But why did they want to kill Kweli?" Sigrun asked in confusion.

"That is an exceedingly long story," Gareth answered before Greer could respond, "which must wait for another night."

Greer got to her feet and stretched wearily. "I must get back."

"I'll come back with you," Kila said purposefully as she too stood. "I can help coordinate forces and fend off the curious."

"No," Greer said firmly at the same time Gareth said, "That's an excellent idea. Greer, did you get any dinner?"

"No," Greer said curtly, "and I haven't the time now."

"Fine," Gareth said. "Kila, make sure she eats something tonight."

"Will do," said Kila. "I'll check on Gavin as soon as I can and get back to you."

"Thank you," Gareth said. "Greer, let me know if I can do anything from here. I'll see that Sigrun goes nowhere apart from the courthouse, and," he added as Greer opened her mouth, "I will be extremely vigilant then."

Greer nodded and turned to Sigrun. "I'm sorry I haven't enough time to fully explain things to you – but will you please believe me that you must be more cautious?"

"Don't worry," Sigrun said, shaken by the account of the evening's events despite her continuing doubt that it pertained to her. "I'll do whatever Gareth thinks is best."

"Good," said Greer, looking relieved. "Festival will be over

Lunae evening, and I expect things to be calmer thereafter. We will talk again then. If you're coming, Kila," she added impatiently to Kila, who was speaking to Gareth, "let's go."

"Be right there," Kila said, handing Gareth a scrap of paper. "May you encounter a felicitous path at the courthouse."

ᴀᴡ Chapter 22 ᴀᴡ
Iustitia omni auro carior
(Justice is more precious than all gold; proverb)

Sigrun was exceedingly nervous. She had insisted that they leave early for the courthouse in case they were delayed at the security check, but everything had gone smoothly. Judge Deemer's courtroom was occupied with another matter, so the three of them had taken seats on the benches that lined the corridor. Sigrun, however, could not sit still and was pacing. It didn't help that Gareth was watching her like a hawk. She hadn't seen or spoken with Zareh since that tension-filled visit in June. So much had happened since; would he treat her differently? Not that they'd have much opportunity to interact, she supposed, since he would of course be in custody. And Philip was here. She glanced down the hallway where he was slouched on the bench next to Gareth, staring fixedly at the floor. She could tell by his posture that mentally he was elsewhere. She had never dreamt that Philip would meet Zareh. Sigrun was still having trouble assimilating the collision of what she had come to think of as her two separate worlds. More to the point, perhaps, Professor Ehrlich was coming. And where was the professor anyway? She checked her watch – it was almost time for the hearing. The courtroom door opened and several people exited. Sigrun anxiously retraced her steps.

"It's nearly ten," she said. "Maybe we should let them know we're here?"

"Don't worry," Gareth said, "the judge is not going to start without us."

"Well no, but ..."

"Sorry, I'm late," said Professor Ehrlich a bit breathlessly. "I was held up in traffic. Hello," she said to Gareth, extending her hand. "You must be Mr. Malama."

"Yes," said Gareth cordially. "I am so pleased to finally meet you."

"And I want to thank you for your generous financial support – it's been such a boon to my program."

"Not at all," Gareth said. "Your assistance has provided me, and Zareh, with an invaluable asset."

"Well, none of us would even be here without your years of dedicated work." She turned to Sigrun. "Are you ready?"

"I'm petrified."

The professor laughed. "Don't worry, I'll do the talking; just tell me if I miss something or misstate an argument."

Gareth opened the courtroom door and peered inside; he then gestured for the others to precede him. The courtroom was empty apart from the court clerk and an anxious-looking young attorney who, Sigrun noted with a stab of pride, was perusing the petition she had prepared.

"When the case is called," the professor explained, "Sigrun and I will move forward. Mr. Fremont will be brought out after we've made an appearance."

"Please rise," the court clerk called out as a tall, grey-haired, black-robed judge stepped behind the bench. "The Court is in session, Judge Deemer presiding in Fremont v. The State of California. Counsel, state your appearances."

"Wonderful," the professor murmured as Sigrun followed her up the aisle. "Emma Ehrlich representing petitioner Zareh Fremont."

"Deputy Attorney General Dominic Cook representing the people of the State of California," said the young lawyer as he took his place.

"Good morning," said Judge Deemer, "is the petitioner present?"

"Soon, Your Honor," replied the clerk. "The bailiff just called and said they would be here in a moment."

"Thank you. Please be seated," the judge said to the courtroom. "While we wait, I want to let both parties know that, although I called this hearing a status conference, I spent my weekend reading the Petition and the transcript that the State," he nodded toward the Deputy Attorney General, "was kind enough to provide me. I trust, Mr. Cook, that you're familiar with the case?"

"Uh ... somewhat, Your Honor," stammered Mr. Cook. "It was assigned to me late last week ..."

"Yes, well," the judge interrupted sternly, "I stated in my notice of hearing that I expected both parties to be prepared to discuss the merits of the case, and I do."

"Excuse me, Your Honor," the clerk said, "the prisoner has arrived."

"Good." The judge donned a pair of reading glasses and began to arrange the stacks of books and papers on his bench.

Sigrun's eyes swiveled as a door behind the clerk's desk opened. A uniformed bailiff appeared and nodded at the clerk before holding the door for another uniformed bailiff who was leading Zareh by the arm. Attired in an orange jumpsuit, Zareh was handcuffed and – she caught her breath – wore leg shackles. She watched as he scanned the courtroom; he nodded briefly at Gareth. The bailiff led him to the seat beside the professor. He did not look at Sigrun.

"Mr. Fremont?" The judge peered over the glasses perched on the end of his nose.

"Yes, Your Honor," Zareh said flatly.

"Please be seated. I'm Judge Deemer, you may recall me from your trial."

"Yes, Your Honor."

"Well, I'm handling your new habeas petition. You may or may not be aware that I did not handle the last petition you filed in this Court. At that time, I was temporarily assigned to a different district. Consequently, this is the first opportunity I've had since shortly after your trial to take a look at the case." He looked at his notes. "Mr. Cook, I'm going to give petitioner's counsel an opportunity to summarize what she sees as the main issues before us. Then I'll give you a chance to respond. I'm aware that you have not had an opportunity to file formal papers in this matter, and I don't expect case citations or polished arguments. I do advise you, however, that the reading I did has left me deeply disturbed. So, Professor Ehrlich, would you care to make a statement? This is informal – you'll note that we don't have a court reporter – so please remain seated."

"Thank you, Your Honor," the professor said. "First I would like to express our profound gratitude for your extraordinary promptness in turning your attention to this Petition. I'm sure you appreciate the injury and injustice that has been inflicted if this man," she gestured to Zareh, "has been incarcerated for nearly 21 years for murders he did not commit. But, before I continue, would the Court permit Mr. Fremont's handcuffs to be removed? I don't believe that he poses a flight risk."

"I have no problem with that," the judge said. The bailiff stepped forward and released Zareh's handcuffs.

"Your Honor," the professor continued, "what we have here is a case of an ambitious and ardent prosecutor blinded by his own belief in the guilt of an obvious suspect. It is likely that he couldn't believe his luck in landing a case with sympathetic victims and a clear-cut culprit. Unfortunately, his hunger for a conviction drove him to make unethical and, we contend, unconstitutional choices. The claim that brought us back to your courtroom today, however, is that Mr. Fremont's counsel was ineffective for failing to investigate a piece of evidence that was right before his eyes and had the potential to, at the very least, cast doubt on his client's guilt. That was but one of a regrettable confluence of errors that, collectively, deprived Mr. Fremont of his constitutional right to a fair trial.

"Not only did trial counsel fail to explore the expeditious arrival of the police – which any reasonable attorney should have investigated irrespective of the unconstitutional withholding of the witness' statement – but he also failed to protest the prosecutor's fanciful fable of cult penetration in the community and failed to object that considerable portions of the prosecutor's closing argument were unsupported by **any** evidence. Further, Mr. Fremont's trial counsel abandoned his duty to investigate and present a potentially meritorious defense for his client. It is undeniable that it was objectively unreasonable for an attorney to altogether fail to investigate and introduce evidence that would have raised significant doubts about his client's actual innocence."

"Hold on," Judge Deemer interrupted. "You're not bringing a separate claim of actual innocence here?"

"No, I merely wish to stress the significance of the evidence that trial counsel ignored. Moreover, the petitioner unquestionably has shown that, but for trial counsel's many errors, there is a reasonable probability that he would not have been convicted. Because of counsel's failure to investigate, the jury was deprived both of the testimony of an impartial witness that Mr. Fremont arrived at the apartment **after** the murders had occurred and compelling evidence that someone other than Mr. Fremont had been in the apartment **before** he arrived and had left a footprint in the wet blood of the victims. Compounding these omissions, counsel – pursuing his objectively unreasonable trial strategy – permitted the jury to be exposed to the prosecutor's unsubstantiated and outlandish theory of satanic activity. In the absence of exonerating evidence, the jury was swayed by the prosecutor's scare tactics. Thank you, Your Honor."

"Mr. Cook," said Judge Deemer.

"Yes, Your Honor. With all due respect to Ms. Ehrlich, I totally disagree with her summation. What we have here is a man who was caught in the act of stealing jewelry from the bedroom of a couple he had just cold-bloodedly murdered. Perhaps Ms. Ehrlich is correct, and the prosecutor was somewhat overly zealous in his interpretation of the motive for the murders – but motive is not an element of the crime. The State didn't need to prove **why** Mr. Fremont killed the victims – only that he did so. Trial counsel's failure to produce iffy evidence that one blurry footprint **possibly** was not made by Mr. Fremont doesn't show that Mr. Fremont is not the murderer. The State contends that it **was** reasonable for trial counsel to decline to introduce shaky evidence that could, in any event, only have led to the conclusion that more than one person committed the crime. And, anyway, it likely was a tactical decision. Additionally, Ms. Ehrlich is wrong in her assertion that trial counsel did not respond to the prosecutor's argument about cult activity. In his closing, counsel tried to deride the theory as crazy, but the jury clearly found the prosecutor's take on the evidence more persuasive.

"Further, petitioner's so-called newly discovered evidence of the footprint was, as counsel said, right before petitioner's eyes the entire time. Therefore, petitioner cannot raise this claim after such a lengthy delay. Finally, most of his ineffective assistance of counsel claims – such as that trial counsel was ineffective for failing to find a witness who had long fled the state – and his claim that the prosecutor withheld evidence have already been considered and rejected by our Supreme Court. This Court has no authority to overrule the highest court in the state. Thank you, Your Honor."

"But, Mr. Cook," the judge asked, "isn't it true that petitioner's expert concluded unequivocally that the bloody footprint could not have been made by petitioner?"

"Well, Your Honor," said the Deputy Attorney General, "I think that the report's conclusion is weak, and I'm confident that – because the footprint was so indistinct – an unbiased expert would conclude that no definitive analysis is possible."

"Your Honor," the professor interjected, "I think the credentials of our expert speak for themselves. If the State has any evidence that she is biased, I certainly would like to see it."

"I agree," said the judge. "My reading of the expert's report differs from yours, Mr. Cook, and I am doubtful that any qualified expert would arrive at a contrary conclusion. Furthermore, isn't the petitioner's delay excusable in light of his argument that counsel abandoned his duty to investigate?"

"But, Your Honor, if petitioner had access to the photographs – which he doesn't dispute – what prevented him from discovering the footprint when he filed his earlier petitions? The Supreme Court has consistently rejected petitions from death-row inmates that are designed to drag out the habeas process."

"I don't think," the judge scoffed, "that a condemned prisoner aware of evidence supporting his innocence has any incentive to delay presenting a meritorious claim."

"But, Your Honor …"

"Excuse me, Mr. Cook," Judge Deemer interrupted. "I want to focus on the merits of the claims. I am quite confident that I can circumvent any procedural hurdles you can construct. Isn't it true that the only evidence linking Mr. Fremont to the murders was his presence in the apartment?"

"No. No, Your Honor," said Mr. Cook as he shuffled his papers on the table, "that's not correct. Uhm … let me see, there was evidence that petitioner had admired the victim's necklace that was in his pocket and … he left fingerprints."

"But his fingerprints were only on the dresser," Sigrun whispered.

"Excuse me, Your Honor," the professor said. "Mr. Cook is misrepresenting the evidence at trial. The prosecutor only **argued** that Mr. Fremont had seen the victim and her necklace before the murders; he presented no evidence to support his baseless speculation. Moreover, the fact that Mr. Fremont's fingerprints were on the dresser in the bedroom only supports his conviction for burglary, not for murder."

"So," queried the judge, "no fingerprints were found in the living room?"

"None that belonged to Mr. Fremont," said the professor.

"What about the front door?"

The professor looked at Sigrun, who said quietly, "Only from the victims."

"No, Your Honor – the only identifiable prints belonged to the victims."

"So," the judge continued, "is the petitioner contending that he happened to see the open door and found the victims after they had been murdered?"

"Yes, Your Honor," said the professor decisively.

Judge Deemer leaned forward in his chair and removed his reading glasses. "Having heard the initial thoughts from both parties and having read the record as it presently exists, I am tentatively leaning toward granting the Petition. It appears to me that the petitioner has met his burden of showing that his trial counsel's performance was rendered deficient by counsel's failure to investigate incontestable evidence captured in the photograph of the crime scene that another person was present in the apartment before the police arrived. I also believe that the petitioner has met his burden of establishing that, had such evidence been presented, there is a reasonable probability that the jury would have acquitted him on both counts of murder. Obviously, if I stay with my tentative ruling, it goes without saying that the petitioner's capital sentence cannot stand."

Sigrun heard Gareth's soft exclamation behind her.

The Deputy Attorney General jumped to his feet. "Your Honor ..."

"Before you protest," the judge admonished, "I am mindful that I cannot issue a formal ruling without allowing the State a reasonable time in which to file a response to the Petition. Let me caution you, however, that I will not permit the State to drag its feet until the case has been reassigned to a new judge. To the contrary, I intend to push this forward as rapidly as is humanly possible. I do not intend to allow this man, whom I personally put in prison, to spend any more unnecessary time behind bars. Based on my new appreciation of the evidence that was before me, as well as that which appears to have been unconstitutionally withheld, I believe that Mr. Fremont has spent 20 years on death row for simple burglary. I don't know about you, Mr. Cook, but that is not something I can live with. Therefore, I advise you in the strongest terms to get on the phone with your boss and find a means of making this case go away. I expect that he will be eager to prevent negative publicity about a prosecutor intentionally withholding evidence and crafting closing arguments based on innuendo and intimidation."

Mr. Cook flinched. "Certainly, Your Honor." He sat down.

"At this point, I have not made up my mind on the petitioner's cumulative error claim. Further, I see nothing that would cause me to question the validity of the burglary conviction, and I believe that conviction must stand. If the parties cannot find a way to dispose of this matter, I will schedule an evidentiary hearing as soon as possible. Moreover, even if I grant the Petition, the State unquestionably will appeal and will have the right to re-try petitioner for murder if my ruling is upheld. Consequently, I make the following suggestion: I think both sides need time to digest my tentative findings and then come together for settlement discussions. Although I realize this is an unusual request, would it be possible for the bailiffs to make a room available for Mr. Fremont to meet with his attorneys in private?"

The bailiff posted behind Zareh said, "I don't see why not, Your Honor. If you give me a little time, I'm sure we can arrange it."

"Good," said the judge. "We will now adjourn, and petitioner will be taken back to the holding cell. At 1:30, petitioner will be placed in whatever room the bailiffs select. Check back with my clerk to find out which one. Mr. Cook, I've cleared my calendar for the rest of the day, apart from a long-scheduled settlement conference. We can use my chambers for that matter, so my courtroom is available for your use. The parties can meet here for negotiations as you wish, and I'm available at any time for consultation. Please let my clerk know if you need me. I hope that some agreement can be reached this afternoon before I need take further action. Court is adjourned." The judge stood and left the bench.

The courtroom fairly reverberated with astonishment. Sigrun was so focused on taking detailed notes that she was not aware of feeling anything.

Then the professor exclaimed, "Congratulations, Mr. Fremont! You won."

Zareh stood slowly, causing the bailiff to edge closer, but she made no move to restrain him. "No," he said softly. "You won. Thank you."

The professor laughed and shook her head. "Your thanks go to Sigrun. Sigrun, you did an amazing job. I'm sure this is just the first of many legal victories."

Gareth approached the counsel table and gestured toward Zareh. "May I?" he asked the bailiff.

At the bailiff's nod, Gareth clasped Zareh in a close hug, whispering something in his ear that Sigrun could not catch. As he stepped back, Zareh said in a slightly trembly voice, "Thank you, Kako."

"Excuse me." The bailiff held out handcuffs. "I need to take the prisoner back."

Zareh nodded and offered his wrists to the bailiff.

As soon as they'd exited the courtroom, Philip turned to Sigrun excitedly and asked, "I can't say I understood all of that, but am I right that you just got Zareh off death row and maybe even released altogether?"

"I think so." Sigrun shook her head. "I'm ... stunned!"

⤳⤳

After lunch at the café where Sigrun had first met Gareth, which turned out to be not far from the courthouse, they waited outside Judge Deemer's courtroom while the professor checked with the court clerk.

"All right," she said as she returned, "we're to go to the jury room down the hall." She headed off and the others followed. The professor greeted the bailiff from the morning's hearing, who was posted outside the last door on the hallway.

"The prisoner is inside," the bailiff explained. "A bailiff will be outside this door at all times while the prisoner is here, and the door must remain locked. You may come and go as you please – knock and we'll unlock the door." She turned the key in the lock.

Sigrun followed Gareth inside. Zareh was standing across the room looking out the window. He turned as they entered; he wore no shackles. For the first time that day, his eyes sought hers, and he gave her a nearly imperceptible smile.

"Mr. Fremont," said Professor Ehrlich, "why don't we have a seat, and I'll briefly summarize our thoughts."

As the professor launched into an abbreviated account of their lunch conversation, Sigrun marveled at the fact that Judge Deemer apparently had accepted most of their arguments. And he seemed prepared to order Zareh's release! Somehow, the idea of Zareh's freedom had never been more than an abstraction. It had seemed … unattainable; she had never quite credited that they could win. She still didn't, really. Maybe it was the accumulated stress from the recent series of staggeringly bizarre events, but she felt strangely dissociated from the day's proceedings. And she couldn't wait to tell Blythe. Blythe would be so … of course, Sigrun stopped herself, she wouldn't be telling Blythe anything if she went to Kaia. Had they …

"Sigrun?" the professor said with a note of inquiry.

"Sorry." She looked up in embarrassment from the notes on the table that she had been staring at without seeing. "I'm afraid I lost track of the conversation."

"That's okay, I just wanted to know if you had anything to add, but I think I covered everything. So, we're waiting to hear from Mr. Cook. I asked him to get back to us as soon as he could with an initial proposal."

"While we wait, would anyone else like some coffee?" Gareth asked. At the general murmur of agreement, he handed some money to Philip. "Philip, would you please locate the cafeteria and bring us some coffee."

"No problem," Philip said, getting up to knock on the door.

Gareth turned to the professor. "In the meantime, Professor, could we step outside for a moment? I wish to discuss a matter with you in private."

"Sure," said the professor, sounding startled. "That is, if you don't mind, Sigrun?"

Perceiving that Gareth apparently wished to leave her alone with Zareh, she said, "No, I'm fine."

As soon as the door had closed behind the others, Zareh said abruptly, "Sigrun, I asked Gareth the last time we spoke if he could try to arrange for me to talk to you. Since we don't know how long I'll be down here, I didn't want to miss this opportunity."

"But, Zareh," she protested, "things are going so well …"

"No," he interrupted, "I've been incarcerated far too long to permit myself to hope before anything concrete has happened. We don't have much time – I want you to know that I'm deeply grateful for your efforts on my behalf. But, regardless of what happens here, you must go to Kaia immediately."

"No, I couldn't …"

"Sigrun," he cut her off, "please don't argue. I'm not important here – you are."

"I don't see why we have to discuss this now when it looks like you'll be released soon."

Zareh sighed, shaking his head. "Gareth warned me that you're as stubborn as your mother was. One day I hope to be able to explain everything to you. But at the moment, it is imperative that you go to Kaia, where you can be protected. Now that your birth has been discovered, you're no longer safe on Earth."

Frustrated at the already too-familiar theme the conversation had taken, Sigrun leapt to her feet and crossed to the window. "So Gareth and Greer keep telling me," she said snappishly. "I understand that things on Kaia are dangerous – but I don't see why that means I …"

Zareh placed a hand on her shoulder. She jumped at the unexpected contact. She spun around and was shocked to see that he had shed his emotionless facade. He gripped her shoulders firmly and said somberly, "Sigrun, I **won't** lose you too."

Stricken by the despair in his eyes, she struggled to form a response. She heard the key turn in the lock. He immediately dropped his hands and stepped away as she pivoted toward the window, fighting to regain her composure.

"Here's the coffee," Gareth said cheerfully.

Sigrun turned to find Gareth, wearing a concerned expression, bringing her a cup. She took it with a grateful smile before heading back to her seat. Although Sigrun assiduously avoided the professor's eyes, she could feel her searching look as they all settled at the table. Great, she thought, she must look as shaken as she felt. She drank her coffee, keeping her gaze down.

Later, the professor returned once more to the room. "I finally reached the District Attorney himself, and I'm pretty sure he's on board. Apparently they want to keep this quiet as much as the Judge does. So, I think we have an unbelievable deal here. Mr. Fremont, if you agree to accept the burglary conviction with a new sentence of time served on that charge, the State will agree to your immediate release and will waive all possible appeals. A condition they insist on is a confidentiality agreement. We'll all be prohibited from discussing the terms of the settlement and any allegations of improper conduct on the part of the prosecutor or the judge. And, of course, Mr. Fremont, you must agree not to file any civil action or claim for damages against anyone connected with the case."

"I have no interest in money," Zareh said disdainfully.

"No, of course not," the professor said. "But it's natural for someone who was wrongfully convicted to want to make someone pay for the lost years."

"I do," said Zareh darkly, "but it does not involve pecuniary gain."

"I think, Professor," Gareth said swiftly, "that your proposal is more than acceptable. If Zareh is to be released, I see no problem with their conditions."

"I committed no crime," Zareh said quietly.

"But why does it matter?" Sigrun asked. "You've already served the time, and we don't have any good claims to challenge the burglary conviction. They aren't asking you to give up anything significant."

Zareh looked at the table.

"Perhaps," the professor suggested, "we should let you and Mr. Malama discuss this alone. Why don't the rest of us go into the hallway?"

"Sigrun must stay," said Zareh flatly.

"Oh, well …" The professor looked at Sigrun uneasily.

"That's fine," she said awkwardly.

"Okay then." The professor got to her feet, giving Sigrun a

troubled look; Philip followed her to the door. "We'll wait to hear from you."

The door closed behind them.

"Zareh," Gareth said with exasperation, "what possible difference does it make if the burglary conviction remains?"

Zareh got to his feet and ran his hand through his short hair. "I know, Kako. It's just …" he shook his head. "I just want this all to be behind me."

"But," Sigrun asked, "what do you care if you're a convicted felon here?"

"Zareh," Gareth said gently, "have you taken in the fact that they've agreed to your immediate release? You shouldn't have to go back to San Quentin."

He stared at Gareth for a second. "They did?"

"Yes," said Sigrun. "The professor said so explicitly."

Zareh sat back down. "I'm sorry, I guess I missed that. Certainly, if they'll let me go now, I agree."

"Splendid." Gareth headed to the door. "Maybe we can get this resolved today."

🪶～🪶

"Please be seated." Judge Deemer took his place behind the bench. "I've read the latest version of the settlement agreement, and I have only one alteration. I've added and initialed a provision that the State has released the prisoner to the custody of the County as of today. Mr. Fremont, I assume that you would prefer not to return to San Quentin to await processing of your release?"

"Definitely, Your Honor," said Zareh.

"In my experience, the State moves with excruciating slowness on such matters. I'm prepared to go out on a limb here and, because you're technically in my custody during this hearing, order that the County process your paperwork immediately."

"Thank you, Your Honor," Professor Ehrlich said, "I certainly will agree to that."

"Mr. Cook?" the judge asked.

"Oh, well, as I understand the settlement," he said, "we've agreed to petitioner's immediate release. So, I guess that's fine."

"Then I believe we are done. If the parties have no objection," the judge gestured toward a court reporter who had taken a position at the front of the courtroom but had recorded nothing yet, "we'll go on the record to finalize this agreement."

Judge Deemer picked up a piece of paper and began to read.

"In the matter of Fremont v. The State of California. The parties are present in court with petitioner present in custody. Following discussions and argument by both sides, and after reading and considering the Petition for Writ of Habeas Corpus filed herein, the Court hereby grants the Petition on the claim that petitioner was deprived of the effective assistance of counsel. Accordingly, the Court vacates and discharges petitioner from all adverse consequences of his two convictions for first degree murder, as well as the special circumstances finding, and vacates petitioner's previously imposed sentence. Further, following negotiations between the parties, they have entered into a settlement agreement that has been read and approved by the Court. Pursuant to which, the State of California has agreed to waive its right to bring petitioner to a new trial on the murder charges and also has agreed to waive all rights to appeal this judgment. Finally, petitioner has agreed to dismiss his pending federal habeas petition and to not file a civil action seeking damages. Both parties have agreed to the imposition of a sentence of time served on the burglary conviction with no further supervision. Let judgment be so entered. Off the record."

The judge removed his reading glasses and waited until the court reporter had finished. "So, that concludes this matter," he said, turning his gaze to Zareh. "Mr. Fremont, nothing I can say will give you back the years you've lost incarcerated for murders you did not commit. I can only offer my sincerest apology for my role in the errors that put you there. My only explanation is my inexperience, but that cannot justify what occurred here. I realize that it will be of little value to you, but I want you to know that I'm deeply shaken by the fact that, had it not been for the dedicated assistance you received from volunteers, I would have been responsible for your death. I suspect that it will be a long time before I sleep easily. And an even longer time before I'll accept a prosecutor's arguments at face value. But, thanks to your friends and counsel, late though it is, we have managed to bring a small measure of justice to this proceeding. I pray that you will be able to cherish the freedom that has been restored to you. Would you care to say anything, Mr. Fremont?"

"Thank you, Your Honor," Zareh said after a heartbeat. "I appreciate your honesty. In return, I can say without hesitation that, had this conversation taken place ten years ago, I would have been furious with you. ... I must also say that I've always blamed you for my conviction. I believed then, and still believe now, that a person with the authority that this justice system vests in judicial officers has a moral obligation to evaluate the truth of matters that come before him and to take actions that are consistent with that truth. But," Zareh paused and threw a glance over his shoulder at Gareth, "I like to believe that I have gained wisdom and maturity in the course of my many years of introspection. As a consequence, I hope that I have overcome my anger. So I thank you, Your Honor, for returning my life to me at a time when I can resume my path and finally be of use to my family and friends."

"Thank you, Mr. Fremont," the judge said. "I promise you that I will reflect on your words and on what occurred in my courtroom. I can only hope that I will be able to derive some insight from this experience as you clearly have. ... Well, the parties need to initial the change I made to the agreement, and then my clerk will make copies for everyone. The court file will remain sealed. Unless anyone has any final details, this matter is adjourned."

"Excuse me, Your Honor," said the unfamiliar bailiff who had been stationed behind Zareh during the hearing. "What is the status of the prisoner?"

"Of course." Judge Deemer hesitated and looked at Zareh apologetically. "I'm terribly sorry, Mr. Fremont, but you will need to return to the holding cell while the paperwork is processed. It may take several hours, but I have instructed the responsible parties that it must be concluded tonight. I will remain here until I receive the final signed statement of your release."

Zareh nodded as he got to his feet. "I understand, Your Honor." He turned to the professor and held out his still-unshackled hand. "My deepest gratitude for your dedication and the time that you have devoted to my claims. Had you not taken up my case, it is most likely that I would never have been released."

"Thank you, Mr. Fremont," the professor said warmly as they shook hands. "I feel so lucky that your case was brought to my attention, and that I was able to interest Sigrun. We have all learned from your fortitude and grace."

"Excuse me," said the bailiff impatiently, "but I need to take the prisoner back."

"No problem." Zareh turned to receive the handcuffs.

"Please excuse me," the professor said to Sigrun, who was watching Zareh being taken from the courtroom, "while I initial the agreement and talk to Mr. Cook about the final details."

As Sigrun collected her paperwork, Gareth joined her at the counsel table, shaking his head. "This is extraordinary! I never anticipated such a rapid resolution. But, if Zareh really is going to be released tonight – my car is rather small for all of us. Since it appears that there will be some delay, perhaps I could drive you and Philip to my house and return for Zareh?"

"Yeah, that makes sense. I think I'm done, but let me check with Professor Ehrlich."

"So, Mr. Cook," the professor said as the Deputy Attorney General closed his briefcase, "thank you for your cooperation. I hope to work with you again sometime."

"Uh ... no offense, Professor, but I'd rather not. It's been a most illuminating experience, but not one I'd care to repeat."

"Do you need me for anything, Professor?" Sigrun asked.

"No," Professor Ehrlich said, "but I would like to talk to you before you leave."

"Okay," Sigrun said, immediately apprehensive. She had been intending to talk privately to the professor today, but it had slipped to the back of her mind. "We can step into the hallway ..."

"No, you stay here," Gareth said. "Philip and I will wait outside."

The professor waited until the door had closed behind them. "Sigrun, is everything okay?"

"Yeah." She managed what she hoped was a natural-looking smile. "Fantastic! I can't believe we won."

"I must say I can't believe how smoothly this went. You did a simply remarkable job. But," the professor added somberly, "on a personal level, is something wrong?"

"No, I'm okay," she responded without meeting the professor's eyes.

Professor Ehrlich reached over and put her hand on Sigrun's. "Sigrun, I don't mean to pry, but I feel responsible for bringing you into this matter. Is there something between you and Mr. Fremont?"

Having anticipated the question, she hoped that she remained expressionless as she shook her head. "Romantically? No, absolutely not."

The professor did not look convinced. "It happens frequently with prisoners. There's something compelling about a man who is so isolated and needy."

"No," she said earnestly, "I promise you that's not the case. I appreciate your concern. I think it's just that I've been upset since the fire, and ... well, I'm rather emotional today."

The professor nodded thoughtfully. "I suppose. But, Sigrun, please promise me that you'll think carefully before doing anything drastic."

"Oh, uh ..." Sigrun stumbled, trying to come up with a way to make her announcement less melodramatic. "Actually ... uh, I've decided to take a leave."

"**No!** You can't – what are you thinking?"

"Uh ... well, Philip and I ... we want to take some time off, and ... well, we both feel we've been thrown off course. So, uhm, we decided to take a break to ... think about the future."

The professor shook her head disapprovingly. "But, Sigrun, you have the makings of a fine lawyer – I'd hate to see you squander your skills. Surely you haven't done anything formal yet?"

"I have," she admitted guiltily. "Late last week, I notified the school."

"And you didn't come talk to me about it?"

"No. I'm sorry. I ... I didn't know what to say."

"Well, I certainly didn't expect this." Professor Ehrlich sat back in her chair and regarded Sigrun with disappointment. "I don't suppose you want to discuss it now?"

She shook her head remorsefully. "No – I've made up my mind."

"Sigrun, neither you nor Philip have any parents left. You're young, wounded, and directionless. But that is precisely why now is **not** the time to do something foolish. You both have the potential to have rewarding and fulfilling careers; you must give careful consideration to your future before destroying that potential."

Sigrun felt dreadful. "We have thought about it. I know it seems foolish ..." She shrugged helplessly, wishing she could explain.

"Well," Professor Ehrlich sighed, "I guess that's it then. I'm very sorry you didn't feel comfortable coming to me. But, please, do take me at my word when I say I'll always be available if you want to talk. Call or write any time."

"Thank you." Sigrun groped in her pocket for a tissue to wipe the tears from her eyes. "I'm sorry I ... well, I wish things were different. Thank you for your concern. Maybe I'll be back after a year."

"I hope so. At least we were able to resolve this before you took off. I would have hated for you to have missed such a wonderful outcome from your hard work."

The professor got to her feet and Sigrun followed. "Thank you for being so kind to me this year," Sigrun said, giving the professor a quick hug.

"I really hate to see you go."

"I'm sorry," Sigrun repeated. She wiped her eyes again while walking up the aisle and hoped she looked presentable as she opened the door.

⤜⤛ Chapter 23 ⤜⤛
Iacta alea est
(The die is cast; Julius Caesar)

"Please do not be upset." Gareth opened the front door of his house for Sigrun and Philip. "I intend to shield the door when I leave, so you will not be able to exit."

"Yeah," Sigrun said with a shrug, "I expected that. I'm not going anywhere."

"Good," Gareth said. "Philip, would you mind if I borrowed some of your clothing for Zareh? He doesn't have anything other than prison garb, and I am certain he will not want to wear that a moment longer than necessary."

"Sure," Philip said readily, "but he's thinner and shorter than I am."

"Yes, but," Gareth said, "your things will fit him better than mine."

"I can go outside, right?" Sigrun asked.

Gareth approached the board in the hallway and studied it thoroughly. He placed his left thumb on an empty spot in one corner, and the configuration of the board changed too swiftly for Sigrun to follow. He studied it for a few seconds, then said, "Go ahead. It was quiet here while we were gone."

So, she thought dazedly as she dropped into a seat at the patio table, it had worked! Better than she could ever have imagined. But her brain seemingly had shut down – she just couldn't quite wrap her mind around the idea that Zareh was at this moment being released from prison. Or that she had taken a leave from law school. Or that she and Philip were waiting around to talk to Greer about Kaia.

"Sigrun," Gareth called from the kitchen doorway, "I am leaving. I don't know how long we'll be but I will call. Do you need anything?"

"A grip on reality?" she quipped. "No, I'm fine," she added at his uncertain look.

"If you're sure?" At her nod, he left.

"Hey," Philip said, coming out a few minutes later, having changed into jeans and a T-shirt, "why don't you get out of that suit?"

Sigrun looked down at her clothing distractedly. "Yeah, I suppose. So ... how do you feel?"

Philip took a seat. "How do **you** feel?"

"Like I've lost my mind."

"Yeah." He leaned back in his chair and contemplated the view. "Well ... I suppose we could consider the possibility of hallucinogenic drugs. But," he turned back with a shrug, "that can't account for the incident at the train station."

"True. So, what did you think of Zareh?"

"Well, I didn't talk to him, so it's kind of hard to say. But he's pretty enigmatic!"

"I just ... I mean, do **you** believe I'm related to him?"

"Uh, yeah, I guess I have to say I do."

"Really?"

"Well, you're the lawyer here. What's your opposing position? I mean, how could they know these things about you if they're not who they say they are? And," he chortled, "I sure don't get a shock when I touch them. Hey, did it happen with Zareh?"

She shook her head. "But we were inside the building, so I suppose there were steel beams."

"Right. So, how else do you explain that box of yours? Your father told you it was a baby gift. I mean, come on – it's got Eireen's mother's name on it!"

Sigrun sighed. "Yeah, I know. My problem is – it makes sense, but I just ..."

"Don't 'grok' it?"

"Yeah." She got to her feet. "Maybe I will change. Do you want anything?"

"Do you think it's uncouth to drink his wine?"

"No. I'll bring some out."

⤚⤙

The exuberance flowing from Zareh's unexpected release carried them through the takeout dinner Gareth had picked up on the way back from the courthouse. Then, in one of those pauses that randomly fall into a conversation, Zareh turned to Gareth and asked, "So, Kako, when are we heading home?"

"Oh," Gareth responded in a voice that sounded strained, "we haven't had time to discuss a schedule yet."

"Soon I hope," Zareh said.

"Well ... a slight complication has arisen, but," Gareth said blandly, "I am sure it will be resolved shortly."

"He means me," Sigrun said. "I'm not sure I want to go with you."

"But there's no question," said Zareh flatly.

"It's not that simple," she said, annoyed that he, like Greer, seemed indifferent to her opinion. "I don't belong there. After all, I don't know anything about Kaia and ..."

"Wait." Zareh held up a hand to stop her. With a slight narrowing of his eyes, he turned to Gareth. "I thought Philip was not one of us."

"That's right," Gareth said, "but much has occurred this past week, and I have not had an opportunity to bring you up to date. Sigrun prevailed upon Greer to tell Philip some of the story. You see, it appears that Gilda killed Philip's family."

Zareh looked skeptical. "Even so, surely his knowledge should be strictly limited; certainly, he should not be present for this conversation."

"As I've told both Gareth and Greer," Sigrun said hastily, "Philip is my best friend, and I won't lie to him."

Zareh shot her a penetrating stare. "Our future plans are of no relevance to him."

"I want him to come to Kaia with me," she retorted.

Zareh looked startled as he threw a brief glance at Philip. "That's impossible."

"I'm sorry," she said guardedly, fighting to control her anger, "but I prefer to participate in decisions about my future."

Philip stood up before Zareh could respond. "I think it's best if I go inside. Really," he added as Sigrun opened her mouth to protest, "this is a family discussion, and I shouldn't be involved."

Gareth closed the back door behind Philip before returning to his chair and leaning forward. "Emotions are running high here," he said in an uncharacteristically serious tone, "and I lack my sister's gift of empathy. I cannot see the right path to bring you two together. But, I want you to know that I will do anything in my power to keep you from hurting each other. Please keep in mind that you both have been through a rough time and, whether you realize it or not, are somewhat fragile."

At Zareh's dismissive wave, Gareth added sharply, "Zareh, you've just been handed your life back after 20 years expecting to die. And Sigrun has learned that the world she has always known is not where she belongs." He continued without allowing them time to respond, "Zareh, remember that, although we keep telling Sigrun how important she is to Kaia's future, she does not fully credit its existence."

"But …" Sigrun began.

"No," Gareth stopped her, "please, hear me out. Zareh, we must be patient with Sigrun's fear of the unknown – despite our urgency to take her home. And Sigrun, you must understand Zareh's need to put this world behind him as soon as possible."

Zareh stood and strode to the back wall. "Kako," he said over his shoulder, "is it safe to go for a walk with Sigrun?"

"Safe enough."

Zareh turned back and asked, "Would you care to take a walk with me, Sigrun? You don't mind, do you, Gareth?"

Startled, she waited for Gareth's response.

"No," he replied cautiously, "go ahead. But I want to keep an eye on you, so stay in my line of sight."

Zareh nodded, giving Sigrun an appraising look. "Can she link to the Grid?"

"No. We thought it best if we waited until we were in more secure surroundings."

"Do you have an extra focus stone I could borrow?"

"Certainly." Gareth reached into his shirt pocket. "I doubt it will work well for you, but you are welcome to use it."

"Thank you." Zareh took the topaz Gareth held out to him. Then he raised his eyebrows at Sigrun.

Feeling as if she'd missed something, Sigrun gave Gareth a questioning look. He nodded encouragingly, so she got to her feet.

Gareth remained seated in his usual chair, which, she suddenly realized, faced the portal. So, he sat where he could keep an eye on the portal! As Sigrun crossed the yard, she saw the neon bursts signifying that Gareth had released the shields. They strolled silently across the deserted pasture in the deepening twilight.

"Sigrun," Zareh said quietly, "I can't begin to express my gratitude for what you've done … I have no words …"

He lapsed back into silence. She was too unsettled to say anything.

After a few paces, he said, "I wanted to talk to you alone, not because I want to keep anything from Gareth – to the contrary, he knows all this – but because, as you no doubt have perceived, I have difficulty discussing my feelings."

They reached the edge of the bluff. Zareh halted and turned

to face her. "I want you to know that your mother's last thoughts were for you." He paused, and Sigrun struggled not to cry at the sudden sadness that swept over her.

Zareh turned to look over the ocean and continued in an intense voice, "Sigrun, I promised your mother as she died that I would keep you safe. I will give my life to fulfill that promise."

She could no longer contain her tears. Impulsively, she placed a tentative hand on Zareh's arm. She flinched, but did not draw back, at the jolt that accompanied the touch. "Thank you," she said, at a loss for a more adequate response.

Zareh turned to face her. He reached out a finger to touch the tears on her cheeks. "You're crying. I didn't intend to make you cry."

Embarrassed, she felt around in her pockets until she located a tissue. "That's okay. I guess I've never really thought about her dying before. It's always been rather abstract to me; a murder, rather than someone's death. If that makes any sense."

Zareh sighed. "Now that I've upset you, I have one more thing to say."

Sigrun caught a change in his tone of voice; she stiffened, finished wiping her eyes, and jammed the tissue back in her pocket.

Zareh held his left hand toward her, palm up, cradling the stone Gareth had lent him. He stared hard at it for a long moment before his face relaxed into a slight smile. Then he looked at Sigrun. "You will not understand what I'm about to say for some time, but, if you listen closely and let your gift guide you, you will know that I speak the truth." He reached out and pulled her left hand over the gemstone he held cupped in his palm. "Do you feel the Power flowing to you from my connection to the Grid?"

Sigrun felt first the now-familiar shock from his touch, followed by a gentle and unfamiliar tingling sensation that began in her palm and flowed up her arm. Her stomach lurched and she jerked her hand, but Zareh held it in place. She gulped and nodded weakly.

He continued solemnly, "You are your mother's daughter. Your mother was a veridictrix, and so are you. You are vital to the survival of Kaia. Your mother understood this, and she made me understand it as well." Zareh paused and touched Sigrun's wet cheek again with a gentle finger. "I don't want to hurt you, but you **must** accompany me to Kaia and learn what you need to know."

Sigrun was shaken by the note of steel in his voice as he finished. She began to ramp up into anger at his implacable insistence that she do what they want. But his words, she suddenly realized with confusion, had been infused with a clear and vivid blue light. Alarm overshadowed anger; she yanked her hand away.

What did it mean? She struggled for understanding in light of Gareth's brief explanation of this … so-called "gift" she seemed to possess. Disquieted by Zareh's steady gaze, she turned away. Somehow, she knew without doubt that his words were true. Brushing aside the questions that suddenly begged to be asked about this "Power" she apparently had access to, Sigrun slowly drew a deep breath.

She rubbed the palm of her left hand; no trace of the sensation remained. But she had to admit that she had both perceived the Power and sensed it guiding her comprehension of Zareh's words. There was no denial … and no logical explanation. So, if she accepted that he spoke the truth, where did that take her? To Kaia? Get a grip, she thought shakily, struggling to quell her rising panic. She forced herself to focus: if Zareh spoke the truth, then she had to concede that there was something she needed to do on – she shuddered – Kaia. And, having accepted that fact, she had to conclude that she must either go with them now or walk away from all of this. If indeed they even let her. … And, the thought gripped her, turn her back on Zareh's sacrifice.

Her stomach knotted. But how could she agree to go somewhere so … nebulous and so … implausible. What if they were all psychotic? And how could she abandon Philip? Especially since **she** apparently had been the intended victim. It was all so unfair, and so frightening. She drew another deep breath in a vain effort to slow her relentlessly racing thoughts. She could see no way around crossing this Rubicon: She had to either agree to go or try to get away. She wavered. She looked at Zareh; his piercing gaze remained fixed on her.

Struggling to keep her voice steady, Sigrun said haltingly, "You're right … I do know that your words are true."

Zareh let out a sigh of relief.

"So, since you believe it's essential for me to go with you … I'll go. But," she added quickly, "you must let Philip come too."

"That, I am thankful to say, is not my decision to make. I know you're frightened, Sigrun, but you'll be welcomed into a warm and loving family." Zareh gave a wry smile. "Believe me also when I tell you that I am not representative. I have, however, retained sufficient social skills to remember to wish you Happy Birthday."

Sigrun stared at him.

"Today is your birthday, correct?"

"Uh, August fourth. Yeah, I guess it is. I had completely forgotten."

"I trust it has been a good birthday."

"Yes," she admitted with amazement as they headed back, "unexpectedly good."

"Sigrun has agreed to return with us," Zareh said as Gareth held open the gate into the yard.

"Excellent," Gareth said mildly, giving Sigrun a close look.

She smiled feebly. "I did, but I haven't yielded on Philip."

Gareth nodded as he returned to his usual seat. "I've brought Greer up to date on today's events. She is elated. She wanted to check on some things and is going to get back to me shortly to discuss timing. She does, however, think that she should make an appearance at Festival this evening. Tonight is Festival Finale, Zareh, in case you've lost track of time."

"I haven't. Did you know, Kako, that today is Sigrun's birthday?"

"No! Neither of you mentioned the date. Well, Happy Birthday, Sigrun."

"Thank you," she said faintly, having trouble fitting something as prosaic and familiar as her birthday into the freakishness of the day.

"So," Zareh asked, "what does Greer want to do?"

"She's conflicted," Gareth said. "As I mentioned in the car, Gavin is still recuperating from his injuries, and everyone else is busy with Festival. But, on the other hand, she feels it might be prudent to time our return with the conclusion of Festival – with the hope that our arrival would go unnoticed in the tumult of late-night departures."

"Do you mean … tonight?" Sigrun asked anxiously.

"Yes. But that would entail an extensive amount of work in a short period of time, and, with the constraints of Festival, I am not sure that we should be so hasty."

"The sooner the better," said Zareh.

"Yes, but," Gareth said calmly, "only if it is safe."

"Of course! But no one is expecting Sigrun. If we do an undetectable transit with her, why isn't it safe?"

"They may be expecting you," Gareth said matter-of-factly.

"Right. Sorry, I shouldn't question your decisions tonight. I'm afraid I'm not entirely rational on this issue."

"No problem," Gareth said. "So, Sigrun, would you like to

join my loquansmente link with Greer?"

"Uh … can I?"

"I believe so," Gareth said. "All you have to do is put your hand on mine – make sure that you maintain contact with my stone – and concentrate. I warn you, though, that we will be able to pick up your thoughts, so be cautious and stay focused. If you want to say something, just think it clearly."

"Okay," she said uncertainly.

"I assume, Zareh," Gareth asked, "that you would like to join the link?"

"Definitely. Of course I don't have my focus stone, so I'll have to link through you as well, which might put some strain on you."

"I forgot!" Sigrun jumped up. "Do I have a minute?"

Gareth checked the clock through the now-open back door. "Several."

"I'll be right back." Sigrun hurried inside and headed to the living room, where she found Philip sitting on the couch with a book in his hands. He looked up as she rushed in. "How are you?" she asked.

He snorted. "The relevant question is – how are you?"

"Okay. I guess. I'm supposed to join them in communicating with Greer." She shook her head in bewilderment. "Gareth seems to think I can do that. Anyway, I'm going to try to get her to agree to your coming with me." She gave him a questioning look. "That is, if you still want to?"

He swallowed hard and nodded. "Yeah."

"Okay then, wish me luck. I've got to run."

"Good luck … I guess."

She dashed down the hall and into the guest room. She had forgotten that she had brought the jewels with her with the intention of giving them to Gareth. One of the stones must belong to Zareh. She rummaged around in her bag until she found the small envelope. Grabbing it, she rushed outside.

"Here." She handed the envelope to Zareh. "I'm sorry. I forgot that I wanted to return these to you. I realized what they were after talking with Gareth."

Zareh gave her a curious look before opening the small envelope and shaking its contents onto the table. When the jewelry tumbled out, Zareh paled. Gareth gasped and asked in a strangled voice, "Where did you get those?"

"I …" Sigrun hesitated, feeling slightly dishonest, but then she rushed on, "well I took them from the habeas file. I think the State included them with the rest of the trial exhibits by mistake. I don't think anyone will miss them."

Zareh reached out an unsteady hand and picked up the ruby. "Thank you," he said quietly. "This is mine. But the others now belong to you." He pushed the quartz and the necklace toward Sigrun.

Gareth reached out a hand, which Sigrun was surprised to see was also trembling, and scooped up the necklace. He held it up to catch the light. "I never thought I would see this again," he said with great sadness. "Here, Sigrun, I had this setting made for your mother's stone for her eighteenth birthday – she would have wanted you to wear it."

Sigrun took the necklace from him and put it on. "Thank you, I'll treasure it."

Gareth took a deep breath and glanced again at the kitchen clock. He picked up his topaz from the table and held it in his cupped hands. "Well … Greer should be contacting me shortly. Sigrun, wait until I call you; then place your hand on my stone. And remember to keep tight control of your thoughts."

"I'll try," she said doubtfully, fingering the emerald at the center of the necklace she now wore.

"Zareh," Gareth continued, "do you think you'll be able to link on your own?"

"Yes. I had no problem with your topaz earlier."

Gareth nodded. He then stared intently at his gemstone. "Now, Sigrun."

Sigrun tentatively placed her hand over the topaz. She felt the same tingling sensation she had felt with Zareh on the bluff, only it spread swiftly. Not knowing what she should do, she focused on her hand. She was dumbfounded to hear Gareth's voice inside her head say, *"We're here, Greer. Sigrun, are you with me?"*

Sigrun thought, *"Yes!"*

Greer responded, *"Excellent. Welcome, Sigrun."*

Sigrun looked around, but of course, Greer was not there. Wow! This loquansmente thing really did work!

"This is Zareh, I'm present as well."

"Zareh!" Greer sounded pleased. *"Greetings. Are you linked through Gareth?"*

"Sigrun just returned my focus stone – I'm linked myself."

"Good!" Greer exclaimed. *"That will make things easier. Gareth, where are we?"*

"Zareh has convinced Sigrun to return with us. He feels that we should do it tonight. I, however, am concerned that someone at the prison will have alerted the Ødeleggers that Zareh is free, and they will be waiting for his return."

"I agree, but I'm loath to give them additional time to prepare. Because of Festival, we may be more organized tonight than they."

"Exactly!" Zareh interjected. *"I think we should grab whatever advantage we may have in moving rapidly."*

"What did Alaric say?" Gareth asked.

"I couldn't reach him." Sigrun thought Greer sounded concerned. *"Extra shields must have been erected at the prison — which adds to my misgivings."*

"When was the last time anyone communicated with him?" Gareth asked.

"Yesterday. And Malie's still staying in town to be with Gavin. We didn't think it would be prudent for her to rush over to visit him."

"No." Gareth sounded thoughtful. *"I agree with that. Why don't we wait one more night? Then you can check with Alaric and have more time to prepare ..."*

"But wait," Zareh interrupted, *"if their intelligence is good enough that they know already that I may be arriving, I think giving them another day is our worst option."*

"I'm afraid I have to agree with Zareh." Greer's thoughts readily conveyed her weariness. *"I believe we must do it tonight. We will meet you, but I think we should time it for after the crowds have thinned."*

"How would you prefer to bring Sigrun through?" Gareth asked. *"Do you want a record of her arrival?"*

"No. I think Makoa should bring her. What do you think?"

"Perhaps." Gareth sounded unconvinced. *"But how hard has he been working? Does he have the strength to do two cross-world, undetectable transits, one of them accompanied?"*

"I'll check with him," Greer replied. *"He should be here shortly."*

"Also, before this plan gets too far along," Gareth added, *"we need to discuss Philip. Sigrun wants him to come with us."*

"I suppose it was too much to hope that that issue had evaporated." Greer sounded exasperated. *"Sigrun, what is your relationship with Philip?"*

"Uh," Sigrun quickly clamped down on her thought that it was none of Greer's business. *"He's my best friend — he's not my boyfriend."*

"So, I'm not seeing the issue here."

"I told you." Sigrun struggled to remain calm. *"I am not going to*

abandon him, and he wants to have a chance to try to hold this Gilda person responsible for the murder of his family."

"Gareth, have you discussed this with him?" Greer asked tersely.

"Some. I believe he truly does wish to come."

"Hold on." Greer's thought was abrupt and was followed, Sigrun was startled to note, by her perception that a presence had left the link.

"Sigrun?" It was Zareh. *"I know you don't understand the circumstances, but it's going to be difficult enough to arrange transits for the two of us. We cannot jeopardize your return because of this friend of yours."*

"I don't see why it makes any difference. I mean — who's going to care if he comes anyway?"

"That's true," Gareth observed. *"It is unlikely that anyone will pay the slightest attention to Philip."*

"That's not the point," Zareh shot back. *"It's a complication that we don't need, and it requires someone to babysit him who would otherwise be useful."*

"I'm back." Greer rejoined the link. *"I must go. Sigrun, does Philip realize that if he comes, he stays? For him, it is a one-way trip."*

"What?"

"Clearly not. All right, I don't think this idea is sufficiently evolved to be realistic. I want to attempt a transit tonight, and I don't see how we can accommodate your desires, Sigrun. I'm sorry to disappoint you ..."

"I won't come," Sigrun thought firmly.

"Gareth, I don't have time for this!" Greer's anger was apparent. *"Can you resolve this, and I will check back in ... about one bell?"*

"Certainly." Gareth sounded as calm as usual. *"Will you be secure?"*

"Yes, I'll come back here."

"If possible, could you have Malie join you? Since she's in Maluhia, that shouldn't be too difficult."

"I'll see," Greer snapped. *"In the meantime, perhaps you could think about your preparations."*

"Certainly," Gareth repeated. *"And Greer, please remain alert. I am confident that you are being watched quite closely."*

"Fair point," Greer conceded. *"I've got both Makoa and JT here, and I'll brief them before we leave. I'll be back in touch."*

"So, Sigrun," Gareth instructed, *"just move your hand, and you'll leave the link."*

Sigrun lifted her hand from the topaz; the table spun beneath her eyes, and she grabbed its edge. "Oh," she gasped as the wave of dizziness persisted.

"You're fine," Gareth said. "Just sit still. Using Power depletes your own energy. One of the first principles you must learn is that all Power comes at a price."

Sigrun was startled at how unsteady she felt given that she had not moved from her chair. "But I wasn't doing anything!"

"Yes, you were," Gareth said, sounding pleased. "Loquansmente between worlds is difficult. And, I must say, you did extraordinarily well."

"I did?"

"Yes." He got to his feet. "You two stay here. I need to talk to Philip."

Sigrun watched apprehensively as Gareth closed the kitchen door behind him.

"You did do well," Zareh said. "Especially since you've had no training."

Sigrun was pleased by his unexpected praise. "Thank you. But I just joined Gareth."

"True," Zareh said, "but the fact that you were able to do so without instruction indicates that you have a strong loquansmente gift. However, I'm afraid that I agree with Greer – I don't see the issue with Philip."

Sigrun sighed. "It's not complicated. You don't know about the fire, but his entire family was killed this spring when – Greer thinks – that woman, Gilda, was trying to kill me. He's been my best friend my entire life. I want him to come with me, and he wants to come as well. What's the problem?"

Zareh shook his head impatiently. "No, I don't know about any fire. But it doesn't matter – we don't invite people from Earth to Kaia. It is, in fact, prohibited."

"But I don't see why anyone would care."

"Perhaps not. But we're assiduous in protecting Kaia from contamination by Earth."

"He's just one person," she said irritably.

"And you're not romantically involved?" Zareh sounded skeptical.

"**No**. We're not."

"That makes it easy. I don't see any reason to even try to circumvent the rules."

"I'm not going to come alone." She jumped up, momentarily forgetting the earlier dizziness, but the ground only swayed slightly. She managed a steady walk to the back wall. She was extremely rattled; things seemed to be spiraling out of control, and she was so out of her element. To all appearances, she had just held a conversation **in her head**! With a woman **on another planet**! She leaned against the wall, wishing desperately that she could just walk out the gate and somehow be back in the comfortable world she had known before the fire. No, she corrected herself, before she had started working on the habeas case. Back then, a bad day was Tony's derision after she botched an answer in Contracts!

"Sigrun?" Zareh said behind her.

She didn't respond.

"You know you must come to Kaia. You have no choice."

She whipped around to confront him. "I do! I don't have to get involved in your battles."

"You are involved, like it or not. Given that Greer thinks Gilda already tried to kill you – exactly how long do you think you'd survive on your own?"

"If I don't have any further contact with you, why would she want to murder me?"

Zareh gave a harsh laugh. "You have much to learn. It is irrelevant what you do. Gilda appears to have discovered that you were born – a fact we successfully concealed from her for nearly 21 years. They will not rest until you are dead."

The coldness and certitude in Zareh's voice chilled Sigrun to the core.

"We can protect you; but only on Kaia."

"I don't see how you can say that!" Sigrun lashed out. "That other woman – Kweli – you didn't protect her."

Zareh flinched. "True. But think about it: If Gilda Gleipnir and the rest of the Ødeleggers are sufficiently fanatical to stage a flagrant attack on an obscure veridictrix on her first visit to Maluhia, how likely do you think it is that they will let you live?"

"I don't understand."

"I know. But you don't need to understand the underlying issues. Just accept that Gilda believes that the mere existence of veridictrices threatens her aspirations. Look, she sacrificed her own son to eliminate a veridictrix who was not, we believe, essential to any future path. You – the daughter of a woman who fervently denounced the path she espouses – you embody her deepest fears. She **will** try to kill you."

Shaken, Sigrun swiveled to stare at the star-filled sky. An image of the Schlichters' house in flames – embellished by her own nightmares of what had happened inside – filled her vision. She closed her eyes but the image persisted. "I don't care," she said fiercely, "I won't go without him."

Zareh's hand on her shoulder jolted her as he pivoted Sigrun to face him. "I regret that this conversation has been so confrontational. And I fear you'll think I'm unappreciative of your diligence in securing my freedom." He sighed. "I only ask that you keep in mind that I've spent most of your life learning how to distance myself from my emotions when I tell you that I can't let your wishes interfere with what I know must happen tonight."

Sigrun recoiled as far as she was able at the not-so-veiled threat. "So ... you'll take me with you by force?"

"If I must," he said, returning to his typically expressionless voice.

"I see. Then why even try to convince me?"

"Because I want you to understand." He took a deep breath. "I should have left this to Gareth."

"Does he agree?"

"Of course not." He laughed humorlessly. "Don't you see ... no. How could you?" He reached out a hand to brush the hair she had let fall forward away from her face. "I've spent 20 years carrying on conversations with you in my mind. I feel that I know you – but of course, I don't."

She was flooded by a cold barren loneliness that stopped her up short. "Why ..."

"Excuse me," Gareth said quietly from the kitchen door.

"Kako," Zareh said, turning to face him, "I've made a thorough mess of things."

"I am sure not," Gareth said easily. "Come and have some coffee. Are you all right, Sigrun?"

"No." She wrapped her arms tightly around herself in an attempt to stop shaking. "I'm not. I mean – why are we even pretending that anyone cares what I want?"

"I care," Gareth said simply.

She leaned against the back wall as Zareh crossed the yard and picked up one of the coffee mugs that Gareth must have brought out. "But it doesn't matter, does it?" She shook her head in an effort to dispel the lingering despondency. "Zareh told me. It doesn't matter."

Gareth threw a look at Zareh, picked up a mug, and carried it over to her. "Have some coffee. What did Zareh tell you?"

She took a sip of the coffee before it occurred to her, as it had during that first visit, that it might be drugged. Then she laughed at herself; she was pretty sure they had no need of drugs to make her do what they wanted. She took another sip and felt some warmth seep into her core. "Zareh's planning on making me go back with you," she said as calmly as she could manage.

"I did say that," Zareh admitted.

"Well," Gareth said reassuringly, "I won't let him. Come sit down."

"I don't believe you."

"Sigrun, I will never let anyone hurt you."

"If what Zareh told me is true – I don't see how you can say that."

"You are correct," Gareth agreed, "I was careless in my language. I will do everything I can to prevent your enemies from harming you. But I **promise** you that I will not let your friends hurt you. We're only trying to keep you safe."

Sigrun shook her head. "Fine, but I don't see how you can prevent it. I don't want to be a pawn in some … contest over the role of veri… dic … trices – whatever they are – in some world I don't want to go to."

Zareh joined them by the back wall. "Sigrun, you must accept that you already are a pawn. And I will not let them kill you."

"It seems to me," Sigrun said sharply, "that my chances are better here if Kweli was one of the last veri–whatevers on Kaia, and you couldn't protect her."

"That's true," Gareth said quietly. "But I assure you that our chances of protecting you on Kaia are vastly better than they are here."

"And," Zareh said, "on Kaia, you can learn to protect yourself."

"I can?" she asked Gareth.

"Definitely. Come sit down."

Really, what could she do? She returned to her seat.

"You must trust us," Gareth said earnestly as he joined her. "I discussed things with Philip and …" He held up his hand and cocked his head, then pulled his stone from his pocket and cradled it in his hands. Zareh did the same. Gareth nodded to Sigrun.

She hesitated and then, reluctantly, placed her hand over the topaz.

"Sigrun?" Greer's voice inquired in her head, startling her anew.

"Yes."

"Good," Greer responded. *"I'm back earlier than planned, and I've brought Malie with me. She's linked as well. Sigrun, if you don't know, Ma-*

lie is the sister of Gareth and Gavin."

"This is Malie. Greetings, Sigrun, Zareh." It was a warm and friendly presence that filled Sigrun with reassurance.

"So, Gareth, what is the status?" Greer asked.

"I have spoken with Philip. He is quite realistic and understands the significance of our sharing any information about Kaia with him. He suspected that, if we permitted him to travel to Kaia, he would not be allowed to return. He does want to come."

"Good!" The thought escaped Sigrun before she could suppress it.

"But," Zareh broke in, *"how do you propose to do this? It's not permitted."*

"Well," Greer responded slowly, *"Malie and I discussed it, and we think we can hide him."*

"You can't hide him forever!" Zareh sounded annoyed. *"What happens when the Concilium finds out it's been duped? You could face an edictum."*

"We can deal with that later," Greer stated irritably. *"But, Gareth, if he and Sigrun are not a couple, how do you propose to account for who he is?"*

"I'll file a postulatum cognationis," Gareth replied.

"Oh!" Greer sounded taken aback. *"Does he agree?"*

"Yes."

"Sigrun, this is what you want, correct?" Greer asked.

"Uh …" The question caught her by surprise as she was pondering what postulating cognationis might mean. *"Yes, yes it is."*

"All right, then. Gareth, I've spoken with Makoa, and he has no hesitation about bringing Sigrun back tonight. He said he's well rested."

"Do you agree with that assessment, Malie?" Gareth asked cautiously.

"I think so," Malie responded. *"After Greer contacted me, I checked with him. He seemed relaxed and confident."*

"He's always confident," Gareth stated dryly.

"Yes, of course." Malie sounded amused. *"But he's pretty realistic in evaluating his vitality."*

"So," Greer interjected, *"what about your end, Gareth? Are you ready?"*

"Well, I plan to come back, say my goodbyes, and take care of things here later, so I don't need time. Zareh, do you have anything you need to do?"

"No," Zareh declared. *"I can go this minute."*

"And you, Sigrun?" Greer asked.

"Uh … I don't know …" Sigrun stumbled, again feeling as if

she were several steps behind.

"*Greer, how do you want to handle the transits?*" asked Gareth.

"*I think you should bring Philip through first, followed by Makoa with Sigrun. And Zareh should come last. Zareh, we'd like a clear record of when you return, and from where, but do you feel comfortable transiting on your own?*"

"*I'm fine,*" Zareh replied quickly.

"*Be precise with your destination.*" Greer sounded stern. "*It's been a long time, and we don't want you popping out somewhere on Earth. If you do, stay there, contact me, and let us come and get you. Don't try to correct a problem yourself.*"

"*Yes, ma'am!*" Zareh agreed with evident amusement. "*You know, Greer, I'm not 18 anymore.*"

"*You might as well be 13 for as much practice as you've had recently!*"

"*Fair point. I promise to be careful and wait for you if I get into trouble. Good enough?*"

"*It will have to be,*" Greer stated. "*So, what have I forgotten?*"

"*What time did you want us?*" asked Gareth.

"*I have to get Makoa over there and check in with everyone here. So far, Festival is quiet, but I want to wait and see. We'll get back to you.*"

"*I have one request,*" Zareh broke in. "*Is it possible for someone to swing by Palepouli and pick up some of my old clothing for me? I'd like something to wear.*"

"*Of course!*" Gareth exclaimed. "*We need something for Philip, too. It won't do to have him show up in Earther clothing. Malie, do you think you could obtain two sets of clothing from Zeroun? Something from Zareh should work well enough.*"

"*I'll send something with Mak,*" Malie promised.

"*Are we done?*" Greer seemed markedly tense.

"*I think so,*" Gareth affirmed. "*We will prepare and wait to hear from you.*"

Sigrun raised her hand from the gemstone and, anticipating the resulting dizziness, immediately grabbed at the edge of the table. Her vision spun, but steadied quickly this time. She looked at Gareth in disbelief. "So … she agreed? Just like that?"

Gareth nodded as he rubbed his eyes tiredly. "She agreed. So, we need to get the two of you packed. You can't take anything with a significant amount of steel – nothing electrical, no watches, razor blades, knives, shoes with steel in the shank. Set out what you want to take with you on your bed, and I'll look it over. Shall we talk to Philip?"

Sigrun's mind was moving at a slower pace. "But, I don't understand," she said as she followed him inside, "there's no problem with Philip coming?"

"There are many problems." Gareth stopped in the doorway of the living room where Philip was sitting on the couch, not even pretending to do anything. "But we are going to do as you two wish and let him come. That is," he added to Philip, "if you are positive this is what you want. It is not too late to change your mind."

Philip blanched and looked uncertainly from Gareth to Sigrun. She gave him a shaky smile. He cleared his throat. "Uh ... I suppose I may regret it someday, but ... I know I only have this one shot. So, yeah, I'm game."

↢ Chapter 24 ↣
Quo fata vocant
(Whither the fates call)

"That's everything, then." Gareth closed the last of the sad-
dlebags he had pulled out of a closet for Sigrun and Philip to pack
their belongings into. "I'll leave these here and collect them when I
retrieve my things. I'll give whatever you've left behind to charity.
And give me your cell phones; my financial manager will cancel
your service."

Sigrun pulled out her cell phone and handed it over. "No
phones, I guess."

"Uhm, what about money?" Philip asked anxiously as he too
relinquished his phone. "I mean, I assume I can't use dollars ..."

"Right," Gareth said absently as he set their phones beside his
on the desk. "You can change money on Kaia – but we don't want
to draw unnecessary attention to your presence. So, just leave
whatever you have with me, and I'll exchange it for gold bullion
when I return."

"But it's mostly in the bank. I mean, I don't have much with
me," Philip said, sounding embarrassed.

"Don't worry," Gareth said, "you can borrow what you need
from me, and at some point we can arrange to convert your ac-
counts to gold. Do you have any money you'd like me to change,
Sigrun?" As she emptied the few bills she had from the wallet she
had tucked into a pocket of a saddlebag, Gareth added, "Your life
on Kaia will be different; you will not have as much need for
money."

"But I don't want to be a burden ..." objected Philip.

"Please," Gareth said, holding up a hand. "We can discuss
this later. Right now I need to worry about our transit."

"Gareth," asked Zareh from the doorway, "have you explained portals?"

"Not yet. Could you do so while I confer with Greer?"

"Certainly." Zareh entered the living room and studied a
bookcase laden with a jumble of papers, books, and tall, unadorned,

bound volumes. "Interesting," he said, seemingly to himself, as he examined a slender volume. "I didn't realize he was keeping these." He tucked it back on the shelf and, after a brief glance around the room, took the desk chair. "Sit," he said. Sigrun sat on the couch; Philip dropped to the floor where he stood by the pile of saddle-bags.

"For our purposes tonight, portals are passageways that permit a person with Power to travel from one to another. They can be shaped at the intersection of any two sufficiently strong Grid lines in the absence of intervening iron ore."

"Oh," Sigrun asked, "so it's not steel that's the problem, but iron?"

"Correct," Zareh said, "iron in any form – such as steel – blocks access to the Grid. So, a portal, if provided with a stable source of Power, can be maintained in an open position – as most are on Kaia. On Earth, obviously, portals are neither open nor marked. A portal here can be used only by someone who both knows its exact location and is capable of accessing it." He fixed Sigrun with a stern look. "You should think twice before you enter a portal here on your own. If you end up somewhere unintended, you'll be unable to leave."

She didn't respond – the thought that she would, or could, ever willingly use a portal by herself struck her as too far-fetched to consider.

"Here, as on Kaia," Zareh continued, "you can transit between any two portals as long as you have an adequate concept of your destination. Unfortunately, only one portal permits passage **between** Kaia and Earth; that is Poholo Portal, which is located in the center of Maluhia. Consequently, our journey must involve two steps: First from here to Poholo's corresponding portal on Earth, and then to Kaia through Poholo – necessitating our arrival at one of the busiest and most-monitored of the portals."

"Excuse me," Sigrun broke in. "But didn't Gareth say that your capital is located where Honolulu is on Earth?

"Yes."

"So we're going to be … appearing in a portal in the middle of Honolulu?"

"Not exactly. You won't need to step out of that portal; any-one who is experienced at Earth-side transits can re-direct their des-tination to Poholo while inside the portal. Physically, you'll be pre-sent in Honolulu only a few seconds. And, more significantly, the portal there is located on the edge of a cemetery – so no one should be around at night."

"You can do that?" asked Philip, sounding torn between admiration and alarm.

Zareh shrugged. "I used to be able to. We'll see. At the moment, the most important thing for the two of you to remember is that you **must** maintain contact with your escort. Before you step into the portal, take a firm grip on his arm. When you transit, you'll feel a sudden and unpleasant lurch as the ground on which you're standing vanishes. You will momentarily contact a solid surface again at the intermediate portal, but do nothing. When you arrive at Poholo, you'll be dizzy, so continue to hold on as you exit the portal."

"How do they work?" Sigrun asked warily.

"That I can't explain now – you don't yet know enough, nor do we have the time."

"What happens if I lose my grip?" Philip asked with consternation.

"Most likely, you'll fall out at a portal, but we won't know which one."

Philip gulped audibly.

Gareth had appeared in the doorway and waited until Zareh finished. "Excuse me," he said, "I caught Greer in an unsecured location, and she reported that Makoa has postponed his visit. So, something unexpected must have arisen. We may be in for a lengthy wait."

"I shouldn't think they'd want us until after aught and two bells, anyway," Zareh said. "It doesn't seem prudent to arrive until Festival has waned."

"True." Gareth glanced at the kitchen clock. "It's barely midnight there now. If I must stay alert at least two more hours, I need coffee. Would anyone care to join me?"

"Splendid," Zareh said. "It's a real treat for me."

⤙⤚

"At last," Gareth breathed at the flash of light across the bluff that Sigrun barely caught out of the corner of her eye. He checked the hallway sentinel. "Zareh, will you stay here while I go meet Makoa?"

Throwing an agitated look toward the now-dark portal, Sigrun got to her feet. Zareh's description of portal travel was less than reassuring. Was she really planning to step into thin air and go whisking across space on the arm of someone she'd never even met before? She swallowed hard as the figures of Gareth and a shorter and slighter man – attired in clothing that resembled Greer's in style, but which somehow faded into the sky when she looked at it directly – took shape in the pale pre-dawn light. Gareth opened the shields, and the two entered the yard.

The younger man immediately approached Zareh, setting down the large bundle he was carrying. "Cousin Zareh!" he exclaimed, extending his hand. "You probably don't remember me – I wasn't quite five the last time you saw me – but I revered you."

"Greetings, Makoa." Zareh clasped the proffered hand. "I could not forget you."

"I'm glad, but I probably don't want to hear why."

"Is there a problem?" Zareh asked.

"Yeah," said Makoa, "but we've created a window for us to slip through."

"They removed our portal keeper from Poholo," Gareth said grimly, "and replaced him with one of the Ødeleggers. As we feared, they appear to be expecting you, Zareh."

Zareh nodded thoughtfully. "So, Makoa, how did you get through?"

"JT outdid himself. He blew up a freak summer storm, with high winds that knocked out many of the lights in town – including a spectacular thunder and lightning show. And – in a brilliant move – he lured a lightning bolt to strike Papalua Portal."

"Admirable," Zareh said.

Makoa laughed. "He's good. The keeper rushed over with a couple of underlings to repair it – leaving Poholo unattended. Haldir is taking out more lights now, so it should be plenty dark by our return. But we have to move fast before they finish fixing Papalua."

"Greer still wants to attempt this?" Gareth asked dubiously.

"Absolutely," Makoa affirmed. "The last thing she said as I came through was: 'Tell your uncle we must bring Sigrun home'. Morgan's posted outside Poholo watching for the return of the keeper, and I'm to check with her before we transit."

Gareth looked displeased. "So, I'd like you to meet Sigrun and Philip. This is my nephew, Makoa."

Makoa turned with a friendly smile. "Greetings, Philip – I've brought you some clothing." He handed one of the bundles to Philip and another to Zareh. "And," he said as he carried the last bundle over to where Sigrun still stood by the table, "my mother sent some of my younger brother's things for you, Sigrun. Aunt

Greer thought they'd be the right size, but," he gave her an appraising look, "I'm sure they'll be too big."

Surprised, Sigrun reached for the package. "I wasn't expecting …"

"An excellent idea," said Gareth. "Leave it to Malie to think of the details. Why don't the three of you go change while I review our plans with Makoa."

"Look, Sigrun," Philip said, holding up a pair of knee-length pants he had unrolled from his bundle, "no zipper."

She studied them uncertainly. They were similar to what Makoa was wearing.

"They lace," Makoa said with a grin. "I'd be happy to help, Sigrun, if you like."

"I think I can manage." She headed into the house while unrolling her bundle. It contained a pair of the short pants that were brown in color and made of an unfamiliar soft and supple fabric; a crisp white short-sleeved shirt that appeared never to have been worn; a hooded cape that was so finely woven it was nearly weightless; and, in the center of the bundle, a pair of soft-soled ankle-high boots. As Makoa had guessed, it was all too large. The pants fell loosely to below her knees and were too roomy at the waist even after she had pulled the center lacing as tight as she could. The shirt hung on her. She tied the cord she found in the bundle over the shirt and off to the side as a belt, as she had seen Lupe do with similar outfits. Lupe, she thought with a pang; she should have at least left her a note. Well, she couldn't concern herself with that now.

She pulled on the boots and hoped she wouldn't have to walk too far. She tried on the cape, but it fell past her hips and extended below her hands, so she took it off. She studied herself in the mirror in disbelief – now she looked as odd as she felt! Her eye fell on the necklace that hung around her neck. She cautiously touched the emerald that glowed softly green against the whiteness of her shirt. Although she felt no shock, its presence underscored her escalating sense of having stepped into someone else's shoes, literally as well as figuratively. She turned away, shaking her head to dispel the disquieting image. She folded her discarded clothing and stopped in the living room to stuff it into a saddlebag.

When she entered the yard, she found Gareth, Zareh, and Makoa clustered near the back wall.

"You are sure?" Gareth was asking gravely.

Sigrun hung back, reluctant to interrupt what seemed to be a serious discussion.

"Positive," Zareh, gossamery in a pale grey outfit, said impatiently. "As long as you two take responsibility for Sigrun's safety. The important thing is to get her home. Otherwise," he shrugged, "whatever happens, I'll be better off than I was at San Quentin."

"All right then." Gareth turned to address Makoa, who was eating some sort of dried food bar. "Makoa, you're accountable for Sigrun. You're responsible for getting her through Poholo and to Palepouli. By yourself if necessary."

"No problem," Makoa said, sounding arrogant to Sigrun's ear.

"And," Gareth lectured, "don't forget that everything will be unfamiliar to her. Don't expect her to understand anything you don't spell out."

"Don't worry." Makoa wrapped the remainder of the bar and tucked it inside his cape. "I've got it."

"What's up?" Philip whispered in her ear, having crept up behind her.

"I gather Gareth is worried about an unfriendly welcoming party."

"Well," Gareth said, "we should get moving since it will be light soon. I'll check with Greer. Are you all prepared to leave immediately if she's ready?"

At everyone's affirmative response, Gareth cradled his topaz in his hands. No one spoke while he stared at it. Soon, he looked up. "She didn't reply."

"May I have some coffee while we wait?" Makoa asked after glancing at the mugs that remained on the table.

"Certainly," Gareth said immediately, sweeping the mugs toward the kitchen with a motion. "I am sorry, I should have offered. Come inside."

"Do you mind if I ask you something?" Philip followed Gareth.

Sigrun watched Philip worriedly as he went into the kitchen. He had sounded disturbingly serious; she hoped he wasn't having second thoughts.

"Sigrun," Zareh said behind her.

Sigrun turned to find him giving her an appraising look.

"Put on the cape," he instructed.

"It's too big," she complained, pulling it on.

"Tuck your hair into the cape and pull the hood forward before you enter the portal – it's best if no one gets a good look at you."

"She rather stands out," offered Makoa, coming out of the kitchen, mug in hand. "As if she feels out of place."

Zareh nodded thoughtfully. Pulling his ruby out of a pocket in his breeches, he held it before him. He looked at it for a few seconds and then looked up at Sigrun. He twirled the ruby in a slow circle; a narrow beam of magenta light flowed from the gem to her left arm.

She felt the cloth on her arm move. She stared speechlessly at the sleeve as a band of fabric midway between her elbow and wrist changed color and shrank.

"Let your arm hang naturally," instructed Zareh.

She relaxed her arm. The sleeve lifted until it fell just below her wrist. The beam of light shifted to her right arm, and the process was repeated. Then the light beam died. Each shortened sleeve now bore a narrow band of gold fabric. She rubbed one gingerly – the band felt different from the rest of the cape.

"Can you shorten the breeches?" Makoa asked. "And maybe tighten the bands?"

"Of course," Zareh said. He held the ruby lower and the magenta beam flowed to the bottom of her left pants' leg.

Sigrun watched, mouth agape, while each pantleg grew shorter and the band at the bottom, which now fit her leg snugly, turned the same gold color as the sleeves. "How did you do that?"

"Nice," said Makoa.

Zareh tucked his stone back into his pocket while studying her approvingly. "Better. I changed the composition of the fabric to shorten and tighten the threads," he said matter-of-factly. "The change in color is simply cosmetic. Do you like it?"

She blinked at him. "Uh ... yeah, I do. Thanks."

"If the three of you are finished," Gareth said, "I'll try Greer again."

"I said I wouldn't question your decisions tonight," said Zareh apologetically, "but don't you think we should wait to hear from her?"

"I suppose," Gareth said with a sigh. "But it is dawning here, and we'll soon encounter early-morning walkers."

"I'm guessing it's someone we'd rather avoid at Poholo," said Makoa. "I expect we'll hear from her shortly."

Sigrun took the opportunity to join Philip where he stood near the back door and asked quietly, "Are you all right?"

"Yeah," Philip said, too casually.

"You look troubled."

He gave a short laugh. "Aren't you? I ... well, it's just ... I've become concerned for your safety."

"Not you too," Sigrun said fretfully.

Philip kicked at the ground in his borrowed riding boot. "I wish these fit better. Uhm, I offered to stay here so I wouldn't get in the way, but Gareth assured me that, in general, he tends to be overly cautious."

"What do you mean, 'stay here'?"

"Only until he comes back for his things," he hastened to add.

"No! I want you to come with me."

"I am," he snapped. "I just thought it might be better if they didn't have to deal with me as well tonight."

"Are you two ready?" called Gareth.

"Yeah ... I guess," she said, instantly filled with dread.

"All set," said Philip.

"Greer sanctioned the transit. Let's go." Gareth held open the gate.

"Wait," Makoa said softly. "I assume we don't want to be seen?"

Gareth turned. "Ah, joggers, as I expected. Back away," he said quietly, closing the gate. "My shields prevent them from seeing more than a few feet into the yard."

"Does it matter?" Philip whispered to Gareth as they watched a couple and a dog jog past the yard. The dog sniffed the air and tried to head toward the wall, but was jerked back by his leash as the group passed. "I mean, you're leaving."

"True, but we prefer to minimize reported sightings of oddly attired individuals."

"It's clear," Zareh said after checking both directions.

"All right then." Gareth opened the shields again.

They filed past him, and Zareh briskly led the way along the path.

Makoa fell into step with Sigrun. "Do you know what to expect with the portal?"

"Sort of. Zareh told us, but ..."

"Don't worry. It's simple. All you need to think about is holding onto my arm. Just don't let go until I say so, all right?"

"But what about the other portal? What if ..."

"You'll hardly notice it," he said dismissively. "I'm fast – it'll just be a flash. If you'd rather, you can close your eyes."

"No!" She recoiled at the thought. "I mean, it's not that I

don't trust you, but, well, have you done this with someone …"

Makoa laughed. "Of course. Do you think my uncle would entrust you to me if I wasn't the best?"

His cockiness grated, but his statement made sense. "I suppose not."

"So then," he said, "just get a good grip on my arm and relax."

"Yeah, sure!"

Zareh had walked past the old bench and was heading back as the rest of the group arrived. "Others are approaching; we'd best not linger."

"Mak," Gareth said, "will you check with Morgan?"

Makoa pulled from under his tunic a long chain that hung around his neck, then briefly studied a bluish-green stone he cradled in his hands. "All clear."

Gareth nodded decisively. "Don't worry, Sigrun. Trust me that you could not be in better hands. Just remember to hang on and follow Makoa's directions. May we all find favorable paths."

Gareth gestured to Philip as he took a position alongside the stone bench. Philip grabbed hold of Gareth's right arm with both hands. With his topaz in his left hand, Gareth nodded once to Zareh before staring at his stone for a long moment.

Then, her skin briefly awash with the same prickly sensation she'd perceived at her first portal opening, Sigrun watched in awe as Gareth and Philip were swallowed in a swell of whiteness.

"All right," Zareh said at her side. "You two step into place. It shouldn't be long."

Sigrun gulped and followed Makoa over to the bench. He turned to face Zareh and pointed to his left side.

"But Gareth did it on the other side?"

He cradled the stone that hung around his neck in his right hand. "I prefer you on my left. Hold on."

Sigrun gingerly grasped his well-muscled upper arm.

"You're not going to stay with me," he said with amusement, "if you don't step closer and hold on tighter."

She edged closer and gripped his arm firmly with both hands.

"Good. Whatever you see or feel, you must not let go. Got it?"

"Yeah," she muttered feebly and watched nervously as Makoa stared intently at the gemstone he held high. She could feel her heart, already racing, increase its pace. She adjusted her grip. She tried to take a deep breath, but found she had trouble getting air.

"Soon," he murmured, eyes on the stone.

She shifted her gaze from Makoa and glimpsed Zareh watching intently.

"We're set," Makoa said calmly. "When I open the portal, you'll see two flashes instead of one. Immediately after the second, I'll take one step forward, and you come with me. Ready?"

"Yeah," Sigrun managed to croak.

Before she had finished, a burst of brilliant light engulfed them. She tensed. Her heartbeat in her ear was so thunderous, she feared it would drown out his words.

The light flared again. "Now," Makoa said as he stepped forward.

Sigrun stepped with him. She felt the ground fall away as her advancing foot moved through what should have been solid earth. Her stomach lurched violently. The early morning beach where they stood dissolved in a nausea-inducing blur of images that disintegrated into absolute blackness – as if bright lights had been turned off, and her eyes had not yet begun to adjust. She could see nothing. Yet somehow she perceived pinpricks of light – mere specks really – all around them. If she tried to look directly at them, however, they receded. Abruptly, the sensation of falling ceased; her legs buckled beneath her. She directed her full attention to hanging onto Makoa's arm, which she could not see. Light blazed in two brief flashes, and the ground fell away again. She fought back a rising tide of nausea and grimly hung on. Her feet encountered something firm; her legs trembled and threatened to collapse.

"Step forward," Makoa said into her ear.

She concentrated hard on her right leg. It moved forward and held her weight. She caught a confusing glimpse of people watching, but she fixed her focus on her feet.

"Let go of my arm," he said, "and let me support you."

It took her a second, but she got her hands to release their death grip. His left arm encircled her shoulders and held her loosely against his side as he led her forward. They passed a small silent group of people and stopped. Makoa turned her around and dropped his arm. She swayed slightly, then found that she was steady.

"Welcome to Kaia," Gareth said at her side.

She stood between Gareth and Makoa. On Gareth's other side was Philip. She caught his gaze – he looked decidedly green – and he gave her a wobbly grin. Her nausea receded, and she looked around avidly.

They were positioned in front of one of two corridors that curved from either end of a cavernous, shadowy, ornately decorated, high-ceilinged, windowless space dominated by two enormous stone archways sculpted in relief in varying bold, angular patterns. Each arch spanned an area of utter blackness that contrasted with the surrounding walls, which were hung with decorative patterned cloth. She realized with a start that these must be entrances to the portal; Zareh had said that they were held open here.

Here! She was on Kaia!

A luminous line of royal blue light blazed skyward from the stone Gareth held before him. Once above his head, the line swiftly spiraled outward and downward, encircling the four of them in a nearly transparent bubble that had a faint pearly sheen. Sigrun swallowed hard as nausea threatened again. She felt a breath of warm, tropical air; the bubble around them undulated in the breeze.

The troubled stillness was shattered by the sound of sharp footfalls in the corridor just as the outer rim of the far arch began to glow before turning a deep golden yellow. A tall figure appeared in the center and stepped lithely between the flanking columns.

"Welcome home, Zareh," said Greer from the group in the center of the room.

Sigrun moved to greet him, but was stopped by Gareth's hand on her shoulder. She felt Makoa, who was uncomfortably close to her other side, tense.

Zareh straightened his shoulders and stood, framed for an instant by the portal columns.

Gareth's hand on her shoulder tightened. "Let's go!"

Sigrun craned her neck around Gareth's substantial figure to see who was arriving and caught a glimpse of a short dark-haired man striding arrogantly into the room, trailed by four brawny men. They brushed by Greer's small group. Sigrun stumbled as she was swept along by Gareth. Makoa remained as if glued to her other side. She looked over her shoulder; Philip was right behind them, followed by a middle-aged woman who bore a strong resemblance to Gareth. Just before Gareth tucked her under his arm, she caught a glimpse of peculiarly pale blue eyes that gleamed icily in the small man's sallow face.

As she was hustled down a nearly dark corridor, Sigrun heard a man's supercilious voice say, "Well, well, look who's back. You're under arrest, Fremont."

⤙⤚ ⤙⤚

～ Afterword ～

Hadleigh Garrard is my pen name. I'm an attorney employed by the United States District Court, where I work on habeas corpus petitions and <u>pro se</u> civil rights cases. By day, I write legal opinions and memoranda for judges; by night, I write contemporary fantasy novels.

If you would like more information about *The Trails of Truth*, or would like to read an omitted excerpt from *Untrodden*, please visit my webpage at www.HadleighGarrard.com. Please join my mailing list if would like to receive news about forthcoming books, quarterly contests, and special offers from Proprio Vigore Press.

If you enjoyed this book, please complete the reader survey at www.HadleighGarrard.com, and you may win a free eBook. Please also consider leaving a review of *Untrodden: Book One of The Trails of Truth* on Amazon.

Proprio Vigore Press thanks you for supporting the work of our authors by purchasing only authorized copies of our books.

Coming in 2012: *Unveiled: Book Two of The Trails of Truth*

A new moon has risen, and Sigrun's path, while revealed, remains as uncertain as it is unnerving.

A publication of Proprio Vigore Press
www.ProprioVigorePress.com

Proprio
Vigore
Press

www.ingramcontent.com/pod-product-compliance
Lightning Source LLC
Chambersburg PA
CBHW020913200626
46814CB00001BA/312